MW00364328

THE WATER CATCHER'S RISE

The Kyprian Prophecy Series

Beginnings – An Origins Novella

The Firemaster's Legacy – Book 1

The Water Catcher's Rise – Book 2

The Air King's Return – Book 3 (coming soon)

Anthologies Featuring Kylie Fennell

Lighthouse

Stories of Survival

THE WATER CATCHER'S RISE

THE KYPRIAN PROPHECY BOOK 2

KYLIE FENNELL

Lorikeet
inK

Published by Lorikeet Ink, Brisbane, Australia.

www.lorikeetink.com

First published in Australia in 2021.

Kylie Fennell Copyright © 2021

All rights reserved. The author asserts her moral rights in this work throughout the world without waiver. No part of this book may be reproduced or transmitted by any person or entity in any form or by any means, electronic or mechanical, including photocopying, recording, scanning or by any information storage and retrieval system, without prior written permission from the publisher, except for the use of brief quotations in a book review.

This is a work of fiction. Names, characters, places, events, organisations and incidents are either the products of the individual author's imagination or, if real, used in a fictitious manner.

ISBN 978-0-6488769-4-6 (eBook)

ISBN 978-0-6488769-5-3 (paperback)

A catalogue record for this book is available from the National Library of Australia.

Cover design by Jo Edgar-Baker

Maps by Dewi Hargreaves

Author photo by Marissa Powell

Ornamental break icon by Freepik via Flaticon.com

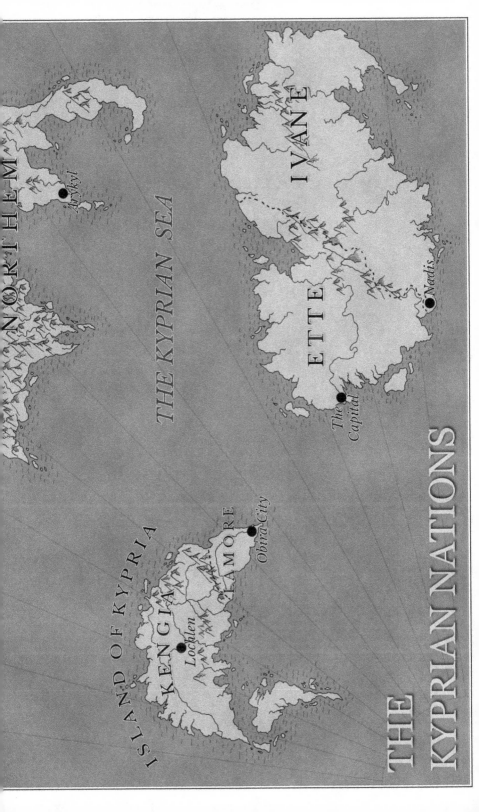

THE KYPRIAN SEA

NORTHEM

Arykyl

IVANE

ETTE

Nadis

The Capital

ISLAND OF KYPRIA

KENGIA

ELAMORE

Lochlen

Obira City

THE
KYPRIAN NATIONS

KYPRIAN SEA

KENGIA NYMOI ALPS

LAMORE

Shizen Falls
Ufon Festival
Shizen Lake
Fisherman's Hut
Riverend Falls

King's Forest

LAKEFORD

Talbot

Lamore River

Lakelands Road

King's Road

LOWLANDS

Calliope

Dunhin Village

Iveness

King's Gate
King's School
Smuggler's Gate
Fortuna
Apothecary
Market
Lion's Den
OBIRA CITY

Obira Port
Lamore Castle

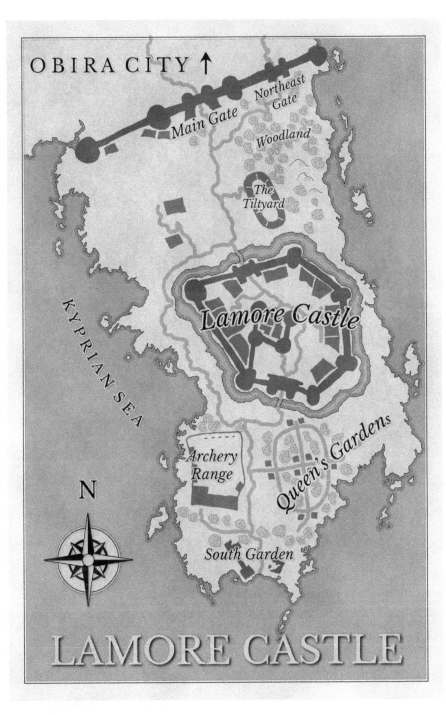

OBIRA CITY ↑

Main Gate

Northeast Gate

Woodland

The Tiltyard

KYPRIAN SEA

Lamore Castle

Queen's Gardens

Archery Range

N

South Garden

LAMORE CASTLE

PROLOGUE

The Kengian snow wolf crept to the opening of her den. She was tucked away in a rocky outcrop at the edge of the castle grounds, as far from the humans as possible. When she had heard the noise, she'd wondered whether they had finally found her hideout. They seemed determined to hunt her down and talked of taking her thick white coat as a trophy.

She sniffed the salt air. Nothing came to her on the night breeze other than the musky earthiness of the nearby woodland with its undergrowth of fallen leaves, pine needles and damp soil. She pricked her ears, but there was no sound. If it hadn't been the humans, it may be a small animal in distress.

The young wolf licked her lips. She hadn't eaten for a few days, as her choices were limited at Lamore Castle. She was used to hunting with her pack in the Nymoi Alps, the mountain range bordering Lamore and her Kengian homeland. She and her brothers and sisters would take down a deer and bring it back to their family to share. While prey was scarce – especially in winter – at the high altitude where they lived, the animals that did cross their path didn't stand a chance against their pack. But here the wolf was alone. Stranded in Lamore without her family, and surrounded by people who wanted her dead.

She yearned to return to her pack in the mountains, far away from the grand stone castle nearby, but some strange power stopped her. It was the same power that had overtaken her body leading up to the night of the blood moon. Many things had changed after the blood moon's appearance, at least in the human world. The Kengian King had fallen ill and later died – at least, that was what must have happened, for that was when the King's protection over the mountain border had disappeared, and she had made her journey across the Alps.

Since she'd been a pup, the wolf had known she could never venture beyond the top of the Nymoi Alps. She'd been told any animal or human who tried to cross the mountains dividing Kengia and Lamore would be forced back by a great trembling of the earth – and that was merely a warning. If they persisted, monster-sized rocks would fall down on them. Chasms would open in the mountainside and gobble them up. She had never dared to see if it was true. That was, until the night the power found her.

That night, it was as if everything she did or saw was through the eyes of another. A force had come over her, reaching into her mind, asking to control her body, yet she hadn't fought it. Somehow, she'd known the energy wasn't evil. The power had chosen her as its vessel and was sending her on a quest – an important one.

So she had left her pack and the warm comfort of their cave to ascend the Alps. She had negotiated the wintry path, thick with several feet of snow, until she'd reached the summit. The power had told her not to fear any trembling of the earth, that it wouldn't come. And without hesitation, she had stepped over the other side and descended into Lamore. The power had led her through the Lamorian countryside and then to Obira City. She'd arrived at the castle the night of the blood moon and had remained at one with the power ever since.

For the most part, she lived as any wolf would. She ventured into the woodland and hunted for food, and she watched. She watched the castle's inhabitants and their comings and goings, always from a safe distance.

Sometimes the power would speak to her with a human voice. If she saw something unusual, or a particular person, she would sense the force guiding her. She wasn't sure what her quest was, exactly, but she accepted that it was important enough not to fight it. That was the way of the natural world in Kengia: humans and animals lived in harmony and balance. But it wasn't the way of Lamore. Here, she needed all her wits to survive.

The wolf trained her ears to the air, and the noise came to her again. A scratching. The sound of twigs being crushed underfoot in the woodland? Her ears twitched. No – it was the sound of gravel and small rocks scuffing along the ground, and it wasn't coming from the woods. It was coming from the jagged hillside that led up to the castle's north-east gate from Obira City.

Her curiosity urged her to edge further out from her den. She looked around and assured herself she was safe. There was a bright full moon in the cloudless sky, its light carving out the craggy outline of the Nymoi Alps in the distance. The wolf could see her path to the boundary wall was clear. She bounded out into the clearing and took a path that hugged the coastline, seeking refuge in the line of rocks running along the cliff's edge.

As she neared the castle wall, a new sound came to her on the wind, but this time from a different direction. She spun her head to the sea, and paused. She could hear waves. Waves slapping against something. Slapping – not crashing like they did on the rocks far below. And she heard human voices; only whispers, but they were definitely voices, carrying from the water. The wolf looked down the cliff face to the murky depths below, scanning the water, her eyes alert for any movement, but there was nothing. She stared out a little further, but saw only the black sky merging into the rippling inky blanket that was the sea.

She was about to turn back when the moonlight caught on

something shiny. Her night vision confirmed it as the hilt of a sword glinting back at her. Now she knew where to look, the shape started to take form.

It was a long, low-set boat.

When the wolf had first arrived in Obira, the surrounding sea and harbour had been heaving with ships, but in recent days it had become a graveyard. The voice inside her mind had explained that all of Lamore's trade relied on resources from a place called Ette and its seaside capital – territory Lamore had since lost to invaders called Northemers. Only the occasional merchant ship that had found other far-flung ports to trade with visited Lamore now. So the appearance of this boat was unusual. More so because it was different to any vessel she'd seen before.

The boat was open to the elements and a dozen or more giants of men were rowing it. The oars slipped in and out of the water with barely a ripple. Each man had a shield strapped to his back, and swords or axes tucked behind him. At the boat's prow was a snarling sculpture of a water serpent.

The boat disappeared behind a rocky formation, a tiny island several hundred feet from shore. The wolf heard the splash of a stone anchor being thrown overboard. She was certain these men in their stealthy boat were not Lamorians. And they weren't Kengians. They could be none other than the invaders from the north: the Northemers. And they were waiting for something – but what?

The wolf's natural instinct was to return to her den, to avoid whatever complicated human business was afoot, but she felt the familiar force wash over her. Energy rushed through her veins, warming her limbs, reaching every muscle in her body, until her golden eyes transformed. She was no longer herself, not entirely. She was the other presence as well as the wolf. Her golden eyes transformed to green, and the voice in her mind told her she must turn her attention back to the noises coming from the other side of the wall.

She loped back toward the boundary wall, clinging to its shadows. The north-east gate was a narrow passage, only wide enough for a single file of livestock to pass. There were only two guards on duty, and they seemed oblivious to the noises intensifying outside the gate. The wolf was certain now that the creatures making the noise were humans. And judging by their overpowering scent, they were close.

She listened as the intruders' feet crunched in the gravel on the slope below. She willed the guards to spot them despite their inferior sense of hearing and smell, but her hopes were in vain. The guards stood motionless in their gatehouse. Neither had noticed the approach of the snow wolf, either. She peered through a crack in the wooden gate, seeing an army of large granite slabs and boulders jutting out from the hillside like broken teeth.

At first the wolf could see nothing out of place, but then she registered the slightest movement from the corner of her eye. Two crouching shadows were fleeing from one rock shadow to the next. Cloaked in black, they were gargantuan-sized men who moved as sleekly as cats. Before she realised it, the pair of men had scaled the castle wall and leapt into the gatehouse.

The intruders were upon the guards before they had even a chance to scream.

The Lamorians' bodies slumped to the ground, blood running freely from gaping slits across their necks. One of the intruders let out a low whistle, and another four Northemers materialised like ghosts. One was carrying a wooden chest. The wolf slunk back into the shadows as the intruders opened the gate. There were too many of them for her to overpower. She contemplated howling to give a warning to the castle, but it would only draw the Northemers' attention, and they would be rid of her as quickly as they had seen to the guards. She would have only one chance to raise an alarm, and she would have to choose the exact right moment. She couldn't sacrifice her life. Her protection was needed beyond this night.

She followed the Northemers as they set off on foot through the castle woodland. They kept a surprisingly swift pace. The wolf trailed them as close as she dared, past the tiltyard and through the castle's northern grounds. They came to a stop outside the outer gate and waited until the patrolling guards on the battlements were out of sight. The intruders silently dispatched four guards at the gatehouse, dragging their bodies inside. Then they did the same thing at the next castle gate.

The Northemers slipped into the inner courtyard, where they came across a hapless servant. The man's mouth opened as if to scream, but a flying axe to the chest distorted his cry into a gurgle of blood. A kitchen boy appeared from a side door of the castle, his eyes wide with horror. His mouth gaped as if he too would scream, but he was quickly stopped by the smallest of the intruders, a hooded figure who muzzled the boy with a tattooed hand – the tattoo an intricate red-and-yellow feather extending up their wrist. With their other hand, the intruder pressed a knife to the boy's throat.

'Do you want to live?'

The wolf stepped a little closer, intrigued. The Northemer's voice belonged to a girl – one who spoke perfect Lamorian.

The boy nodded vigorously.

There was a flash of white teeth, a grin, from under the Northem girl's hood.

'Good.' She pointed to the chest one of the Northemers was still carrying. 'Do you see that?'

The boy nodded again, his chest heaving with muffled sobs.

'Deliver it to the man they call Horace.'

The chest was dropped at the boy's feet.

At that moment, another of the castle's inhabitants appeared at an open window along the west wing. The wolf's fur bristled.

It was *her*. The one she must protect.

Arisa looked like she was only passing through, heading

toward the main keep, but she stopped at the window and peered into the darkness, as if sensing the intruders' presence.

The Northern girl clamped her hand over the servant boy's mouth and stared at Arisa. She tilted her head curiously. One of her fellow Northemers raised a loaded bow and pointed it at Arisa. The wolf advanced to attack the man, knowing she had little chance of covering the distance in time, but she froze when the Northem girl held up her free hand and, with a flick of her wrist, stopped the arrow in mid-air.

The wolf pushed aside her curiosity about the magic she'd just witnessed to focus on Arisa's safety. *Go now,* she thought, planting the words in Arisa's mind. *Your guardian is waiting for you.*

Arisa appeared to hesitate. She stared intently for another moment, before giving a slight shrug and disappearing out of view.

The Northem girl released the servant boy. 'We're going now. Count to two hundred before you leave this spot. Do not raise an alarm, or we'll be back for you. Do you understand?'

The boy nodded frantically.

'A wise choice.' The razor-sharp edges to the girl's voice didn't invite defiance. She thrust a closed hand toward the arrow that was still suspended in the air and flicked open her fist. The arrow burst into flames and disintegrated.

The boy choked back sobs. His legs shook violently. His eyes fell to his feet, planted in the pool of blood spreading from the slain servant, but he didn't move. And as stealthily as they had arrived, the Northemers were gone.

1

*a*risa found her guardian pacing the floor in front of the fireplace, his wiry hair and beard a mass of brown frizz flecked with grey. She'd arrived at Erun's rooms bubbling with questions and ready to share all the strange things that had happened to her recently. The visions of the silver-eyed man, who may have conjured up that wild storm at the marketplace and saved her from Guthrie's sword. The Kengian wolf that appeared to speak to her. On her way here, while passing through the eastern wing, she had heard what she thought were the wolf's words in her mind, telling her to go to Erun. She was sure the voices of the natural world were growing louder to her.

As she stood waiting for Erun to stop pacing, she swore she could hear the fire speaking to her, too. *The time is coming*, it hissed. What time? She didn't know, but she was sure Erun could help her understand. He could help her harness her powers.

'Erun,' she began eagerly, 'I have so much to tell—'

Her words were cut short by her guardian's shattered look as he stopped before her. She couldn't recall a time when she had seen him this agitated, and she had been in his care for almost all of her seventeen years.

'It's hopeless.' His torment was clear in his strangled voice.

'What's hopeless?'

Erun took a deep breath. He took off his eyeglasses and rubbed his nose. Only then did she notice the parchment clutched in his hand. It was one of her practice tests for the College of Surgeons.

'Your practice examination.' He thrust the parchment into her hands. 'It's riddled with mistakes. Simple mistakes that, frankly, I'd never expect from you, Arisa.'

She cast her eyes over the test and winced.

'For a start, you calculated the incorrect quantities of hemlock and henbane for anaesthesia. What you've calculated there' – Erun gesticulated at the parchment – 'is enough anaesthetic to kill twenty men several times over.'

Arisa hung her head, unwilling to meet her guardian's eyes. She hated disappointing him. He was the closest thing she had to family.

'I know,' she muttered.

'You finally have a chance to become a surgeon. It's how you've always said you can help people. But you will never pass the entrance examination with work like that.'

She looked up and sighed. 'You're right. It isn't good enough, and I can do much better. But there are other ways I can help.'

Erun narrowed his eyes. 'Other ways?'

'I could use my silver-eyes magic,' she said brightly, 'if you could show—'

He rubbed his nose again. 'You're not ready.'

'But I am,' she said, raising her voice in protest.

'I still see the darkness in you. You carry too much hate. You seek revenge for what happened to Rea. To Hyando. To your father.'

'No,' she cried. 'I'm finding other ways to get justice.'

'Like poisoning someone at court?'

Arisa froze.

'Horace? The King, perhaps?'

'How did you know?' she said in a low voice.

'What,' he raised an eyebrow, 'you didn't think I'd notice that a vial of strychnine was missing?'

'It was a stupid plan,' she said. And it had been – she knew now that her scheme to poison the King would never have worked. 'I'll give the strychnine back.'

'It was beyond stupid. It was dangerous, as is practising magic at the castle.' His voice rose. 'Your eye drops won't be enough to conceal your identity if there is even a whiff of silver-eyed powers about you.'

'But maybe the King will be more understanding of silver-eyes now the Queen has his ear. There is already a great amount of talk that it was silver-eyed magic that conjured up the storm and freak wave that saved the court that day in the marketplace.'

Erun frowned. 'I have heard that talk as well, and I suspect if that silver-eyed boy they think is responsible is ever found, he too will end up a prisoner at Lamore Castle, tasked with using his magic to further Lamore's cause.'

'But—' Arisa was about to explain that the boy hadn't conjured the storm, that she thought it had been the silver-haired man from her vision, but Erun held his hand up to silence her.

'As I said, you're not ready. You've given no signs to indicate you are, and the darkness remains in you.'

She folded her arms. She wanted to scream at Erun that there *had* been signs of magic. Plenty of them. But it was point-less. Erun was decided. He wasn't going to help her, so she wasn't going to share her secrets.

'And whose fault is it that I'm in danger?' she cried instead. 'The whole reason I'm stuck here, masquerading as some "lady", is because of you. You're the one Horace wanted. You're the one tasked with delivering an unthinkable weapon to him. You're the one who put me in this position.'

Erun blanched, and took a step back. He paused for a long moment before speaking in a gentler tone.

'You're right. It is my fault you were brought here, but you also had a chance to leave. I begged you to escape when Horace discovered the key to the secret messages. But you came back here, knowing the danger it put you in. Knowing he would use you against me.'

Arisa shook her head vigorously. Erun hadn't been there in the marketplace. He didn't understand.

Just over a week ago, her guardian had sent a warning that the King's former Chancellor, Horace, intended to imprison her, to try to force Erun to create and weaponise firesky. He'd also told her that Horace may be able to decode his messages from the Kengian Queen, revealing Erun's true identity as a Prince of Kengia and placing both of them in further danger. So Arisa had agreed to flee to the Lamorian countryside. And she'd had every intention of going through with it – she knew it was the only way to keep the power of firesky from Horace. But on the day of the planned escape, when she'd joined the King and his court on progress, everything had changed.

When the progress had stopped in Obira City, the rebel leader, Sergei, had incited a riot. The entire royal party had been under attack and Prince Takai had come dangerously close to being killed, until a freak storm had given them enough time to find temporary shelter. Arisa had eventually stood up and addressed the crowd. She had called on all Lamorians to be united and refrain from violence. Somehow, she'd won support from the royal court and the Lamorians alike. She'd saved the Prince's life – and probably the King's with it.

Arisa could easily have slipped away in all of the mayhem, but something the Prince said had stopped her. His words were still etched in her mind.

'The people have all the hope they need now,' Takai had said. 'They have you. We have you.'

Prince Takai believed she could unite the troubled kingdom.

Arisa didn't think so, but she did believe the newly reunited Lamorian King and Queen were ready to make change. More so, the Prince's words and actions on that day had shown a new side to him. She had seen a glimmer of hope that Takai could become the kind of leader Lamore needed. She dared to believe there may be some salvation for the troubled kingdom. So she had returned to the castle, figuring it was worth the risk.

Evidently, Erun didn't support her decision.

'Everything has changed,' she tried to reason. 'Horace no longer holds any power; he has been demoted to a lowly Secretary. The King will never imprison me while I'm under Queen Sofia's protection.'

Erun didn't look convinced. 'The Queen's protection is only possible while she and the King remain reconciled.'

'Which they are. They're in total agreement. King Delrik is committed to improving the lives of his people.'

Arisa didn't add that she was prepared to renew her plan to kill the King if he didn't do as he'd said he would – so yes, the darkness was still alive in her. But for now the Queen trusted the King, and Arisa trusted the Queen.

'The King is planning on reducing the tax burdens on the poor and punishing any nobles who hoard grain and other supplies,' she went on. 'He's ordered Horace and any other lords to reopen the lands they enclosed and reinstate them as common lands.'

'That is admirable, but the King and Queen's reconciliation is temporary. She can't maintain the facade forever.'

'The Queen says she sees the kind and generous man that she married, and he's no longer Horace's puppet. Only today we visited an orphanage in Obira to help sick children there. The King provided funds from his personal coffers and sent his own physicians to tend to them.'

Erun frowned. '*We* visited an orphanage?'

'Yes. The King, the Queen, Lady Gwyn and me.' She didn't point out that Prince Takai had been noticeably absent. It was irrelevant to Erun, but it stung Arisa. She hadn't seen Takai since the council meeting shortly after the riot, when he'd indicated he wanted to help his people.

'You let them trot you out as their poster girl for peace,' Erun was saying. 'Don't you realise, Arisa, that the King is using you to further his personal cause?'

'So what if he is?' Arisa retorted. 'Peace is a good cause! If the King starts taking care of the people, there will be no need for Sergei or his rebels to challenge the regime. There will be no more attacks or violence. There may very well be peace in Lamore.'

'Peace!' Erun's voice went high and wobbly. 'The kingdom is on the brink of war with the Northemers. Lamore is desperate to take Ette back – and Ivane, for that matter.'

'Not anymore. The King wishes to form an alliance with Ivane and restore Ette to its people.'

Erun exhaled loudly. 'Yes, I have heard the Queen sent Lore to her brother's palace in Nadis. That she is calling on King Laskar to pay the Northemers to leave Ette. But we don't know these Northemers. I fear it is a dangerous strategy.'

'Haven't you always said there are no winners in war, and urged me to advocate peace before violence? That is what the King is trying to do.'

Erun looked back at her with knitted brows. 'I'm afraid the King can't be trusted to keep his promises.' He grimaced. 'He never has before.'

Her guardian didn't need to say out loud that he was referring to the Kengian Prince, Alik – Erun's brother, who had died because the Lamorian King betrayed him.

Erun slumped into a chair in defeat. Arisa sat down beside him and put her hand over his.

'It's different now. The Queen has the King's trust again. They both want peace with Ette and Ivane, and there is no more talk of invading Kengia.'

Erun gave a thin smile. 'I hope you're right. Truly, I do. But even if Lamore succeeds in the alliance with Ivane, it does little to help our situation. I'm still required to deliver firesky for the King's celebratory tournament. It is Horace's only task, his only means of regaining favour with the King.'

'Yes, but we have time. We have the rest of winter to come up with a plan, and maybe the King won't want it after all…or at least, not as a weapon. Not now that he has the Queen by his side again.'

Erun's face darkened. 'The promise of firesky will remain irresistible to the King. I know this…'

There was something in the way that he said it that sent a chill through Arisa. 'You know it?'

Now, her guardian's eyes had started to shine. 'I did it, Arisa. I conjured up firesky in a secret test, the night of Sar's knighting. It was…magnificent. The sky was alive with great explosions of light and colour. It is how I know I can never hand it over. Once anyone sees it, it isn't hard to imagine weaponising it, and that would guarantee the King power over any of his enemies. With it he could have Ette. He could have Ivane. He could have Kengia. He could rule over all of the Kyprian Empire. He would leave a greater legacy than any Lamorian King, even Emberto, the so-called Conqueror. And with that kind of inducement, not even his love for the Queen would be enough to make him abandon such an opportunity.'

To learn Erun had succeeded with firesky struck fear in Arisa's heart. Yes, there had been moments when she'd been just as fascinated as her guardian, even helping him in his quest, but the sudden reality of firesky and its potential as a weapon was terrifying.

Nervously, Arisa twisted the silver medallion that hung around her neck. Inside it was a Kengian coin engraved with a koi; the fish symbolised water and the power that came with it. It was the only thing she had left of her father. She normally drew strength from the medallion, but now the cold silver sent a chill through her. Erun was right. Firesky was a powerful attraction.

'Don't you see?' her guardian went on. 'No matter what happens, no matter what the lovesick King says, he will want firesky. Horace still demands it, and with us here, and the secret messages from Kengia, he has the means of getting it – and much more…' His voice trailed off.

Arisa would have pressed him to explain what he meant by 'more', but the terrified look on her guardian's face made her want instead to allay Erun's fears for his beloved homeland. Her father's homeland. Devastatingly, Erun shouldered the burden of creating the means of victory over Kengia. If only they had escaped there before Horace had detained them and forced Erun to work for him. Then there would be no firesky. But here they were: Erun, who was prepared to sacrifice his own life to avoid delivering firesky, but not hers. And Arisa, who had refused to leave when he had begged her to. She could be the cause of Kengia's demise as much as Erun. They were treading a treacherous path, with both of their lives hanging in the balance.

'I'm sorry,' she whispered. She truly was sorry for refusing to escape and giving Horace the leverage over Erun he needed.

Her guardian gazed back at her with tear-brimmed eyes. 'You were doing what you thought was right. Anyway, Queen Mira still believes Kengia will prevail if Lamore or the Northemers attack.'

She shuddered as she caught Erun's meaning. 'She can't believe the Water Catcher will still come. You must tell your mother to prepare Kengia's defences. There isn't a Water Catcher. There never can be. You know this. You know the Water Catcher prophecy died with Prince Alik.'

Erun shook his head adamantly. 'We must have faith.'

Arisa still didn't understand how he could be so certain the prophecy would come into being, when all evidence pointed to it being impossible. She wanted to tell him he couldn't deliver firesky under any circumstances. That she was prepared to give her life too if it meant protecting Kengia against the weapon; that this was the only way, because there could never be a Water Catcher. She would have said all of this, but she was interrupted by the sound of a primal howl piercing the air. It sliced through the gaps in the wooden shutters and reverberated off the stone walls, reaching all the way into her chest.

'The snow wolf!' Erun swung his head in the direction of the window.

The wolf howled again. The hairs on Arisa's arms stood on end.

Erun's grey eyes grew wide. 'There is something terribly wrong. You need to go.'

2

'Father, I can help,' Theodora said with as much confidence as she could muster.

She knew she had disappointed her father by not securing the Prince's heart. But there were other ways she could help re-establish her family's power at court – if her father would just trust her enough to share his plans with her. If he would just see her as more than a pretty face and a pawn in his schemes. She had all of Horace's nous and ambition; she just needed him to give her a chance.

Given his recent fall from grace, Theodora figured that chance was now.

Horace glanced up from the papers on his desk. Looking past his daughter, he surveyed his new chambers with distaste. The wood-panelled walls were made of the same fine oak found in his previous apartments. His ornately carved furniture and finely embroidered tapestries had also come with him, but they seemed out of place in the new rooms. The apartments consisted of a study and a privy chamber, and were actually no different to those allocated to the highest-ranking nobles – a fact that Theodora knew irked others at court, since Horace was lowborn. To them, he was nothing more than the King's

18

childhood companion, and he had used this friendship to ingratiate himself into a position of power and influence. Further, he had taken advantage of this connection to secure a fortunate marriage to the King's distant cousin, Countess Datanya.

But in truth, Horace could credit more than nepotism for his success. He owed much of his power and influence to his wits – wits Theodora prided herself on having inherited – as well as his commitment to doing whatever it took to get what he wanted, no matter how distasteful the task. These qualities had served him well – at least until now.

A few days before, Theodora's father had occupied the grand apartments next to the King's rooms in the main keep: a series of anterooms and chambers fit for royalty. They were traditionally the Queen's rooms, and provided unrivalled access to the King. Horace had occupied those apartments for nearly two decades, ever since the Queen had exiled herself to the far-flung south-east tower. But when the King and Queen had reconciled, Horace had been removed to more modest rooms in the north-east tower, a stone's throw from the stables and build-ings set aside for soldiers and servants. He had fallen far, and his advice was no longer valued or sought.

Theodora could point to the exact moment the balance of power had started to shift. The Queen had publicly declared her loyalty to the King in a bid to save a Kengian woman's life. The woman, a nobody, was to be executed for speaking out against the King and enlisting support for the rebels. Inexplicably, the Queen had spoken for her. After almost twenty years of separa-tion, Queen Sofia had reconciled with the King in exchange for the Kengian's life. She had been willing to dismiss the fact that her husband had invaded Ivane shortly after their marriage, and that he was responsible for the death of her father King Arlo, the former Ivanian ruler. She had put all of this aside for a poor woman of no importance. But while the Queen may have been prepared to forgive the King – or at least give the appearance of forgiving him – she clearly hadn't forgotten Horace's part in everything.

Theodora detested Queen Sofia, who she thought was pathetic and weak. After King Delrik's failed attempts to conquer her homeland, the Queen had retreated to the abandoned south-east tower to mourn her personal losses. For years, Sofia had been no more than a shadow of the warrior princess she once was. As an absent Queen, she had posed no threat. Not until now. Not until she had inexplicably decided to worm her way back into the King's favour.

One of her first acts had been to eject Horace from his grand apartments. To add further insult, the Queen remained in the south-east tower, leaving the stately chambers next to the King's as empty as the look in Horace's eyes.

Theodora had never seen her father in such a state: a state of defeat. Theodora's mother was no hope, the Countess far too absorbed in the frivolities and gossip of the royal court. Theodora's brother, Guthrie, was nothing more than a dim-witted thug and an acknowledged coward. So it must be her. She must restore herself and her family to power.

'I can help,' she repeated to her father.

Horace looked at her for the first time and sighed. 'There's nothing you can do, unless you can discover the clue to decode Erun's messages. The key is in there somewhere.' He jabbed at the parchment laid out in front of him.

Theodora leant over her father and began reading.

Darkness and defeat, a King is to blame;
A regime must fall for everything to change.

Heed the three signs by looking to the skies:
The first will be seen in a blood moon's rise.

On the brink of war, the next is firesky:
Promises of destruction, many sure to die.

It was the nonsensical Kyprian prophecy that some – mostly Kengians – believed foretold the coming of a Water Catcher to 'save' them from the Lamorian King's regime. Her father was convinced the prophecy was the key to the messages he'd found in the Kengian healer's house.

'Why is this so important?' she asked.

Horace clicked his jaw, seemingly trying to decide how much to share with his daughter. 'I must know what is in the messages. I know they will give me what I need to guarantee Erun's compliance. Then I can deliver on my promise to the King and regain our power.'

'What exactly have you asked Erun to work on? Surely it is something more than some pretty lights in the sky. What must he deliver?'

Horace waved his hand dismissively. 'Some specific scientific knowledge that is important to the King.'

Theodora gritted her teeth. So her father didn't trust her enough with the truth. She would have to prove her worth to him somehow.

She read on:

An empire's fate uncertain, until comes the third:
A catcher of water. Kengia's firstborn returned.

Hopes will be tested; some will be betrayed.
Fire or water – the choice must be made.

Theodora frowned. She knew nothing about deciphering codes. She cared even less about the Water Catcher prophecy, dismissing it as irrelevant since the Kengian firstborn line had died with the Kengian Prince, Alik.

'I don't know why this prophecy is so important,' she said. 'I thought the Water Catcher could never come to being.'

'It can't. I made sure of it.'

'So why the prophecy?'

Horace rolled his eyes. 'The prophecy is symbolic only. It is just used as a key for the code itself...I wouldn't expect you to understand these things.'

Theodora took a deep breath, pushing down the rising anger inside her. 'Father, if you would just trust me with your plans, I could help.'

'Like you *helped* with securing the Prince's hand?' he spat. 'One simple task, and you failed.'

'There was nothing simple about it. How am I supposed to compete with that stupid peasant girl? Takai and the whole of Lamore is obsessed with Arisa. Send her and her guardian away from court and I may just succeed.'

'That is not an option. Win the Prince over and you will have my full trust.'

'Then you will let me be part of the rest of your plans?'

He nodded.

'Perhaps, in the meantime, there are other things I can help with—'

Theodora was interrupted by the sound of a wolf's howl.

'Haven't they caught that wretched thing?' her father wondered aloud.

The wolf howled for a second time. There was a sense of urgency in its call.

Theodora and Horace moved to the window and stared out into the darkness. Almost immediately, a hurried set of footsteps sounded outside Horace's rooms. Theodora heard a muffled conversation between the visitor and her father's guards before the door swung open to reveal a dishevelled servant boy clutching a wooden chest.

A guard stepped forward and addressed Horace. 'Secretary, the boy says he was attacked by a gang of Northemers.'

The Northemers were the fearsome army that had invaded Lamore's territory, Ette. From overheard conversations, Theodora knew her father had been seeking an alliance with the Northem leader, Malu, against the wishes of the King's Council.

The King, at the Queen's urging, had instead made an alliance with Sofia's homeland, Ivane, and sent an ambassador, Lore, to negotiate with Malu.

'Northemers!' Horace cried. 'How ridiculous.'

'Beggin' your pardon, m-me lord,' the boy stammered, 'but I saw it...with me own eyes.'

Theodora's gaze fell on the trail of bloodied boot marks the boy had left in his wake. Her heart quickened. Horace nodded for the boy to continue.

'Half a dozen or more invaders...in the inner courtyard... killed a man...put a knife to me own throat.'

'A fanciful tale,' Horace hissed. 'If it was in fact the Northemers, I can't imagine why they would leave you alive, boy.'

'They said I had to deliver this chest to you.'

Horace's hawklike eyes scrutinised the casket. It was inlaid with several types of stained wood, as well as metal and something that looked like bone, all creating an intricate geometric pattern. At the centre of each panel were diamond-shaped cavities, where precious stones had probably once been set. Theodora had only seen a chest like it once before. There was one in the Queen's bedchambers. It was an Ivanian casket.

'Open it,' Horace ordered.

The boy complied with shaking hands.

A rank stench of decay struck Theodora in the face. She recoiled, covering her nose and mouth. The boy slammed the lid shut and began to dry retch.

Theodora watched her father collect himself and motion for the boy to open it again. He obeyed, holding the chest as far away from himself as possible. Horace peered back into the chest, pinching his nostrils. Over her father's shoulder, Theodora could see a large object wrapped in dark cloth. On top of it was a note with Horace's name written on it. The wax seal was a serpent-head symbol she didn't recognise.

Horace reached in and snatched the note, and the boy dropped the lid closed again.

Theodora's father broke open the seal and scanned the note quickly, not noticing or caring that his daughter was reading over his shoulder.

Secretary Horace,

As you know, a short while ago I met with your distasteful 'friend'. A vile man I would have killed on sight, had he not held my brother hostage.

Theodora groaned inwardly, remembering the pirate her father had entrusted with his message to the Northem leader.

He delivered your proposal to join forces and invade Kengia. I have heard of this land and its many riches, and I don't believe we need Lamore's assistance in conquering it, or any other lands. Our performance in Ette is testament to this.

That being said, your claims of having a powerful new weapon are intriguing.

A weapon? Was that the real secret her father was hiding from her?

I would have liked to have learnt more about it, but I'm convinced it was a lie used to distract us until your Ivanian ambassador arrived.

It could be a lie. Horace wouldn't stop at anything to get his way. But Theodora filed away the idea of a weapon in her mind, just in case.

The Ivanian claimed he was representing both your nation and Ivane and had an altogether different proposal. He offered us money. A great deal of gold, in fact, to leave Ette. He appeared to be making the offer in good faith, which led me to believe he was unaware of your promises. Quite an odd business. I left the man in no doubt of what I thought of the proposal.

We won't be leaving this new land of ours – such a fertile and prosperous nation – or running back to Arykyl with our tails between our legs. And we have kept the Ivanian's gold as payment for Lamore's duplicitous behaviour.

I care not for your motives, Secretary, and have a message for you.

By now you will know my men are capable of making it into the heart of your Lamorian fortress, and it serves as a warning that we will not be trifled with. Lamore may not have been in our immediate sights, but it is now.

As soon as the conditions are favourable to mobilise my forces, you and the rest of the Kyprian nations will experience the full force of the Northem army.

The note was signed 'Malu, King of Northem and Ette'. His name was written in what looked like dried blood.

Horace folded the note and slipped it into his cloak. Theodora couldn't fathom how her father managed to look so unrattled.

He looked to the nearest guard. 'Go to Lakeford immediately and tell him a party of Northemers breached our defences. The Duke must ensure the castle is secure and send men to the port to catch sight of any Northemer boats…but it is to be done quietly. There is no need to alarm the entire court, for I'm sure these intruders are long gone. Their mission has been achieved.'

The guard nodded and hurried from the room.

'And me, Secretary?' The servant boy's shaking hands still clutched the Ivanian chest.

Horace took a deep breath and waved his hand at the boy,

indicating for him to open the chest once more. The boy complied, averting his eyes and dry retching again.

This time Horace seemed prepared for the smell, and after only a moment of hesitation he reached in and moved the cloth aside to reveal the chest's grisly contents.

Theodora's stomach turned at what she could see from her position. Bile rose in her throat, yet a smirk tugged at the corner of her father's mouth. He clicked his jaw back and forth.

'Close it,' Horace barked. His eyes fell on the boy's bloody boot marks on the floor. His lip curled in distaste. 'Remove your boots and follow me.'

Theodora made to follow as well, and only then did Horace seem to remember she was there. He nodded to a second guard. 'See that my daughter gets back to her rooms safely.'

'But, Father—'

'This is no business for a girl.'

Theodora swallowed the bile in her throat, determined to prove that she had the stomach for all of the kingdom's 'business'. But first she would do as her father bid and seduce the Prince. She would be the one who secured a crown – and it would be her giving the orders to her father when she became Queen.

3

*E*run ran his hands across the book's embossed cover, tracing the gold detail that depicted a phoenix rising from flames – the symbol of the last Firemaster, who had had the power to transform into a phoenix. He opened the book to reveal its blank pages, then looked around himself and through the doorway to the small anteroom. Erun was certain he was alone, but he couldn't be too careful. He murmured the Kengian protection spell.

'Thoughts to words
Words to action
Reveal thy words
Speaketh your secrets.'

Erun spoke the words over and over, until his fingertips glowed. The light spread more with every word he uttered, until it covered his whole hand and leapt from his palm. Under the glimmering light, the Firemaster's words materialised on the pages before him.

The book held the secrets to firesky. It held Erun and Arisa's fate. And it held not only Lamore's future, but also that of

Erun's homeland – Kengia. Erun dreamed one day of returning to Kengia but if and when he did, it would be a different place. His father, King Leo, had died only months before, something Erun tried not to think about. He couldn't allow himself to surrender to grief, not until his work was done. His work that was firesky.

The power of firesky was indisputable. Using the Firemaster's book, Erun had successfully conjured up its magic in secret. He had filled a paper tube with the exact chemical composition outlined in the book. With the help of Klaus, a trusted guard, he had snuck out to an unseen area of the castle grounds and ignited the tube's contents. There had been a great explosion and the sky had come alive with bright lights.

Erun had conducted many great scientific experiments in his time, but they were all overshadowed by the spectacular display of light that was firesky. He understood completely why the King wanted it for his great celebrations. And if the King had only wanted firesky to impress his subjects, Erun wouldn't have hesitated in delivering it to him. But that wasn't the only reason why nearly every King in Lamore's history had coveted it. King Delrik knew the real power of firesky was in its explosive abilities, and that weaponising it was a natural progression. It would give him the means to dominate all of the Kyprian nations.

Fortunately, every King before him had failed in their attempts to unlock the power of firesky. Its secrets were believed to have been lost with the demise of the last Firemaster, in King Emberto's time, centuries before. So when Erun and Arisa had discovered the Firemaster's book, it would have been prudent to *lose* it again – to hide it as quickly as they had found it. Erun's rational mind told him everything possible had to be done to stop the King and Horace – in fact, *anyone* – from getting their hands on the book and the key to firesky.

But Erun had kept the book and used it, for one reason alone. Firesky was the second sign in the prophecy.

The first was the blood moon, which had appeared this very

winter. After that was firesky – and only after those two signs would the Water Catcher come.

The prophesied Water Catcher, a descendant of the Kengian King's firstborn line, would unite Kypria, delivering peace and prosperity to all. Erun was sure of it, despite all evidence to the contrary. Most people believed Kengia's first-born line had ended with the death of Erun's brother, Prince Alik – the Kengian King's firstborn. Alik had perished at Delrik and Horace's hands. Yet none of this prevented Erun from believing the Water Catcher would come…they *had* to come. But there would be a price – and that price was firesky.

He hoped his own tests had been enough to trigger the prophecy, but failing that, he was prepared to deliver firesky for the King's celebrations in spring. At best, he was counting on the Water Catcher arriving before then. At worst, the Water Catcher would come later…hopefully, though, before anyone had the chance to weaponise firesky.

There were risks, of course. Great risks that only intensified when Horace had discovered the coded messages Erun had been sent from Kengia – messages the Secretary could eventually decode using the prophecy as the key. Horace could discover Erun was actually the Kengian Prince, Amund, and this would compromise Erun and Arisa's safety even further. But it was possible Horace could learn even more from the coded notes. Erun couldn't be sure, but enough might have been said in the correspondence with his mother to incur far greater consequences.

Despite all of this, Erun was prepared to stay the course with firesky. He just wished Arisa had escaped when he'd urged her to do so. The fact that his ward was under the King and Queen's protection was only a temporary reprieve. Erun knew this regime well enough to understand the thirst for power, the need to dominate – and the pursuit of firesky would eventually outweigh any sentimentality and affection the King felt for the Queen.

Arisa was on borrowed time, and there was nothing he, the Queen or Gwyn could do to protect her. Not even his wolf friend could help if the King decided to act against them. All Erun could do was hope the Water Catcher would arrive soon. He felt sick from the knowledge that firesky was equally as capable of saving Kypria as it was of destroying it…and its power lay entirely with him.

Erun sighed, a sigh filled with fear and dread, and waved his hand over the book's pages.

'Words begone.'

4

$\mathcal{A}$risa lifted the bottom of her skirts as she raced up the stairs of the south-east tower. She shivered, partly from the wintry air that was accentuated by the bare stone walls common in this part of the castle, but mostly from the sense of foreboding she had felt since hearing the wolf howl. Like Erun, she was sure it was a sign of something awful.

She hadn't told anyone about her encounter with the wolf, the day it had sought her out in the woodland. Arisa had felt as if the creature had stared all the way into her soul with its peculiar green eyes. She hadn't seen the animal since that day, yet somehow she knew its message tonight had been for her.

Erun's reaction had told her he knew something about the wolf – something he hadn't shared with her. It was another of the many secrets that lay between them. Secrets she believed he shared with Gwyn, yet wouldn't share with her. None of it made sense.

Arisa reached the Queen's deserted presence chamber and continued into the privy chamber that led to her own rooms. She had expected the inner chamber to be empty at such a late hour, but it was quite the opposite. The room was alive with warmth and chatter. The smell of mulled wine wafted toward her, and a newly stoked fire crackled away in the hearth. A quick scan of the room revealed the King and Queen in deep conversation in front of the fireplace. Gwyn was nearby, reading the book of Kyprian tales that was rarely far from her hands.

In the darkness Arisa could just make out two noblemen playing cards in the corner. One of the men was obscured from her view, but there was something familiar about the one with his back to her – a loftiness in how tall and upright he sat, his broad shoulders rigidly straight. Her breath caught in her throat as she realised his identity.

What was *he* doing here?

The Prince rarely bothered to visit his mother, and certainly not late at night for a game of cards. He hadn't bothered to seek any of them out for days, but now he was here. Arisa frowned as Takai turned toward her, a tentative but warm smile on his face, as if he had been waiting specifically for her.

'Arisa!' came a bright voice behind the Prince.

Her eyes were drawn to the man awkwardly leaping from his chair and stepping out of Takai's shadow.

'Lord Willem!' She couldn't hide the joy in her voice as the Earl of Talbot moved haltingly toward her with a crooked grin. 'I thought you were in Lakeford?'

'I was. I'm only here for the day, I'm afraid. Father had me deliver some timber to the shipyards. I'll be leaving for Talbot first thing in the morning.'

'I'm sorry you have to leave so soon.' Arisa meant what she said. She liked Willem's company. 'Surely the Duke could have found someone else to deliver timber?' she teased.

'He could have asked Sar, but he's far too busy chasing down a certain rebel leader.'

Willem gave a wink that only Arisa could see. She was well aware that neither Sar nor Willem were interested in capturing Sergei, at least while there weren't any riots. They were, in fact, sympathetic to the rebels' cause.

'In any case, I was quite keen to see for myself how my

cousin was putting the timber to use.' Willem shifted his gaze to Takai, who was now standing beside him. 'And I have to say, I was impressed. It's going to be the finest naval fleet we've ever seen.'

'Naval fleet?' Arisa didn't know anything about a naval fleet. Why would they be building more ships, given Lamore and Ivane were negotiating peace with the Northemers? Was the fleet the reason the Prince had been absent?

Willem glanced between her and Takai and shifted his feet. 'I must get to bed. I've got an early start tomorrow, but I couldn't go without seeing you first, Arisa.' He bent over and kissed her hand. 'It's always a pleasure.'

'As it is to see you, Willem.'

Willem bid farewell to Takai, leaving the Prince and Arisa to stare at each other in silence.

Takai spoke first, his dark eyes boring into her. 'How have you been?'

'Fine.' She wasn't sure whether she was more annoyed that Takai had been avoiding her, or that he'd been preparing for a war they didn't need or want.

He wrinkled his brow at her blunt response. 'I hear you were with my parents today, visiting an orphanage.'

She gave a small nod and looked around for Gwyn to relieve her of the Prince's company, but Gwyn was speaking to the King and Queen.

Takai followed her gaze. 'Gwyn will be busy making plans with my parents for the great tournament. They have been discussing it all night.'

She resisted the urge to roll her eyes at him. 'Yes, celebrating your eighteenth birthday and the King's twentieth year on the throne must be the most pressing matter for the kingdom.'

Takai's face crumpled, as if she had physically stung him with her words. 'They've been discussing how to best engage the people in the celebrations, and how Lamore can benefit from it,' he continued hesitantly. 'They have quite a marvellous plan for putting the profits from all the stalls on the day into benevolent institutions.'

'A worthy plan,' Arisa admitted begrudgingly.

Takai gave a broad smile. 'I'm glad you approve.'

'It was your idea, then?'

He nodded enthusiastically. 'Like we talked about in the marketplace that day. I think the people can be brought to our side, especially with your support.'

A surge of anger flooded through her veins. 'And that's where you're wrong. You think it's all about forcing the people to come around to your way of thinking. To comply with whatever the Lamorian court demands of them, and not to cause any more trouble for you.' Her voice rose indignantly. 'But what you *should* be doing is trying to make amends for all the wrongs already done to them by your father's regime.'

Takai lifted his chin defiantly. 'I have no problem with offering charity where it is deserved, but I do not forget easily that some among the people have taken up arms against us. And those individuals are probably planning further attacks, when we need their support now more than ever. We can't fight among ourselves – not when we're on the brink of a real war with Northem.'

'There you go, wishing for war when we have the means of brokering peace with the Northemers.'

He flung his hands up in exasperation. 'I don't wish for war. Like you, I wish more than anything that Lore and the Ivanians are successful in their negotiations with the Northemers. But we must be prepared for every eventuality.'

Arisa raised a brow. 'I suppose that's why you've been over-seeing the rebuilding of the naval fleet, instead of *helping* your people like you attest?'

'Unfortunately, I don't have the luxury of refusing responsi-bilities that may not be to my personal taste,' he hissed. 'Someone must protect this kingdom, whether the people want our protection or not.'

Incorrigible. Arisa couldn't believe she had ever thought the Prince could change. He was as arrogant and misguided as the day she had met him, and she would have told him so in no uncertain terms, had she not been interrupted by Gwyn's hand on her arm.

'Arisa, I'm so pleased to see you.' Gwyn had an uncanny ability for diffusing conflict with nothing but her kind words and gentle touch. 'Did you hear the wolf howl earlier? It sent quite a shiver up my spine.'

The wolf! Arisa was immediately brought back to the reason she had returned to the rooms. 'I did hear it,' she replied. 'Tell me. Is everything as it should be here?'

Takai and Gwyn exchanged a perplexed look.

'I'm not sure what you mean by *"as it should be"*, but nothing unusual other than the wolf howl has occurred tonight.' Gwyn's voice was thick with concern. 'Is there something we should be aware of?'

Arisa shook her head. 'I don't think so. An odd feeling, I guess. It's probably nothing.'

Gwyn exhaled loudly. 'Good. Good.'

But it appeared as if they had spoken too soon, for the next moment the Secretary strode into the room unannounced, a barefoot servant boy in tow.

'I have news,' Horace addressed the room at large.

King Delrik's lips thinned, but with an indifferent wave of the hand, he indicated for Horace to continue.

The Secretary took a moment to cast a grave look at each of them. Arisa was sure she saw a small smirk form when he made eye contact with the Queen, before he adopted a worried frown.

'Your Majesty, it pains me to inform you that a small group of Northemers made it into the castle grounds tonight.'

'Northemers!' the King cried, standing up from this chair.

'This boy' – Horace pointed to the servant – 'saw them with his own eyes.'

The boy nodded vigorously.

That was what the wolf had been trying to tell them. But why had the Northemers ventured to Lamore and into the castle grounds when Ivane was seeking an alliance with them? It didn't bode well.

'And where are they now?' The Queen sounded surprisingly calm, though Arisa noted her hands tightening on the arm of her chair.

'We are sure they are gone, but Lakeford is securing the castle and port as we speak.'

The King was silent and disturbingly still. Arisa felt the same. She had heard the stories of the fearsome Northemers.

'What do you think they hoped to achieve, then?' the Queen pressed.

'They wished to deliver a message.'

Queen Sofia stood up and outstretched her hand. 'I will see it.'

'Your Majesty, I have no note for you.' There was the hint of Horace's smirk again. 'But their message was clear. They do not wish to negotiate with us or Ivane.'

'And how can you be sure?' the Queen demanded, her steady gaze locked on the Secretary.

'I am sure.' Horace's matter-of-fact tone was beyond irritating.

'How convenient that you, Secretary, the very person who doesn't support Lamore's alliance with my homeland, who has always done everything within his power to undermine Ivane and me, now claims the negotiations have failed.'

Horace didn't even blink an eye at the Queen's direct words. 'Your Majesty, you must trust me. I am sure of it.'

'Trust you!' the Queen scoffed.

'I suppose if Your Majesty cannot trust the word of her husband's most loyal and closest adviser,' Horace began in a conciliatory tone, 'I must provide *proof.*'

Arisa's stomach churned wildly. Horace was up to something. He was baiting the Queen for some reason.

'Yes, I shall have your proof.' The Queen jutted out her chin, ready to meet his challenge.

Horace motioned to the servant boy, who stepped shakily toward the Queen. Arisa noticed for the first time that he was carrying something – a casket.

The Queen's eyes widened as he approached her. 'An Ivanian chest!' She paused, as if contemplating the significance of the object's presence. 'What's in it?'

The question was directed at Horace, but he just inclined his head toward the casket.

'Open it.' The Queen spoke directly to the boy now, who slowly opened the chest in front of her and the King.

Immediately they both recoiled. The reason for their reaction was clear as a sickening stench wafted toward Arisa.

She knew that smell. She had experienced it many times before in her work assisting Erun as a healer, but its effect never lessened.

The Queen grimaced as she stepped forward and reached into the chest. Sofia's eyes widened in shock. She was silent for what felt like a full minute before she spoke in a tiny voice.

'*Lore.*'

The smell of death and decay emanated from what was left of the Queen's friend and physician – nothing but a blackened, rotting head.

To the King's credit, he put his arms around his wife, whose face was glistening with tears. Gwyn, who had also known Lore since childhood, reached out and grasped Arisa's hand. Arisa squeezed back, but the attempt at comfort was futile. She glanced over at Horace. He stood firm and tall, his face inscrutable. Was it only her imagination, or did the Secretary have an air of victory about him?

Arisa looked around to see if anyone else had noticed, and Takai caught her eye. She expected to see in his face the same pain and devastation they all felt. That he mourned the loss of Lore. That he grieved the breakdown in negotiations – but she saw none of that. Takai's face was flushed bright red, his chin raised, his eyes narrowed.

'I'm going to Lakeford,' he announced angrily, before storming out of the room.

She should have known his first thought would be to go to the Commander of the King's forces. The Prince's mind was never far from war.

Arisa clutched the silver medallion in her hands and willed herself to hold back the tears threatening to come. She lamented Lore's brutal death. She mourned for everything they had lost – including their hope for peaceful negotiations. But she knew better than to cry in front of the others. She knew better than to cry in front of anyone – tears would be her undoing, in more ways than one.

5

It was on days like this that Takai felt Sar's absence most.

Since they were children, the pair had rarely been apart. Like any highborn son, Takai had been sent away from the age of eight to be brought up in the household of a landed family. In his case, the household was Talbot, and he'd been raised under the guidance of the Duke of Lakeford. Sar and Willem, Takai's cousin, had been his companions.

As the son of a King he was entitled to set up his own household at Talbot, but the Duke had insisted Takai be treated like anyone else. For a near decade, he had attended lessons, practised riding daily, and mastered swordsmanship, archery and all the other skills of a warrior knight. His upbringing had been focused on preparing him to be King one day – a leader worthy of his people – but it also meant he'd spent little time at court. Takai's parents had been virtual strangers to him, until he'd returned to the castle a few months ago. He was only just beginning to re-establish his relationship with his father and mother. It would take time before he was comfortable confiding in them. In the meantime, he needed someone he could speak openly to, who could help him navigate Lamore's troubles and the threats it faced. Someone he trusted to advise him on what he must do. That person was Sar.

His best friend was an experienced soldier who had been in Ette when the Northemers attacked. Sar would have stood to the last had the Duke not ordered a retreat. He understood the enemy that hadn't hesitated in slaying an emissary sent to negotiate in good faith. If Sar were here, Takai could ask him why the brutes had taken the life of the Queen's Ivanian physician, who'd bravely agreed to open negotiations with the Northemers. If Sar were here, he could help Takai make sense of why a good man such as Lore had met such a tragic end. If it weren't for Lore, Takai wouldn't be here now.

Maybe Sar could also have tempered Takai's desire to seek swift revenge on the Northemers. He could have been the lone witness to Takai's grief, as Takai struggled to come to terms with everything they'd lost. But Sar wasn't here. And Willem – the only other person Takai considered a real friend – had left. The Prince was alone, his desolation compounded by the fact that the girl who consumed much of his remaining thoughts – whether he liked it or not – could barely tolerate being in the same room as him.

Takai hadn't lied to Arisa. He had been hopeful the Northemers would accept the Ivanian payment and leave Ette. He had wished he would never need to launch the naval fleet he had been tasked with rebuilding. He had hoped, more than anything, that a Lamorian army would never need to set foot on the battlefield.

But the peace in Lamore was fragile. The court was still on edge after the Northem party's invasion. Sergei and his rebels were quiet, but that could only last as long as the King's coffers did. With no trade from Ette, Lamore, with its finite resources, would have to reinstate austerity measures and rely on Ivane's goodwill to support them – a risky strategy. The pragmatist in Takai, the soldier tutored under a great military leader, told him Lamore may have no choice but to seek other territories.

And if it had been a year earlier, even a few months earlier, Takai would have accepted this scenario. He had always known Lamore's future probably lay in invading other lands; that its survival relied on conquering territories like Ette and Ivane. And when the Kengian King had died, the perfect opportunity had arisen to invade the neighbouring nation – the richest territory of them all. Now, though, everything was different.

The King, under the influence of the Queen, was favouring alliances over invasions. Takai's parents were confident in the Ivanian King's indefinite generosity toward his sister. They were also determined to show benevolence to the Lamorian people, no matter the cost. Kengia appeared to be the last thing on their minds. And Takai wanted more than anything to share his parents' confidence. He wanted the Ivanian alliance to be enough. He wanted to believe that together, Lamore and Ivane's forces could defeat the Northemers, if it came to that. He wanted to be a different kind of leader than he'd been raised to be. Different to the leader his father had been before his recent transformation. He wanted to be the kind of leader that some – *someone* – believed he could be.

But the Northemers had essentially declared war on Lamore. So now what?

Lacking someone he trusted enough to share all of this with, Takai grabbed his favourite longbow and quiver of arrows and headed for the archery oval. There, he could clear his head and, for a short time, forget about the responsibilities that lay so heavily on his shoulders. This almost daily ritual was one of the only things that gave him any semblance of comfort at court.

His heart lightened as he walked through the castle grounds and the silver sun's rays warmed his body. The guards nodded in recognition as he reached the southern gatehouse leading to the archery oval. Takai stepped out onto the bridge that crossed the castle moat, noticing with a pang of annoyance that a cloaked figure stood in the middle, blocking his path. He was about to order the person to stand aside, when they turned toward him and removed their hood.

'Theodora?'

The Secretary's daughter was the last person he had expected to see. In truth, he'd been avoiding her since the riot at Obira's marketplace. He had seen Theodora's character in full light when she had refused to mix with or help the people. She had been rude and dismissive. It confirmed that she had the same cruel streak as her father. Takai was starting to wonder how he could ever have considered marrying her.

'Your Highness.'

Theodora curtsied, looking up at him from under lowered lashes, her black eyes shining. She was remarkably pretty. There was something in her looks that reminded Takai of an exotic animal. He'd heard of great cats called lynxes that lived in Ivane, with distinctive markings and sharp eyes. Takai had never seen one, but he imagined they held the same allure as Theodora. A beauty to be admired…from afar.

'I'd hoped to find you here.' She even purred like a cat.

'Was there something you needed, Theodora?'

'I thought I could join you at archery. You're so busy these days – this was the only way I could see you.'

Takai scratched his head as he searched for a suitable reason he could give for refusing her.

She tilted her chin upward. 'You see, Father thinks it's important we spend time together. After all, we are—'

'I prefer to practise my archery alone,' he interrupted. He didn't want to hear that her father expected them to marry. 'Less distractions that way,' he added, with a thin smile.

Theodora pouted, but was undeterred. She moved closer to him, until her lips were almost touching his ear, her breath hot on his cheek. 'All the better that we'll be alone,' she whispered. 'No one can disturb us.'

Takai stumbled back. 'Theodora, when I say alone – I mean only me.' He tried to sound as forceful as possible.

She screwed up her lips, her cat eyes narrowed. 'I warn you, I'm not the sort of girl to be trifled with. I'm the Chancel—Secretary's daughter,' she corrected herself, 'which may not mean much now, but my father will not always be out of favour. Soon enough he will be restored, and he will not have forgotten those who were against him, or who reneged on their promises.'

Takai bristled at her impudence. 'You presume too much. Good day.'

He turned on his heel and strode back toward the castle, not looking back to see if she was following him. He was intent only on putting as much distance as possible between himself and Theodora. She had brought the realities of his position crashing back to him. She was a painful reminder of his previous self. The person he had been before...before everything changed.

Takai marched unseeingly through the grounds, his chest constricting with every step. Was there nowhere at this castle he could be alone? Was there no escape from his responsibilities?

Before he realised it, he was back at the inner courtyard and stables. A stable boy led a fine-looking stallion past him. The boy bowed awkwardly and mumbled, 'Your Highness', as he let the horse take some water. The stallion was saddled and covered in a fine lather of sweat, as if it had just been ridden.

'I'll take the horse,' Takai said.

The boy tilted his head in confusion.

'Here.' Takai handed over his bow and gestured for the reins in return. He mounted the horse with ease, and after reclaiming his bow, he was on his way.

They galloped through the castle's bailey and northern gate-house, and past the tiltyard, the snowy caps of the Kengian Alps in the distance. Turning a little to the north-east, Takai rode toward the thicket of trees on the horizon. The further from the castle they got, the easier it became to breathe.

Before long, they had reached the edge of the woodland, but Takai didn't stop. He urged the horse onward, galloping through the trees at a dangerously frantic pace. He ducked under low-hanging branches and gripped the reins tighter as they jumped over gullies. He knew he should slow the horse, but he was determined to leave his thoughts and old self behind.

Caught up in his inner turmoil, Takai was completely unprepared when the horse pulled up suddenly. Before he knew it, he was flying through the air. He came down hard on the ground.

The Prince sat up shakily, thankful he'd fallen into a deep layer of leaves and soft undergrowth, which appeared to have cushioned him from major injury. He stood up slowly, ready to admonish the horse. The stallion was stepping backward, his nostrils flared and the whites of his eyes showing. Takai grabbed the reins and calmed the horse enough to check if he had been hurt. He was relieved to find no obvious injuries.

Takai stepped back to gain his bearings. He'd never been this deep into the woodland, at least not alone. He looked around for landmarks or a way out, but could see none. He searched for the sun, but the canopy above was thick. Takai spun around in frustration – not noticing the creature until it was already upon him.

Its enormous chest flashed before his eyes, its front hooves beating high in the air. A glimpse of golden coat confirmed it was the wild Kengian horse, Meteor.

Takai retreated to the other side of his horse and instinctively reached for his longbow and arrow. Meteor was snorting and stamping at the ground. She looked as wild as all the stories he'd heard about the out-of-control mare. Takai pulled back his bow string and trained an arrow at the centre of the horse's neck. He took a breath to be sure he wouldn't miss, for he had only one chance at most to release an arrow—

'No!'

A cry rang through the forest, and a hand reached out to still his arm.

'*No,*' Arisa repeated, her amber eyes blazing.

'Stand back, Arisa!' His arrow remained trained on Meteor. 'That horse nearly killed me.'

'*That horse* saved you.'

'What?'

'Look.' Arisa pointed to the ground.

Takai was standing on the soft piles of leaves he'd landed in earlier. Arisa indicated to his right, where the undergrowth was piled even thicker, but there were also layers of sticks. Then it hit him. How hadn't he noticed?

He lowered his bow and arrow. 'It's a trap.'

Arisa nodded, her lips tightly pursed. 'A wolf trap.'

Takai wasn't surprised. The castle groundskeeper had reported losing a flock of chickens and livestock to the snow wolf.

Arisa bent down and pulled the branches aside to show him the long spikes embedded in the bottom of the pit. The smell of carrion wafted upward. 'And such a trap.' She shook her head to herself. 'Cruel and unnecessary. There are many other ways to trap an animal more humanely, if it must be done at all.'

Takai nodded silently. It would be a grisly death for any animal that fell into the pit.

Arisa moved all of the branches aside until the trap was fully exposed. 'In any case, they'll never catch the wolf. It can look after itself.'

'How can you be sure?'

'I'm sure,' she said confidently. 'But the wolf isn't the only living thing that comes out here.'

'You're right. I will see that the trap is filled.'

She nodded her head approvingly. 'Now, show me that.'

'What?'

She pointed. Takai looked down and registered, for the first time, the trickle of blood oozing from his right arm.

Arisa examined his limb, as expertly as she had done the first time they'd met. She took out a flask of water from Meteor's saddle bag and washed his wound.

'A decent cut, but not too deep. We won't have to amputate.' She gave a half-smile.

Takai froze. Even the smallest sign of affection from Arisa managed to unnerve him. He could barely make sense of it and was still unsure where they stood with each other. There had been so many misunderstandings between them. She had the highest expectations when it came to Takai, but he was never able to meet them, no matter how hard he tried. She'd made her disapproval of him clear from the moment they met.

Not long after his accident – the accident that would have killed him, had it not been for Arisa and her guardian – Takai had had a chance encounter with Arisa when he'd snuck out from his sick room. Stupidly, he'd injured himself falling down a stairwell, but Arisa had found him. It was the first time they'd properly spoken, and she had accused him and the King of being arrogant and selfish in their mistreatment of the Lamorian people. She was the first person who had ever spoken to him with such forthrightness. He had hated it, and her…at least initially.

Even now he still didn't fully understand her, or the secrets that hid behind her changeable eyes. He knew her guardian was a suspected Kengian and had been tasked with delivering forbidden magic in the form of firesky – something Takai didn't support. He feared all forms of Kengian magic, even if it might have been what saved the court in the marketplace a few weeks ago. He preferred to think instead about what *Arisa* had done that day. How she had saved them all. How, when she had spoken to him, she'd made him feel like he was the only person in the world – and simultaneously made him want to be a *better* person.

Takai took a good look at her and smiled to himself at her unkempt appearance. Her bronze hair escaping from a gold silk scarf tied loosely around her head. Her skirt crumpled and dirt-stained.

'You're making quite a habit of saving me,' he offered hesitantly, trying to catch her eye.

Arisa kept her gaze from him. 'Your arm needs a bandage.' She dug into her saddle bag again, retrieving a small swatch of linen and placing it over his wound. She rustled around for more and frowned, before untying her silk scarf.

'You can't use that.'

'Of course I can. It will do the job perfectly.'

'What are you doing here?' he asked, as she wound the scarf around his arm.

'I'm doing something for Willem.'

'Oh.' Takai's face fell as a strange pang of jealousy rippled through him.

Arisa tilted her head curiously.

'I mean...why would you need to come out here,' he stumbled, 'for Willem?'

'I'm collecting some herbs to mix some medicine. I think it will help with his pain.'

Takai's heart swelled. Willem had been born with a condition that affected his movement. Most people just noticed a limp, but those closest to him were aware of the pain he endured on a daily basis. No amount of the Duke's money or help from Royal Physicians had managed to ease his condition. But if Arisa had even a fraction of the healing powers and knowledge her guardian possessed, perhaps she could help his cousin.

'Do you need help?' he asked. 'Finding the plants you need?'

'I'm quite sure I'm capable of finding them myself.' She couldn't have sounded more dismissive.

Takai restrained himself from sighing. 'I know you're capable, Arisa. You're one of the most capable people I have ever met.' He wanted to add *intriguing* and *frustrating* to her list of qualities, but stopped himself. 'I merely wondered if you would *like* some help.'

Arisa shrugged. 'Suit yourself,' she said, and led Meteor back into the woods.

Takai grabbed his horse's reins and hurried to catch up.

'What are you looking for?'

'Henbane. It has—'

'Sharp-toothed leaves with sticky hairs,' Takai supplied. 'The flowers, which come out in spring, are bell-shaped and usually yellow.'

Arisa's eyebrows shot up.

'I did learn a thing or two from the Kengian farmers...the few who talked to me when I was at Talbot.'

She shrugged again. It appeared nothing would sway her preconceived beliefs about him.

'I don't know if there's any here, but I'm sure my mother mentioned once that Lore grew some in a garden near his rooms.'

'Lore.' Arisa's voice was soft, as if it were coming from far away.

Takai resisted the urge to talk about Lore and the extent of his grief. Arisa had made it obvious she didn't care for him or his feelings. 'I'll get the henbane for you,' he said matter-of-factly.

'Thank you.'

They walked in silence until he mustered up the courage to say something he'd been wanting to say for days now.

'What you did in the marketplace was quite remarkable.'

'Which part?' It sounded as if she were surprised to hear him say so.

'All of it. Saving me and my family. The way you calmed the people. The way you tended to the injured and sick.'

Arisa was silent.

'And what you said about how all Lamorians are the same.'

She stopped and glared at him. 'I said what had to be said to stop unnecessary deaths. I did it for the people. It was only they who would have suffered if the riot hadn't been quelled.'

Takai bristled, the truth cutting into him. He took a deep breath.

'You're right. Our people have been wronged, and we can do more.'

'We?'

'Me. I can do more.'

Arisa started to walk the horse again, but Takai could tell from how her shoulders relaxed that her mood had softened.

'That seems like a change of heart,' she said.

'Maybe I wasn't *listening* to my heart before.' His voice stuck in his throat. 'After all, it is my job to protect the most vulnerable. Someone wise once told me that.'

Arisa's cheeks flushed at the reference to her own words. They continued in awkward silence for some time before she spoke again.

'What do you propose?'

'Sorry?'

'What will you do to make change? How will you help, as you say you want to?'

What exactly *was* he proposing to do that wasn't already being done by his mother and father? Takai hadn't a clue.

'Figures,' she muttered to herself.

'Pardon me?'

She turned on him again, her eyes on fire. 'It figures. You say you want to help. You're in a position to help. But you do nothing.'

'But I'm powerless,' he protested. 'I don't run the kingdom.'

'You're the Prince, the future ruler of this kingdom, and you sit on the King's Council. You're hardly powerless.'

'What exactly should I do?' The Prince genuinely wanted Arisa's opinion – for he was at a loss – or was he looking for her approval?

'If you mean what you say, you'll come up with something.'

'And I will,' he said with conviction. 'I'll put my mind to it this instant.'

Arisa gave a hint of a smile in acknowledgement, and Takai's heart felt as if it would burst.

'Maybe once you're done with archery.' She indicated his bow and quiver.

'Archery can wait. As I said, I have some thinking to do, because if I don't...I fear what you may do to me.'

She laughed and slapped him playfully on the arm. The heat of her touch penetrated his sleeve and warmed the innermost part of his soul.

A spontaneous thought occurred to him.

'I don't suppose...' He faltered. 'I mean, would you like to try archery some time?'

Arisa stopped abruptly. Her smile had vanished. 'Oh...I don't know...'

It annoyed him that she was searching for an excuse. Takai's joy vanished. He wondered why he had asked in the first place. He was never going to be able to please her. The injury her refusal had dealt, though, made him determined to make a point.

'Arisa, I *wish* for you to join me at archery.'

She folded her arms. 'You wish, or you order me?'

'They are the same thing for a Prince.'

Arisa's eyes burned with hate. He regretted his words immediately, but stubbornness prevented him from taking them back.

Takai mounted his horse and looked down at her. 'I will send instructions for you to join me at the archery oval the next time I go.' He dug his heels into the horse's belly and rode off before Arisa could protest further.

Takai felt a thousand times worse than when he'd set off into the woodland. He was furious with himself. He had proven to Arisa that he was as arrogant as she accused him of being. Somehow, he would have to make it up to her.

At least he would have a chance to argue his case in person at archery. Takai would prove his worth to her then...if she turned up. If only he hadn't let Arisa get under his skin, but for whatever reason he lost command of himself every time he was around her.

6

$\mathcal{T}$heodora was as angry with herself as she was at the Prince for snubbing her. She had been sure Takai would invite her to join him at archery. She had taken care to look her most becoming when she'd sought him out. Not one warm-blooded male at court would have baulked at spending some time with her – not one except Takai, it seemed. She'd been furious with him, so angry she had lost her temper and threatened him – an unwise decision, she realised now. She would have to find another way to get the Prince's attention.

If only her father had given her some other task. She wasn't surprised that he hadn't entrusted her with something else, though. He had fixed views about the roles of the 'fairer sex'. Theodora believed these views dated back to when Horace had first met Gwyn – independent-minded and warrior-trained – and fallen in love with her, only to have his heart broken by her. It was why he'd sought a compliant beauty for his wife, someone who wouldn't upstage or challenge him. He'd got everything he'd wanted in the Countess, including her noble pedigree and her ancestral lands.

Theodora had tried to talk to her mother about the injustice of her never being able to inherit the lands she was entitled to –

Lamorian law dictated that they would be her husband's, and her son's after that. But the Countess had merely giggled as if it were a great joke, saying, 'A woman *owning* lands – how ridiculous. She wouldn't know what to do with them.'

It wasn't, of course, the first time Theodora had become aware of the stark differences in how the sexes were treated in Lamore.

For their fifth birthday, Guthrie had been given a sword, and Theodora a doll.

Her brother had been trained in swordsmanship while she was taught deportment, learning critical skills like how to walk with a book on her head.

While Guthrie practised jousting with a quintain in the tilt-yard, she was instructed in elocution and dance.

All the while, Horace would applaud his son for brutally injuring his swordmaster, while chastising Theodora for not being quiet enough at the dinner table. 'Just smile sweetly,' he would say. 'No one likes a lady with an opinion.'

When Guthrie had been sent to live with Sir Marcus in Ette, Theodora had hoped that she would fill her brother's place and learn about the running of the kingdom. She'd even read a book on military tactics, hoping to impress her father, but he'd said, 'No man likes a woman who's smarter than him.'

So Theodora had spent her early teenage years giving the appearance of being a 'lady' – making herself attractive to every young nobleman at court, but secretly listening to their conversations. Over games of cards and chess, which she deliberately lost more than once ('Because you cannot show up a man,' her father reminded her), she would take in their assessment of politics and the like, gaining the schooling her father denied her.

She was certain that one day he would see her real value, but in the meantime she would use the only power at her disposal: her beauty. She would use it to secure a crown and, in turn, *real* power – power she'd wield better than any man. She just needed to bring the Prince to her side…unless her father was finally giving her a seat at the table.

Today, he had invited her to accompany him on a secret outing. Theodora rode beside him as they passed the city's central stores. The place was a hive of activity, with dozens of wagons coming and going, and teams of labourers loading and unloading bulky sacks and pallets of goods. When the King had banned nobles from hoarding supplies and selling them back to the people at impossible prices, he had presented them with an attractive alternative. The King agreed to purchase grain and other produce above the market rate, on the proviso that the landowning lords shared the increased profits with their tenant farmers. The King was paying for the supplies from his personal coffers, except for a portion paid from the national treasury, for supplies being stockpiled for the Lamorian army. Food supplies were being sold back to the citizens at a fair price, and some were donated to the poor. The nobles were pleased with the arrangement, as were the people.

Theodora had heard her father describe it as a populist move – the Queen's idea – but short-sighted. The King's coffers were full thanks to Horace's canny management over the years…but they wouldn't stay that way, according to her father. At this rate, the King would expend his personal funds within a few months.

The Secretary looked away from the stores with distaste and continued toward their destination – a destination unknown to Theodora. All she had been told was that her father had received an important message to meet someone, and a demand that she be in attendance at that meeting. Theodora couldn't imagine who would insist on her being part of her father's business, but she relished the fact that someone had.

When they reached the steep path that led down to Obira's dockyards, Theodora followed her father's lead and pulled her hood up over her head – whatever their mission, it was a secret. But they needn't have worried. At any other time they would have had to jostle their way through the bustling community servicing the port and its visitors; there were usually merchants, bankers, clerks, shopkeepers, foreigners, stevedores, fishermen and sailors hurrying about. Now, it was a ghost town. The port's warehouses, custom houses, open markets and inns were all but abandoned. The harbour cranes stood stationary, their usually creaking arms eerily silent. There were no ships to unload. No cargo of livestock, cloth, precious metals – none of the goods Lamore relied on. The bounties Lamore had previously acquired from Ette were now Malu's. The best of the riches were diverted back to Northem. What little Lamore had to trade itself could no longer pass through Ette's port, at least not officially. The kingdom had to rely on a handful of merchant ships with trading partners in little known lands, well beyond Ette.

Theodora watched as a lone fishing vessel unloaded its catch of flounder and herring under the watchful eyes of the Royal Guards. The guards vastly outnumbered any other people on the docks – a necessary presence since the Northemer ship had snuck into port.

Horace urged his horse further along the stone dock, passing the only other source of industry: the shipbuilders tasked with rebuilding the King's naval fleet. Theodora noted with disappointment that the Prince didn't appear to be on site. She imagined her father had deliberately timed their visit to avoid him.

They passed Custom House. An official leant back on his chair against the wall, lazily picking his teeth. Theodora shivered as a salty breeze cut into her, rattling a wooden sign that hung precariously above them. The sign read *Smith & Son, Merchants* in faded gold lettering. The merchants were long gone – their warehouse empty, its wooden shutters broken and hanging loose from their hinges. The walls were thick with grime, but the word *Sergei* was etched into the outer stone wall, alongside a depiction of a raised fist.

Theodora saw her father grit his teeth at the sight of the rebellion leader's name.

Sergei was the former reeve of Horace's estate at Calliope and had been displaced after Horace enclosed his lands. In retaliation, Sergei had rallied the peasants and Kengian farmers and incited several uprisings against their landholding lords. The King and the nobles blamed Horace for the threat Sergei posed, and for his failure to capture the man. Sergei continued to elude all of the Royal Guards and provided further cause for Horace to remain in the King's disfavour. After the riot in the marketplace, the Prince's friend Sar had been sent to capture him.

Sar was a sentimental fool in Theodora's eyes. She suspected the young knight actually sympathised with the rebel cause, so it was unlikely he would capture Sergei. Horace said the same, and was convinced the rebel leader would remain a thorn in his side. So it was strange that a smile suddenly appeared on his face.

Horace urged his horse to pick up its pace to a trot until they came to the only other ship berthed at the docks – a sleek-looking schooner. A motley crew was cleaning the deck and tending to the sails. Horace stopped and dismounted, removing his hood and handing his reins to the nearest guard. He indicated for Theodora to do the same.

'Secretary, as ordered, we have not allowed anyone to leave the ship,' the guard said. 'We were about to send word to the Duke on how to proceed with its unauthorised arrival, but the ship's captain demanded to see you, and the Lady Theodora. I explained it was impossible, but he was quite insistent.'

Horace gave a brisk nod that didn't invite further discussion and made his way to the ship's gangplank. He stepped carefully onto it, advancing slowly across the narrow beam, his eyes intent on his fine leather boots, which had been designed with style rather than function in mind. Theodora followed slowly.

Horace exhaled loudly as he took his last step off the beam, only to lose his balance at the last moment. He waved his hands around frantically, but a meaty paw grabbed his arm and pulled him safely to the deck.

'Looks like you owe me again,' the owner of the hand chortled. 'But this time it's *your* life I saved.' The man tipped his hat to Theodora. 'My lady,' he said, offering his hand to help her off the gangplank.

Theodora groaned inwardly, recognising the pirate, Goldman, who'd aided Guthrie's cowardly escape during Northem's invasion of Ette. She slapped his hand away.

Goldman was as she remembered. Dripping in gold chains and rings, his large frame threatening to spill any moment from his vest, he had one beady eye fixed on Horace. The other was swollen shut.

'What happened to your eye?' the Secretary asked.

'The same thing that happened to your Ivanian-born ambassador. Though I think I fared a little better than him, no?' The pirate's gold teeth glinted in the sun's silvery light.

Horace clicked his jaw impatiently in response.

'Below decks!' Goldman bellowed, and the crew immediately complied.

Horace looked around, clearly assuring himself they couldn't be overheard. 'That' – he pointed at the pirate's injury – 'was for delivering my message?'

'Your message didn't exactly help matters. Malu was as perplexed as I was when Lore arrived in Ette offering money for the Northemers to leave, and within days of me delivering your proposal of an alliance. What exactly was your strategy?'

Horace shrugged. Like Theodora, it seemed the pirate would be in the dark when it came to her father's plans.

Goldman narrowed his eye and gave a knowing smile. 'While your mixed-up business didn't help me, Malu was less impressed with the other purpose of my visit.'

Horace smirked. 'Did you really expect him to *thank you* for holding his brother to ransom?'

'It's my experience that people are prepared to pay anything for their loved ones.' The pirate looked frustratingly pleased with himself. It was a reminder that Horace had paid the fine sum of ten thousand gold pieces to Goldman to secure Guthrie's escape – money wasted, in Theodora's opinion.

'So Malu didn't meet your demands?'

Goldman screwed up his mouth. 'He did not. From what I could tell, Malu's actions are paid in violence, not coin.'

Horace barked a laugh. 'I could have told you that.'

'I suppose you could have. I hear he sent a little invading party to the castle to deliver the Ivanian's head.'

'He made his stance very clear in that respect, as well as in a written note – curiously crafted in perfect Lamorian. I understand from a witness that there is a girl among the Northemers who speaks our tongue as if it's her own.'

A strange flicker flared in the pirate's eye. 'Didn't see much of the girl myself.' He waved a hand dismissively. 'A Lamorian runaway or something, I expect.'

Theodora frowned. It intrigued her that a girl had been at the head of the invading party. Perhaps the Northemers were far more advanced than Lamore and her father when it came to a woman's 'place'.

'So, *pirate*,' the Secretary went on. 'Tell me how you stand before me now with nothing more than a bunged-up eye.'

Goldman grunted. 'Malu let me leave with my life on one condition…I'm to report back to him on all of Lamore's plans.'

'You have the gall to tell me you are acting as a Northem spy?'

'I'm his spy as much as I'm yours.'

'Let me guess. You'll align yourself with Malu, as well as me. So no matter what happens you will be on the winning side?'

The pirate retrieved a pipe from inside his vest and lit it, taking a long puff.

Horace sighed. 'What's your price?'

'As before. A knighthood and governorship of Ette when you reclaim it.'

Horace nodded, though Theodora knew he had no intention of ever meeting the pirate's demands.

'And…' Goldman looked in Theodora's direction and gave a wolfish smile.

'And?'

'And your daughter as my wife.'

Theodora made a loud scoffing sound. There was no limit to the pirate's brazenness.

'Yes.' Goldman's good eye gleamed at Theodora. 'I was quite taken with your fine looks when I met you.'

The man was serious! Theodora's skin crawled, remembering how he had leered at her when he had come to the castle before his trip to Ette.

'I'm already promised to another,' she said quickly.

The pirate chuckled to himself. 'That's not what I hear. In fact, *I* hear the Prince prefers another. A girl from Obira, who the whole kingdom is practically in love with.'

Theodora wondered how Goldman had heard of such matters, especially since he'd only just got back to port. She lifted her chin defiantly. 'The Prince favours me above all.'

Goldman chortled. 'That's the thing. I know that you and your father, the *Secretary*, are in fact very much *out* of favour, and that right now, you need me more than I need you.'

Theodora's palms felt suddenly sweaty inside her kid gloves.

'You will go back to Malu and assure him the Ivanians don't represent us,' Horace said. 'And my original offer still stands.'

The pirate puffed a ring of smoke in Horace's face. 'If I am to do that, you will allow my ship and crew to come and go from the port as we please?'

'So you can sell questionably acquired goods to the unsuspecting people of Lamore?'

Goldman flung his free hand to his chest dramatically, as if to say, *Who, me?*

'Very well. You can come and go as you please.'

'And your daughter?'

Horace nodded slowly. 'If you help me succeed, you will have everything you asked for.'

'Father!' Theodora protested, but he did not even look at her.

'I would like to hear it from the lady's own mouth,' the pirate insisted. 'That she agrees to marry me as part of this deal.'

The word *never* was on Theodora's lips, but it froze there as her father gripped her arm tightly.

'My daughter will gladly comply.'

Goldman cast a hungry gaze at Theodora. 'From her mouth.'

Horace dug his fingernails into his daughter's arm.

'I agree,' she hissed through clenched teeth.

The pirate's face broke into a wide smile. He twirled his hand in a mock flourish. 'I'm at your service, Secretary.'

'How could you?' Theodora screeched at her father as soon as they were out of earshot.

'I did what had to be done.'

'But agreeing to hand me over to that…that *pig* of a man—'

Horace turned to her then, his gaze cold. 'Secure the Prince and you need not worry about marrying the pirate.'

Theodora's stomach clenched. It was clear now that Horace would stop at nothing to further his own cause, and that he would hand her over to the pirate without hesitation, if it came to it.

And given how things were with Takai, it may very well come to it.

Knowing this only magnified Theodora's determination to win the crown at all costs. Not just to avoid marrying the vile pirate, but to see the day that her cruel father would have to bend the knee to her – the day that he would be *her* pawn.

7

*A*risa had given Takai much to think about. What could he actually do to help Lamore? How could he prove he was the leader he wished to be? She made it all sound so simple, but it wasn't. There was nothing simple about running a kingdom – especially a kingdom on the brink of war. And while Takai wished to help people who were suffering through no fault of their own, it wasn't so easy to support those who threatened the kingdom's interests: the likes of Sergei and his rebels, those who practised forbidden Kengian magic, and those who had their own agenda – namely Horace.

Takai's brief encounter with Theodora had been a chilling reminder that the Secretary and his daughter's schemes were still alive, and that Arisa was an obstacle to all of them. With this in mind, the Prince had decided to speak to his father.

The King greeted him with a delirious grin. 'Son, it's so marvellous to see you. I've been meaning to talk to you about our great celebrations.'

'Actually, Father, I was hoping to talk to you about the Northemer strategy.'

The King sighed, as if annoyed to be bothered with any real

business regarding the kingdom. 'The Ivanian alliance will assure us victory. Your mother's brother is certain.'

'I know, Father, and with their forces and our new naval fleet, I believe it is our best strategy.' He took a deep beath. 'I'm just concerned that...alternative schemes may undermine our chances.'

'Alternative?'

'Horace's plan to side with the Northemers instead. His quest for firesky. His aim of weaponising it.'

The King got up from his chair and patted his son on the shoulder. 'Don't worry, my boy. It is just insurance...just in case.'

'But I don't think Horace sees it that way,' Takai persisted. 'It is the only way, as far as he is concerned, and he will stop at nothing to get it. And the stakes are even higher for him now that you've tied his future position at court to delivering firesky. No one will be safe from him and his ambition. No one.'

'What are you saying?' The King inclined his head. 'That I should abandon plans for firesky? It will be quite the spectacle for our celebrations—'

'Father, I think it is dangerous to rely on anything that involves Kengian magic – especially magic that hasn't been seen in hundreds of years. It's an impossible task. I'm just worried about what lengths Horace will go to...and who he'll destroy along the way.'

The King frowned. 'If there's even the slightest chance of creating firesky and weaponising it, I must take that chance. This is bigger than our celebrations. It is bigger than this spat with the Northemers. It is *my* legacy. It is your legacy. We will be the greatest leaders the Kyprian nations have ever seen.'

Takai's heart sank as he realised his father hadn't changed as much as he'd hoped. The King wasn't really interested in helping Lamore; beyond keeping the Queen happy, he was concerned only with himself and his own ego. And with this realisation, Takai knew it was up to him to represent the kingdom's interests. It was up to him to make sure that the King never needed firesky – that between Takai, Lakeford and Ivane, they would be well equipped to face the Northemers. And it was up to him to keep Arisa safe.

8

---

*G*iven that Theodora was yet to come up with a new strategy to capture Takai's heart, she focused on a comment he had made to her some time ago. The Prince had told her that any woman who was capable of riding a particular horse was worthy of being his wife.

Theodora was a skilled rider. She was capable not only of keeping pace with the best equestrians at court, but also outriding many of them. Side-saddle or astride, it didn't matter; she was a superior horsewoman, and being the best at something gave her immense pleasure. Her riding prowess had never failed to garner her the recognition she sought…that was, until the arrival of Arisa.

Somehow, the ridiculously inexperienced rider had managed to tame the horse the Prince had spoken of. Meteor was a rare Kengian mare who'd been left at the castle when Prince Alik had died. She was a beautiful beast, with a coat of liquid gold and a fiery nature that prevented anyone from riding her. Not even Sar had managed to sit on her for more than a few moments – but Theodora had been determined it would be she who broke in the bad-tempered creature. She'd wanted to show

Prince Takai she had succeeded where everyone else had failed. She'd wanted to show him her strength and superiority. But she had been beaten to it...by Arisa.

But now, if Theodora too could just ride the Kengian mare, the Prince may favour her again. He would see she had many more virtues than that lowborn and frankly plain-looking peasant girl. If Theodora were being truthful with herself, she would admit that the plan was a long shot, and that it had become more about proving to herself that she could equal Arisa. But even so, she was failing dismally.

Lately she had noticed she'd lost her ability to inflict her will upon any steed. Annoyingly, the most docile horses in the stables now reared and pulled against her, whinnying as if they were laughing at her – as if Arisa and Meteor had whispered some spell in their ears. Today, Theodora had hit an all-time low when a delicate-looking pony had thrown her to the ground in the mounting yard. She had stormed off, humiliated, the stable boys' laughter still ringing in her ears.

As she marched away from the stables, she was keenly aware of her dishevelled appearance. Her purple velvet riding habit – the colour usually reserved for royalty – was dirt-stained, its ermine trim crushed. Theodora was still picking chunks of gravel from her hair when a messenger arrived. Her father was demanding her immediate presence.

Instinctively, Theodora's kid-gloved hand tightened around her riding crop. He was the last person she wanted to see.

She arrived at the Secretary's rooms to find him pouring himself a large cup of wine. He glanced up at her entrance, and raised an eyebrow at her appearance.

'Don't ask,' she responded sharply.

'I wasn't asking.'

Horace sat down in a high-backed, upholstered chair, motioning for Theodora to sit opposite him. She sat hesitantly, mentally preparing herself for her father's displeasure. He put his wine down on a side table and steepled his fingers.

'The Prince.' He didn't need to say anything more.

Theodora shook her head. 'I've barely seen him since the marketplace.' She didn't tell her father how Takai had openly snubbed her a few days before on his way to archery. 'He occasionally comes to the Queen's rooms, but I understand he is much occupied with overseeing the rebuilding of the fleet.'

Her father leant forward in his seat. 'He's not spending time with the ward?'

'Not to my knowledge.'

Horace relaxed back into his chair again. 'That is good news, though we must be sure of it. You will need to watch the girl closely.'

Theodora groaned.

Horace reached out and grabbed her arm tightly, his dark eyes narrowing.

'You have already failed me by not making friends with the ward, as I previously instructed. I accept that friendship is no longer possible, but you must be vigilant. You must know where she is, who she is with, and what she is doing. She is critical to our plans. Do you understand?'

He tightened his grip. Theodora winced. She wanted to scream that she did *not* understand, because her father refused to share all his plans with her. She wanted to ask him if Arisa had anything to do with the weapon he'd promised the Northemers, or if it was just another one of his lies. But instead she nodded.

'I understand. I'll bring the Prince back to my side, and watch the girl, as well as those close to her.'

'You must try to find whatever secrets bind Arisa, and the healer, to the Queen and Gwyn.'

Theodora nodded. 'Trust me. I will not be outsmarted by a peasant girl, a pathetic excuse for a Queen or her trumped-up guard dog.'

'Good. Good.' Horace released his grip on Theodora's arm.

Theodora had meant what she said. She was determined to do whatever it took to become Queen. 'What of you, Father?'

she ventured hesitantly, wishing to know whatever it was he'd been keeping from her. 'What will you do?'

Horace raised a brow before deigning to speak. 'I am fighting for us on several fronts, but the most important of those may take some time to come to fruition. In the meantime, I must do everything I can to undermine the Queen's power. The King must see he is badly advised by her peace-loving policies, that his people continue to work against him, and that Lamore needs a firm hand. It cannot be ruled with benevolence and mercy. The King must see this. He must realise there is only one person he can trust to bring his subjects to order.'

'And that person is you?' *When I'm Queen, it will be me,* she thought.

Horace smirked and took a sip of his wine.

Theodora was about to ask how he intended on undermining the Queen, when an urgent pealing of bells rang through the air. She raced to the window and looked out toward Obira, her eyes drawn to a tower of smoke billowing from the edge of the city. Bright red flames licked the sky above the port.

'There's something on fire,' she cried. 'Something big!'

But her father didn't join her at the window. Instead he calmly sipped his wine.

'Father, you must see it. Goodness, I think it's coming from the grain stores.'

Horace didn't budge. He merely smiled at her.

Theodora looked out the window again, to the castle grounds filled with onlookers below. Everyone was pointing and shouting; guards were mounting horses and rushing toward Obira. She could hear screams in the distance as the cloud of smoke grew, its blackness devouring the city. It was horrifying. And in all the chaos, no one appeared to notice the lone rider on the grey stallion as he galloped through the castle gate. The rider's hood was pulled up over his head and there was nothing to distinguish him, but Theodora recognised him immediately. She would have known him anywhere.

'Guthrie,' she whispered.

Theodora would have told Horace of her brother's unexpected arrival, but she didn't need to. Nothing about this was a surprise to her father.

9

*A*risa's mind was awhirl as she left her lesson with the Schoolmaster. He was visiting regularly to help her pass the entrance examination for the College of Surgeons. Although the King had made it clear he would waive the testing requirement as a sign of gratitude for what she'd done the day of the riot, Arisa was determined to earn her place. And since she wasn't a noble or a man, she had more to prove.

But that wasn't the only reason the Schoolmaster was still meeting with her. He was the conduit between Erun and a Shaman who was in communication with the Kengian Queen via starling messages. The Schoolmaster had reported that tensions were still high in Kengia among the nation's leaders, who were understandably fearful of a Lamorian invasion. Queen Mira was still advocating peaceful means, but the Kengian Mountain Chief and his tribes were preparing for war. Mira was losing support from her tribal leaders, who were starting to question her right to rule as Queen, since she only held the position through marriage. Now King Leo was dead, there had been talk of a leadership challenge as well as a pre-emptive attack on Lamore. With the support of her daughter,

Princess Kairi, Mira was only just maintaining power – but she needed assurances from Erun.

Arisa knew Erun had told his mother he remained confident war wouldn't come to Kengia. He'd reminded Queen Mira that Lamore was fully occupied with the Northemer threat. This only bought them time, though. Whether it was Lamore or the Northemers, someone would come for Kengia. The Northemers had already demonstrated what a threat they were, making it all the way into the castle grounds. Arisa had heard that among the Northem army was a girl with unusual powers who spoke perfect Lamorian. Her instinct told her there was much more to this girl.

Erun and the Kengian Queen must know of the whole breadth of dangers they were facing, but for some inexplicable reason, they were holding fast to the hope that matters would be resolved...given enough time.

Arisa had also asked the Schoolmaster for news of the Kengian woman who had been spared from execution after speaking out in support of Sergei, the rebel leader. Arisa hadn't forgotten Lina, who had lost her son, Hyando, the night of the blood moon. The boy with the startlingly silver eyes – the colour only a few Kengians possessed – an innocent child who had died at the reckless hands of the Royal Guards. The boy she and Erun had failed to save.

The Schoolmaster had assured her that Lina was under Sergei's protection, and that she was safe – as safe as anyone could be hiding out with Lamore's most wanted man. Fortunately, Sergei didn't seem inclined to upset the current peace in Lamore. Through the Schoolmaster, Erun and Arisa had given their own assurances that the rebels had support at court, and would be given warning of any plans to move against them. And if there was an immediate threat to Sergei and his support-ers, Erun had promised to send an unmistakable signal.

When the great fire had happened at Obira's stores a few days before, Erun sent an urgent message to Sergei to say that it wasn't the signal they'd been waiting for. The blaze had been devastating. Several Lamorians had died; dozens more were badly injured. Arisa was frustrated that she and Erun couldn't be there to help. She was hopeful the King would allow her to visit some of the victims soon and offer what little medical treatment she could.

Arisa and Erun had sworn the Schoolmaster and Shaman to secrecy about what the real signal was. A signal Arisa hoped would never be needed.

The launch of firesky.

It would be the quickest way to get a warning to Sergei. Erun would only launch it if all other options were exhausted – that was, if the Queen's protection over all of them was gone. But if firesky were launched, that meant Horace could gain control of its power, and its potential to become an unstoppable weapon.

'It won't come to that,' Arisa said to herself, with as much confidence as she could muster. She pushed the idea of war from her mind. She tried not to think of her contingency plan to kill the King. She tried not to give in to the selfish thoughts of her and Erun's lives on the line. Right now, she had some other unpleasant business to deal with.

Begrudgingly, she made her way to the archery oval to meet Prince Takai.

Arisa couldn't understand why the Prince had ordered her to spend time with him. They had been getting along well enough when they'd met in the woodland, until he'd started pulling rank and insisting she do his bidding. If he had only asked her kindly to join him at archery, she might have agreed. Something about Takai made her want to be around him, but not when he reverted to his default state of arrogance.

In the marketplace, that day when everything had changed, the Prince had indicated that he wanted to be a better leader, though his actions more recently had led Arisa to question whether he could be. But part of her still believed that with the right guidance, he could change. It was this belief that had stopped her from leaving the castle and drove her today to meet his order.

Arisa passed through the central courtyard and the southern gate after telling the guards she was 'taking a turn in the gardens'. But after taking the path leading to the Queen's gardens, she wasn't sure where to go. She only had a vague idea of the direction of the archery oval, but she hadn't wanted to ask for directions. Arisa didn't want to reveal her meeting with Takai to anyone. She wasn't quite sure why.

She wandered along a pebble path that stretched beyond the gardens. A line of oaks lay straight ahead, bordering the south garden. She knew the landmarks from the view she had from her bedroom, but they looked different at ground level. Arisa stopped to gain her bearings, training her ears to the breeze rustling through the trees.

Come this way, the wind whispered to her right.

She took the path in the direction of the voice. Soon she was surrounded by a small woodland, and a further few steps brought her to a clearing. It was a large, open space overlooking the sea. To the north-west, she could see the point of land that jutted out from the Lamorian peninsula peeking out from behind the castle boundary wall, offering glimpses of Obira City in the distance. Arisa stepped onto a perfectly manicured lawn, noting the hessian-covered targets at its far end. She'd found the archery oval.

A glance to her left found Takai pacing. He was completely alone. There was a jittery feeling in her stomach. She wasn't sure if she felt excited, or anxious, or both. Suddenly confused, she made to retreat to the castle—

'You're not leaving already, are you?' Takai's voice trembled slightly, as if he were nervous.

'I've got to...' Arisa grasped for an excuse, but couldn't think of one. 'Is no one else joining us?'

'Just us.' The Prince smiled brightly. 'I should have thought to tell you I practise archery alone. It's the only real time I have to myself. It gives me a chance to think – think for myself, that is. Not have someone telling me I need to do this or do that.'

Arisa relaxed at his honesty. 'If you wish to be alone, me being here would be at odds with your purpose...wouldn't it?' she teased.

Takai raised an eyebrow in amusement. 'When I say alone, I mean away from...' He trailed off, as if he were choosing his words carefully. 'Away from the usual company I have to keep.'

Arisa felt a flutter in her chest, wondering whether he was talking about avoiding Theodora.

'You mean to say I'm not the *usual* company you have to keep?' She flung her hands dramatically to her chest. 'I'm mortally offended.'

'There is not one ounce of *usual* about you, Arisa.'

'I will take that as a compliment.'

'As you should.'

His dark eyes fixed on her a little longer than necessary, and she looked away.

'Here, take this.' Takai handed her a longbow as tall as she was, and picked up an even larger one, closer to his height, for himself. He pointed to her bow. 'That's one of my favourites from when I was younger. It's a bit old and tired-looking, I'm sorry, but all my other bows are probably a bit large for you.'

She turned it over in her hands. The bow was worn smooth in places. She could see where Takai's palm and fingers had left a shallow imprint in the wood. Its aged appearance only made it more beautiful.

Takai noted her interest and ran his palm along the upper and lower limbs of the bow. 'It's made of a single piece of yew wood. The wood is dried for several years, and slowly worked into shape during that time. The yew is soft enough to mould and bend, but strong enough to withstand the tension of the string.'

Arisa liked hearing that something could be so strong, but soft and yielding at the same time.

She began to lose herself in the gentle murmur of Takai's voice. Here was another side to the Prince she hadn't seen before. He was like the changing seasons: one moment, as harsh and cold as winter; the next, full of light and the promise of spring. He was unpredictable, and it intrigued her. With him she could experience every season. But that was the problem — she never knew when a summer storm was brewing.

Takai examined his own bow, thankfully unaware of her intense stare. 'You see, a bow is an amazing thing. It must be equally proficient in maintaining tension and resisting compression. Part of the bow comes from the sapwood, or the outside of the tree, and the remainder comes from the heartwood.'

Arisa was mesmerised by the intensity of his voice. By the fact that he could experience such passion for a seemingly simple object. 'You said it's made from yew?' she asked. 'How unusual.'

'The yew is one of the only trees that can provide such properties in equal measure,' Takai explained. 'Unfortunately, you would be hard-pressed to find a yew tree, or a bow made from yew, these days. The yew tree is practically extinct...well, in Lamore, at least.'

She nodded knowingly, not mentioning that the yew held a special place in all Kengians' hearts. The silver yew tree in Kengia's capital, Lochlen, was the source of all magic. The source of the silver-eyed magic that was in her. Every Kengian was born with some magic in their veins, which enabled them to become one with nature. Silver-eyes like Arisa could learn to hear the voices of nature at a heightened level. With the right training, they — *she* — could learn to manipulate the natural elements in small ways, albeit not to the extent of the prophesied Water Catcher or any of the Kengian firstborn lines. Arisa may never be a Kengian Scholar like Erun, who had learned science and spells to harness the lifeforce known as *kira*, but with the visions she'd been having, she was beginning to wonder if she had Shamanic abilities within her. She couldn't know for sure…not without talking to Erun. But there was no point while he still refused to help her harness her powers.

Takai looked out toward the Nymoi Alps on the horizon. Arisa wondered if he was thinking about how his future lay in invading the neighbouring land – that was what *she* was thinking about. Then a sadness fell over his face, like autumn leaves fluttering to the ground. She wanted to bring back the light she'd seen in him earlier.

'What are bows made of now?' Her voice sounded overly bright.

Takai gave a strained smile. 'They are a composite of different woods, but the longbow is practically a lost art form. Armies these days have crossbows capable of piercing a soldier's armour. Anyone can pick up a crossbow and use it reasonably well. That is the future of war. Armies of warriors absent the skills and discipline that come with the bow.'

A chilly breeze blew across Arisa's face. If only the Prince knew of firesky and how its explosive powers could be harnessed for devastating new weapons. Weapons capable of bringing down a castle and city walls, and probably used even more indiscriminately to cut through masses of soldiers. She wondered what kind of future he would see then.

'Why a longbow?' she asked.

'Pardon?'

'If a crossbow is much more powerful and effective in battle, why would you want to use a longbow?'

Takai's eyes brightened. 'A crossbow is more accurate at a closer range, but they are heavy and cumbersome, and, as I said, don't require as much skill as a longbow. Skill is something that should be admired and aspired to. If a life must be taken, let it be done at the hands of someone who trained hard in their craft. If you must go to war, at least be able to respect your fellow combatants' skills. A battle should be decided by the training of its soldiers and the strategy of its leaders, not by who has the most powerful equipment. The longbow forces you to respect life and bravery.'

Arisa smiled to herself. The Prince was practically quoting the Kengian and Ivanian warrior codes without realising. His mother had influenced him more than he probably realised.

Takai plucked an arrow from his quiver. 'Someone skilled in the longbow can shoot twelve arrows a minute and pierce armour like the crossbow. The longbow is lighter and quicker to load, and can go a much longer distance. It can also be used on horseback.' A lightness had returned to his voice.

The Prince loaded his bow and pulled the string back toward his jaw. He raised the bow, one eye closed, the other focused on the target, which Arisa estimated was about two hundred yards from them.

'How's your arm?' she asked, remembering the injury he had sustained in the woods.

'Thanks to you, it's fine.' A smile tugged at the side of his mouth, but his gaze never left the target.

'It must be accuracy, then, that lets the longbow down,' she said.

Takai released the string, sending the arrow decisively to the centre of the target. Arisa couldn't repress a gasp.

The Prince grinned. 'It's not inaccurate in skilled hands. If you're prepared to practise, you can master the longbow. And practice is something I have done plenty of.'

He put down his bow and motioned for Arisa to lift hers.

'Your turn. You take the bow like this.' Takai stood behind her, guiding her hands. Her breath quickened at the warmth of his body. 'Take an arrow' – he pointed to the feathered end – 'and lock its end on the string. Take hold of the string with your index, middle and ring fingers. The arrow should be between these two fingers.' He touched her fingers lightly. 'Pull on the string and the arrow and it will hold itself in place. Now, draw the arrow back to here.'

Takai pulled the string back toward her jaw and the corner of her mouth, then released her hands.

'Focus your attention on the smallest spot on the target you can find,' he whispered. His lips were almost touching her ear. 'Pull back and hold, until that spot becomes clear and all else around it becomes a blur.'

Arisa squinted at the target, willing everything around it to go hazy. Her arms had started to wobble from maintaining the tension on the string. Her bow was shaking. Takai reached out and steadied her.

'Take as long as you need.'

Her heart thumped wildly – she was sure Takai could hear it. She closed her eyes and willed herself to focus. She could hear the steady inhaling and exhaling of Takai's breath, feeling it in her chest until her own breath slowed to match it. She opened her eyes and refocused.

'Relax your fingers and release,' Takai whispered.

Arisa let go of the string with an outward breath. The arrow left her bow and travelled a hundred yards or so before falling to the ground, well short of the target. Her heart fell with it.

'Good,' Takai declared. 'A good start. We'll have you ready to compete in the tournament in no time.' He gave a cheeky smile.

Arisa rolled her eyes in response.

Takai guided her through a few more attempts. Her arrow gained a few more yards each time, but her technique was clumsy, and the arrow refused to fly cleanly through the air as Takai's had done. Yet the Prince was delighted with her progress, and she couldn't help but share in his enthusiasm.

After they had exhausted all the arrows, they started the arduous task of retrieving them. Arisa felt confident enough now to broach certain matters with the Prince. She wanted to test how serious he was about helping his people. She began with what she thought was a rather innocent remark.

'I expect the King's Council is quite occupied…with the fire and all.'

Takai's face darkened. 'You could say that.'

Arisa raised a questioning brow.

'We lost nearly all of the supplies set aside for the army, as well as what the King had hoped to donate to the people. Grain will probably have to be rationed. Many of the nobles are calling for taxes to be increased again so supplies can be purchased from the few merchant ships we still have access to.'

A lump formed in Arisa's throat. Her immediate thoughts had been for the victims of the fire. It hadn't occurred to her that it could also mean the end of the recent gestures of good-will from the King. 'Surely it doesn't have to come to that,' she ventured.

'Not yet. We are holding strong to the alliance with Ivane, and we can call on their generosity, but it's a lot to ask.'

'And what of the fire victims?'

'The King has left their care to the city – until he is sure of who lit the fire.'

'What!' She looked up sharply from the arrows she was collecting. 'You mean to say it wasn't an accident?'

Takai shook his head adamantly. 'They think it was Sergei.'

'Why would they suspect him?'

'His name was plastered all over what was left of the build-ing's walls.'

'That doesn't mean he did it.' Her voice began to rise. 'Even if he did, he wouldn't be foolish enough to leave his name behind. Regardless, I can't think of any possible reason he would want to do it.'

Takai folded his arms. 'I can think of plenty of reasons. To undermine us and incapacitate our army so they can't come after him. To distract us while he plans an attack on the castle. Should I go on?'

Arisa frowned. The Takai she liked the least was returning.

'Think about it, Takai. Sergei has only asked for one thing, and that is for all Lamorians and Kengians to be treated fairly. The people are what matters to him. Nothing would induce him to jeopardise their food source and income.'

Takai tilted his head. 'I hope you're right. But I don't know what I, or anyone else, can do.'

'You need to convince the council that regardless of who caused the fire, they need to go to the people's aid. You need to…' She paused. A plan was starting to form in her mind, but she wanted it to be Takai's idea.

The Prince looked at her with a mix of curiosity and annoyance.

'If you put your mind to it, I'm sure you can come up with an idea that would help everyone – the victims of the fire most of all.'

He scrunched up his face. Arisa continued, undeterred.

'Perhaps you could take a lead from your parents. What was one of the first things they did when they married?'

She could almost see his mind tick over as he tried to recall what they'd done. 'They opened the King's School,' he offered tentatively.

'To all children in the city. Not only the nobles. What else?'

'They opened the College of Surgeons.'

'To ensure there were qualified medical professionals to care for the people.' Arisa bit her tongue to stop herself from adding that it had been only for those with money.

Realisation dawned across Takai's face. 'A hospital! What if we were to build a hospital to care for those who couldn't afford physicians?'

The bright smile she gave him in response was only a tiny indication of the joy she felt.

'Of course, the council may not agree. They may not support the cost, but I'm sure there could be a solution. Lakeford has quarries, and forests. He could supply sandstone, slate and timber.' The Prince spoke with rapid confidence now. 'And there is plenty of granite around the castle and cliffs. Labour could come from the evicted farmers and peasants who haven't been able to find new employment.'

Arisa's heart swelled. Takai's plans had developed quicker and further than she'd hoped. Further than even she had considered.

The Prince looked out past the oval, to the peninsula jutting out beyond the castle wall. 'We will build it there. On the edge of the city. The land is no use for anything else.'

'Almost on the castle grounds?' She wondered if Takai was now being overly ambitious.

'Of course. I must go at once.'

'Where?'

'To speak to my parents. I'm not sure if the council will agree, but I will do everything in my power to make it happen.'

Takai hastened to pick up the last of the bows and arrows. He was about to rush off but suddenly stopped.

'Thank you, Arisa.'

'You don't have anything to thank me for. It is your plan.'

'I mean, thank you for coming today. Will you meet me here again tomorrow?'

'Yes, I will.' The words had left her mouth before she even realised.

Takai gave her one last smile before sprinting back to the castle.

10

Takai practically floated back to his rooms. After spending time with Arisa, he felt like anything was possible. For those precious few moments that he was drawn into her world, he could see everything as she saw it. He could see Lamore flourishing without mounting wars. He could believe that compassion was a sign of strength, not weakness. That forging alliances with Ivane, Ette and even Kengia, instead of invading them, was the path to prosperity. When he was with Arisa, these were more than ideals; they were possibilities, and real plans could – no, *must* be put into action. When Takai was with Arisa, his responsibilities to the kingdom didn't weigh him down. They reminded him he had the power to make change.

Now, alone in his privy chamber, the same rooms occupied by generations of Princes and Kings past, he remembered the realities of his position. First and foremost, he wasn't the King. It would be difficult to convince the council to build a hospital for the people – the same people they believed were acting against Lamore. While the council suspected Sergei of causing the fire, every lowborn Lamorian would be tarred with the same brush. All were suspected rebels. Takai would have to get his parents' support and approach each of the councillors separately to secure their votes.

He would appeal to them on terms they would understand. Takai knew every one of them. He knew what made them tick, what drove them, their strengths and weaknesses. But instead of using this knowledge against them, as Horace had done before him, he would work *with* them. He would prove to the councillors that his plan was a good strategy for them, as well as the kingdom.

There was only one stumbling block.

Takai slumped into a chair in front of the fire as he realised how difficult it would be to convince the council that the arsonist may not be Sergei or any of the suspected rebels. He stared into the flames, wondering if this was how every King had felt before him. Knowing what needed to be done. Knowing what was right. And knowing that, even as the ultimate ruler of Lamore, one was helpless without the support of a court that was more often driven by self-preservation than justice.

The buzz of excitement that had overtaken Takai earlier had vanished. Evaporated into the night air. How could he face her? How could he tell her he had failed before he had even begun?

The answer came to Takai as the door to his chamber swung open. A towering silhouette stood before him. The visitor's features were in darkness, but Takai could distinguish a travel cloak and mud-splattered boots. He could see enough to know, with all certainty, the identity of his unannounced visitor.

'Sar!' He leapt from his chair to greet his friend.

Sar took two giant strides and threw his trunklike arms around Takai's shoulders, pulling him into a bear hug and thumping him on the back.

'Steady on,' Takai said, and Sar released him. Takai rubbed his shoulder. 'That's no way to treat your Prince!'

Sar removed his hood, his blonde hair flopping in his eyes.

He gave his familiar dimpled smile. 'I think I've earned the right,' he said. 'I am, after all, the same person who has been saving your princely behind for as long as I can remember.'

'Good to see you haven't changed.'

Sar winked at him. 'Someone has to keep that massive ego of yours in check.'

Takai laughed. He had missed his friend. 'What are you doing back here?' he asked. 'Don't tell me you've captured Sergei?'

The smile disappeared from Sar's face. 'I haven't.'

'I expect many at court will be disappointed to hear that.'

'From what I've learned at Talbot, Sergei is not the man they accuse him of being. None of the people in Lakeford County pose a threat, from what I can see.'

'How can you be sure?'

'I've spent time with Sergei's supporters. I've worked alongside them, visited with them in the villages and their homes, and confirmed they do not act against the crown. Your cousin Willem and the Duke are well respected in their own lands and further afield. They're known for being fair and just, to Lamorians and Kengians alike. I could never imagine any of them rising up against Lakeford or the King – for now...at least while the King is also being just to the people.'

'But what of Sergei?'

Sar shook his head. 'I understand he has been in Lakeford, and other counties, but he is well hidden. No one is likely to give up his whereabouts. Even those who don't condone his means support his intentions. They dare not believe the current peace will last. They're scared the King will have to reinstate food and wage restrictions...meaning they will need Sergei.'

'So Sergei is waiting to see if the King lives up to his promises?'

'He's waiting for more than that. There is talk that the King and Horace are working on some great weapon, and if they succeed, they will have the means of bending not just Lamore, but the whole known world to their will.'

Takai made an exaggerated scoffing sound. The fewer people who knew about Horace's firesky plans, the better. 'A great new weapon? I'm in charge of the fleet with Lakeford. If there were such a thing, I would know about it.'

Sar shrugged. 'That is what they say. Anyway, for now Sergei poses no danger. As long as the people aren't under threat and there is no weapon.'

'It doesn't matter. The council is coming after Sergei anyway.'

Sar nodded. 'That is why I've come. I heard reports it was Sergei who lit the fire in the city, but that's impossible. I've brought some men from Lakeford with me – trusted men who will swear Sergei was with them at the time of the fire. Even knowing the danger it puts them in.'

'But if it wasn't Sergei himself, it could have been one of his supporters.'

'It wasn't,' Sar said with conviction. 'One of the men who came with me is Lakeford's Master of Horses. He was in the city that day, to inspect a new steed. And he saw the culprit fleeing the stores.'

Takai tilted his head. 'He recognised the arsonist?'

'Not the person. The horse. It was a grey stallion he'd sold recently to Calliope. A fine-looking horse with distinctive white markings on its chest.'

Takai's brow crinkled. 'A grey horse, you say? With what looks like a white shield on its chest?'

'The very same.'

'But that's Guthrie's horse. I saw him ride in on it...' Takai thought for a moment, trying to recollect when he'd seen Guthrie on the horse. His eyes widened. 'I saw him ride in on the day of the fire. The Master of Horses is sure of this?'

'Did you ever know him to mistake a horse the whole time we were at Talbot?'

Of course it was Guthrie. Horace and his foolish son would do anything to destroy their enemies. 'You're right,' Takai said, 'but will the council believe it?'

'They know Horace well enough, so they should know he and his son are capable of such a thing.'

'It makes sense to frame Sergei and discredit my mother's plan for peace. To deplete the grain store so we are forced to look to other lands for resources. It all feeds into Horace's strategy to form an alliance with Malu and invade Kengia.'

Sar nodded sagely.

'But if Horace would stoop to such measures, what more would he do if we accuse him of it?' Takai rubbed his chin. 'It will have to be managed carefully.'

'Do you think you can persuade the council of Sergei's innocence?'

'I will find a way.' Takai grinned at his friend. 'Sar, you have no idea how glad I am that you brought me this news.'

'I'm always at your service, Your Highness.' Sar gave a mock twirl of his hands, and they both broke out in laughter.

'Secretary. *So* honoured you could join us.'

The King's clipped tones at Horace's late arrival to the council meeting spoke volumes. In reality, it probably wasn't Horace's fault he was late, given no one told him when the meetings were taking place these days. Takai almost felt a little sorry for the former Chancellor as he watched Horace register that the Queen was sitting in the position usually reserved for him.

'Your Majesties. Councillors. My sincerest apologies.' Horace bowed and hurried to the only spare chair – the one next to Takai at the opposite end of the table.

Takai leant over to him and spoke in a low voice. 'I see Guthrie is back at court.'

Horace nodded briskly.

'I couldn't help but notice the fine stallion he rode in on,' Takai continued. 'Such a distinctive-looking horse.'

Horace turned to look at the Prince, clearly searching for meaning in what he had said, but Takai diverted his attention back to the meeting.

'Lakeford was telling us how preparations go for an attack on the Northemers,' the King was saying.

'Your Majesty—' Horace tried to interrupt, undoubtedly to protest the plan and insist on an alliance with Malu instead, but the King held up a hand to silence him.

'I'm told the fleet is close to being finished,' he continued. 'In fact, our ships are bigger and better than before – isn't that right, Lakeford?'

'It is, Your Majesty.' A triumphant smile spread across the Duke's usually humourless face. 'They are the finest ships I have ever seen, thanks to the Prince's leadership.'

The councillors nodded at Takai in acknowledgement.

'We are also recruiting new soldiers so we will be prepared in case further peace negotiations with the Northemers fail,' the Duke went on. 'The new recruits will start training at Talbot under Sar and me, and our long-serving soldiers will assemble for training with the Baron of Iveness at his property.'

The Baron nodded. 'We will be ready by early spring.'

'Your Majesty, you cannot agree to this,' Horace cried. 'Going up against the Northemers is a hopeless mission.'

'We won't be going against them alone,' Lakeford said. 'We will have Ivane's army by our side.'

'Even so. The majority of our forces will be made up of untested soldiers, men who've never been on the battlefield.'

'You forget your place, Secretary,' the King hissed. 'You would be better served *supporting* my wishes instead of questioning them.'

'It is my job to advise you on the best strategy.'

'That is no longer your job. It also strikes me that your advice isn't in the interests of the kingdom, and never has been.'

'But Ivane can't be trusted to live up to its promises,' Horace insisted, in what was clearly a last-ditch attempt to sway the King.

'And you can?' Takai's father thundered. 'You, who have failed me on so many fronts? You, who cannot deliver on promises to your King?'

'Your Majesty,' Horace leant forward in his chair, 'I will deliver everything promised by spring – in time for your great celebrations.'

Several councillors raised questioning brows. Takai knew, of course, that Horace was referring to a weaponised firesky, but he still believed it was an impossible quest.

'I will believe it when I see it,' the King said, his voice low and dangerous. 'In the meantime, our army preparations go ahead as planned.'

'Your Majesty, I can see you are set on this,' Horace said. 'But I wonder how you propose to feed the army, since the fire destroyed much of the supplies. Will you reinstate rationing and increase taxes again? This will ensure you can replenish the stores.'

A chorus of mumbling rolled around the table. The King drummed his fingers on the armrest of his chair, glaring at Horace. The Queen reached out and stilled his hand.

'Any supplies will be paid for out of my own personal treasury,' he said. 'There will be no need to increase taxes. I will continue to support the people, as a good King should.'

Horace bowed his head in submission. 'Your Majesty.'

'What other business is there?' the King asked.

'I have a proposal,' Takai said.

Horace seemed surprised to hear the Prince's voice beside him. Takai rarely contributed anything to these meetings. But the King gave a knowing smile and motioned for his son to continue.

Takai looked around the room, briefly making eye contact

with each councillor. Lakeford tipped his head in acknowledgement.

'We should build a hospital in Obira,' he said.

Horace snorted out loud, but otherwise there was silence.

The Prince continued. 'The hospital will be a gift to our people. It will give the victims of the fire a safe and clean place to get medical help and recuperate. It will remain a place where all Lamorians, regardless of birth or wealth, can get the care they need.'

'The expense!' Horace cried.

'Not as expensive as you think. To build the hospital, Lakeford has offered timber from his lands and stone from his quarries. Other stone can be sourced from the very hill this castle sits on.'

There were murmurs of agreement.

Horace's eyes bulged. 'What about labour?'

'You see, that's the best part.' Takai looked pointedly at the Secretary. 'It seems many of our people lost their livelihoods when some among us evicted them from their homes and farms. These people desperately need work, and we could employ them. It would only cost us food and the right for some of them to camp onsite.'

'I think it's a commendable plan,' the Duke said, fixing an unwavering gaze on Horace.

'I agree,' the King said. 'It will be called Prince Takai's Hospital, and we will build it north of the city wall.'

'Your Majesty, that is too close to the castle,' Horace said.

'We have nothing to fear from our people.' The Queen's dark eyes bored into the Secretary. 'Not when we're helping them.'

'Work will begin immediately.' The King beamed at his son, then his wife.

'Sire,' Horace said, 'I don't understand how you can consider rewarding the people, especially when we know their beloved Sergei was the arsonist behind the devastating fire.'

Takai turned toward Horace with raised brows. 'You must have missed that part of the meeting, *Secretary*. Before you arrived, I was telling the council we have it on good authority that it wasn't Sergei – that the perpetrator was trying to frame the rebel leader and destabilise Lamore.'

Horace clicked his jaw. 'How ridiculous. Of course it was Sergei.'

'Besides the fact that there's no motive for Sergei to hurt the people he fights for, we have a reliable witness who can identify the real criminal. Lakeford's Master of Horses says he recognised the horse the man was riding. He says it was one he sold recently.'

Takai watched the realisation wash over Horace's face. The Secretary shifted in his seat. 'Can this Master of Horses be trusted?'

'Above all men.' Lakeford's clenched jaw appeared to be set in stone. 'He has been in my service for more than twenty years.'

'Who does he say he sold the horse to?'

'He is currently checking his records – he brought them with him to the castle. I can have him report to the council if you like,' the Duke said.

Takai was certain Horace wouldn't want him to do that. Indeed, Horace shook his head slowly. 'I trust you have the matter well in hand, Your Grace.'

The Prince clapped his hands together. 'So, we have unanimous support for the hospital?'

'After hearing your arguments...I do see some merit in it.' Horace appeared to nearly choke as he said the words. 'Well done...Your Highness.'

Takai smiled. There was no chance the King would listen to Horace now unless he delivered on his promises. The Secretary's reckless plans to form an alliance with Malu could be abandoned once and for all.

---

11

*T*here were several obstacles to Theodora capturing the Prince's heart. Not the least of which were the rumours of Takai and Arisa's secret meetings the last few weeks, and the fact that Takai's eyes rarely left the peasant girl when he visited the Queen's chambers – which was often these days. If Theodora could just spend some time alone with him, she knew she could plant seeds of doubt about the girl and her questionable background. She knew she could undermine Arisa. She just needed the opportunity.

On this particular day, Theodora waited until she knew Arisa was occupied by lessons with the visiting Schoolmaster. Then she headed to the stables, figuring she would look for the Prince first at the archery oval and, failing that, the naval shipyards. Reaching the west wing, she wandered onto the great stone breezeway that ran along the main building's perimeter, and was about to descend the marble stairs that led to the courtyard and stables. She stopped short, though, when she noticed a familiar figure standing at the base of the stairs.

It was the Baroness of Iveness, standing cross-armed and tapping her foot impatiently. A tower of travelling chests was stacked beside her. Theodora found the Baroness as vapid and annoying as her own mother – perhaps more so. She did an about turn, but it was too late.

'Theodora!' the woman called out.

Theodora turned back and flashed her most polite smile at the King's former mistress. It would be extremely short-sighted to upset the woman married to the second most senior noble in Lamore. She went down the short flight of stairs to greet the Baroness.

'Baroness. I'm sorry, I didn't see you there.' Theodora gave a sickly sweet smile. 'Where are you off to?'

It was a rhetorical question. Everyone at court – except perhaps the Baron himself – knew that with the King and Queen reconciled, having the Baroness around was an awkward reminder of past indiscretions. Theodora was only surprised the woman hadn't left the castle sooner.

The Baroness pursed her painted lips. 'I'm to go back to Iveness, if the carriage is ever ready. I couldn't stand the dreadful noise and dust coming from that hospital site.' She screwed up her nose in distaste. 'And have you seen the likes of the labourers camped there?'

Theodora nodded knowingly, indulging the Baroness's cover story for leaving.

'I blame your father, you know.'

Theodora raised a brow. She had her own problems with her father, of course, but she wasn't about to stand back as someone else besmirched her family's reputation. 'How so?' she said through clenched teeth.

'Bringing that healer and his ward here, of course. All the trouble started with them. Surely you can see that?'

Of course I know that, you silly woman, Theodora thought, but she adopted her best smile again and said, 'My father always acts in the best interests of the kingdom.'

The Baroness made a *harumph* sound. 'I'm not sure having the Queen reconciled with the King is in anyone's best interests...I would have expected you to share my view.' It was the

Baroness's turn to give a sickly sweet smile. 'If that girl and her healer had never come to the castle, you would have your promise of a crown by now, and I'd still be a favourite at court.'

Theodora bit her lip, acutely aware that the next words from her mouth may be to tell the Baroness to shut hers. The Baroness either didn't notice Theodora's reaction or didn't care, because she continued to rabbit on.

'...And the whole thing is ridiculous. This folly of your father's, trying to get the healer to create firesky...convincing the King he can weaponise it – ha! I've never heard anything more—'

'*Weaponise?*' Theodora's mind immediately went back to the message from the Northern leader about promises of a new weapon. Could this be it?

The Baroness's hand flew to her mouth as she realised she had shared too much. 'Silly me. I was just remembering a funny conversation I had with the King once – a jest, more than anything. It meant nothing. There's no weapon.' The woman clutched Theodora's arm and squeezed tightly. 'It's probably best you don't mention that to anyone. The King bade me never to reveal any of our conversations...even those spoken in jest... You will forget what I've told you, won't you?'

'It's forgotten already,' Theodora said breezily.

The Baroness exhaled and released her grip as her carriage arrived. 'I must be going, my dear.' She pressed her cheek to Theodora's and made a kissing sound.

Theodora bestowed a grateful smile on the woman and offered her genuine best wishes. She owed the Baroness a great debt. Unknowingly, the woman had handed Theodora the leverage she needed to get rid of her ultimate obstacle.

THEODORA WASTED no time using the information she'd learned. She went straight from the courtyard to the north-west tower.

'Me lady!' A Royal Guard with stringy hair, who had been

leaning against the wall outside the healer's rooms, leapt to attention at her unexpected arrival. He dipped an imaginary hat to her.

'I am here to see the healer.'

'I'm sorry, me lady. Orders are no visitors, other than his ward.'

'And whose orders are they?' she sniped.

'Your father's.'

'Exactly. So you wish me to tell my father that you refused my entry?'

The guard scratched his stubbly jaw.

Theodora gave her most beguiling smile. 'I would really appreciate this one small favour.'

'Well, I s'pose I could let you in…for a quick minute…No one else would need to know, would they?'

She leant a little closer to the man, ignoring the sour smell of his body odour, and dropped her voice to a whisper. 'It will be our little secret.'

The guard gave a black-toothed smile and winked at her.

'Tell me, are you usually posted here?'

'Most days, me lady, but only the graveyard shift. I finish up after the next shift has broken their fast – which is soon, me lady.'

'Good to know. I'll see the healer now.'

The guard nodded and let her into a small anteroom. Theodora waited until the door was locked behind her before she let the frozen smile leave her face.

The first thing she noticed was the acrid smoke hanging in the air. Then the sounds of the healer banging around in the next room. The clinking of glass. The man muttering to himself.

She moved into the main room. There was a long table laden with books, equipment and flasks of brightly coloured liquids set up on stands over flames. The healer buzzed around the room like a disoriented hummingbird. He hadn't noticed her appearance.

She cleared her throat and the healer – Erun – looked up at her. He did not blink. He did not frown. He gave no indication of anything, other than the tightening of his grip on a vial in his hands, until his knuckles were white.

'Erun. I don't think we've been formally intro—'

'I know who you are,' he said calmly, putting the vial away.

'Good, because I thought I'd get right to the point of my business with you.'

'Please do.'

Theodora made a show of walking slowly across the room, taking her time, collecting her thoughts. She only had one shot at getting the information she sought – she needed to have her wits about her. She lowered herself into a chair and gave a courtier's smile.

'I understand you are creating firesky for the King's celebrations.'

Erun shrugged. 'I understand it is supposed to be a surprise for most.'

'I also understand my father wishes to weaponise it.'

Erun tilted his head in question.

'There is no need to deny it. I know this to be true.'

'Then why are you here?'

It was a valid question. Initially she'd come to Erun on a fact-finding mission, but now she was there, she sought confirmation of a growing suspicion about the healer's task.

She cast her eyes across the room, taking in every detail. Erun was certainly giving the appearance of trying to conjure up firesky, but she wasn't fooled by his industrious behaviour. Theodora had grown up at court – watching, studying the kingdom's most powerful men and their mannerisms. She knew when a man was lying. She knew when a man was bluffing. And she knew when a man was hiding something.

'I'm here to make you an offer.'

Erun grunted in what may have been a laugh of sorts.

What Theodora said next, and how she said it, was critical. She lifted her chin and looked the healer squarely in the eyes.

'My offer is simple. I won't tell my father that you have already mastered firesky, on one condition.'

It had been a bluff, but Theodora got exactly the response she'd been hoping for. Erun's reaction was slow and deliberate. He pushed his glasses up the bridge of his nose before speaking. That one movement told her everything.

'I have no idea what you're—'

Theodora waved her hand dismissively. 'Yes you do. But I have no interest in sharing this information with my father.'

Erun looked at her warily. 'Let's entertain this ridiculous notion for a moment...Why would you make such an offer?'

'Simply because I want Arisa gone from here, and I suspect you want the same. You get her out of the castle and out of my way, and I will keep your secret.'

'But how am I supposed to make that happen?'

'I know you have supporters here at court. Appeal to them. Find a way to get her away from the castle.'

Erun frowned. 'I still don't understand why you don't want to help your father.'

Theodora laughed. 'My father doesn't need my help. He will get what he wants from you...eventually. But in the meantime, I need your ward gone.' She stood up and dusted off her skirt. 'I'm so glad we understand each other,' she said, before Erun could protest. 'Good day.'

A ripple of excitement rushed through Theodora as she strode from the healer's rooms. She had the feeling she had just got what she needed to succeed in her impossible task.

12

'*W*hat do you think?' Takai asked, tapping his fingers nervously on the rolled-up building plans in his hand.

The Prince had brought Arisa to the hospital site on the outskirts of Obira City, where construction was already underway. A delivery of timber had just arrived from Lakeford. Masons were carving stone into large bricks as the Lamorian labourers dug the foundations. Jobs were being created; displaced farmers had a new purpose and means of making a living. It was a hive of activity. A visible sign of hope on a troubled horizon.

'It's magnificent,' Arisa said, meaning every word.

Takai's grin was so wide that it went all the way to his dark eyes.

For weeks the pair had been meeting for archery lessons, and had formed a tentative friendship. Of course, they still argued about almost everything, from who wrote the finest poetry to the merits of Kengian farming practices. Each debated with equal passion, ending only when they agreed to disagree. Occasionally – not that either would admit it – one of them would make such a compelling argument that the other would be convinced to change their point of view. The hospital was one topic, though, that they always agreed on.

Takai had been modest enough to credit Arisa for leading him to the idea, and he spoke animatedly about how she could work at the hospital – if she wanted to – once she had completed her studies at the College of Surgeons. Neither of them brought up what would happen to the hospital and Arisa's plans once Lamore was at war. Instead they lived in the moment; lived in hope.

As they looked at the building site, Arisa realised how far Lamore had come in just a short time. She sniffed back the tears threatening to fall. Tears she couldn't let escape – not unless she wanted Takai to know who she really was.

'Are you alright?' Takai asked her, his eyes darting across her face for signs of pain or injury.

She gulped, pushing the salty tears back down her throat, and nodded. 'I was just thinking about how things might have been different if Lamore had always been the way it is now… How it would be different for some people…'

'For some people?' Takai asked, in the softest of voices.

Rea. She was thinking about Rea. But could she talk about her friend with Takai? Could she mention a silver-eyes to him? Would he see that what had been done was wrong? Maybe she *had* to tell him. Maybe this would be the only way she'd ever know if Takai was the kind of person she believed he was, or was becoming.

'When I was a little girl,' she began, 'I had a friend called Rea. She was my only friend…and she was a silver-eyes.'

Takai didn't wince or give any look of distaste. He just nodded, like he understood what it was like to only have one friend.

So Arisa opened up to the Prince, telling him how she and Rea had been kidnapped from school by Sir Marcus, the Governor of Ette at the time. And how Guthrie had been with Sir Marcus, an eager supporter of the Governor's cruel plans to force poor Lamorians and Kengians into 'service' in Ette. She explained how she had escaped, but her best friend hadn't been so lucky. She told him how Rea was supposed to be under the Duke's protection, but before word could be sent to Lakeford, Horace had refused all appeals to help her.

As she told her story, she noticed Takai's fingers clenching tighter and tighter around the hospital plans in his hand.

'I'm sorry that happened to you and your friend,' he said, when she had finished. 'It was wrong, what Sir Marcus, Horace and Guthrie did. But just as wrong that my father allowed this to happen. Things like that must never happen again. I will make sure of it.'

There was a conviction in Takai's voice that made Arisa believe him.

After a moment, the Prince frowned. 'I knew of the girl you speak of. She was the adopted daughter of some Kengian farmers at Talbot. Kind people. Good people. They were even kind to me when all the other Kengians were...' He paused, shrugging away whatever he'd been planning to say. 'Yes, the Duke wanted to help the family and sponsored the girl to go to school in Obira. Everyone was devastated to learn what happened to her. The Duke was furious, and he saw that no stone was unturned looking for her, but—'

'They never found her,' Arisa finished. 'You know, the saddest thing of all is that she was sure she would be saved...she was sure the Water Catcher would come to save us all.'

Takai frowned. 'That kind of false hope is dangerous. What could a Water Catcher even do...assuming it was even possible they existed?'

'Which it isn't.'

Takai nodded.

'No one really knows. Like any of the firstborn royal line in Kengia, they would have an incredible ability to harness a natural element – water, in their case. But what other powers they'd have would depend on whether they had Shamanic or Scholar tendencies.'

'But essentially they would use their ability to command water like the last Kengian King controlled earth, using his powers to protect Kengia's borders?'

'Yes,' Arisa gave an approving smile, 'and his son commanded wind and air. He controlled the mountain passages into Kengia before he died and his father closed the path once and for all.'

A troubled look came over Takai's face. 'Very powerful, then,' he said, almost to himself.

Knowing the Prince's fear of Kengian magic, Arisa wondered whether she'd said too much. But Takai placed his hand gently on her arm, his touch warm and soothing.

'I'm sorry there wasn't a Water Catcher to save your friend, Arisa.'

She wanted to thank him for comforting her and showing her hope still lived, showing her that Lamore was different now – that *he* was different now – but the words caught in her throat. Tears were hanging like a storm cloud in her chest, threatening to burst at any moment. It took everything she had to keep them there.

13

Theodora watched nervously as her father poured himself a large cup of wine and sat down heavily behind his desk. Horace was still smarting from the humiliation he had been dealt at the last council meeting he'd been allowed to attend. At that meeting, the King had refused to listen to any of her father's advice, and Takai had only just stopped short of openly accusing Horace and Guthrie of arranging the fire at the grain stores. Trust her buffoon of a brother to get caught out and fail so dismally at his task.

Not that Theodora could talk. The healer hadn't acted yet to arrange Arisa's escape – though she wasn't sharing that with her father. In the meantime, she was no closer to seducing the Prince.

'Do you have anything at all to report?' Horace asked accusingly, after Theodora had informed him of that fact. 'Anything to actually help our cause?'

'I have done what you asked. I have tried to keep an eye on Arisa, the Queen and Gwyn, but they are vigilant around me, never speaking about anything of any consequence.'

Horace clicked his jaw.

'But I am sure, from the little I've seen and already reported to you,' she pressed on, 'that there is some form of relationship between Gwyn, the Queen and Erun – that they knew each other before the Kengian healer came here to help the Prince. They seem too invested in the healer and Arisa's welfare for there not to be some relationship. I am certain of it.'

'Your certainty means nothing. I need proof.'

'How about those coded messages you have? Have you found anything yet?'

Horace waved toward his desk and took a large gulp of wine. 'See for yourself.'

Theodora ignored the mocking edge to her father's voice. While she had no wish to help him hasten the realisation of firesky, she wanted more than anything for him to see her worth. She looked at his notes, willing herself to see something her father had missed.

There were strings of letters, but none that made sense to her. Then a name: *Leo*.

'Leo?' she wondered out loud. 'The late Kengian King?'

Horace waved his hand. 'Yes, Erun mentioned him a few times in his messages. It is one of the only things I've successfully translated. The rest of it is in some Kengian dialect I don't know.'

She looked up at her father triumphantly. 'But if you could translate one name, you could translate any—'

Horace's eyes widened. 'Of course.' He rushed to his desk. 'A name would be the same regardless of the dialect,' he mumbled to himself, his eyes darting all over the pieces of parchment. 'I was looking for something more complicated. It took a simple girl to point out the simple answer.'

Simple! Even after she had helped him, he still thought she was simple. Theodora's hands clenched into fists by her sides.

Horace pulled out the next note in the pile and set to work on it. Theodora watched over his shoulder as he ran his finger along the lines of numbers. Two lines in, he stopped and wrote G – W – Y – N. *Gwyn!*

The hairs on Theodora's arms stood on end. She'd been certain Erun and Gwyn had known each other before the healer came to the castle, and she was right.

Horace scanned further and wrote down more letters: A – L – I – K.

Alik. The Kengian Prince. Theodora wasn't sure what Alik and Gwyn had to do with each other. She did know that Alik had spent time at the castle with the King, and had also kept the company of the Queen and her ladies. But why he would be specifically mentioned alongside Gwyn's name, Theodora couldn't fathom. Her father, though, tapped his chin thoughtfully.

From what Theodora had been told, it was her father who had once been associated with Gwyn. The rumours around court said they had been more than friends. From the moment he had first met her in Ivane – when he had accompanied the newly crowned Delrik on his journey to broker peace with Sofia's father and ask for her hand in marriage – Horace and Gwyn had been close. But Gwyn had turned on him soon after the King and Sofia's marriage. She had been angry that Horace had convinced the King to break his alliance with the Ivanians and invade his wife's homeland. After their relationship soured, had Gwyn aligned herself with the Kengian Prince?

It wouldn't have surprised Theodora to learn that Gwyn sympathised with the Kengian cause – especially after the blood moon massacre, where many Kengians had died. She was pathetically soft-hearted, and Ivane and Kengia had been allies. But why would Erun have received messages mentioning her by name?

Horace leant back in his chair and clicked his jaw. Theodora could see her father's mind whirring over.

'Did I ever tell you about how I got this injury to my jaw?'

'No, Father.' Theodora's heart quickened. Her father had never shared anything personal with her. Did this mean he was beginning to trust her?

'It was the Kengian Prince. Once I discovered that he meant to turn the King against me, I acted against him. I convinced the King that Alik had tried to bewitch him. And when the blood moon appeared – the first time – I used it to convince the King that the Water Catcher prophecy was upon us. I invited fear into Lamore. I incited the Kengian massacre. I made sure the firstborn Kengian line died with Prince Alik – but not before he gave me this injury.' Horace gave a wry laugh. 'You know, I almost welcome the pain that is always there. It's a reminder that I got my revenge on the Prince, and on Kengia.'

A chill ran through Theodora at hearing exactly how far her father would go – and had gone – to get what he wanted and stop all those who stood in his way.

'I understand why you acted against the Prince, but why Kengia? Why do you hate the country so?'

Horace narrowed his dark eyes at Theodora, then waved for her to take a seat.

'I have hated Kengia for a lifetime. It is the country that took my father from me as a boy. He had loyally served the last King as his Master of Horses for many years. He was returning from Ette, where he had purchased twenty new destriers for the King, when his ship got caught in a storm. The squalls had blown up from nowhere in the Kyprian Sea, and the ship was blown off course toward Kengia's coast.' Horace's voice caught on something. He cleared his throat and then continued. 'Witness accounts cited that the Lamorian ship would have survived the storm had it not landed within the Kengian King's protective reach. King Leo used his magic over the coastline to create a massive tidal wave that devoured the ship. There were no survivors.'

Horace took another drink of wine.

'The Kengians expressed regret that the ship had been targeted – they said they had mistaken it for an invading party. They sent Delrik's father a payment of gold in compensation, but no amount of gold could bring my father back.'

Theodora's hands curled into fists. 'I am glad their King and his son are dead, then.'

'But it's not enough.' Horace's mouth formed a bitter sneer. 'I will have my revenge on all of Kengia. It is why I must have this alliance with the Northemers. It is why I will use these mentions of Gwyn and Alik in the secret messages to bring the King to my side and force the Kengian healer to comply.'

But not before I have made sure Arisa is gone from here, and made the Prince mine, Theodora thought.

'Father, what have you promised to the Northemers?' She was testing him, seeing whether he was beginning to realise her use.

Horace narrowed his eyes at her again. 'I have had word from the pirate, Goldman, and the Northemers will agree to the proposed alliance. But I must deliver something for them. Something you need not worry about.'

Theodora prickled with anger. Her father still didn't trust her. 'I am smart enough to understand your plans, Father. I can help.'

'The only way you can help is by living up to your promise to secure the Prince. And if you don't succeed, there *are* others who will take your hand.'

Theodora shuddered at her father's thinly veiled threat – or more accurately, his promise – to hand her over to the pirate if she failed. Her only hope was to get that irksome peasant girl to leave the castle. She would have to take matters into her own hands.

14

*T*akai's book lay idle in his lap as he gazed out the window. There were signs of the coming spring every-where. Outside in the castle gardens, the plum and pear trees were sprouting the first buds that would soon become pink and white blossoms. In the woodland, wildflower buds had started to emerge from the ground. In a week or so, the season would offi-cially change – but winter wasn't surrendering yet.

A biting cold wind howled outside the south-east tower, shaking the glass of the windows. The giant fire blazing away in the Queen's privy chamber struggled to eliminate the chill from the air. No one was complaining, though. Least of all Takai.

Every minute left of winter meant another moment he could spend with Arisa. Spring came with uncertainty. The new season would separate them indefinitely. Takai didn't want to think about the grisly possibilities of what lay ahead. Instead he would focus on what he did know for sure.

He knew war was inevitable. Whether it would be on Ette's or Lamore's shores, he couldn't say, but with the Northemers still refusing to enter peace negotiations, it was only a matter of time before Malu made his move. As soon as the weather warmed, the Northem invaders would be in a position to mobilise their forces and ships. Then they wouldn't have to contend with the unpredictable winter squalls at sea. On land there would be spring harvests, prime for raiding – provisions for an invading army.

Lamore and Ivane had been feverishly preparing their forces. Whether they would be mounting a defence or a pre-emptive attack was undecided. Most expected Malu to make the first move. In any case, Takai would be charged with launching his newly built fleet, and he and Sar would lead their units into battle against a monster-sized army. A battle that was likely to cost Lamore – and Takai – dearly. Of that much he was certain.

In the rare moments he was alone, Takai could admit it to himself: he was terrified. He wasn't necessarily scared for his own life; death was an inevitable consequence of war, and he was prepared for it. What he wasn't prepared for was the possibility that he may never see Arisa again. He couldn't bear the thought of leaving her – not when he was only just getting to know her.

All the current uncertainty had at least one positive aspect, though: it emboldened Takai and the castle's inhabitants to savour every last second before war. It was a merry court. There was an air of eager anticipation for the great celebrations and tournament being held on the first day of spring – the Prince's birthday. The court's ladies and gentlemen basked in the King's newfound happiness with the Queen, and peace was secured within Lamore. And at the centre of it all was Arisa.

Takai noticed how others, high- and lowborn alike, were drawn to her. She didn't need to put on airs and graces, or flirt. She had a curious mix of humility and righteousness that attracted people to her. As if she had an inner light or power that pulled them in. He had overheard the admiring whispers about her bravery during the riot at the marketplace, as well as her compassion and skills as a healer. And like the rest of Obira who'd fallen under Arisa's spell, Takai needed to be near her.

So despite the wretchedness on the horizon, he could find

happiness. He only needed to surrender himself to the bright energy that came with Arisa's company. He wouldn't waste a minute of his time with her.

The Prince scanned the room, seeking her light. His ears trained to the music of her voice. His heart ached to hear the trill of her laugh. The Queen and Gwyn sat by the fire, embroidering linen shirts for the poor. Theodora and her companion, Selina, were playing cards in a corner. Musicians strummed lazily on their lutes. Across the room was Arisa — a faraway smile on her face, an open book before her. Her free hand twirled the silver medallion hanging around her neck. She looked completely at ease, as if she belonged nowhere else but here.

Arisa caught his gaze. She didn't look away. She didn't furrow her brow. She smiled at him. A smile that went all the way to her remarkable amber eyes. Eyes that still held so many secrets; secrets Takai wished he had more time to uncover.

'I asked you to dance with me,' came a brisk voice.

Takai looked up with a start to find Theodora, who had abandoned her game of cards and was staring at him with crossed arms. 'Sorry?'

Theodora's lips thinned. 'I'm asking you to dance with me.'

'I thought you were playing cards.'

She sighed. 'Cards bore me. We've been locked up in here all morning because of the horrid weather. You must dance with me.' She grabbed Takai's arm, pulling him up from his seat while motioning to the musicians to play something upbeat.

'No.' He dug his heels into the floor. 'I'm fine here, thank you.'

She tried to drag him again. 'I refuse to take no for an answer.'

Takai pried himself from her grip. 'But no is the answer you must accept.' He didn't bother trying to soften his tone.

Theodora's black eyes flashed.

'You mean to tell me you would rather sit there staring into space than dance with me? Unless, of course, something else has caught your eye?' She looked back over her shoulder at Arisa.

'I don't know what you mean.'

'Don't play me for a fool. You've been making puppy-dog eyes at that commoner for weeks,' she spat. 'What is it you could possibly admire? Her *easy* temperament?' Theodora laughed. 'I daresay not...Obviously not her beauty or talents, either.'

Instinctively, Takai's hand clenched by his side. 'You shall not speak of Arisa in such a manner.'

But Theodora would not be stopped. Her voice had risen, and every person's eyes were on her. Arisa stared too, but her gaze was on Takai.

'No. I know what it is.' Theodora's eyes narrowed. 'I think she has offered you other favours – the kind of favours that a *true lady* could not.'

'You shall stop at once.' Takai's voice rose. 'Arisa is more of a lady than you'll ever be.'

Theodora's eyes widened before she dropped her head in submission. 'Forgive me, Your Highness.' She looked up at him through lowered lashes.

The hard look he gave in return told Theodora she'd gone too far and would not be excused. She curtsied hurriedly and retreated. Thankfully, the others in the room quickly returned to their previous occupations.

'What was that?' came a low voice.

Takai turned to see Sar standing behind him. What was it with people sneaking up on him today? In all the commotion he hadn't noticed his friend's entrance. Now, Sar stood watching Theodora, his head tilted.

'I think you'd better fix that.'

'Did you hear what she said?' Takai demanded.

'Believe me, I'm not defending Theodora. But don't forget, she is Horace's daughter. And given the opportunity, he will go to great lengths to make sure you – and others you care about' – Sar glanced over at Arisa – 'remember that.'

Sar was right. Horace could never be underestimated, especially after the humiliation Takai had served him over the hospital. Takai would have to somehow placate Theodora.

'Sar!'

Arisa had bounded toward them and thrown her arms around the new arrival. Sar lifted her off the ground and spun around in a circle to her delighted squeals.

A stab of jealousy ripped through Takai. He had forgotten how close the pair were.

'Or should I say *Sir* Sar, after your knighting?' Arisa teased, after Sar had released her to the ground.

Sar's face reddened. Not long before the riot, the King had knighted him for his bravery during the Northemer invasion of Ette. 'Sar's fine, thanks.'

'It's been too long. What are you doing here?' Arisa asked. 'Takai told me you came back not long after the fire, but I didn't get a chance to see you.'

'Sorry, it was a brief visit. I didn't even have time to see my mother.' He looked over at Gwyn, who smiled back at him. 'I wish I could have been back earlier, but the Duke has kept me busy in Lakeford.'

'Training the army?' Arisa asked.

Sar nodded. 'And working with Willem to manage Talbot lands.'

'Is Lakeford County as beautiful as they say?' There was a note of wistfulness in Arisa's voice. Takai remembered that she had never been past Obira City's gates.

As Sar regaled her with a vivid description of the Duke's lands, an idea came to Takai.

He excused himself and sought out Theodora, who was sitting with Selina. Her face pinched at his approach.

'Lady Theodora. May I have a word?'

Her eyes darted nervously before she nodded and came to stand with him a small distance away.

'While I wish you hadn't said those things about Arisa, I am sorry I upset you.' He took a deep breath before continuing. 'I'm not quite myself lately. There is a lot of talk of war and such. I'm afraid it may be taking a toll.'

She lifted her chin and pursed her lips. 'These are difficult times for many of us.'

'You're right. But I know exactly how we can forget our troubles…for a small while, at least.'

Theodora arched a brow.

'We will take a trip to the countryside. Soon after the tournament, if the weather is fine.'

The colour returned to Theodora's cheeks. 'That would be the perfect remedy.'

'You should invite Selina.'

A flash of irritation crossed Theodora's face. 'Must I? I thought we could go alone. You and I.'

Takai shook his head. 'We couldn't possibly deprive our friends of such an outing. Selina and Sar will come…and Arisa.'

Theodora scowled, but Takai had already brushed her from his thoughts. His mind was filling with plans for a trip to remember. Takai wanted – no, he *needed* to bask in Arisa's light a little longer, and the trip would give him that opportunity.

And maybe she would gaze at him with the same look of joy she was now bestowing upon his friend.

15

_T_heodora marched into the healer's rooms, fuelled by anger and humiliation at the Prince's words. He'd said Arisa was _more of a lady_ than she'd ever be. Never had she been spoken to in such a manner.

The only saving grace of the whole encounter was the opportunity to be rid of Arisa once and for all.

'It's time for your ward to go,' she barked at Erun, who'd jumped from his chair in surprise at her entrance. 'The Prince is organising a trip to the countryside, and Arisa is invited. You must arrange for her to escape then – or I will tell my father you have mastered firesky.'

'I have already told you, I haven't—'

Theodora strode toward the healer until she was mere inches from his face.

'Do not play with me. We both know the truth, and I am my father's daughter. I _will_ carry through with my threat.'

Erun pushed his glasses up his nose and took a step back. Theodora relaxed a little, knowing they understood each other.

'I expect the trip will be soon. You have until then to make all the arrangements you need.'

The trip was the only way Theodora could ensure Arisa disappeared without it somehow pointing back to her. And it couldn't come soon enough.

16

*A*risa arrived out of breath outside the King's presence chamber. The King and Queen were hearing petitions from the people, being asked to rule on everything from neighbourhood disputes to complaints about the price of grain. The anteroom was buzzing with conversation as the merchants, farmers and peasants waited their turn. It had been a long time since the King had heard petitions himself, and a longer time since the Queen had been by his side. It looked like half the kingdom was present, whether they needed to be or not.

Arisa would have preferred to avoid the crowd, but had received an urgent message to meet someone here. The servant boy who'd delivered the message didn't know who the 'someone' was. The person hadn't given a name, but had said Arisa would know them when she saw them.

She scanned the crowded room, but no one jumped out at her. Then she felt a tug on her arm. She turned to see the Prince, his dark eyes smiling back at her.

'What are you doing here?'

'I'm not sure,' she said. 'I got a message that someone needed to see me. What about you?'

'I was looking for you, actually.'

'Oh?' Arisa tried unsuccessfully to sound disinterested.

Takai dropped his voice to a whisper. 'I wanted to tell you that Horace has been to see my father. He had some news for him…news about some messages he decoded.'

She froze. 'Messages?'

'I don't know the exact contents, but it has something to do with your guardian and Gwyn. I thought you should know.'

This surprised Arisa. Why would Erun's messages from Kengia mention Gwyn? Was it another secret her guardian was hiding from her?

'That's odd…' she said slowly.

Takai's brow crinkled. 'I don't know what it all means, but I'm worried about you. If you just told me what might be in these messages, I could help.'

'I'm sorry, but I don't know.'

Takai's eyes dulled, the hurt within them clear. Arisa didn't like being the cause of it.

She was about to make an excuse to leave so she could inform Erun of Takai's news, but her eyes fell on a flash of curly red hair and a familiar face smiling back at her.

'Lina!'

The Kengian woman approached and Arisa embraced her. She hadn't seen Lina since the day of the riot, when she had spoken in favour of Arisa. Lina had convinced the angry crowd to listen to her. If it hadn't been for her, Arisa wouldn't have been able to address the people and quell the violence as she had done. She was pleased to see Lina, but there was also a sick feeling in the pit of her stomach as she thought of Hyando.

She made to introduce Lina to Takai, but remembered he would have recognised her as the woman he and the Queen had saved from execution.

Lina curtsied. 'Your Highness.'

'Good to see you.' Takai sounded formal, but not unfriendly.

'What are you doing here, Lina?' Arisa asked.

Lina compressed her lips. 'I have come to ask the King to release my husband from the dungeons.'

'*Cynfor*? He's in custody?'

'For some time now. He was involved in a disturbance at the Secretary's property at Calliope. Several of the King's knights were injured.'

Takai frowned. 'I remember that. Guthrie was hoarding grain, and Sergei and some of the farmers protested. Guthrie was a little heavy-handed, from what I heard.'

'That he was. Sergei got away, but Cynfor and some of the others were taken to the dungeons. It was one of the reasons I was speaking out against the King when I was arrested.' Lina smiled at Takai. 'You, of course, know the rest of that story.'

Takai reached out and laid a hand gently on Lina's shoulder. 'I'm sure if you speak to my father and explain the circumstances of your husband's arrest, he may be willing to consider your request. He is most merciful these days.'

'Thank you.'

'Was that why you wanted to see me?' Arisa asked.

'No, there was something else.' Lina cast a nervous glance at Takai, but continued. 'I have something I was hoping you could give the Queen. I don't dare to give it to her myself...especially in front of everyone.'

Arisa nodded, looking down at the bag Lina held. Lina retrieved a small drum from within it. Ribbons and bells hung from it in the Kengian fashion.

Takai visibly stiffened at its appearance. Ignoring his reaction, Arisa picked up the drum and examined it with interest.

'It's a gift from our Shaman,' Lina said.

'Is this one of the drums she uses to—'

'Communicate with the dead,' Takai finished in a deadpan voice.

'Yes,' Lina said. 'We know how hard it must have been for the Queen to lose Lore, and we all thought this may give her some comfort. Ivanians have a similar custom to Kengians when they wish to speak to their loved ones in the spirit world.'

'I suggest you don't go waving that thing around too much in here.' Takai spoke in clipped tones. 'The King doesn't take too well to Kengian hocus-pocus, especially after the Kengian Prince tried to bewitch him all those years ago.'

Arisa shot an annoyed look at Takai. She couldn't believe he thought the rumours about Prince Alik were true. He was still so close-minded when it came to Kengian and Ivanian customs.

Lina opened her mouth, looking like she wanted to correct the Prince, but stopped herself. She turned instead to Arisa. 'If you wouldn't mind passing it on to the Queen privately?'

'I'd be honoured. Thank you, Lina.'

After a quick hug, Lina disappeared into the crowd.

Arisa spun on Takai. 'What exactly is your problem?'

Takai's nostrils flared. 'I was going to ask you the same thing.'

'What makes you think Kengians mean any harm toward you and your family? They pose no threat to Lamore.'

'I suppose you didn't hear me the first time. Their Prince tried to use magic to control my father and take Lamore for himself.'

'I can't believe you actually think that is true!' Arisa couldn't conceal the frustration from her voice. Just when she thought Takai was changing for the better.

Takai shrugged and looked away, a bored expression on his face.

'Kengia wishes for nothing but to live in peace with Lamore and all of its neighbours,' Arisa pressed.

'By using witchcraft!' he snapped.

'Having an affinity with nature and respecting its elements has nothing to do with witchcraft or harming anyone. The Kengians' ability to work with nature was why they were asked to come to Lamore in the first place. It's the reason they continue to cultivate Lamore's crops and care for the land today.'

Takai scoffed. 'You know as well as I do they use their powers for other things. Your guardian – who everyone knows is Kengian – practises his mysterious "science" daily.'

Arisa jutted out her chin. 'Yes, he harnesses the healing powers from herbs, trees and plants. He spends every waking hour perfecting his science experiments for the better of all Lamorians. And he saved your life, remember?'

Takai's eyes narrowed. 'You speak with such conviction, Arisa. What aren't you telling me?'

'Nothing. I have nothing to say to you!'

Arisa turned on her heel and stomped off, silently berating herself for ever thinking the Prince may have changed, or that he was starting to be the kind of leader his people needed. She had never been so wrong.

ERUN RUBBED the nape of his neck nervously as Arisa's amber eyes bore into him.

She stood with arms folded, glaring at her guardian. 'Well?'

Arisa had stormed into his room to tell him about the message Horace had decoded. She'd wasted no time demanding an explanation for why Gwyn's name appeared in a coded note from the Kengian Queen.

'And don't try to tell me you don't know why Gwyn is mentioned, because of course you know,' she added. 'I've heard you two speaking in secret before. There's something you're both hiding from me – something important. And I want to know. I deserve to know!'

'You're right.' Erun appeared to deflate under her gaze. 'You do deserve to know what we've been speaking about, and why she appears in the message...but I can't share it with you. Not yet. And not if I want to keep you safe...which is getting harder to do every day.'

Arisa flung her hands in the air in exasperation.

'In any case,' Erun went on, 'the more pressing matter is that Horace actually managed to decode a message, or at least some of it. This puts us all in real danger. If he finds out I'm Prince Alik's brother, he will have no trouble getting the King to agree to drastic measures against us. Who knows what else he may learn?'

'Exactly! *Who knows?* Certainly not me.'

Erun clutched Arisa's arm, his eyes wide with concern. It had been almost a week since she'd seen her guardian. She had blamed her studies, when in fact it had been due to her spending so much time with Takai. It surprised her now to see Erun so agitated – a level of agitation she couldn't put down to the coded messages alone.

'I truly am sorry I have to keep this thing from you, Arisa, but I haven't got a choice.' He tightened his grip on her arm. 'It's to keep you safe. You need to trust me.'

Arisa pursed her lips. Why was Erun always asking her to trust him? It was infuriating.

She walked across the room to the window looking over the castle grounds and opened the shutters, hoping the fresh air would relieve her anger. It was late afternoon, bordering on dusk. Her eye caught on a movement in the shadows at the base of the tower. She couldn't quite make it out from its outline – but she knew from its flashing green eyes that it was the Kengian snow wolf.

Trouble? The wolf's question planted itself in her mind.

How was it possible for her to hear the animal? She knew silver-eyes were supposed to be able to speak to animals, but not without training, and this seemed different. Like something more powerful.

Arisa is in danger. It was Erun's voice in her mind now, but not speaking to her. Speaking to the wolf. *She has to leave. She has to escape.*

The wolf blinked in reply and bounded away in the direction of the woodland.

Why was Erun speaking to the wolf about an escape plan? What exactly was in those messages? And how could she hear Erun's thoughts as well? Arisa knew she should speak to him. She should ask him again to train her to harness her silver-eyes magic. But she couldn't, for one simple reason…she didn't trust him.

'We have to do something about those messages,' Erun said, bringing her back to the matter at hand. 'They have to be destroyed.'

She shook her head vigorously. 'They will be in the Secretary's apartments. We can't get to them.'

'You'll have to find a way.'

'Can't you use your suggestive powers?'

'You know as well as I do that I can only use them on people who are inclined to help. Horace has ensured I'm only surrounded by his people. My powers wouldn't work on them.'

Arisa considered the matter. Getting into Horace's rooms was no easy feat.

'I suppose I could ask for Sar's help,' she said. 'He is back at the castle, preparing for the tournament.'

'Good, but don't tell him what it's for. We don't want to put him in any more danger than is necessary.'

'He can probably buy me a few minutes with the guards so I can get in and out of Horace's rooms, but there's still a chance the Secretary will catch me.'

'You will need to get him to leave his chambers for some errand,' Erun mused. 'A message from someone who won't arouse suspicion.'

'In that case, the Queen or Gwyn won't be much help. He'd never come if they summoned him.'

'The Prince?'

Arisa rolled her eyes and groaned.

'What? You don't think he'd help? I thought you two were on good terms.'

'So did I...but I was wrong about him.'

Erun gave her a curious look. 'He can't be trusted?'

'It depends on who's asking him for help. I'll speak to Sar.'

Erun breathed a sigh of relief. 'You should go to him straight away.'

Arisa nodded and turned to leave.

'And be careful,' her guardian added. 'Please.'

17

'Your Highness.' A guard stood in the doorway to Takai's bedchamber. 'There's someone here to see you.'

Sar poked his head around the door and bounded past the guard into the room.

'Thank goodness it's you!' Takai said. Sar tilted his head in question as the guard left them alone. 'I thought it might be Horace.'

Sar visibly shuddered. 'Why would he be looking for you?'

'Ever since my father ousted him from his position, he has been harassing me endlessly. When I'm not down at the port overseeing work on the fleet, he is here, trying to meet with me.'

'What does he want to talk to you about?'

'Anything and everything. When he's not dropping hints about marrying Theodora, he's trying to secure a meeting with my father. The last time it was about some Kengian message he'd decoded.'

'What message?'

Takai shrugged. 'I'm not sure what exactly, but he seems to think Gwyn has something to do with it.'

'Whatever he wants to accuse her of is complete rubbish.' Sar clenched his fists. 'And if he does anything—'

Takai held up his hands to calm his friend. 'It's alright. He's not doing anything yet...as far as I know. And even if he tries, I won't be helping him.' He didn't add that he wanted to get to the bottom of it himself – to find out what Arisa may be hiding from him.

Sar relaxed his hands and nodded.

'I'm afraid I don't have the energy or inclination to deal with Horace right now,' Takai went on. 'In fact, let's get out of here before he thinks about showing up.'

'Where?'

Takai winked, then strode across his room to the wall. He stopped and tapped on the wood panelling.

Sar's eyes lit up. 'The top of the north-west tower?'

Takai nodded, searching for the spot that should return a familiar hollow sound.

'I'd almost forgotten about the secret passage,' Sar said. 'It's been years since we used it.'

'I *had* forgotten about it until a couple of months ago when I was laid up in bed, recovering from my accident. With all that thinking time, I remembered its existence.'

'And you used it? You made it up to the turrets?'

'Sadly, no. I got a little waylaid.' Takai didn't explain the reason: he had fallen in the tower stairwell and had to be rescued by Arisa. It had been the first time he'd met her.

Takai tapped the wall until he heard an echo. He nudged the panel with his shoulder and felt it shift slightly. He shoved it harder, and it gave way to a black void.

Grabbing a torch from the wall, Takai bid Sar to follow him into the passageway. They closed the panel behind them and followed the passage for a few minutes, brushing the cobwebs from their path as they went. After another hundred yards or so, the passageway ended at another wood-panelled wall.

Takai leant against it until it swivelled, allowing them to exit into a disused corridor. A quick glance up and down the hallway confirmed no one was around. They could speak freely here.

'What news from you, Sar?' Takai led his friend down the corridor toward the north-west tower.

'A lot, actually. I've been going back and forth every couple of days between Lakeford and the castle, training the new army recruits and helping Willem and the Duke with anything they need, but it's been good – especially my time at Talbot. I'm learning a lot about how to manage the farmland and properties.'

'And how to manage the Kengian farmers, I suppose.'

Sar paused for a moment. 'It's actually they who are helping me. They are extraordinarily knowledgeable about the land, and friendly.'

Takai thought back to how most of the Kengian farmers had treated him, a bitter taste forming in his mouth. 'Not in my experience.'

Sar gave Takai a sympathetic look. 'I know things were different for you when we lived at Talbot, but it was because you were the Prince. They feared you because of your father.'

'Whatever you say. I'm glad you found some time to visit me while you're here, though.'

'Me too. But…I do have something…'

'What is it?'

Sar scratched his head. 'I need your help with something.'

'Anything. What do you need?'

'I was hoping you could get Horace away from his rooms for a few minutes.'

A knot formed in Takai's stomach. He'd only just told Sar he wanted to avoid the man. 'Horace…why?'

'I'm sorry, Takai, but I can't tell you.'

Takai wasn't sure if he was more angry or hurt at his friend keeping secrets from him.

'I can't tell you because *I* don't know the reason for getting Horace away from his chambers,' Sar went on.

'I don't understand.'

'It's to help someone else.'

Takai clenched his jaw. He was sure he knew who Sar was referring to, but he asked anyway.

'Who?'

'Arisa.'

Takai stopped abruptly. They had reached the spiral staircase that led to the top of the tower. He pushed open the door into the stairwell.

'What is it with that girl? She seems to have put a spell over the whole kingdom. Everyone seems to think she's above reproach.'

Sar gave a perplexed look. 'I thought you liked her. You did invite her on the trip to the countryside.'

'I don't know. I don't feel like I can trust her. She has some agenda or secrets she's not sharing with the rest of us.' Takai was talking mainly to himself. 'And she's forever lecturing me.'

Sar shrugged. 'I kind of like what she has to say.'

'Of course you would. She is full of fanciful ideals about how the kingdom should be run and how people should be treated, but none of them are practical. It's wishful thinking.'

'Is it? Why can't we do the right thing by all of Lamore? Isn't that what you're trying to do with the hospital?'

'Yes...' Takai hated how reasonable his friend was making everything sound, '...for the most part, but not everyone is deserving of such mercy and charity. Not everyone is kind and just, like you and Arisa seem to think they are. Think of Sergei and his rebels, and the Kengians in Lamore who still practise forbidden magic. They are a threat to the kingdom.'

Sar frowned. Evidently Takai's friend didn't agree with him.

'Alright, Sar.' He sighed. 'Against my better judgement, I'll get Horace away from his rooms.'

Sar's smile returned.

'For you, Sar. I'll do it to help *you*.' Takai stressed the last word. He hadn't forgiven Arisa for her most recent outburst. 'But be careful.'

Sar laughed, as if to say, *Do you know who you're talking to?*

Takai was readying himself to climb up to the turret when a scratching noise at the base of the stairs stopped him in his tracks. The pair followed the sound to the bottom of the stairwell.

'What is that?' Sar asked, pressing his ear against the stone wall.

Takai joined him. It sounded like the scratching sound was coming from the other side of the wall. Something, or someone, was clawing at the stone.

'Here.' Takai passed the torch to Sar as he examined the wall. There was nothing unusual about it. The stone was cold to the touch and a little damp, but nothing was out of place.

He pushed against the wall and was surprised to feel it give a little. Takai shoved it again and it groaned as a shower of dust and mortar fell to the ground. Together, he and Sar pushed it until it opened all the way.

It was another secret passage.

Sar held up the torch to show the long, narrow tunnel that lay ahead of them, and the creature responsible for the noise. The Kengian snow wolf.

Takai stumbled backward at the sight of the creature's unsettling green eyes shining back at him. There was something disturbingly human about the animal and the way it looked at him. The wolf moved its head to the side before turning and running back into the darkness. It stopped and looked back at them once, as if beckoning them to follow.

A swift look at Sar confirmed he was as curious as Takai to see where the tunnel led. Cautiously, they stepped into the passageway. Behind them, the stone wall closed of its own accord with a thud.

They followed the wolf's path into the dark unknown, a

welcome distraction from Takai's troubles and the confusing thoughts about Arisa swirling through his mind.

Takai and Sar followed the tunnel for what seemed like miles. In parts they were forced to bend right over and almost crawl, but the wolf kept turning back, beckoning them to continue.

Eventually, they emerged in the woodland and the wolf slipped away among the trees. Takai looked down at his dirty clothes, frustrated that his attempt at escaping from everything had resulted in nothing but a sore back and the need for a good bath.

18

*S*ar and Arisa stood in the shadows of the hallway outside the Secretary's rooms, waiting for the signal. She couldn't believe the Prince had agreed to help, especially after the argument they'd had after seeing Lina. In fact, she still wasn't willing to believe Takai would go through with helping them, until it actually happened. But a moment later, at the exact agreed time, a servant boy from Takai's rooms approached Horace's guards.

'I have a message for the Secretary from the Prince.'

The guards admitted the boy into Horace's chambers.

Sar turned to Arisa. 'This is it,' he whispered. 'Are you ready?'

She nodded. It was a show of assuredness she didn't feel, but she had to forge ahead. The messages had to be destroyed.

As expected, Horace and the servant boy emerged after a moment and headed toward the main keep. With a final squeeze of Arisa's hand, Sar emerged from their hiding place and strode purposefully toward the guards.

'Sar?' the men said in unison, standing up straight.

'At ease. I have been visiting all of the Royal Guard units to ensure the security measures for the King's tournament are well understood and in hand.'

Arisa hadn't heard her friend speak with such authority before. He must have sounded serious enough, because the guards nodded earnestly and started repeating the orders they had been given. Sar manoeuvred himself into a position so the guards had to move away from the door to speak to him, their backs facing Arisa.

She took her opportunity to sneak behind them, her delicate slippers sliding soundlessly across the stone floor. Turning the brass doorknob without so much as a whisper, she opened the door just wide enough to slip into the Secretary's rooms, then closed it carefully behind her.

Arisa's heart hammered in her chest, beating so loudly she was sure the guards could hear it. She paused, willing herself to remain calm, then made a beeline for Horace's desk. The room was eerily silent, save for the slight rattling of the window's wooden shutters.

It didn't take her long to locate the messages. Horace must have been working on them when the messenger arrived; the heap of parchment scraps was in a neat pile in the centre of the desk. One sat by itself with an abandoned quill beside it. He had marked it up in several places – Arisa immediately spied the names *Leo*, *Alik* and *Gwyn*.

Bundling up all the messages, she tucked them inside her dress. She would have to destroy them as soon as she got safely back to her room. She did a final sweep of the whole desk and a nearby shelf to make sure she hadn't missed any messages. It appeared she had them all.

As Arisa was about to leave, a thought occurred to her. While there was no escaping the fact that Horace would note the absence of the messages immediately, it would help if there was at least one plausible reason why they were missing, other than having been stolen.

She walked to the window and opened the shutters. *The time is coming,* the breeze outside whispered. *What time?* she wanted to reply, and the wind appeared to hear her, as it answered, *You will know.*

A gust of wind blew into the room, scattering the papers on Horace's desk. Arisa picked up a handful of the documents and threw them through the window, watching as they fluttered through the air.

She tiptoed back across the room. Pressing her ear to the door, she listened for Sar and the guards. From what she could hear, they were still deep in conversation. Sar was reciting a list of orders in great detail and clarifying the men's understanding. Arisa noted with relief that he was speaking in his usual booming voice. She opened the door a crack and peeked out. The guards were in the same position as before, their backs to her.

She slid back through the door, closing it quietly behind her. Sar's voice had risen even louder, as if he were deeply passionate about the instructions he was giving regarding the exact amount of polish the guards should use on their uniform buttons.

One of the guards cocked his head to the side, but neither turned toward Arisa. Sar, of course, gave no indication he had seen her. She snuck past them and scooted as quietly as possible back to her hiding spot in the shadows. Safely out of sight, she allowed herself to take a deep breath.

She had done it. The secret messages were out of the Secretary's clutches. She and Erun were safe again. For now.

19

*I*t was only two days until the tournament and great celebrations, and there had been no news of firesky. While not surprised, Takai was apprehensive. Horace had met with the King and intensified his demands to take action against Erun and Arisa. The King had maintained his original stance. The healer and his ward were not to be touched, unless Horace could find evidence that they were working against Lamore.

'But I saw the evidence,' Horace cried. '*You* saw the evidence. The messages that showed a connection between the Kengian Queen, Erun and Gwyn.'

'And where is that evidence now?' the King spat. 'Disappeared on the wind, you say – flew out of a window like it had wings?'

'That is my understanding, sire.'

Takai held his tongue. It hadn't taken much thought to figure out that the diversion he'd been asked to create had been for Arisa to get rid of the messages. What exactly had been in them? And why was he happy that he'd helped her dispose of them?

It was difficult for Takai to reconcile that Arisa held so many secrets from him, but that he still wanted to help her. The reason, of course, was simple. She enchanted and intrigued him as much as she infuriated him.

'Father, we do not need firesky,' he said to the King now. 'The celebrations the Secretary has so diligently prepared are enough to dazzle all of Lamore.'

Takai's father nodded his agreement.

'But sire,' Horace interjected, 'if you have firesky, you also have the key to defeating the Northemers and all of your enemies. It will be the weapon I promised you. Your legacy to be the greatest leader Kypria has even seen.'

The King's eyes flared with hunger.

Takai spun on Horace. 'I thought you wanted to align yourself with the Northemers. Even after they invaded the castle grounds with a Lamorian-speaking girl helping them – a girl rumoured to have powers.'

'As I have said,' Horace rolled his eyes at Takai, '*many* times, we will only join the Northemers for as long as it takes to get Kengia. Then we will turn on them and take back what is ours.'

'Father,' Takai protested. 'Our navy and forces are well prepared to face the Northemers. Combined with Ivane's forces, we can defeat Malu, *without* relying on something that may or may not eventuate – something born of Kengian magic.'

'Sire, just let me have the ward taken from court. It will be enough to guarantee the healer's compliance – I know he can do it. The girl can stay at Calliope under Guthrie's watch.'

Takai's heart began to race. 'Father, that is a fate far worse than being thrown into the dungeons. And you promised Mother.'

'Enough,' the King said. 'Horace, you will get me firesky by the celebrations, but you are not to act against or harm the Kengian or the girl. The Queen will not forgive me if a hair is touched on either of their heads.'

'What if I find some proof of their treachery?' Horace demanded.

'Then I will reconsider your request.'

The King dismissed the Secretary then, leaving Takai to exhale with relief. He had kept Arisa from being harmed...as long as Horace didn't find any damning evidence that could be used to force Erun to conjure up firesky. He needed to warn Arisa – but that would involve speaking to her. Did she even *want* to speak to him after their last argument? He would have to get Sar to pass on the message, because as much as he wanted to help Arisa, he feared he was the last person she wanted help from.

20

The first day of spring arrived exactly as it should. The cerulean sky was clear and cloudless. The silver sun shone brightly overhead, its light warming Arisa's skin. It was a welcome change from the cold, wet and miserable weather of recent days. Only the night before, a wild thunderstorm had howled ominously outside the castle windows, shaking the shutters and keeping Arisa awake most of the night. In contrast, today's weather should have been a reason for rejoicing.

Instead, Arisa was consumed by dread.

It was the day of the King's long-awaited celebrations and the Prince's eighteenth birthday. It was also the third and final day of the tournament, which was supposed to end with a spectacular surprise – firesky. But there would be no firesky today… or any other day, she hoped.

Reportedly, Horace hadn't taken the news well that Erun would not deliver firesky for the celebrations. He had blustered around Erun's rooms, smashing glass beakers and vials and upturning furniture. Erun had told Arisa he'd been sure the Secretary would have killed him had the Queen not pre-empted Horace's reaction and assigned her own personal guards to protect him. The Secretary had eventually calmed, but not before launching a volley of unspeakable insults and promises of retribution.

Surprisingly, both Erun and Gwyn had downplayed the confrontation. They were sure of the Queen's influence, confident that the King wouldn't allow Horace to deliver on his threats. Arisa didn't share that confidence. They'd known stringing Horace along for all this time came with significant risk. Erun may have avoided punishment – for now – but Arisa felt it was only a temporary reprieve. There would be consequences for defying Horace. It was only a matter of time.

Erun had tried to allay her fears by reminding her that Horace's leverage from the coded messages no longer existed, thanks to her. She had taken the stolen messages back to her rooms and tried to decipher them herself, curious about the mentions of Gwyn and the other secrets they may contain, but despite knowing the key to decode the notes, she wasn't fluent in the Kengian dialect Erun and his mother used, so couldn't decipher them. She had thrown the messages into the fire, watching bitterly as the flames consumed the answers both she and the Secretary had been seeking.

After this, though, Sar had told them that the King would withdraw his protection if Horace uncovered any other proof of treachery. Erun had said he would send the Firemaster's book away from the castle – and the secrets to firesky with it. The next time the Schoolmaster was at the castle, Erun planned to ask him to deliver the book to a Kengian Shaman. But until then, there was a risk Horace could get his hands on the very thing needed to create firesky. And even once the book was gone, Erun still wanted Arisa to leave the castle, to slip away on the upcoming trip to the countryside.

'There are just too many risks now,' he'd said. She'd argued bitterly, saying she would never leave him behind – and she meant it. But it didn't make her feel any safer for herself or Erun.

For all these reasons, Arisa found it difficult to celebrate the spring day, but she couldn't show signs of her inner turmoil. For anyone to understand it, she would have to speak about the true nature of Erun's work. She would have to reveal his true identity. She would have to share that she was half-Kengian herself – but she couldn't share that with anyone.

She forced a smile as she sat down next to Gwyn in the Queen's pavilion. The Queen glanced over at Arisa's arrival and offered a reassuring smile. An aura of peace and tranquillity had surrounded her since she'd received the Shaman's gift – the one Lina had brought to court. Trying to draw comfort from the Queen, Arisa took a deep breath, taking in the scene around her. The Duchess of Lakeford, the Baroness of Iveness, Countess Datanya, Theodora and Selina sat in the row behind them. Everyone in the pavilion was bubbling with excitement, waiting for the main joust.

The pavilion offered an unobstructed view of the tiltyard. The King, the Duke and his son Willem, and the Baron of Iveness were sitting on a dais on the opposite side of the grounds. They were performing the role of judges, while Horace hovered in the background. Willem waved to Arisa enthusiastically. She responded with a smile and nod, conscious of the Secretary's hawklike eyes drilling into her. She broke Horace's gaze, determined to fix her attention on anything but his angry glances.

Brightly coloured banners representing each noble house lined the outer edge of the field, rippling in the ever-so-slight breeze. The stone castle dazzled in the background, its gates open to the nobility and lowborn alike. As the Prince had suggested, a small entrance fee was being charged, to go toward the hospital project.

A line of tents and pavilions had been set up for the nobles, and rows of timber stands were in place for invited guests. The hundreds of other Lamorians who'd made the trek to the castle claimed spots of grass, jostling for the best vantage points, and wandering to and from stalls selling everything from pies and ale to sweets.

On the tiltyard, Arisa counted at least two dozen competitors in full armour. Their shields, emblazoned with house emblems, glinted in the morning sun. Their destriers and stallions were dressed in elaborate caparisons, with the cloth bearing each knight's heraldry. Squires and pages laden with bundles of weapons and armour scurried around surprisingly quickly.

This morning, the younger nobles and knights who'd excelled in the previous two days of swordsmanship and archery were due to take a turn at the tilt. As expected, Sar and Takai had both fared well in swordsmanship, with Sar edging out the Prince, while Takai had bettered everyone in archery. Guthrie had secured his place in the joust by beating Willem on points in archery, eliminating the Duke's son from the tournament. Takai, Sar and Guthrie would all compete today to determine the overall winner of the tournament.

Sar would joust against a young squire who was currently in fourth position, and the victor would compete against the winner of a joust between Takai and Guthrie. Arisa was worried about Guthrie facing the Prince. She hadn't seen Horace's son since he'd been back at court, but memories of him were fresh in her mind. She knew firsthand he wasn't the type to play fair.

Guthrie had taken a dislike to her the day he and Sir Marcus had come to take Rea away. He'd convinced the Ettean Governor to take Arisa as well, and if it hadn't been for Erun, she could have ended up...She dared not think about it. Just a few months ago, Guthrie had beaten her up in Obira for trying to save a Kengian starling. Arisa had retaliated by breaking his nose. Ever since, Guthrie had targeted her – and had tried to kill her during the riot in the marketplace. She knew exactly what the Secretary's son was capable of, and while she was still angry with Takai after their recent argument, she didn't want him to get hurt.

Guthrie must have read her thoughts. At that moment, he rode past the pavilion and caught her eye. His lip curled into a knowing smile before he pulled down his visor and cantered away.

A cold shiver ran up her spine.

'Have you seen a joust before?' Gwyn asked Arisa.

'No. My experience is limited to what I've read about it. It sounds terrifying.'

Gwyn patted her hand. 'You'll be relieved to hear it's not quite as bloody and gruesome as you may have read.' Spying the long-tapered lances the knights held, Arisa was unconvinced. But Gwyn went on, 'For a start, the lances you see are blunted, meaning it's unusual these days for a knight to be seriously wounded.'

Seriously wounded. Waves of nausea rippled through her. She swallowed back the bile that had risen in her throat.

Gwyn read her discomfort and offered a distraction. 'Would you like me to explain the rules?'

Arisa could only manage a nod.

'When the trumpet sounds, the two riders charge with levelled lances and attempt to unhorse each other. They must aim at the shields and nowhere else, and have three opportunities to knock the opponent from their horse. It's more difficult than it sounds, as the saddles have a back piece designed to keep the knight in their seat.'

Arisa had an awful vision of Takai being knocked to the ground, just like Lina's son, Hyando. She could see clearly in her mind the moment Hyando had flown through the air – thrown from a cart after a Royal Guard had forced the horse to bolt. The boy had landed heavily, sustaining injuries that would claim his life.

She realised with a shudder that she couldn't lose the Prince too.

Again, Gwyn must have sensed her anxiety, because she squeezed Arisa's hand. 'The knights don't need to be completely unseated. Points are also given for breaking a lance on an opponent's shield.'

'It still sounds dangerous. Why even do it?'

'In older times, the victor would win his opponent's horse and armour, but today they fight for honour and a purse of gold. Tradition also dictates that the ladies of the court sponsor individual knights by offering favours, such as a scarf or veil.'

In the distance, Arisa could see Takai taking his place at the end of the tiltyard. He wore the insignia of the King: a silver falcon on black. The Queen had said the King's earlier plans for an emblem depicting the falcon surrounded by flames – presumably to represent firesky – had been abandoned. Guthrie wore red with a yellow cross for his mother's house.

Arisa thought she saw Takai look for her a moment before pulling his visor down. She watched on nervously as the horses snorted and pawed at the ground.

The trumpet sounded.

She held her breath as Takai charged toward Guthrie, his lance levelled. The crowd erupted in cheers. The horses' hooves thundered down the tiltyard as the competitors neared each other. Arisa resisted the urge to look away when they came alongside each other.

She exhaled as Takai's lance struck its target, cracking loudly as it connected with Guthrie's shield. The lance split right down its centre.

Guthrie fell back in his saddle, but managed to right himself. The crowd roared with excitement as the pair returned for their second round and a new lance was handed to Takai.

The Prince's head turned in Arisa's direction and he appeared to nod at her, as if to say, *I have him. I have Guthrie beat… for you.* The cruel and horrible Guthrie, who had tormented her ever since the day he'd taken Rea from her. It was no consolation for all the pain the Secretary's son had inflicted on her and countless other people, but seeing him beaten so decidedly in front of practically the whole kingdom would go some way toward making her feel better. And she was sure now that the Prince would beat him – that everything she thought she'd seen in her mind a moment ago had just been her imagination.

Arisa sat forward in anticipation as Takai and Guthrie charged at each other again – she was so close to the tiltyard that she could see the sweat lathering on the horses' necks. Wet clumps of dirt sprang from the ground, released by the horses' hooves. Their beating echoed the pounding of Arisa's heart. She tried to block out the roar of the crowd to focus on Takai, to somehow will him to beat Guthrie, but the sound was deafening. Splinters of silver armour and a flutter of the knights' colours flashed past Arisa until the riders were upon each other.

Her heart stilled as they came within reach, and once more she had to force herself not to look away. But with an ear-splitting crack, the Prince's lance found its target again. This time, Guthrie was knocked off-centre and looked sure to fall from his horse, but after a considerable struggle he managed to get back in position.

There was much murmuring and even laughter among the crowd as Guthrie galloped his horse unnecessarily quickly back to the end of the tiltyard. He threw his lance to the ground, yelling abuse at his squire. It took several minutes of Guthrie examining and trying new shields and lances before he was ready to face the Prince again. All the while, Takai sat still and tall in his saddle, at the ready. He was the picture of confidence and calm.

The final round began as the others had. The crowd. The horses. The noise. The excitement as the riders barrelled toward each other with their weapons aloft. But then Arisa noticed something.

She saw it happen in her mind's eye, just like she had with Hyando. The pair charged at each other. The world appeared to slow. Arisa could see every muscle in the horses' flanks and legs, rolling, flexing, contracting, sinews and veins popping from their lathered coats. Takai's steady and deliberate movements as he tightened his grip on his lance and adjusted his aim. The shift in Guthrie's weight as he appeared to change the angle of his lance – aiming it a little higher.

'*No*,' she screamed, her voice lost in the crowd.

This time, the cracking sound ricocheted through Arisa's ribcage. The sound of a lance not striking the unyielding iron of a shield, but connecting with something more vulnerable.

Guthrie's lance had struck the Prince's helmet. Takai's head flung back at an awkward angle and his body followed, catapulting through the air, a whirl of metal-covered limbs, finally smashing to the ground with a crumpled thud.

There was a collective gasp among the crowd, and Arisa leapt to her feet. Guthrie dismounted and removed his helmet, his face drawn with shock.

The Queen ran toward her son, her dress drawn up to her knees. The King was running, too. Arisa felt as if she were frozen to the spot. She barely noticed as Theodora shoved past her to get to the Prince.

It was Hyando all over again.

'Arisa,' came Gwyn's voice. It was as if she were speaking to Arisa from a long way away. 'Arisa,' she said again, and clutched her arm. After what felt like forever, Arisa slowly turned toward her. Gwyn was mouthing the words, *Go to him.*

She nodded and rushed toward the crowd that had gathered around the Prince, hearing someone say Takai was unconscious. Somehow, she managed to push her way to the front.

Sar was bellowing at everyone to get back. The King was shouting for one of his physicians. The Queen clasped Takai's limp hand. After a moment, the physician arrived and removed the Prince's helmet. There was a bloody, jagged cut on his forehead, a black bruise already forming around it. The physician bent over to listen for Takai's breathing.

His lips thinned, and he shook his head.

'Shush!' Arisa ordered the crowd.

The physician put his ear to Takai's chest again. He grimaced as he sat back on his heels.

King Delrik grabbed the physician by his collar. 'Check again!'

The physician held up his hands in surrender and offered condolences to the King. Gwyn was by Sofia's side, trying to comfort her. Theodora stood next to her father, away from the crowd; neither showed any emotion in particular. Guthrie hid behind his father and sister as Sar marched menacingly toward him.

Not this time, a voice said in Arisa's head. *Not after Hyando.*

Whatever the connection she had with the Prince, it wasn't going to end this way. Not today. She would not have it.

She fell to her knees beside the Prince and reached for his free hand, not caring who was watching. Her other hand was planted firmly on the wet grass. 'I will not have it,' she whispered, and squeezed his cold palm. 'I will not have it,' she repeated, more loudly.

The ground under her hand was damp. Her fingers drew life from the earth. A warm energy formed in her palm, running up her arm, through her chest and down her other arm before transferring into Takai's hand, until all the coldness was gone.

Takai's chest suddenly heaved. His eyes flew open, and he gasped. His eyes darted around until they fell on Arisa, and his breathing slowed. He held her gaze as someone shouted in the background, 'Long live the Prince.'

There were more shouts of celebration, and a collective sigh of relief. Arisa felt her own breath return – she hadn't realised she had stopped breathing – and squeezed Takai's hand tighter. She had an urge to tell him something. Maybe she wanted to admonish him for trying to leave her before they had a chance to settle their argument – or was it simply that she…cared about him?

That was when she realised every eye was on the two of them. Arisa dropped the Prince's hand as if it were a hot coal and retreated into the crowd. She watched from afar as Sar stepped forward and enveloped his friend in a bear hug.

The crowd turned its attention to Guthrie.

'Lord Guthrie must be disqualified,' a noble declared.

'It was the horse,' Guthrie said, his voice edged with fear. 'Something must have spooked him and pushed me off balance.'

Loudly, the crowd voiced their doubts.

'Guthrie won't be disqualified. Let him prove whether he can win fair and square.'

It was Takai who had spoken. He was propped up in a standing position by Sar; a bandage had been hastily wound around his head.

'You cannot joust again,' the Queen protested.

'I'm fine.' Takai's tone didn't invite further discussion.

Arisa wanted to protest herself but bit her tongue, not wishing to draw any further attention to herself or how close she'd just been to Takai.

The King frowned, but after a brief discussion with the physician, he nodded. 'There will be one last tilt in this joust. The previous round is declared forfeit.'

Guthrie's eyes darted around, as if looking for an escape, before he returned to his page and horse. Takai released himself from Sar's hold and made his way back to his own horse, slowly and somewhat unsteadily.

The crowd returned to their seats. After a few minutes, Guthrie and Takai had taken their positions for the final tilt.

The trumpet sounded and they charged headlong at each other. Arisa held her breath for what felt like the millionth time today.

She needn't have worried. Takai's lance struck Guthrie's shield with such force that it lifted Guthrie up and out of his saddle. He appeared to be suspended momentarily in mid-air before he fell to the ground, landing squarely on his backside with a *thud*. His helmet flew through the air and the crowd roared with laughter, which only got louder as Guthrie stood and wobbled from the tiltyard. The red look on his face was murderous.

Arisa didn't join the jest. She realised how close she had come to not only losing the Prince, but to publicly declaring herself to him. She tried to convince herself she had lost her mind for a moment. That she didn't love Takai. That she could never love him. Her rational mind told her he was still the arrogant and misguided Prince she'd first met. He was still the future King of Lamore, a country with a troubling history of invading other lands and persecuting its own people. If that weren't bad enough, Arisa knew Takai could never care for her. She was an unsuitable match. Even if the vast difference in their positions could be overcome, any affection he may hold for her was based on secrets and lies. Takai didn't know her. The *real* her. And if he did know she was half-Kengian – if he knew she was a silver-eyes – he would be rid of her in an instant. She dared not think what he would do if he knew Erun was a Kengian Prince, and brother to the man Takai thought had tried to bewitch his father.

Unsure if these realisations made her more sad or angry, Arisa stood up and stumbled from the pavilion.

'Where are you going?' Gwyn cried out after her. 'You're going to miss Sar's joust.'

'Tell Sar I'm sorry,' she called back over her shoulder, 'but I can't...I can't do this.'

She sprinted away, heading to the castle, across the moat and through the gates to the inner courtyard. She ran all the way through the south gate and past the Queen's gardens before slowing her pace. There she continued, half walking, half running, wanting to get far away from the tournament, far away from Takai. She only stopped when she reached the archery oval, where she crumpled to the ground, biting back the tears threatening to fall.

The same series of thoughts cycled through her mind. It was

hopeless. She had fallen in love with someone who could never love her back. If by some miracle he did love her, what future was there for them? Would the Lamorian kingdom survive, or would it become a territory of Northem? And would Takai even be alive after the war that was sure to come? Arisa felt no hope. No hope for her and Takai, no hope for her and Erun, and no hope for all of Kypria. She breathed heavily in and out, trying desperately not to give in to crying. She didn't hear the approaching footsteps until it was too late.

'Arisa! What is it? Are you alright?'

She opened her eyes to see an out-of-breath Takai crouching in front of her. He was still clad in the padded gambeson he'd worn under his armour.

'Takai.' She rushed to wipe her eyes, where tears were ready to be released, threatening to reveal her true eye colour.

'I was looking for you. Gwyn said you were upset. What happened?'

She wanted to tell the Prince to go away. Her head told her to stay as far away from him as possible, but her heart constricted at the concern in his voice. She placed a hand on his forehead. An egg had formed under the bandage. Takai winced, but didn't back away from her touch.

'It seems I'm making quite the habit of injuring myself in front of you.' He gave a lopsided grin.

Arisa returned his smile. Perhaps she could enjoy the moment. Enjoy whatever this was while it lasted.

Takai stroked her face. Her cheek tingled under his touch. He held her gaze with an intensity that was both addictive and unnerving. Her breath quickened. They stood motionless. Part of her wanted to stay like that forever, but part of her was chiding herself for feeling any joy when there was so much danger and uncertainty ahead.

She dropped her hand and pulled away from Takai's reach.

His brow furrowed. 'I'm sorry. Did I upset you?'

She shook her head vigorously.

Takai exhaled loudly. 'Good. Because I was afraid this was about to become the worst birthday ever.'

Arisa flung a hand over her mouth. 'I'm sorry, Takai, I've been so distracted – I completely forgot to wish you a happy birthday.'

Takai shrugged. 'It's alright.'

'No, it's not alright.' Arisa cursed herself internally, thinking of the token she'd been meaning to give him today. 'I've been working on a gift for you, but—'

'It's alright,' he repeated. 'I already have a gift from you.' He reached under his gambeson and pulled out a gold scarf. It was the one she had used to wrap around his arm the day he'd been thrown from his horse in the woodland. 'It's my good luck charm. I think it's what saved me today.'

Her cheeks flushed. 'I think your head injury is affecting your judgement. You should take care.'

'I'm not worried about me. I'm worried about you. I'd like to think you came running out here because you thought that I may have…well, that doesn't matter, because I know there's something else troubling you.'

Arisa nodded. 'I'm worried about Erun.'

'Why? What's happened?'

'Nothing…yet.' She wondered how much she could tell Takai, whether she could trust him. 'You know he has to deliver firesky for Horace and the King, but he won't do it…he can't.'

'I know. But you have my mother's protection…and mine.'

She bit her lip. Would he feel the same way if he knew the whole truth about her?

'Is there something else?'

Arisa didn't respond. Takai reached out and lifted her chin, his dark eyes searching her face for an answer.

'So many secrets,' he whispered. 'What are you hiding behind those strange eyes?'

She clasped his hands in hers and lowered them from her face. 'No secrets.'

'I accept that you're not ready to tell me. But one day, Arisa…one day soon I hope you will trust me enough to share the burdens you carry.'

'Why do you care so much?' she asked softly.

'I don't know. You're one of the most aggravating people I've ever met…but also the most enchanting.'

She couldn't help a laugh bursting from her at the back-handed compliment. 'Thanks…I guess.'

Takai smiled back at her, but his expression became serious after a moment. 'All I know for sure is that I care about you…I care a lot.'

These were the words Arisa suddenly wanted to hear, more than anything else in the world. But she couldn't accept them. She would never be able to share her secrets with Takai. Not if she wanted him to still care for her.

It was better to end this before it went too far.

'We should get back to watch Sar's joust.'

Takai's face dropped. 'Alright.' He held out his arm, but she hesitated. 'What is it?'

'I wonder if we should go back separately.'

Takai's jaw tightened.

'We wouldn't want anyone to think—'

'No, we wouldn't…would we.'

Takai turned his back and strode away from her. And like a wordless whisper on the wind, the moment was gone.

21

*T*akai and Sar were the last two competitors left standing at the end of the day's events. They faced one another in the final joust, but neither of them unseated the other. Takai was declared the overall winner of the tournament on points, beating Sar by a whisker. A feast in the Great Hall had followed, and now the Queen and her inner circle were relaxing in her privy chamber.

Takai wished he were there. He was desperate to see Arisa again, to try and get to the bottom of what was going on between them...or wasn't going on. He felt that they had had some kind of breakthrough. That Arisa cared for him – but she had put up a wall. Why? What was she hiding? Why was she so scared of letting him in? He had to get answers, but they would have to wait for now, because he'd been summoned by his father.

He had presumed the King wished to enjoy a celebratory drink with him, so was surprised to discover that Horace had also been summoned. Outside the King's privy chamber, the Secretary greeted Takai with uncharacteristic deference – not surprising, given Guthrie had nearly killed him today. Takai grunted his acknowledgement and the pair were admitted into the King's private rooms.

'Your Majesty.' Horace bowed low.

'Father.'

Takai's father was standing with his back to them, gazing out the window that overlooked the castle's northern grounds. His hands were clasped behind him.

Takai and Horace waited for the King to acknowledge them, but he was silent, his stillness unnerving.

'Sire?' Horace ventured.

'I heard you the first time,' came the cold response. The King didn't bother to turn when he spoke. 'What exactly am I looking at, *Secretary*?'

Takai and Horace followed his gaze. The grounds below were still, other than a few servants and stallholders packing up the last remains of the tournament in the distance. The purplish dusk sky was clear. There was nothing out of the ordinary.

The King didn't wait for an answer. 'Nothing. The answer is *nothing!*' Delrik spun toward Horace, nostrils flared and cheeks flushed. 'No great display of light, and certainly no promise of a great weapon.'

'Your Majesty. Please accept my apology again. I was sure Erun would deliver firesky—'

'But he didn't.' The King's clipped tones cut like a knife.

'Not yet, sire. I'm sure he would have done it if I had been able to take action against his ward.'

'Enough!' The King thumped his fist down on the table in front of him, shaking it. 'I have had enough of you and your pathetic excuses. You have not fulfilled your promises. No firesky. No alliance with the Northemers. No Sergei. And as a further insult, your son nearly killed mine today.'

Horace hung his head. 'Again, sire, I apologise for Guthrie's recklessness, but it was not intentional.'

'You owe your apology to my son.'

Horace turned toward Takai and bowed from his waist.

'Your Highness, please accept my sincere apologies for the role Guthrie played in today's terrible accident.'

Accident! Takai could have argued with Horace that it had been no accident. He could have demanded that Guthrie be punished, but he suspected by the King's manner that some form of justice was to be served. He merely nodded.

'I wonder if you're more of an enemy than a friend to me, Horace,' the King hissed.

'A friend, sire.' Horace appeared unrattled as he calmly placated the King. 'Always your friend and trusted adviser.'

'That's just it.' The King stepped out from behind his desk and moved alarmingly quickly to stand before Horace. 'I *don't* trust you. You have taken advantage of our childhood friendship and manipulated me for longer than I care to recall. You have urged me to act against my council's advice on many occasions, and you had me convinced firesky was possible.'

Horace didn't so much as flinch. He raised his chin and spoke with confidence. 'It is possible. You can have firesky, and with it the power to defeat all your enemies. You will have the power to take Kengia – a feat no other King before you has managed.'

'And that is why I supported this quest in the first place. For Kengia alone. I don't need firesky to feign an alliance with the Northemers. I will defeat them with Ivane's help. I don't need firesky to defeat Ivane, or Ette, and claim them as my territories…for those nations will be my allies. Thanks to my wife's intervention, we will be able to live in peace and prosperity with our neighbours across the sea.'

'What about Kengia, sire?' Horace pressed. 'You owe nothing to them, especially after one of their Princes tried to bewitch you. The whole country and its riches lay ripe—'

The King held up a hand to silence him. 'I no longer desire Kengia.' His eyes shone momentarily. 'The Queen would be against it. And after your failure today, I am decided. We will give up on firesky.'

'So you're forfeiting the chance to be the most powerful ruler in all of Kypria – ruler of the whole known world?' Horace's voice rose indignantly. 'Because the Queen would not like it?'

'I know you think I'm weak.' Delrik was unblinking. 'But it is you who is the weak one. You who have lost the ability to control me.'

'It is not *I* who is controlling you, Your Majesty.'

'What?' the King roared. 'No one controls me anymore!'

Horace shifted his feet. 'I have said too much. My apologies.'

The King took a step closer. 'No. Don't stop there. Say exactly what you were going to say.'

Horace sighed. 'Sire...it pains me to be the one to point out that you *are* being controlled, and by the person closest to you. The Queen.'

'Father!' Takai protested. 'My mother has done nothing but act in your and the kingdom's best interests. If it weren't for the Queen, we would be facing the Northemers alone. Thanks to her we have an alliance with Ivane.'

'The Queen is too close to your enemies, sire,' Horace pressed. 'She urges you to listen to no one but her, and has convinced you to shut me out. I, who have done nothing but devote my entire life to you and your legacy.'

'Yes, my mother speaks against you,' Takai said, 'and rightfully so. You're the one who convinced my father to attack her homeland as soon as they were married. You advised him to execute her father – my grandfather!'

The King stood up to his full height. 'My son is right. You have been the one controlling me. You single-handedly destroyed our marriage.'

'But you know it had to be done,' Horace insisted. 'Ivane is your birthright. It was Lamore's territory for centuries before, and it should be yours again. As for the Queen's father – he had to be removed. He could never be trusted…like her brother can't be now.'

A shadow of doubt passed over the King's face.

'Don't listen to the *Secretary*, Father,' Takai spat. 'King Iskar is committed to the alliance.'

The King nodded rapidly. 'Yes. Yes, he is. He has forgiven me, as has Sofia. I can hardly believe the extent of her mercifulness toward me.'

'Exactly, sire,' Horace said, his tone conciliatory. 'She couldn't possibly have forgiven you.'

Delrik compressed his lips. 'But she has. She is back by my side. She has publicly declared she is my true wife.'

Horace clicked his jaw and looked at Takai, then back at the King, as if calculating what to say next. 'That is something I'd like to discuss with you further, sire…in private.'

'Whatever you have to say to me, you can say in front of my son, your future King.'

Takai watched Horace grit his teeth. 'Is Sofia your *true* wife, as you say? She hasn't returned to her apartments next to yours. Can you say she is your true wife, in every sense of the word?'

Takai's hands formed fists at his sides as the King grabbed Horace's cloak and pulled him close, his face only inches away from the Secretary's. 'You have overstepped!'

Horace cringed as a spray of spit spread across his face.

'You will not make light of my private relations with the Queen.' The King released his grip and pushed Horace away roughly.

A smirk played at the corner of the Secretary's mouth. Takai assumed he had got the answer he was seeking.

'Your Majesty, I don't make light of the situation at all,' Horace said. 'Especially since it exposes your weaknesses. While she refuses to be your wife in every respect, you can assume the reunion is a charade. A charade to manipulate and control you. She is using her position to protect her friends and family, many of whom are your enemies.'

'She is my wife,' the King muttered, as if he were trying to convince himself.

'Of course, Your Majesty. But you need to be sure of her motivations. You need to be certain she really does want to be reunited. She must be willing to be your wife in every sense of the word. Only then can you trust her completely.'

Takai's hands shook with rage over how Horace had spoken of his mother. 'Father, you can't pay heed to anything the Secretary has said. My mother is devoted to you.'

But the King had sunk heavily into his chair.

'And,' Horace continued, 'in the event my fears about the Queen are true and the alliance fails, I will get you firesky and Malu as an ally. Some insurance.'

'Insurance?'

'In case I am right about the Queen, which I hope I am not. I'm sure Malu will agree to my proposal. I have told him about firesky's potential. He will not be able to resist it, and he will see an alliance as a much better option than going up against Lamore and Ivane's forces.'

'Without the Queen, everything will be lost…' The King's voice trailed off.

'You will have firesky. I need a little longer. A day…two at the most.'

'Is it really possible?'

'Yes. All I need is some leverage over the healer. Let me take his ward into my keeping.'

A hard lump formed in Takai's throat. He couldn't let anything happen to Arisa. 'Father, you can't hold Arisa against her will. She will be leaving for the College of Surgeons shortly – it was your promise, in return for what she did to stop the riot.'

The King nodded slowly.

'Surely she is expendable,' Horace said. 'She is no one.'

'She is *someone* to many in Lamore,' Takai said. *She is someone to me.*

Horace ignored him and addressed the King. 'She is the key to firesky, sire.'

The King tapped his fingers on the arm of his chair. 'The Queen will never forgive me if I let harm come to the girl. But…I do see the sense of securing firesky…for insurance only, as you say…The healer is yours to do with what you wish. Do whatever you need to get him to comply.'

'Thank you, sire.'

'Father, nothing Horace can do will secure firesky,' Takai protested. 'It is not in the healer's ability to—'

'I have made my wishes clear,' the King said, in a tone that didn't invite further conversation. 'You're both dismissed.'

Waves of nausea rolled in Takai's stomach. He may have saved Arisa, but what of Erun? And for how long would Arisa be safe? Horace had laid serious seeds of doubt about the Queen's fidelity in the King's mind, and if Takai's mother couldn't quash those doubts, there was no knowing what might happen to Arisa.

Takai had to speak to his mother and get Arisa to safety – away from the castle, until the matter was decided. He would bring the trip to the countryside forward to tomorrow, and pray that his mother could allay the King's fears.

22

*A*risa sipped the mulled wine she'd been given. It wasn't to her taste, but she hadn't wanted to dampen the celebrations in the Queen's privy chamber. She watched with a forced smile as Sar demanded a rematch with the Prince, and attempted to rally support from Willem and others in the room. Spirits in the Queen's chambers were high. Except for Arisa's.

Willem had tried to cheer her. He'd thanked her for sending the medicine she'd made for him, saying it had helped a lot with his pain. She was always happy to see Willem, and would have enjoyed his company immensely on any other occasion.

It had been a long and emotional day, in more ways than one. Her meeting with the Prince, and how she'd felt when she thought she'd lost him, confused her. They had crossed a bridge in their friendship, and there was no turning back. Now they must move forward – but it was impossible to imagine a happy ending for them. The realist in her said there could never be a 'them' at all, but it didn't change the fact that she *wanted* there to be.

She hated herself for being distracted by thoughts of the Prince, especially when she knew Erun was in grave danger. His failure to deliver firesky couldn't go unpunished for long. She had to see her guardian to be sure he was alright.

Choosing a moment when she was sure no one's eyes were on her, Arisa slipped away. She reached the door to the privy chamber – and ran straight into Takai.

'You're not leaving?' He tilted his head and cast an earnest look at her.

'Sorry, but I need to leave.'

'Please don't go.' Takai reached out to grab Arisa's wrist but she stepped out of his reach. She couldn't let Takai cloud her thoughts – Erun needed her.

Hurt rippled over Takai's face but he took a breath and continued. 'I have to speak to my mother about – some urgent business, but after that…please stay.'

Arisa's heart lurched but she had to stay strong. 'You don't need me here.' *He didn't need her at all.*

'Maybe I do. Maybe I want—'

'I must get to my guardian. I told you earlier today – I'm worried about him.'

Takai's face softened, but there was a nervousness in his eyes she couldn't entirely fathom.

'Of course you should go to him. Until tomorrow, then.'

She raised a quizzical brow.

'Our adventure to the Lamore countryside,' he explained. 'I've decided we should take advantage of the fine weather. I have brought the trip forward to tomorrow.'

'Right. Tomorrow, then.' Maybe a trip to the countryside was exactly what she needed to take her mind off things.

Takai compressed his lips and nodded. 'Good.'

Arriving outside Erun's rooms, Arisa was surprised to find Klaus on sentry duty, instead of Horace's guards.

'Klaus. What are you doing here?'

'The Queen has ordered the Secretary's guards be relieved.'

He frowned. 'I understand there is some concern for your guardian and his wellbeing.'

She didn't respond, not knowing how much to reveal to Klaus. Fortunately, he held up his hands before she could speak.

'It's fine. I don't wish to know what Erun is up to. I figure if the Secretary wishes harm upon him, then it is better for your guardian if I can truthfully deny all knowledge.'

'A wise strategy,' Arisa said. Klaus opened the door and let her into Erun's room.

She found her guardian huddled over the Firemaster's book with the Schoolmaster. They were speaking in hushed tones as they leant over the open pages. Their conversation halted immediately as she entered.

'Arisa,' they cried in unison.

'Good to see you haven't been arrested,' she said to Erun with forced brightness.

He gave a wry smile. 'Not yet.'

'I expect it's only a matter of time.'

'Undoubtedly. Horace is sure to try every means at his disposal to extract firesky's secrets from me. Which is why I have asked the Schoolmaster here. I need to get the Firemaster's book to safety, so Horace can never get his hands on it.'

'Where will you take it?' Arisa asked the Schoolmaster.

'To the Shaman, Laurel.'

'The one who came for Hyando,' Erun said in a quiet voice.

A tingle ran up Arisa's spine. She'd known the Schoolmaster was close to a Kengian Shaman, but she'd had no idea it was the same one. It felt like an age since Arisa had met the woman who had spoken so cryptically about the Water Catcher prophecy. The day Hyando had died, the Shaman had peered into Arisa's unmasked Kengian eyes, as if she could see into Arisa's very soul. She'd urged Arisa to have faith...in what, exactly, Arisa didn't know.

'It's alright. She can be trusted,' the Schoolmaster said.

'That's fine for the book. But how is it going to protect you, Erun?'

Erun released a great sigh. 'I'm afraid there is nothing I can do to avoid Horace's wrath. All I can hope for is the Queen's continued protection.'

'Or the Water Catcher,' the Schoolmaster said, his voice overly upbeat.

'Yes. As foretold,' her guardian said. 'The Water Catcher will come.'

Here Erun went again, pinning all of his hopes on a prophecy that could never come to being. Arisa wanted to scream at him to be realistic. To stop dreaming. But she knew her words would be wasted.

'In the meantime, it's you I'm worried about,' Erun was saying. 'I can withstand anything Horace has planned for me, but I couldn't bear it if something happened to you.' He locked eyes with her and frowned. 'You must leave the castle. Escape, as we discussed.'

Her heart lurched. She couldn't do it. She couldn't leave her guardian. And she couldn't leave Takai – not until she knew what they were to each other.

'When is the trip to the countryside?' Erun asked.

Arisa responded in a daze. 'Tomorrow.'

'You can slip away and go to Laurel. She can protect you. She can help you get to Kengia. There are fishing boats smuggling Kengians back home ahead of war – Laurel can find you a place on one of them.'

'What makes you think I'll be safe there?'

'The Schoolmaster brought a message from Queen Mira. The Kengian tribes are campaigning to pre-emptively invade Lamore, so you'll be safer there than here. I will send her a message to say you will be joining the Queen in the capital.'

Arisa shook her head adamantly. 'No! I'm not leaving. Queen Sofia will keep us safe.'

'You will go. You *must*. I have to keep you safe…as well as the book.' Erun clutched the Firemaster's book so tight his knuckles turned white. He appeared to be savouring his final moments with it before handing it over to the Schoolmaster.

'I'm not leaving you,' she said.

Erun looked as if he would protest, but they were interrupted by the sound of raised voices outside the room. The door flung open to reveal Horace and Guthrie. Two of Horace's guards stood behind them, blocking Klaus from getting inside.

'And what exactly is transpiring here?' Horace's eyes went straight to the book being handed over to the Schoolmaster.

Arisa saw Erun start to utter what must be the Kengian spell to hide the book's contents. 'It is as you see, Secretary,' she said. 'I'm here visiting my guardian and Schoolmaster for my regular lessons.'

'Get that book,' Horace ordered Guthrie, and Guthrie snatched the Firemaster's book from Erun's hands. Horace pointed at Erun and the Schoolmaster. 'Arrest these two men.'

'On what charges?' Arisa cried, bile rising in her throat.

Horace looked down his nose at Arisa. 'I don't need to explain myself to you, or anyone else, for that matter. Think yourself lucky you won't be joining them in the dungeons.'

Arisa shot Klaus an urgent look. He nodded in acknowledgement and left immediately.

Erun folded his arms. 'I think I deserve an explanation for this ridiculous charade.'

'Since you ask.' A smirk tugged at the corner of Horace's mouth. 'You're being arrested on suspicion of witchcraft and possessing forbidden books. The same charges I was kind enough to defer after you saved the Prince's life – but you no longer deserve such mercies. I can no longer overlook your continued failure to deliver on your promises to me and to the King.'

'And me? What have I done?' the Schoolmaster asked.

'We have had our eyes on you for a while, Schoolmaster. You're known to be a Kengian sympathiser and supporter of the rebels, and I believe you've been conveying secret messages between Erun and Kengia. And right now we've found you about to take possession of a book that I suspect is devoted to sorcery. Show it to me.' Horace held out his hand to Guthrie, who was flicking through the book's pages with a perplexed look on his face.

'They're blank.' Guthrie scratched his head. 'The pages are blank. Not a thing on them.'

'Give it to me,' Horace barked impatiently. He too flicked through the empty pages. His eyes narrowed and he flashed an angry look at Erun. 'Search the rooms for anything linked to sorcery.'

The Secretary waved at the guards, who started tearing Erun's quarters apart. Over the next ten minutes, they searched every book and roll of parchment in the rooms, smashing Erun's equipment and vials in the process.

'What exactly is the meaning of this?'

The Queen had appeared in the doorway, her face flushed from running. She was flanked by Sar and Klaus. Gwyn and Takai stood behind them.

Horace clicked his jaw back and forth. 'Nothing for *Your Majesty* to be concerned about.'

The Queen squared her shoulders. 'The false arrest of the man who saved my son's life is my concern.'

Horace met the Queen's gaze. 'I have every right to arrest this sorcerer and his rebel friend.'

The Queen lifted her chin. 'On what evidence?'

'I urge you to recuse yourself from matters that are beyond your jurisdiction.'

Takai stepped forward. 'Are they beyond my jurisdiction as well, Secretary?'

'These were your father's orders,' Horace smiled at Takai, 'as you well know, Your Highness.'

Arisa raised a questioning brow. What orders? What hadn't Takai told her?

'I do not recall my father ordering you to destroy all of the healer's important work.' Takai waved his hand around the room. 'In fact, I think such an act is against the King's wishes. As your Prince and future King, I order you to release these two men immediately.'

Horace glared at the Prince, but gave a small nod. The guards released Erun and the Schoolmaster.

'And the book?' Arisa asked.

Horace's mouth formed into a half-smile. Too late, she realised her mistake in jumping in with so much zeal.

'The book warrants further investigation,' Horace said.

'I don't think the Secretary needs to waste his time with an insignificant book,' the Queen said.

'I don't care what you think. I'm taking the book. You are free to raise the matter with your husband. As I will do when it comes to Erun's arrest.'

The Queen stood a little taller so she was eye-to-eye with Horace. 'I *shall* take it up with the King, and alert him to your wrongful and disrespectful behaviour.'

Horace shrugged.

'In the meantime, the Schoolmaster is free to leave the castle,' the Queen continued. 'Erun will reside in my apartments, where I can be sure of his welfare. He will no longer be your prisoner.'

'As you wish.' Horace gave an exaggerated flourish of his hand. '*While* you're the King's wife, I'm your servant.'

Arisa wondered why Horace appeared so smug, given the dressing down the Queen had just given him.

'Your Majesty. Your Highness.' Horace bowed to the Queen and Takai before leaving with his guards in tow.

Guthrie, though, stopped on his way out to snarl in Arisa's face, 'You'll keep, guttersnipe.'

Klaus appeared by Guthrie's side and, with a death stare and a grunt, prompted the Secretary's son to leave the room with him.

'I'm surprised Horace left as easily as he did,' the Queen said, after they had gone.

'But now he has the book,' Gwyn said miserably.

'The book is useless to him without someone who knows the —' Erun cut himself off, glancing nervously at Takai.

'Does the book contain information that is dangerous for Horace to know?' Takai asked.

Arisa could tell the silence in the room was enough for him to know the answer. He ran his hands through his dark hair.

'I won't let anything happen,' the Queen said with confidence. 'I have the King's ear.'

Takai opened his mouth as if to say something, but appeared to change his mind. He gave Arisa what he probably intended to be a reassuring smile, but the dancing shadows in his eyes said that he was just as scared as she was. *Why* he was scared, she didn't know – but it was enough for her to feel more worried than ever for her guardian.

23

*T*heodora admired her reflection in the mirror. She wore a green-and-gold brocade skirt with matching sleeves. Her black velvet bodice was trimmed with fine satin ribbons and ebony pearl fastenings. She had ordered her maid to take extra care fixing her long raven hair. The girl had worked on it for several hours before dawn, and it was now perfectly curled and arranged in pretty waves that fell down past her shoulders. Completing her look were a feather-bedecked hat, kid gloves edged with fur, and soft leather boots. The outfit had cost as much as most other noblewomen spent on their entire wardrobe for a year. The expense wasn't lost on Theodora – but she needed to dress according to her ambition and the task at hand. She had chosen the outfit explicitly with the Prince in mind.

The maid had now left, but Theodora's mother, the Countess, continued to buzz around her like a pesky fly, trying to ensure Theodora looked her best. She winced as her mother tightened her corset.

Countess Datanya stood back and surveyed her. She tilted her head appraisingly before stepping in front of Theodora and hoisting up her breasts.

'Mother!' she cried.

'You must show the Prince exactly what he is missing.'

'Your mother's right,' came Horace's voice behind them. Neither had noticed his arrival. 'This trip to the countryside may be your last opportunity to snare the Prince.'

Theodora raised an eyebrow. 'The last opportunity?'

Horace nodded to his wife, indicating she should leave them alone.

'Have fun today, my dear,' the Countess threw over her shoulder before closing the door behind her.

'Don't listen to your mother. Fun should be the last thing on your mind,' her father said. 'Any moment the balance of power is going to tip back toward us. I have reason to believe I will be back in the King's favour imminently.'

'Really? What reason?'

'Nothing to worry your pretty little head about.'

Theodora pursed her lips. It irked her to no end that her father still believed she was too *pretty* to understand his schemes – and by *pretty* he meant *silly*.

Horace appeared oblivious to the insult he'd given. 'We will be at war any day, but how we fare depends on whether my plans pay off,' he went on. 'I'm certain I will succeed, but in the event that I fail, you will be our only hope of saving this family from disaster. We will need to call on your power, as the future Queen, to ensure matters go our way. You must secure your position, before the Prince's attention moves to the battlefield.'

Theodora rolled her eyes. Her father had made it abundantly clear how important it was to secure the Prince, and what was at stake if she didn't...namely, that she would be handed over to the pirate.

Horace clicked his jaw. 'I mean it, Theodora. You must make it happen.'

'I know.'

'You and Guthrie must stay close to the girl today. Don't let her out of your sight for a moment. The ward is the last part of the puzzle and the leverage I need…unless I can uncover the secrets to…' His voice trailed away as he caught her sharp eyes.

There he went again, referring to his secret plans, oblivious to the fact that Theodora already knew about them and had her own plans in place. One way or another, Arisa wouldn't be returning to the castle. She would make sure of it. She would prove she was more than capable of managing a lowborn peasant girl, and she would secure their family's future in the process. She would tell her father that the healer already knew how to create firesky, and he would find some other way to force Erun to reveal his secrets.

'Do you understand what you need to do?'

'Perfectly, Father.'

'$\mathcal{M}$ake haste,' Guthrie barked as he pulled up beside Arisa on his horse.

She had fallen behind the other riders almost as soon as they had left the castle grounds, holding back to admire the progress on the hospital. The foundations had been laid and the site was a bustling hive of activity. It was a beacon of hope in an otherwise uncertain future. A reminder of everything she had worked for. In a world where Lamore and Kengia weren't at war, Arisa would practise medicine at that hospital. At least, that was her dream. She was only days away from sitting for the entrance exam to the College of Surgeons, if war didn't come first.

But that wasn't the only reason she had stayed back. She had been reluctant to leave Erun, even if it was only for the day. After Horace's attempted arrest, Erun had found refuge in the Queen's apartments, but Arisa feared it provided a false sense of security. Instead of focusing on his own welfare, Erun had spent the entire night fussing about her safety. He had begged her to use today's trip to escape to the Shaman, Laurel. He had insisted she was in more danger than ever, but wouldn't say why. Gwyn had sided with Erun, but neither would elaborate on why she needed to leave, other than saying it was for her safety. She'd dismissed their fears, sure the Queen would continue to protect her. Nothing they said could have changed her mind. She wouldn't leave Erun behind. She wasn't ready to say goodbye to him, or to others she'd grown close to at Lamore Castle.

Now, as she left her guardian for the much-awaited trip to the country, Arisa couldn't shake a nagging feeling that something terrible lay just beyond the horizon. While she had waited her whole life for an opportunity to leave the city and see what was beyond, part of her wondered if she was in real danger.

'I said *move it*,' Guthrie growled, when she didn't make a move to hurry up. And now she had to put up with *him* as their escort. She expected he wouldn't miss any opportunity to try to intimidate her throughout the day.

The hard look Guthrie gave her, coupled with his insult as he'd left Erun's rooms the previous night, told her he hadn't forgotten their history. He must be seething that she'd narrowly missed being on the receiving end of his sword mid-riot at the marketplace. The slight bend of Guthrie's nose was a humiliating reminder of their other chance encounter in the city. It felt like it had happened a lifetime ago – and in a way, it was another life. A life before Lamore Castle, before everything.

Arisa rolled her eyes at Guthrie before nudging her heels into Meteor's flank and pressing the mare forward until she reached the group ahead. At the front were half a dozen Royal Guards. They weren't dressed in their usual regalia, as it would have attracted unwelcome attention. Takai rode directly behind them. He sat tall in his saddle, his broad shoulders stiff as he looked straight ahead. Other than the bruise and lump on his forehead, he showed no other signs of serious injury from his accident during the joust. Theodora rode alongside Takai, her feathered hat bobbing as she attempted conversation with the silent Prince. Selina rode behind the pair, chatting away mindlessly to a handsome young guard, who didn't seem to mind the attention in the least.

Arisa had hoped Willem would be able to join them. He

would have given her someone to talk to, and acted as a buffer between her and Takai if needed. While Arisa wished to discover why the Prince too seemed fearful for Erun's safety, she didn't trust herself to be alone with him, and was scared she would get foolishly close to declaring her feelings for him. She was thankful Theodora was monopolising his attention, but she knew Takai would seek her out eventually, like he always did. Unfortunately, Willem wouldn't be here to save her. He was representing his father's interests at the castle while the Duke was back at Talbot, overseeing the army preparations.

Sar rode ahead of her, his eyes alert and ever-moving, scanning the streets as they rode through Obira City. Arisa could sense the unease in him. The city had remained peaceful ever since industry and employment had been created with the hospital construction, and Sergei and his rebels had been quiet. But there were still plenty of Lamorians, particularly those outside the city, who harboured ill will toward the King and his regime. If anyone spotted and recognised the Prince, there was no knowing what kind of reception they would get.

'I hope you're not going to be sullen all day and ruin my first ever trip outside the city gates,' Arisa teased as she rode up beside Sar.

He gave a dimpled grin. 'You're right. There are plenty among us who are sullen enough.' He glanced back over his shoulder to Guthrie, who was riding with the last of the Royal Guards.

'I'm glad to hear it.' Selina had fallen back to fix her hat and was riding by Sar's other side. 'You have been ever so dull until now.'

'Ah. But my being dull is completely intentional, and for your benefit, Selina.'

'My benefit?'

'My dullness only magnifies the gaiety and joy you bring to our outing.'

Sar gave Arisa a wink, unseen to anyone else. Selina smiled

brightly and urged her horse to catch up to her handsome guard.

Sar leant in closer to Arisa and dropped his voice.

'With all seriousness, I will try to be less *sullen*, as you put it. But it's important we're vigilant. We can't have a repeat of the attack we had in the marketplace. If it weren't for Takai's insistence, this trip would never have gone ahead.'

They had all been lectured on safety prior to leaving. They must stick to the King's Road at all times and be back before dark. The King's Road was the main route through the countryside: very public, heavily trafficked and easily guarded. They were only to go as far as the Secretary's manor at Calliope, in the lowlands. It was said to be an easy ride of a couple of hours.

As they reached the city gates, Arisa noticed that Takai had pulled the hood of his cloak over his head. They passed the line of farmers, fishermen and merchants entering the city with their wagons, wares and livestock, ready for market. A few stopped to peer curiously at the group, but when they didn't recognise anyone, they went back to their business.

Arisa tingled with excitement as they rode through the gateway, all her fears overshadowed for a moment. Getting a glimpse of the countryside and the Nymoi Alps from the other side of the city wall was more than she had experienced in her lifetime. Erun had always insisted it wasn't safe beyond the gates – in the anonymity of the city, they could hide in plain sight. But as the riding group made clear of the line of people heading into the city, Arisa looked around, trying to hide her disappointment. The other side of the gate didn't look vastly different from the side they'd come from. Like the city, it was a sea of brown and grey, the difference being that the dullness here came from the landscape, not the buildings.

The group followed the King's Road as it snaked its way through murky wetlands, passing woody reeds and grass-lined swamps that smelt of stagnant mud. It appeared uninhabitable except for giant, croaking bullfrogs that could be heard over the clip-clopping of the horses' hooves. Swarms of dragonflies hovered above the marshes and flocks of cormorants flew over-head, but otherwise the area was lifeless. It was nothing like Arisa had pictured.

On the edge of the marshlands, they passed a handful of cottages. Farmers watched the travellers from their doorways and muddy fields.

'What do you think?'

Arisa hadn't noticed that Takai had slipped back to ride beside her, while Sar had pushed forward to join Theodora. She wondered how she could respond. Takai had gone to great pains to organise the trip.

'Well?' Takai swept his hand across the flat brown landscape.

'I've never seen anything like it,' she said truthfully.

The Prince frowned, catching her meaning. 'You're right – there's not much to see here. Actually, there's not much to see at all along the King's Road. It's a trade route that passes mainly through moors and marshes. Not really designed for sightseeing.'

'I expect Calliope will be different,' she said with exagger-ated enthusiasm.

'The landscape is much the same there, I'm afraid. If only you could see...'

Takai didn't finish his train of thought. He nudged his horse forward to call Sar aside. Arisa watched as Takai waved his hands, speaking with great animation. She couldn't catch his words, but she could tell by the shaking of Sar's head that his idea wasn't received well. The pair glanced back at her. The look was followed by more discussion and shaking of heads. They turned again, this time looking at Guthrie, and Sar finally nodded. Takai's face broke into a huge grin.

'I'm tired,' he announced loudly. 'We will stop in the village ahead for refreshments.'

It seemed an odd suggestion, as the Queen had seen that

they were provided with food before they left, having the castle kitchens pack them a picnic for the day.

'We have not been authorised to stop,' Guthrie said. 'And there is nothing ahead except a tavern or two – nothing fit for royal company.'

'But today we're not royal,' Takai said. 'We're a group of young adventurers enjoying the sunshine and everything the countryside has to offer.'

Guthrie made to protest, but Takai cut him off.

'It is an order.'

Guthrie was left with no option but to mutter something unintelligible under his breath and comply.

Takai fell back again next to Arisa. 'Follow my lead,' he whispered.

After a mile or so, they came to the outskirts of a village signposted as Dunhin. Takai told her it was at the crossroads of the King's Road and Lakelands Road, not far from Iveness. The group stopped outside a hodgepodge of stone buildings that constituted a tavern. A pair of young women with crudely rouged faces and heaving cleavage beckoned them to enter the establishment.

The guards shot Guthrie earnest glances.

'I suppose I do feel a little thirsty,' he said.

'Go ahead,' Sar said. 'I'll see to the horses.'

Guthrie and the other guards didn't take much convincing. They were led into the tavern, to a table in a dimly lit corner. Takai, Theodora, Selina and Arisa followed a few steps behind. The tavern keeper, who may not have recognised the Prince but clearly knew wealth when he saw it, hastened toward them.

'My good man. Do you have a private room for my companions and me to break our fast?' Takai asked.

'Yes, yes, of course, my lord. Follow me.'

'Stay here and keep an eye out,' Takai called out to the guards as one of the rouged ladies took up a position on Guthrie's lap.

Guthrie gave an uncharacteristic smile. 'My lord.'

The tavern keeper led them through the premises toward a narrow hallway.

'On second thought…' Takai halted. 'I'm in need of some fresh air. Is there a back door out of here?'

The keeper gave a gap-toothed grin and pushed open a door to reveal Sar standing next to their horses, beaming from ear to ear.

'Oh, and please ensure our friends back there are well fed and occupied for some time.' Takai pressed a pouch of gold coins into the keeper's fleshy palm.

'With pleasure.'

Takai grabbed Arisa by the hand. 'Come on.'

She hesitated, trying to ignore the buzzing sensation his touch sent up her arm.

'You wanted to see the real countryside, didn't you?'

Next to Arisa, Theodora bit her lip, looking back into the tavern and then at the Prince. After another moment of consideration, she shrugged and took her horse's reins from Sar.

'But we can't leave the guards,' Selina cried.

'Oh, do shut up, Selina,' Theodora sniped. 'Anything is better than visiting that dreadful manor of ours and putting up with my scowling brother all day.' Selina dropped her head.

Arisa let Takai lead her to Meteor, and within minutes they were back on their horses and travelling down Lakelands Road at a fast gallop.

Once they were a fair distance from the village, they slowed their pace, and she could take in the scenery. In that short time, the marshy landscape had given way to lush green pastures, broken up by meadows of wildflowers in every colour imaginable. They rode over gurgling streams and passed sparkling lakes that sprung up between the rolling hills. The Nymoi Alps and their snow-capped peaks grew larger on the horizon. The closer they got to the Kengian border, the more Arisa's heart fluttered with excitement, and the more Meteor pulled at her bit.

The whole time, Takai rode by her side, drinking in her elated reactions to everything she saw.

After about an hour, they came to a directional sign for Talbot. 'Could we stop?' Arisa asked. 'I would love to see Talbot.'

Takai shook his head adamantly. 'The army is still training there. We don't want to alert anyone to our whereabouts.'

His face was alive with mischief, but Arisa was disappointed. She had heard so much about the picturesque manor where Takai and Sar had spent much of their childhood and teenage years with Willem.

Takai seemingly read her mind. 'Another day, I promise. Today, I have something else to show you...something to take your mind off things.' He tapped the pommel of his saddle nervously.

She asked the question, even though she wasn't sure she wanted to know the answer. 'Do you really think Erun will be alright?'

Takai stopped tapping his fingers. 'He has my mother's protection.' He flashed her a bright smile. 'Just a few more miles to my surprise.'

Arisa believed that the Queen would do anything to protect Erun. So why couldn't she shake the sick feeling in her stomach?

Soon enough, they came to the edge of a forest. 'The King's Forest,' Takai said.

Sar led them in single file through the thick woods. The further they ventured into the forest, the more the light seeped away to almost nothing, and the higher the trees reached above them. The darkness was more beautiful than it was ominous. Obira City and the castle were worlds away as they weaved their way through the shadows and dappled patches of light penetrating the canopy high above. The only noise was the sound of undergrowth and twigs crunching beneath them, and the crashing hooves of a large stag as it ran across their path. Even the trees that usually murmured to Arisa were silent.

Just when she thought they would never see light again, the forest thinned out. Arisa could hear a soft rumble that slowly grew louder and louder. She was burning with anticipation. Eventually, the forest wall opened up to reveal what she'd been waiting for. She gasped at the same time Meteor whinnied with pleasure.

They were standing in a clearing, beside what she guessed from her lessons must be Shizen Lake. To the right of the lake were the Shizen Falls, with the Nymoi Alps towering above. It was exactly as Erun had described to her in his stories. Yet his words hadn't done it justice.

The lake winked back at them, the silver sun's rays catching on the surface of the clear water. Arisa could see the bottom as clearly as if she were looking through glass. The Shizen Falls soared hundreds of feet above them, the roar of water almost deafening.

Her whole body prickled as she gave in to an impulse to reach out toward the falls. Every inch of her body fizzled with energy. It was the same unsettling feeling she had experienced at the marketplace – right before the sky had erupted in great thunder and lightning – and on the day she'd first seen the wolf.

And just as the feeling grew to fever pitch, an apparition materialised before her.

The silver-haired man stood on the ground beside her, holding onto Meteor's reins. This time, Arisa didn't feel dizzy or scared, as she had done the other times he'd appeared to her. The man was more like a friend to her now. She felt completely at ease. As if she were coming home.

She closed her eyes and breathed in deeply, savouring the crisp air as it filled her lungs.

'What do you think of the countryside now?'

She opened her eyes with a start, to see Takai – standing where the silver-haired man had been – gazing up at her.

She looked back at the falls and the lake. 'Magical,' she said, and turned back to the Prince.

'Yes, magical.' Takai's eyes were intent on her, as if they were the only people in the world.

ARISA, Theodora and Selina abandoned their slippers to navigate the slippery rocks around the edge of the lake. Arisa's eyes were drawn repeatedly to the Shizen Falls. The forest went right to the edge of the lake, preventing them from getting any closer to the falls, but she couldn't discard the yearning she felt. Before they left, she *had* to reach out and try to touch the surging wall of water.

When the sun was directly overhead, Takai suggested they find somewhere to eat their picnic. Arisa hadn't realised until then how hungry she was. They remounted their horses and followed the edge of the lake for a few minutes before reaching a stretch of pebbly beach, where the lake flowed into a stream. She gazed further up the stream, marvelling at the rolling rapids stretching ahead as the water widened into a faster-moving river.

'The perfect location,' Takai declared.

They let the horses loose on the grassy bank above the beach and sat down to feast on a picnic of salted meats, fruit, cheese and bread. Theodora had all but dragged the Prince away to sit at a distance from Arisa and the others. The sick feeling in Arisa's stomach had been replaced with a niggling pang of jealousy that she was trying to ignore.

She was brushing the last crumb from her lap when Sar came to sit beside her. 'The Shizen River.' He pointed at where the stream widened. 'One of my favourite places. Apparently, when I was young, my father would bring me here to fish. I don't remember, of course...' There was a wistful tinge to his voice.

Arisa sometimes forgot Sar was an orphan. Early in her time at the castle, he had shared that Gwyn wasn't his birth mother, and that he, like Arisa, had lost his mother as a baby. His father,

Elos, had been a great warrior, but had died during the same massacre that had claimed Arisa's father. It didn't matter that their fathers had been on different sides; their shared grief was enough to bind them. She valued her friendship with Sar, as he was only one of a few who knew of her Kengian heritage. He had seen the Kengian coin inside the silver medallion that hung around her neck. The koi fish coin that had belonged to her Kengian father.

But Sar had kept her secret safe. And, almost as importantly, he could always put her at ease with one of his stories.

'What kind of fishing?' she asked.

'Shizen trout, of course. There's no better river fish.' A conspiratorial smile spread across his face. 'How about we go fishing?'

Arisa laughed. 'We haven't got any rods.'

Sar winked at her before standing up and walking to the water's edge, saving a grin for Selina as he passed her on the way. He held up his hands. 'This is all we'll need. Now we have to find the fish.'

'Over there,' Selina squealed, pointing toward a large rock in the river.

Arisa peered through the crystal-clear water, and sure enough, she could see a shoal of trout. Their speckled skin gleamed back at her, betraying their hiding spot in the shadows of the rock.

Takai jumped to his feet, as if he had kept one ear on their conversation the whole time he'd been sitting with Theodora. 'Challenge accepted.'

'You can't!' Selina said. 'The water will be freezing.'

She was right. While the day was warm, they were barely out of winter, and it was a glacial lake, fed from the summit of the Nymoi Alps.

Takai and Sar would not be deterred. They removed their boots, rolled up their breeches and took off their doublets, revealing their undershirts. Selina and Theodora erupted into fits of giggles. Arisa's cheeks burned.

The pair waded out until they reached the rock. Standing waist-high in the river, Takai and Sar started grasping through the water, attempting to catch fish with their bare hands.

Arisa joined in with the others' laughter. There was much splashing and glimpses of fins, but neither Takai nor Sar came close to catching anything. Arisa noticed with surprise that Theodora had stopped laughing and was tapping her fingers on her forearm. Theodora caught her eye and raised an arched brow – and, with a smirk, she drew her skirts up to her waist and walked toward the water.

'Come on.' She beckoned for Selina and Arisa to join her.

Selina's jaw visibly dropped. 'We can't. It's not proper.'

'Don't be daft. If we all go in, it will be proper enough.'

Selina tried another tack. 'Shouldn't we be getting back to the castle?'

'Yellow-bellied coward!' Theodora spat.

Selina's eyes widened with fear. 'But I'm not a good swimmer.'

Theodora was either oblivious to Selina's terror or didn't care, for she started to drag her shaking friend into the shallows.

'Leave her alone, Theodora,' Arisa said. 'She doesn't want to swim.'

'You keep out of it.' Theodora pulled the sobbing girl further out until the water was above their knees.

Arisa looked out to Takai and Sar, appealing for help, but they hadn't seen or heard Selina's cries over the sound of the splashing trout. Arisa's heart thumped wildly as Theodora hauled Selina into the faster-moving water. She had never swum before and could imagine Selina's horror. She felt no attachment to the girl, but she couldn't stand by and watch Theodora put her in such danger.

Without another thought, Arisa pulled up her own skirts and waded out after them. She willed herself to stay upright as the current gripped her calves and her bare feet slipped along the river floor. *I will stay standing,* she said to herself, over and over. The risk was great – not just because she couldn't swim, but because the coloured drops could be washed from her eyes. And then they would know who she really was. A silver-eyes. Something even Sar didn't know about her.

She reached out and grabbed Theodora's arm. 'Leave her alone!'

'I said keep out of it!'

Theodora wrenched her arm free and shoved Arisa away. She stumbled backward at the same time her foot slipped on a mossy pebble, sending her into a tangle of skirts. She fell back toward the middle of the river, her head remaining above the surface only long enough to register the wide-eyed shock on Theodora's face and to hear Meteor's neigh.

Panic raced through her mind as she was fully submerged in a deep pocket of water.

The current was already dragging her further away from the shore and into fast-moving rapids. The water yanked at her, stealing her breath away. Somehow, she managed to push her skirts away from her face so she could see, but it was hard to tell from the whitewash whether she was up or down. She couldn't reach the bottom, and could only guess she had been pulled a fair distance downstream.

Arisa twisted from side to side until she spotted what she thought was sunlight breaking through the water's surface. She tried to paddle toward it. Her efforts were futile. As she paddled in one direction, she was pulled the opposite way and then pushed back again. Then she was being spun in a full circle, tumbled over and over. The water churned wildly, throwing her around like a rag doll. She was in fully fledged rapids now.

Her chest screamed out for air. Her ears felt like they were going to explode. She caught another glimpse of light above and tried to push her way up again, but she was exhausted. Her eyelids were heavy, and she resigned herself to the fact she couldn't make it back to the surface.

Arisa gave herself up to the jerking movements of the water until it pushed her down into the river's depths.

Everything gradually became darker. If there was a current, she couldn't feel it anymore as she sank toward the bottom of the river. Her arms floated above her head. Her hair billowed around her face. She felt like she was floating. Everything was silent. The tumultuous sound of the whitewash was gone. She felt strangely peaceful, as if she were at one with the water.

A dreamy smile came to her face, and she closed her eyes. This was it. This was how it would all end.

But Arisa didn't have time to ponder her death further, because at that moment, her feet struck the riverbed, and her eyes flung open.

This was her chance.

She mustered every last ounce of energy she had and bent her knees, then extended her legs to propel herself upward. She kicked hard, over and over, until she felt her legs might drop off. Finally, she surfaced in a torrent of white water, gulping in a lungful of air. She spluttered as the rapids smacked her in the face, but somehow, she managed to stay afloat. Above the crashing water, she could hear cries.

She spun around in the water until she could see the river-bank. It seemed miles from her. The voices were coming from far away. Arisa felt the pulling of the current again as it dragged her down the river. Every surge of water pummelled her closer and closer to the rocks. Some were round and smooth, but others had jagged edges that caught her limbs. Each was capable of seriously injuring her, or worse, as she hurtled toward them uncontrollably.

It's alright, she kept telling herself. *Help will be here soon.* She only needed to keep her head above water until someone could get to her. Surely the rapids would end soon.

The rapids would end…

The falls and lake were well behind her and out of sight. *Where does the river go? Think, Arisa. Think.* She desperately scanned her memory for anything that may provide some bearings. *What's beyond the rapids? Where am I being pulled so violently?*

The cries came again. She swung around and caught sight of Sar and Takai riding on the bank, Meteor galloping ahead of them. They were trying to catch up to her, but the water was moving too fast. Arisa thought she heard Sar yell, '*Hold on.*'

Maybe she could hold on. Incredibly, Sar and Takai were gaining ground, and she noticed the water had slowed as she approached a small bend in the river. She paddled toward the bank, putting out of her mind that she didn't know how to swim, because by some miracle she was doing it, as if she'd been born to it. All she had to do was get closer to Sar and Takai and they could reach her. She could conquer the impossibly strong current. She had to.

A new sound rippled across the water. It started out as a low hum and grew to a rumble.

Now it was a roar.

Ignore it, Arisa told herself.

She focused her efforts on getting closer to the bank. Takai was ahead of Sar, and his eyes were fixed on her, seemingly oblivious to his surroundings. She tried to yell out to warn him, but it was too late. An overhanging branch knocked the Prince to the ground, his horse abandoning him.

Arisa's heart leapt into her throat. Sar made to pull up, but Takai waved his friend on. Sar reached the riverbend ahead of Arisa's position and leapt from his horse. He pushed his way through the white water as far as he could remain standing. His long, muscular arms were outstretched, ready to catch her. It was her best shot of getting back to shore.

She reached out with one arm, the other paddling to keep her afloat. The timing was critical.

Everything seemed to slow as she reached the riverbend. Sar's fingers grasped hers, and for a fraction of a second, she thought she was safe. But the current was too strong, her hands too slippery. She saw the terror in Sar's eyes as he lost his grip on her hand, and she was pulled further downstream.

Arisa spun back around, unwilling to believe Sar had failed. *It's alright. The rapids will end,* she told herself. *They will end—*

Then, her geography lessons flooding back to her, she remembered where the river went. The rapids did end. So did the river.

It all ended in a waterfall.

Erun had described the Riverend Falls to her once. A tremendous waterfall that was the same towering height as the Shizen Falls and fell into the ocean. If Arisa miraculously survived going over the edge, she would most likely drown in the sea below.

The riverbend and Sar were now specks in the distance. He looked as if he may be running back to his horse, but he would never be able to reach her in time. The water was rushing faster than ever. Meteor had disappeared from sight.

All hope was gone.

The roar of the falls crescendoed, and Arisa resolved to face her fate. Up ahead she could see where the frothy water dropped away. There was only a few hundred feet between her and death.

She was beyond tired. She was angry. Angry, because she would never see her beloved Erun again. Angry that she hadn't lived out her dreams, that she had failed to help Lamore's people. But most of all, she was angry that she would never know what it was like to be loved. The kind of love she'd been denying for too long.

She wanted to know what it was like to be loved by Takai, and to love him back.

Arisa closed her eyes, urging herself to let go. She gripped her medallion in her hand. Somehow it was still around her neck. She searched for solace in the rhythm and hum of the waterfall. It sounded like it was calling her name, over and over.

Another beat began. This time the sound came from the earth. A pounding that grew louder – along with the call of her name, coming from a new direction.

Arisa opened her eyes with a start to see Takai riding Meteor toward her. She wanted to scream out, but she couldn't find her voice. She wanted to tell him it was too late, that he couldn't save her. But Takai urged Meteor onward. He locked a determined gaze on Arisa, and Meteor lengthened her already magnificent stride. The Kengian mare found inexplicable speed to cover the ground between them. Arisa could see the horse's nostrils flaring, her flank glistening with sweat as they gained on her. Meteor soon brought Takai alongside her position.

With no thought for his own safety, Takai swung his left leg over the horse's back and dived into the water. He surfaced nearby and swam toward her, wrapping one arm around her waist.

'What are you doing?' she spluttered.

'Saving you!'

'Hardly – now we're *both* going to die!'

Takai looked frantically from side to side, registering the violence of the rushing water, and the fact that they were nearly upon the end of the river.

'We may go over the edge, but we're not going to die.'

Arisa didn't have the energy to argue, and found some morbid comfort in the prospect of Takai being by her side when she did perish.

The Prince grasped her chin and turned her face to him. 'We'll be alright. I—' Takai's pupils dilated. 'Arisa. Your eyes!'

She tried to avoid his gaze, but Takai still held her face in his hands. He scrutinised her silver eyes, her Kengian eyes, and shook his head abruptly. 'We'll talk about that later.'

'There won't *be* any later—'

'There will be!' He had to shout to be heard over the white-wash. 'Even if it's to prove you wrong for the first time ever.'

She gave a weak smile.

'We will be fine. You believe me. Don't you?'

Arisa forced herself to nod. She wanted more than anything for Takai to be right.

He tightened his grip on her waist. She wrapped her arms around his torso. Neither of them looked ahead. Their fate wasn't beyond the falls; it was upon them, there in each other's arms.

Their eyes remained locked as they plummeted over the edge.

THE WATER POUNDED down on Arisa as she was swept down the Riverend Falls. It hammered every inch of her body. Yet she had a feeling of weightlessness.

Her stomach lurched into her throat. She was terrifyingly alone. She'd been torn from Takai's arms almost as soon as they'd been pulled over the edge of the falls.

She tried to see where she was being pummelled to, but it was impossible. There was nothing but blinding white water and snatches of dark shadows looming beneath her. The darkness approached rapidly, and she could make out the shapes of jagged rocks below. She put her hands out in front of her in an attempt to protect herself. She had just closed her eyes and braced herself when she felt a tugging sensation on her body.

Her eyes sprang open to see Takai, pulling her into his embrace. Enveloping her in his arms, he would take the full force of the impact. She opened her mouth to protest, but it was too late.

As she reached the bottom of the falls, Arisa was thrown out of Takai's grip again, flung away from the rocks and plunged deep into the sea.

She spun around. Suspended in the depths, she searched for any light, but there was nothing. Not knowing which way was up or down, she turned in every direction, knowing she would soon run out of breath. She stopped moving, but could feel her body sinking under the weight of her sodden gown. At least she knew which way was down. She looked up – a long way in the distance, she could see a dim light.

She made small kicks upward, her calves burning from exertion. Inching her way away from the darkness, she eventually broke the surface, gasping for breath. A rocky shore stretched out beneath the falls. Somehow, Arisa had to summon enough strength to swim to it. But what about Takai? He was nowhere to be seen.

'Takai!' she shouted, over and over, her voice hoarse from the salt water. She scanned the water for a sign of the Prince, but he was gone.

Her gaze caught on something bobbing in the water. An item that looked out of place near the rocks. Bolstered by adrenaline and her aching need to find Takai, Arisa paddled toward the object, using what little energy she had left. It was a long piece of gold material, snaking its way through the water. The gold scarf she had given him – the same one he had tucked under his armour at the tournament. He must have kept it with him.

Arisa retrieved it from the water and stuffed it into her bodice. Takai believed this scarf had saved him once, that it was his good luck charm. Maybe it would help her find him now.

She dived back under the water. She looked again into the darkness, and this time she could make out the shape of a person, far below. It was Takai – but he was sinking fast. Arisa's heart constricted – she knew she didn't possess the strength to pull him back up. She would need help. She surfaced, but there was no one in sight.

Taking a huge breath, Arisa dived again.

'*Takai!*' she screamed helplessly into the water as she followed his limp body. She kicked downward, further and further, but Takai was sinking faster than she could swim. '*Nooo!*' she gurgled, her arms outstretched after him as he was swallowed up by the inky depths.

A ripping sensation suddenly tore through her torso, radiating down her arms and into her fingers. A warmth pulsated through her, throbbing as if there were fire running through her veins. She held her palms up in front of her, almost expecting them to be consumed by flames – and they began to glow white.

Flashes of light shot from her fingertips, and another beam leapt from her chest. Another erupted from her mouth, until her whole body was aglow and the water around her was bathed in bright light. Arisa had no idea what was happening. Nor did she have the energy to question it. The only thing on her mind was Takai.

Looking downward, she could see him clearly now. He had stopped sinking and was facing up toward her, his face icy blue. She reached out to him, until the shaft of light from her fingers fell on his face and warmed his features.

Takai's eyes flung open, widening in disbelief as he caught sight of her.

He was alive. Arisa didn't know what had just happened, but he was alive. She wanted to cry with relief – but Takai was far from safe, and so was she.

Every part of her was screaming in pain, her breath expended. She was sinking as fast as Takai, unable to find the energy to paddle upward again. On impulse, she opened her mouth to get more oxygen, but it was water that filled her mouth, that spilled into her lungs. Was this the end? Had whatever powers she'd seemed to summon only manifested so she could see Takai one last time before they both died?

No! She would not give up. She would not risk losing Takai again. Arisa knew there was something more ahead for them. Every inch of her being knew it. Just as she knew it was she who would have to find a way to get them both out of the water. It was up to her to find the strength to save them both.

As if the sea had read her mind, it started churning.

A small whirlpool formed under Takai, circling them both and expanding. It was as if the water were hers to command –

as if she were harnessing its lifeforce. The whirlpool surged upward, lifting them both and pulling them into its eye. Its cyclonic force heaved them to the surface, shooting them high into the air. Takai and Arisa were momentarily suspended in a light-filled waterspout that slowly subsided, lowering them gently back to the ocean's surface. The light was gone, as if it had never been there, but a soothing warmth remained in the water.

Takai looked around panicked, gasping for breath before locking eyes with Arisa.

'What happened? What did you do?'

Arisa pulled her gaze away from him and started swimming to the shoreline. She didn't know the answers to his questions. 'We need to get to land.'

'Wait!' Takai grabbed her arm. 'I was sinking...drowning... but then I felt − no...I *saw*...' He shook his head. 'What was it?'

'I don't know,' she said softly.

'But the light. And you. Your eyes. They're...'

Arisa gave him a pleading look and he loosened his grip on her arm. 'We need to get to shore.'

They paddled toward the shore, until their feet could touch the bottom. They had survived. Unbelievably, Arisa had nothing other than a few minor cuts and bruises. Takai reached out and grasped her hand. She squeezed it back and turned to look at him, noticing his torn shirt and some bloody scratches on his chest and arms. The gash on his forehead from the tournament had reopened. Without thinking, she reached up to touch it with her free hand.

He gave a boyish smile. 'It's nothing.'

'I thought I was going to lose you.'

Takai cupped his hand around her chin. 'Me too.'

Arisa sighed, leaning into his chest, and closed her eyes. She sank into the warmth of his fingers locked over her hand. Then there was a feeling of cold − coming from something pressing against the back of her hand.

She opened her eyes to see Takai holding her medallion, the silver chain wrapped around his wrist. Its clasp was broken, but otherwise it appeared intact. Her hand went instinctively to her bare neck.

'I must have grabbed it when we were separated in the water.'

Arisa smiled and reached into her bodice to retrieve the gold scarf she had fished from the sea. Takai's eyes lit up.

'My good luck charm,' he murmured.

They stood hand-in-hand, letting the waves roll gently around them. It was as if they were under a spell that kept them fixed to the spot. They could go nowhere, neither back out to sea nor toward the shore. They rolled with the waves, as if they were suspended in time. In a time when their differences didn't matter. When questions didn't need to be answered. When secrets could remain secrets.

They didn't need to say out loud that everything had changed, that they could never go backward, or forward, without consequences neither of them wanted to face. Instead they stayed in the moment. Drinking in the silence, aware only of each other, barely cognisant of the distant sounds of a lone gull squawking to its mate, and of Riverend Falls crashing down into the sea and breaking on the rocks nearby.

Takai and Arisa held each other's hands for what seemed an eternity, until Arisa became aware she was shivering from the cold water and her soaked gown. Takai tightened his embrace and looked back to shore. Feeling him tense, she followed his gaze.

There was a lone figure standing on the shore, watching them.

25

Takai felt as if his skull were about to burst open. His reopened wound throbbed and his thoughts were a swirling mess. He wasn't sure if he'd been imagining things, or if a magical light and giant waterspout had indeed saved him from drowning – all emanating from Arisa. An Arisa he didn't recognise. She had looked at him with those piercing silver eyes, the colour of Shizen Lake.

Kengian eyes.

Takai had wanted to know the secrets Arisa had been hiding from him, but he'd got more than he bargained for. She was a silver-eyes. Knowing that made him question everything he believed.

He'd been told since he was a child that silver-eyes couldn't be trusted – that they could, and would, use their magical powers for their own gain, like when Prince Alik had tried to bewitch his father. But this was at complete odds with his own experiences with Arisa. In all the time he'd known her, the only time he'd ever seen her do anything that might be called *magic* was to save him – to save a Lamorian Prince. If silver-eyes were as bad as he'd been led to believe, then why hadn't she used her powers for her own benefit – to try to save herself and her guardian somehow? Had he been wrong all this time about silver-eyes, or was Arisa different to the others? She had to be different. There had to be a reason he'd grown to care for her so much.

He had a thousand more questions than answers, but they would have to wait. Instead he must focus on the stranger standing on the shore, staring at them.

Hand-in-hand, Takai and Arisa waded to shore, drawing on their last reserves of energy. Each step was more laboured than the last, but Takai couldn't show any sign of weakness. He didn't know whether the man was friend or foe. He didn't know what the stranger had seen.

As they reached the shallows, Takai noted with a shudder that the man was huge – menacingly huge. Takai estimated he was half a head taller than Sar, and Sar was the tallest man Takai knew. This giant of a man wore a simple grey tunic, his weathered face unflinching. More concerning was the long fishing spear he held in one hand, and the knife strapped to his muscular calf. The tools and nets on the ground indicated he was a fisherman, but there was no mistaking from his stance that he had once been – and perhaps still was – a warrior. Takai knew he was outmatched.

The water was only ankle-deep now. The man remained unmoving a half-dozen yards from them, watching with steady eyes. Takai squeezed Arisa's hand reassuringly, but instead of returning his gesture, her hand went limp in his. He spun around to see her crumple before him. Her eyes rolled back in her head, her face draining of colour. Takai made to catch her, but his impaired reflexes rendered him useless. At the same time, he registered a rapid catlike movement in his peripheral vision. The stranger from the shore had sprung to action and caught Arisa before she hit the sand.

The fisherman carried her with ease to a dry part of the shore and laid her down gently. Takai rushed to her side and knelt down beside her, trying to rouse her.

'Arisa!'

She groaned softly in reply. The fisherman grunted, seemingly satisfied Arisa was alright. He stepped away and retrieved his spear.

Takai bent down to listen to her chest and was relieved her breath and heartbeat were both steady. She'd probably fainted from exhaustion.

He looked around to gauge the likelihood of rescue. A sick feeling formed in the pit of his stomach as he comprehended the difficulties of their situation. The top of the falls was a hundred or more feet above them. In the distance, a long, winding track snaked its way up the side of the cliff face, but Takai couldn't guess where it led.

'Where are we?' he demanded of the fisherman, with as much authority as he could muster.

The fisherman gave him a black look. Takai thought he saw the man tighten his grip on the spear. He was about to reveal his identity, in hope of compelling the man to assist them, when he heard a shout from above.

'Ahoy down there!'

With relief, Takai looked up to see Sar, Theodora and Selina standing beside the horses at the cliff edge. Meteor whinnied loudly down to them.

'Ahoy *up there*,' Takai hollered back.

Sar's eyes went to Arisa on the ground and then to the fisherman. He moved closer to the edge and started scaling down, but struggled to find safe footing on the sheer cliff face, unsettling rocks and sending them hurtling down to the shore.

'Stay up there,' Takai shouted. 'It's too dangerous.'

Sar shook his head in defiance and continued downward, his foot slipping repeatedly.

'Sar, *stop*! That's an order!'

Sar froze, but his gaze was intent on the fisherman.

'Even if you make it in one piece, we'll never get Arisa back up there,' Takai called.

Sar scrambled back to the top of the cliff and nodded toward the fisherman. 'Who's that?'

'A fisherman who found us here. He will help us get to safety.' At least, that was what Takai hoped. 'You can't help us.'

Sar was unmoving. 'But what about Arisa?'

'She's fine.'

Sar shook his head. 'She doesn't look fine.'

'It's alright. She's tired and needs to rest, but she'll be fine.'

The fisherman was staring back at Sar, but his look spoke more of intrigue than threat. The stranger furrowed his brow, as if he were struggling to decide what to say. Finally he spoke, shouting above the constant rush of the falls.

'You.' He pointed at Sar. 'Get your friends back to the castle before it's dark. It's not safe for your kind out here.'

For your kind? The fisherman must have picked them for nobles.

Sar looked over to the winding path in the distance, but the fisherman shook his head.

'That way is nothing but boggy marshland. You'll end up in a swampy pit up to your neck, if the locals don't get to you first. You can't cross the river safely. You need to go back through the forest and take a path behind the falls, and it won't be safe for you until tomorrow morning.'

Sar puffed out his chest. 'I'm sure a Captain of the Royal Guards can manage.'

The fisherman's lip curled in amusement. 'And I'm just as sure you wouldn't survive an hour. I know for a fact there is a large gathering of farmers on the other side of the forest.'

'A gathering...is it the rebels?' Takai asked, but the fisherman ignored him.

'You won't be able to protect yourself, least of all your friends.' He pointed at Arisa and Takai.

'And they're safe with *you*? A complete stranger?'

'They will be safer with me. I know this land and the people who live here. My home is not far along that track over there.'

'I'll go back to Talbot and get help.'

'You'll never make it back before dark. And trust me, the last thing you want to do is send the army into these parts.'

Sar remained fixed to the spot. 'I'm not leaving my friends.'

'It's alright, Sar. We will be fine.' Takai tried to sound convincing. He didn't want to mobilise the army either.

'Takai is right. We're fine,' came a soft voice. Arisa had regained consciousness and was sitting up, still pale but awake.

'Your friends can stay with me for the night,' the fisherman called up to the group. 'You need to get back to safety before dark. Send help at first light.'

Sar tilted his head but eventually nodded. 'What's your name?'

'I'm the Fisherman.'

'That's not a name.'

The Fisherman shrugged. 'That is how I'm known around here. You'll have no trouble finding me by that name.'

'You lay one hand on either of them and I will have your head impaled on that spear of yours.'

For the first time, the Fisherman smiled broadly. 'I would be disappointed if you didn't.'

Sar mounted his horse. Theodora cast a look at Arisa – even from this distance, Takai could tell it was filled with hate – before she too mounted her steed. Meteor gave a final whinny, and the group disappeared from sight.

Takai swallowed back the bile that had suddenly risen in his throat. He hoped he hadn't mislaid his trust in this stranger, despite having little choice.

The Fisherman bent down to eye level with Arisa. He grasped her jaw gently and scrutinised her face.

'Get your hands off her!' Takai demanded.

'It's alright.' For some reason, Arisa seemed to have no trouble trusting the stranger.

Eventually the man released her face and nodded silently to himself. 'Arisa? That's your name?'

She nodded.

'Arisa, do you think you can walk?' The Fisherman spoke with a gentleness Takai hadn't expected.

'Yes, I think so.'

The Fisherman stood up and retrieved his fishing gear. 'Follow me, please, Arisa.' He indicated the winding path in the distance. 'Your Highness.'

Takai started. 'How do you know—'

'Even a simple fisherman knows enough to recognise the kingdom's heir and Prince. In any case, you are your mother's son through and through.'

My mother? This man knew the Queen?

Takai refused to show that he was rattled by this revelation. 'And even a simple Prince knows enough to recognise a seasoned warrior when they see one, even if that warrior disguises themselves as a fisherman.'

The Fisherman chuckled. 'Come on, not-so-simple Prince. I, for one, would like to get home before dark.'

The silver sun had gone from above them and was hovering somewhere behind the top of the Nymoi Alps. The Fisherman led them up the sandy path to the top of the cliff. Arisa struggled, collapsing into Takai's arms as they reached the top. The Fisherman reached out to carry her, but Takai pushed him away. He shrugged indifferently before walking on.

Takai carried Arisa as they continued along a boggy track that weaved its way through the marshland. The Fisherman had been right. Sar and the others would never have made it through. Takai was struggling to stay on his feet, and he had the Fisherman as his guide.

Thankfully, the terrain eventually gave way to sandy grassland. It was easier to walk on, but Takai found himself succumbing to his own exhaustion. His wet undershirt clung to him and his body shivered from the icy wind that had picked up across the barren landscape. His bare feet were frozen and sore, but he was determined not to show any sign of weakness.

The Fisherman maintained his silence. He didn't seem interested in how they had come to be at the bottom of the falls, which was good, since Takai lacked the energy to speak. He also needed time to think. Had he done the wrong thing, sending Sar away and putting his trust in this man? All he knew was that he had to get Arisa to safety. But in his weakened state, how could he be sure of protecting her?

He was about to admit defeat and ask the Fisherman to carry Arisa when a hut appeared on the horizon. As they got closer, Takai saw it was made of roughly cut stone with a thatched roof that appeared to be in good repair. The Fisherman pushed open a rickety wooden door and indicated for Takai to enter.

'It's no castle, but it will do. You can put her down there.' He pointed toward a stretcher. Takai lay Arisa on it, then shook his aching arms in relief.

The Fisherman hung his nets up over the low rafters, expertly ducking his head as he manoeuvred his towering frame around the hut. He moved his attention to the embers in the fireplace, stoking them and adding kindling until the fire came back to life. Takai shifted Arisa's stretcher closer to the fireplace and rubbed his hands gratefully before its warm glow. The Fisherman kicked a crudely made wooden stool toward him and Takai sat down on it heavily.

He watched the Fisherman remove an earthen jug from a shelf, pull its cork and take a large swig, before settling himself on a second stool. He offered the jug to Takai.

Takai eyed him suspiciously for a moment before taking a drink. The harsh-tasting liquid burned its way down his throat.

'Urgh!' Takai spluttered. 'What is it?'

The Fisherman smiled and took another swig. 'A homebrew of sorts. This one is made from potatoes. You get used to it.'

'Why would you want to get used to it?' Takai grimaced as he took another gulp.

'As you know, *Your Highness*, the best ale, mead and wine is requisitioned for your royal court.'

Takai winced as he accepted another swill.

'How's that cut on your head?'

Takai reached up to his forehead, feeling the dried blood beneath his fingers. 'I can't feel the throbbing anymore, but I'm not sure I'm feeling anything, thanks to your home brew.'

They both laughed, somewhat awkwardly.

The Fishermen's eyes scanned Takai. 'For the most part, your cuts look alright, but your feet – they're another matter.'

Takai glanced down at his mud-splattered feet.

'You can't be messing up my place with those.' The Fisherman laughed at his own joke as he wet a cloth in a bowl of water and offered it to Takai.

Takai dabbed the cuts on his limbs and chest before cleaning his feet, grateful to wash the stinging salt water from his wounds.

'Here.' The Fisherman threw a giant-sized tunic at him. 'You can dry your shirt and breeches by the fire.'

Takai surveyed the hut and its single stretcher as he changed. 'You live here by yourself.'

'I like to be alone.'

'I know that feeling,' Takai said to himself.

The Fisherman took another mouthful.

'You told Sar it was too dangerous for us out here,' Takai said. 'I thought the uprisings had stopped.'

The Fisherman's grip tightened around his jug. 'Trouble is closer than you think. It won't take much for tensions to escalate again.'

Takai shook his head. 'Surely no one would dare to attack the King's son and his guards.'

'Many don't trust the King.'

'What do you mean?' Takai was genuinely perplexed. 'My father has gone out of his way to make amends.'

'Yes.' The Fisherman handed the jug to Takai. 'Thanks to your mother. But no one believes they will stay reconciled forever, and if your father returns to his former ways, all bets are off.'

Takai took another swig. He couldn't argue with the Fisherman's reasoning.

'But you say *you* won't hurt us?'

The Fisherman shrugged. 'I have my reasons.'

'And you can't guarantee our safety away from your house?'

'I can't. And your friend...' there was a lengthy pause, '... the royal guard who was with you, should not be so sure of his ability to keep you safe, either.'

'Sar is well respected in these parts. He is a knight and a man of honour.'

'A knight, you say?' The Fisherman tilted his head curiously. 'Still, let's hope you're far away when the full rebellion begins.'

A cold shiver ran down Takai's spine. 'What do you know of a rebellion?'

'All I know is that there will be one.' The Fisherman spoke with a conviction that didn't invite question. 'The rebels have done what the King has failed to do. They have united Lamorians and Kengians in a common cause.'

'A common cause?' The Fisherman sounded eerily like Arisa.

'To fight against injustice and persecution of the people.' The Fisherman narrowed his gaze. 'The moment the King appears as if he will move against the people, or looks like he's about to invade Kengia, is the same moment the rebels will mobilise.'

'My father's sights are on an alliance with Ivane and beating the Northemers, nothing else.' He refrained from adding, *As long as Horace has nothing to do with it.*

The Fisherman shook his head. 'That's what the King says, but in truth, your father covets much more than regaining Ette. He will never stop wanting Ivane, and Kengia is too tempting a prize now its King is dead.'

'How would you know such a thing?' The Fisherman's know-it-all attitude was starting to irritate Takai.

The Fisherman leaned forward in his seat. 'I know, the same way you knew I was a warrior. Whether you're willing to admit it to yourself or not, you and I know how to read a person's heart and mind, as you would in battle. And you know what I say of your father is true.'

'Not anymore. The King is changed.'

'A man can't defy his true nature forever. The question, though, is what will you do to protect your people? What will you do to protect the person you love and their homeland?' The Fisherman glanced over at the sleeping Arisa.

Takai felt like he'd been slapped in the face. The nerve of this man to presume anything about his relationship with Arisa...

'And what's in *your* heart and mind, mysterious Fisherman, who's not merely a fisherman?' he challenged.

A shadow passed over the Fisherman's face. 'I have my secrets, as you and Arisa do.' He took a large gulp of his brew.

How much of what happened in the water had the Fisherman seen? Takai was about to ask him outright when he heard a groan from Arisa's direction.

The two men jumped up simultaneously to check on her. The Fisherman reached her side first. 'Go out to the well and get some water,' he ordered Takai.

Takai hesitated, not wishing to leave Arisa alone with the stranger.

'Go on. I haven't killed either of you, yet.'

Takai left the hut, stopping for a moment outside the window, wanting to assure himself of Arisa's safety.

'How are you?' Takai heard the man ask her.

'Alright, I think,' Arisa said weakly.

'Don't worry. I'm a friend.'

'Where's Takai?'

'Arisa.' The Fisherman dropped his voice. 'Something unusual happened to you today in the water, didn't it?'

There was no answer.

'It's incredibly important that you tell me the truth. I can't tell you why, but I need to know. You'll have to trust me.'

'I'm not sure I can.'

'I understand, but I have reason to believe you're in immediate danger, and I want to help you.'

'We're in danger?'

'Yes. You and Takai, but mostly you.'

'Why do you want to help me? You don't know me.'

'But I think I do…Know you, that is.'

'I'm afraid that's impossible. I'm no one,' Arisa mumbled, as if she were dazed. 'I have no family other than my guardian Amund— I mean…Erun.'

She had corrected herself quickly, but the slip hadn't gone unnoticed by Takai – or by the Fisherman, he expected. Takai had heard the name Amund before, but he couldn't recall when, or where.

'Where's Takai?' Arisa asked.

'I don't mean to scare you, but you're in more danger than you can imagine.'

'I thought you said we'd be safe here.'

'You are safe, while you're in my keeping.' The Fisherman gave a laugh of disbelief. 'I can't believe you're here. I was beginning to lose faith. I had started to think I'd made the wrong choice. I thought I had sacrificed everything for no reason – but then I saw you, and the horse, and I knew. You're here. You're living proof I chose the right path.'

'What am I proof of?' Arisa's voice was strained. She sounded as confused as Takai felt.

'You mean you don't *know* it?' The Fisherman's voice rose in surprise.

'I have no idea what you're talking about.'

'Another time, Arisa. Soon it will all make sense to you. You will *know* it. Now, you should rest. Where's that water?'

Takai hurried from the window. He wasn't sure how it was possible, but now he had even more questions than he'd had before.

26

*A*risa stood in her smock in front of the hearth, willing the fire to dry the thin linen of the garment and warm her body. The Fisherman had gone to get more firewood, giving her privacy to remove her wet gown and lay it before the fireplace. As she rubbed her hands together, she fought the fog in her head, trying to make sense of the strange comments the Fisherman had made about knowing her and Meteor, and about 'making the right choice'. She wondered exactly what he had seen when she and Takai were in the water. Strangely, her gut told her to trust him…But why? Who was he?

She was so consumed by her thoughts she didn't hear Takai enter the hut.

'Sorry,' he blurted out, on realising her semi-dressed state. He spilled some water from the jug he was holding as he averted his eyes.

Arisa reached for a fur rug and wrapped it around herself before sitting back down on the stretcher. 'It's alright. You can look again.'

'Here, have some of this.' Takai lifted the rim of the jug to her lips and she gulped the water down gratefully.

She wiped her lips with the back of her hand. 'Thank you.'

Takai sat down next to her and cupped his hand under her chin. He stared intently into her silver eyes. She felt her strength returning at his touch. He furrowed his brow before removing his hand.

'How are you feeling?'

'Much better.' Arisa was telling the truth. She felt strangely energised. Yes, she was tired, but something burned inside her. She felt more alive than ever. 'And you?'

He folded his arms and grinned. 'Despite your best efforts, dragging me down a waterfall and all, I'm still in one piece.'

She laughed. 'You seem to forget it was I who saved us from drowning in the sea.'

Takai moved in closer, lowering his voice to an urgent whisper. 'Yes, you did, but how exactly did you do that?'

Arisa couldn't answer him. Because she had no idea what she'd done, or how. She deflected by picking up her medallion, which was sitting on a block of wood next to the stretcher. She rolled it around in her hand.

'The chain is broken,' she said to herself.

Takai put out his hand to take a look at it. She hesitated for a moment before handing it to him.

'It can be easily fixed once we're back at the castle.' He squinted. 'It's a locket. I never realised. May I?'

Arisa nodded. There was no point trying to hide her identity from him now. She watched as Takai carefully prised open the medallion to reveal its contents.

His eyes widened. 'A Kengian coin.'

'It was my father's.'

'There is no doubt, then. You're Kengian.'

She took the medallion back from him. 'Half-Kengian.'

Takai's face crumpled. 'Why hide it from everyone? From me?'

'You really need to ask?' she cried. 'You know as well as I do that Kengians are outcasts in Lamore. I would never have been able to go to school. I would have been sent to the fields to work, or sent to serve in Ette. I would have been under constant watch to make sure I wasn't practising witchcraft.'

She didn't need to point out that as a silver-eyes, she would have been even more feared – and Takai had made it clear how he felt about her people and their purported powers.

'What happened to your father?' he asked.

'He died soon after I was born.'

'And you're seventeen, right?'

She nodded. 'I turn eighteen in a couple of weeks.'

Takai put his hand to his chin and looked up to the ceiling, as if he were calculating something in his mind.

'Around the time of the last blood moon,' he said quietly.

'Yes. My father was killed at the same time as many of his countrymen and women.' Arisa didn't need to specify that he had died in the massacre instigated by Takai's father and Horace.

'I'm sorry,' he said. 'Your father shouldn't have died.'

'You're right. None of those people should have died. But it's too late. You can't change the past.'

Takai reached out and grabbed both of her hands, his dark eyes earnest. 'But it's not too late to create a better future. Isn't that what you've been trying to tell me all this time? That together we can change everything?'

'*We?*' She liked how Takai thought of them as 'we' even if it could never be.

'Enough of that, lovebirds.'

They hadn't noticed the Fisherman's entrance and jumped apart at the interruption.

'There'll be plenty of time for that later,' he went on. 'You two hungry?'

Arisa was ravenous, but didn't want to say so. Takai shrugged indifferently.

'I guess I could eat.'

The Fisherman produced a loaf of bread and what

appeared to be small, pickled fish, which they accepted gratefully. The food was surprisingly delicious.

'I know it isn't exactly a feast,' the Fisherman said. 'But I can
fix that.'

Arisa raised a curious brow.

'I was thinking you two may like to join me and some of my
friends for a celebration tonight.'

Takai shook his head. 'I thought you said it wasn't safe for us
out here.'

'It wouldn't be safe if it were an ordinary celebration, but
tonight is Ujej.'

Arisa prickled with excitement. 'I've heard of Ujej. It's a
Kengian festival to celebrate spring and call on Mother Nature
for a good harvest.'

'That's right. The official ceremony was held earlier, but
tonight is the festival's feast.'

'And I suppose this festival is the reason so many farmers
and *rebels*' – Takai's voice rose angrily – 'have gathered out
here?'

The Fisherman stared coolly at Takai. 'It is.'

'The festival has nothing to do with a rebellion,' Arisa said,
trying to calm Takai. 'It's an important rite in Kengian culture,
where the Shaman blesses the harvest and livestock and offers
protection.'

'You're well informed,' the Fisherman said. 'We have a
Kengian Shaman who settled here before the mountain pass
closed, and she will be there tonight.'

Arisa didn't mention that Erun knew a Kengian Shaman,
Laurel, and had been sending messages to her. She wondered if
this was the same woman – the Shaman who had come to
perform rites for Hyando to pass into the afterlife. The Shaman
who had spoken to her about the importance of believing in the
prophecy, of 'knowing' it. Hadn't the Fisherman used almost the
exact same phrase earlier? He had said Arisa would soon 'know'

it. Could the Shaman explain what happened to her today? Could she tell Arisa what she had to 'know'?

Arisa turned to Takai. 'We have to go.'

'No.' He shook his head adamantly. It's not safe.'

'Please, Takai. I really want to go.'

'You've both lost your minds.' Takai paced the room. 'I can't attend a festival full of Lamore's enemies – people who might want to kill me,' he stopped in front of Arisa, 'and possibly you, because you're with me.'

'I won't let that happen,' the Fisherman said.

'And what makes you think I want to support a festival that celebrates banned practices? I can't condone the conjuring of mythical spirits and other hocus-pocus.'

The Fisherman folded his arms and glared at Takai. 'The more I get to know you, the more my original opinion of you stands.'

Takai took two steps toward him. 'And what opinion is that?'

'That you're as close-minded and arrogant as your father.'

'That's not fair.' Arisa shot the Fisherman an admonishing look. 'You don't really know him.'

'No. The Prince doesn't get off that easily. Going to this festival could give him real insight into the kingdom and its people.' He turned to address Takai again. 'If you want to make real change, this is your chance.'

Takai ignored the Fisherman and turned to Arisa instead. 'You're talking about attending an event hosted by a Shaman. The very word in Lamorian means "half human and half spirit". They are said to have supernatural powers. How can we be sure we'll be safe?'

'From the little you have seen of Kengian magic,' Arisa said gently, 'has it ever harmed you?'

'Well…no, but…' Takai's words trailed off.

Arisa gave an encouraging smile. 'Please, Takai.'

His expression softened. 'What if I'm recognised?'

'That's the best part about Ujej.' The Fisherman started

rummaging around in a chest. Arisa realised with a start what he was looking for.

'Masks!'

'Exactly.' The Fisherman held up a handful of masks made in the likeness of demons and animals.

Arisa immediately reached to try one on as the Fisherman held one before his own face. 'Of course,' she said. 'Masks are used to drive away the evil spirits and winter's darkness.'

'You are well versed,' the Fisherman remarked again. 'What do you say…To be merry or not to be?'

'Shouldn't Arisa get some rest?' Takai pressed.

'I'm surprisingly fine,' she insisted. 'Better than fine.'

'We have a couple of hours for you to rest before we need to be there,' the Fisherman added.

Takai sighed loudly, before reaching for his own mask. 'You will be the death of me, Arisa. I swear it.'

'Excellent!' The Fisherman clapped his hands together. 'To be merry!'

27

*E*run dropped his quill. He was partway through writing a message to the Schoolmaster. He wasn't sure how to get the note to the man undetected, but he must. The Schoolmaster had narrowly escaped imprisonment and had been there when Horace had taken the Firemaster's book. Erun was worried the Schoolmaster, out of fear, would run to Sergei and tell him that Horace was close to harnessing the power of firesky.

Up until now, they had managed to keep the rebels at bay and hadn't needed to share anything about firesky. But if Sergei knew Horace had access to a potential weapon – a weapon as terrifying as firesky promised to be – he might go through with his threat to mobilise his rebels against the castle. It would be the start of civil war, which could only lead to disaster for most Lamorians. Erun needed to convince the Schoolmaster to keep the latest development between himself and Laurel only. The Schoolmaster had to be reassured that the rebels didn't need to take action, and that the Queen guaranteed their protection. At this moment, the Queen was with her husband, securing Erun and Arisa's safety. While Sofia was by the King's side, they were safe, and Horace had no leverage to uncover firesky's secrets.

Erun picked up his quill to resume his task, but was distracted by a disturbingly familiar sound.

The snow wolf released a protracted howl. And another.

A wave of nausea washed over Erun, wrapping around him, choking him. An unseen force was squeezing the oxygen from him. He leapt from his chair, knocking his inkwell to the floor. He clawed desperately at his throat, but couldn't get air to his lungs, no matter how hard he tried.

Gwyn raced toward him from where she'd been sitting on the other side of the room. 'What is it?'

Erun couldn't speak.

'Guards!' Gwyn cried.

The doors to the Queen's privy chamber flung open and Klaus ran into the room.

'Get a physician,' Gwyn said, 'and tell the Queen what is happening. She is with the King.'

Klaus left the room at a sprint.

'Here.' Gwyn tried to get Erun to drink from a goblet, but his flailing hands knocked it to the ground.

He gasped repeatedly, willing air to come to him, but it was useless. He slumped to the floor, sure he was going to die—

A vision appeared before him.

It was Arisa. Clambering over rocks, next to a silver lake. Then she was in water – thrown around in rapids, being dragged toward…something. Erun tried to call out to her, but no sound would come. He reached out to touch her, but she disappeared, as if she'd never been there. At the same time, the choking sensation in his throat vanished. His breath came back to him in shallow bursts.

'That's it. Take some deep breaths.' Gwyn put her hands under Erun's arms and helped him to his feet. 'To bed.'

'It's alright,' he rasped. 'I'm fine.'

Gwyn frowned. 'What was it?'

His eyes widened in fear. 'Something's happened to Arisa.'

Gwyn's grip on his arm tightened. 'Are you sure?'

Erun nodded miserably. 'Something dreadful—'

'More dreadful than you could imagine,' came a small voice.

Erun and Gwyn spun around to see the Queen, her hands clasped in front of her.

'Sofia?' Gwyn said.

'My truce with the King is over.'

'What do you mean?' Gwyn asked.

'I could no longer keep up the pretence that we were fully reunited.'

'I don't understand,' Erun said.

Realisation dawned over Gwyn's face. 'He insisted on resuming—'

'—marital relations.' The Queen's voice was devoid of life. 'I tried to assure Delrik that I am his true wife. I pleaded for more time, time to completely rebuild trust between us. And I meant what I said…truly, I did. These past couple of months he has been a changed man. I was beginning to see more of the man I married. I may have even returned to him, given more time, but he would not have it. He was livid. He accused me of manipulating him – said that all this time I've been advising him to act against the best interests of the kingdom. He declared me his enemy. I'm afraid my word to protect any of you means little now. Erun, Horace will waste no time in coming for you. You have to escape. Immediately.'

Erun shook his head. 'I can't leave. Not without Arisa. I have to wait until she's back.'

'I don't think we have that much time.'

'Not without Arisa,' he repeated.

'Sofia's right. You need to go now,' Gwyn said. 'As soon as Arisa returns, we will get her to safety as well.'

'You can't guarantee that.'

'Takai will speak for her,' Gwyn said. 'The King will listen to him.'

'From what the Queen has said, the King may only listen to Horace now,' Erun replied. 'And Horace is closer to being more powerful than ever. If he realises the exact nature of what he has in his possession…we're all doomed. Without the Queen's protection, Horace will be able to use Arisa to force my compliance. He will make me reveal firesky's secrets.'

'The King said as much,' Queen Sofia confirmed.

'They'll be back from Calliope soon,' Gwyn insisted. 'Any minute, I expect.'

Erun shook his head. 'I don't think they're nearby. I think they're in Lakeford, near Shizen Lake. I have seen it.'

The Queen clenched her fists. 'Willem. He is still here at the castle. He will know how to find them.'

Erun and Gwyn nodded in unison. Willem was their best and only hope.

AFTER WHAT SEEMED LIKE HOURS, the Duke's son arrived, and delivered the devastating news that he couldn't help them find the group.

'I wish I could do something. Truly, I do.' Willem's voice cracked. 'As I said, I too am under watch. Horace has ordered that no one be allowed out of the castle. He claims it's for our safety.'

'Safety,' Gwyn said. 'What could he mean by that?'

'Horace is moving quickly. He has convinced the King the army should be mobilised to hunt down all of the rebels. He is planning on declaring martial law in Lamore.'

Erun spun around to face Willem. 'Martial law! Your father would never agree to it.'

'You're right, he wouldn't. But I've just heard from one of Father's clerks that the King is refusing to hear or meet with anyone other than the Secretary. I expect Horace's next move will be to remove my father as Lord Commander, and after that he can do anything he wishes.'

Erun wrung his hands. 'Can you get a message to your father at Talbot? Get him to help find Arisa and the others?'

Willem shook his head. 'Horace has placed guards on me, and they are watching my every move. They're outside these doors as we speak. Horace says it's a precaution, since I'm next in line for the throne after Takai and my father. But I think we all know better than that.'

Erun rubbed the nape of his neck. His worst fears were coming to being. Arisa was missing. Horace had the Firemaster's book, and if he got to Arisa before anyone else, he would be able to force Erun to uncover its secrets. On top of it all, Horace was about to send the army after his own people. And there was nothing...*nothing* Erun could do to stop Horace—

Or was there?

An idea was forming in his mind. He recalled what he'd said he would do if it ever came to this. It had only been spoken of as a last resort...if they had no alternative. But wasn't that the exact situation they faced now?

'Do you think they're alright?' Gwyn's grip on the book in her hands tightened until her knuckles were white.

'I'm sure they'll be fine,' Willem said. 'Sar is with them. I expect they'll be back any minute.'

As if summoned by his name, a travel-worn and flushed Sar burst into the room.

'You're back!' Gwyn ran toward her son, but he held up a hand and shook his head.

The Queen's eyes darted around the room. 'Where are the others?'

Sar's gaze fell to the floor.

'What is it? What's happened?' Gwyn cried.

'Everyone is fine. But Takai and Arisa...' Sar's voice was shaking.

Erun fought the panic that was overtaking his body and addressed Sar in his calmest voice. 'It's alright, Sar. Tell us about Takai and Arisa.'

'They're safe, but they're not here.'

Gwyn slumped into a chair, knocking a book to the ground

with a thud. Erun reached out to comfort her. The Queen was silent.

'I'm sorry,' Sar mumbled as he rushed to pick up the book. His brow furrowed as he handed it to Gwyn.

'Sar, where are they?' Willem asked.

Sar tilted his head in Willem's direction, as if he hadn't noticed his friend's presence until now. 'We were separated at Shizen Lake.'

'What were you doing at Shizen Lake?' The Queen's voice rose angrily. 'You were supposed to stick to the King's Road.'

'We did…at least initially. But Takai wished to go elsewhere.'

'And you and the other guards agreed?' Gwyn was out of her chair – it was her turn to be angry.

'Not exactly. We gave Guthrie and the other guards the slip at Dunhin Village. I understand they have been looking for us ever since and have only just returned to the castle.'

'Why didn't Guthrie send word that he'd lost you all? We could have done something,' Gwyn cried.

'I'm probably the last person to defend Guthrie, but I can only imagine the strife he would have been in if he had sent word,' Sar replied. 'I suppose he thought he would find us and wouldn't have to face the trouble he faces now.'

Erun resisted the urge to shake Sar. They were no closer to discovering what had happened to Arisa and Takai. He took a deep breath. 'Arisa and the Prince?'

'They got caught in the river that's fed from the lake and were washed downstream.'

'Downstream?' Erun's voice was thick with fear. 'But the only thing downstream—'

'—is Riverend Falls,' the Queen finished.

A cry escaped Gwyn's mouth.

Sar waved his hands frantically. 'They went over the falls, but they survived. They are fine, I swear. I saw them on the shore below and they were alright. I tried to get down the cliff face to them, but it was too steep. The only way to get to them was to go around the King's Forest and through the marshland, but by then it would have been dark.'

'He's right,' Willem said. 'I know the area, and Sar couldn't have got to them safely.'

But Erun was incredulous that Sar, of all people, would have abandoned anyone, least of all his best friend. 'You left them?' he asked.

'Not alone. There was a fisherman who said he would take them to his hut.'

'The Fisherman.' Willem nodded. 'I know of this man. He is well respected in Lakeford, and I believe him capable of protecting Arisa and Takai.'

'Judging by his size and manner, I'd say he's capable of protecting them against an entire army, if necessary,' Sar agreed.

'Do you believe they are safe with this…Fisherman?' the Queen asked Willem.

Willem nodded slowly. 'Yes. They will be fine.'

'I will go to them at first light.' Sar's face was etched with pain.

'I doubt the Secretary will let you go,' Erun lamented. He knew Horace wouldn't trust anyone but his own men to bring Arisa back. She was key to his plans. 'We have to stop Arisa from returning to the castle.'

'Stop her?' Sar frowned. 'Why would we do that?'

'It's a long story, but if Arisa comes back here, Horace will have the means to destroy all of his enemies,' Erun said. 'He will become unstoppable.'

Willem's face crumpled. 'But we can't even send a message. We won't be able to stop her from returning.'

'There is *something* we can do,' Erun said. 'We can send a warning to Arisa and the rebels at the same time.'

The group turned to look at him expectantly.

'I had promised to send a signal to Sergei if it looked like

Horace would act against the rebels,' he explained. 'Arisa knows the signal and the danger it warns of.'

'A signal?' the Queen asked.

'Yes…firesky.'

Sar and Willem exchanged confused looks.

The Queen shook her head. 'No. We can't. You would be giving Horace proof that you know its secrets.'

'He has the proof already. He has the Firemaster's book, and he will find a way to figure it out. This is why we have to act now.'

Erun could see the Queen weighing it up in her mind. 'It's madness. The idea of using *firesky* to stop Horace from getting his hands on it…'

'It's the only way.'

The Queen drew an audible breath. 'Arisa will know, from this signal, to stay away?'

'I believe so.'

'But you will still be here at the castle,' she said. 'Horace will make you weaponise firesky.'

'It's alright,' Gwyn said. 'We will find a way to get Erun out of here. We will have time to do that.'

'In any case, Horace won't be able to weaponise firesky if he doesn't have Arisa,' Erun added. 'I will give my life if I have to…but not hers. We must launch firesky. Quickly. Tonight.'

'I'm not sure what any of you are talking about,' Sar said, 'but if this is the only hope we have of saving Arisa, we have to do it.'

The Queen looked out to the darkening sky and gave a small nod. 'It will be as it was foretold. There has been a blood moon, and firesky will follow.'

'And then the Water Catcher will come,' Erun and Gwyn whispered in unison.

28

*A*risa and Takai followed the Fisherman along a track that meandered its way inland toward Shizen Lake and the Alps. He led them by torchlight, a bag of fish slung over his shoulder. He'd given Takai a jug of his home-brew to carry. They had to watch their steps carefully, as the track ran alongside peat bogs. The trio walked for some time in silent concentration, until the moorland gave way to drier land.

It was a warm night, but Arisa shivered as a burst of alpine air blew across her face. Takai's free arm went around her. She was wearing the same slippers and gown she had set out in from the castle. Fortunately, they had all dried out in front of the Fisherman's fire. The slippers were a little grubby, and the gown had some splatters of mud and grime along the hemline. There were also a few tears where rocks had caught the fabric, but it helped her appearance. Dressing too finely would give them away. Takai had only been wearing his undershirt and breeches when he went into the water, so was wearing one of the Fisherman's gigantic tunics over them. He had belted it tightly around his waist and accepted the Fisherman's offer to use his only pair of worn boots. The Fisherman favoured the same sandals he had worn all day. They were a motley-looking crew, but the Fisherman thought it would help them blend in at the festival.

'Not much further,' he said.

Arisa recognised the sound of Shizen Falls, though it was much louder than she remembered. She couldn't see the waterfall in the darkness, but she could sense it was close. The path started to climb a rocky hillside. She wondered whether the Fisherman had taken them the wrong way, and Takai must have had the same thought.

'Are we going up the mountain range?' he asked.

'Not much further,' the Fisherman repeated.

The roar of the falls was deafening as they continued upward. A spray of cold water hit Arisa's face and she stopped in her tracks. She wasn't sure what it was, but she suddenly had the same desire she'd had earlier in the day to reach out and touch the unseen falls.

The Fisherman turned to them and held his torch out in front so they could see the path ahead. Arisa gasped.

Before them was a narrow passage that hugged the mountainside and slipped directly behind the falls. She estimated it to be wide enough for a single cart. This must have been the way the Fisherman had told Sar to come in the morning.

He waved them on. 'Come on.'

Arisa looked to Takai, who squeezed her hand comfortingly.

The Fisherman held the torch closer to them so they could keep their footing on the slippery path. As soon as they were behind the falls, the roaring sound became muffled, echoing off the rocky walls. For a few moments it felt as if they were in a wet, mossy cocoon. They came to the end of the path and emerged back onto the rocky hillside, leaving the falls behind.

'There it is.' The Fisherman pointed straight ahead to a clearing at the base of the mountains. A towering bonfire was ablaze at the centre of the field, its flames licking the inky sky. Shadowy figures danced around its base.

Arisa grinned to herself as she detected the strains of music and laughter in the air, but Takai's hand tensed in hers.

'I'm not sure this is a good idea.'

'Come on, you two.' The Fisherman was already several paces ahead of them, his demon mask pulled over his face.

Arisa looked up at Takai. 'Please. We're here now. They'll never guess who we are.' She put on her own mask, covering the upper part of her face. It was a rabbit, a symbol of fertility for the harvest.

Takai sighed. 'I knew you were trouble from the moment I met you, Arisa.' He shook his head to himself as he put on his fearsome-looking mask. It resembled something between a fox and a cat, with a wicked smile and horns.

'The same goes for you,' she teased back.

Takai took her hand again and led her toward the Fisherman, who was approaching the edge of the gathering.

The smell of wood burning and roast meat was the first thing to hit her – a rich, smoky deliciousness. Children wearing masks, with flowers in their hair, danced around the fire as ash floated through the air. A group of men sat on stumps of wood and barrels, singing between gulps from mugs or jugs. Other revellers sat around flat tray carts used as tables, the largest of which was laden with a display of eggs, wheaten cakes and sheaves of corn – an offering to nature, from what Arisa knew of the festival's traditions. The tray was also decorated with budding twigs, wildflowers, greenery, feathers and shells: a perfect homage to spring and all of the natural elements. A group of musicians played an up-tempo song on fiddles, pipes and drums. Arisa was transfixed by the simple beauty of the scene. Takai's eyes, though, were fixed on the bounty of food.

'Where did all this come from? I thought the people were supposed to be starving.'

'Since the Queen has been back, no one has starved,' the Fisherman said. 'She has seen to it that everyone has enough to eat.'

'I'd say quite enough to eat, looking at that,' Takai scoffed.

'What you're seeing isn't an everyday occurrence. This is a collection from people all over the county, to celebrate the festival. We won't see food like this again for another year.'

Takai didn't have a chance to respond. A man in a ghoul mask wandered purposefully toward them, ale sloshing from the mug in his hand. He was as wide as he was tall.

'Oi, Fisherman. There you be. What took you so long? Making quite the entrance.' He thumped the Fisherman good-naturedly on the back.

'What makes you think I'm the Fisherman?'

'Anyone could recognise you, mask or not. You're the only man of that size in all of Lamore.'

'You can talk!' The Fisherman grasped the man's hand and shook it vigorously. 'Good to see you, Sergei.'

Arisa felt Takai's hand stiffen in hers as the Fisherman greeted the famed leader of the rebellion.

'We're about to serve the roast meat. The finest venison you've ever had…courtesy of the King's Forest.' Sergei chuckled to himself.

Takai grunted, and Arisa kicked him in the leg.

Sergei fixed his gaze on them for the first time. 'Who may you be?'

'Friends from the city,' the Fisherman said. 'They have been curious about the festival and wanted to see it for themselves.'

'Friends from the city, you say?' Sergei's interest was clearly piqued. He appeared to ponder it for a moment before dismissing his thoughts with a flick of his arm. 'The more the merrier.'

'This is Sergei,' the Fisherman announced to Arisa and Takai. 'He is a…' He paused, as if choosing his next words carefully. 'A friend of the people.'

'Pleased to meet you.' Sergei gave a mock bow. 'Any friends of the Fisherman's are friends of mine. Welcome to Ujej.' He shoved his mug into Takai's hands.

'Here.' The Fisherman handed over his bag of fish to

Sergei. 'For the feast.'

'Thanking you. To be merry.' Sergei gave a wink before disappearing back into the crowd.

Arisa and Takai let out a simultaneous sigh of relief.

'Come on,' the Fisherman said. 'Best we take a seat and not draw further attention to ourselves.'

'Venison? From the King's Forest?' Takai pressed.

'Must have wandered into the nearest village.' The Fisherman grinned back at them as he took his jug of home-brew from Takai and wandered off in the direction of the festival-goers.

Arisa was under no illusions; this festival would be difficult for Takai. From what she knew, his only real experience of interacting with non-nobles had been the ill-fated progress ending in the riot at the marketplace, and his time living at Talbot as a child. She recalled his stories of how some farmers and villagers had treated him with suspicion or downright dislike because he was the King's son. She also remembered how he felt about Kengians and their forbidden practices, seeing it as an open defiance of the King's rule. Arisa wondered how to get him to relax and enjoy himself. He needed a break after a whirlwind couple of days, with the King's celebration and Takai's birthday — His birthday!

She plunged her hand into a pocket in her gown, hoping by some miracle the item was still there. Her fingers swept over the familiar face of her medallion on its broken chain. But she was searching for something else. Arisa breathed a sigh of relief when she felt the cold metal arm of the pin that she'd used to fix it to her dress.

Takai's eyes went to her hand rustling around her pocket. She held up her other hand to say, *Wait*.

Arisa ran her fingers along the pin's arm and, with a flick of her fingers, unclasped it to release the item. She hesitated for a moment. What if he didn't like it? Had she presumed too much?

She closed her fingers around the object and held out her fist to present it to Takai.

'I meant to give this to you on your birthday, but it wasn't ready. I stayed up most of last night to get it finished.'

Even in the darkness, she could feel Takai's eyes boring into her. The intensity of his gaze was intoxicating.

'Can I see it?' he asked.

'It's nothing much.' She still refrained from unclenching her fist.

Takai put down the mug Sergei had given him and gently uncurled each of her fingers, one by one, his touch sending sparks through her body, his eyes never leaving hers until her last finger was prised away.

In her hand was a braided strip of silver-coloured silk cord. In the middle was a large knot that resembled a five-armed snowflake. Each arm was made of intricate, almost geometric knots. The arms were knotted onto the sides of a pentagon, with an empty void at its centre.

Takai lifted his mask and picked up the knotted cord, examining it closely.

'What is it?' His voice was edged with wonder...or was it disdain?

'It's a Kengian good fortune bracelet.' Arisa was glad she was still wearing her mask, so he couldn't see the fear she felt. The fear that he would reject her gift...reject her—

'It's beautiful,' Takai said.

'*Really?* You like it?'

'Of course.' His brow crinkled in a way that made her feel her heart would explode. 'Why wouldn't I?'

'It's just...I thought...'

Takai took both of her hands in his and stared directly into her eyes.

'I know you think I hate all things Kengian...And maybe there was a time that I did, or thought I did. But that was before. I'm trying to show you I have changed. I'm seeing things differently. Ever since Lina came to see my father, I have been speaking on her behalf. I implored him to release her husband from prison. And I did it, Arisa...I did it! Yesterday, Father gifted me any wish for my birthday, and that was it...that was what I asked for. Cynfor was being released today. I imagine he is on his way back to Lina as we speak.'

Arisa extricated herself from Takai's grip to clasp a hand over her mouth.

His face distorted with hurt. 'I know it's only a start, but I thought you would be pleased. I wanted to do the right thing for once.'

She reached out and grasped his hands again. 'You *did* do the right thing. You did more than I ever...Thank you.'

Arisa couldn't bring herself to tell Takai the real reason for her surprise. She had been so absorbed in her own problems that she hadn't spared a thought for Lina for days...weeks, perhaps. She was the one who always went on about helping people. She was the one who had ranted at and chastised the Prince for his heartlessness...but it was he who'd done something selfless. It was he who was good and just. It was Arisa who was self-involved. Had she been wrong about him? About everything, all along?

She looked down at the ground in shame, but Takai lifted her chin.

'You see, I was scared of what I didn't understand.' She was struck by the rawness in his voice. 'And when I look into your silver eyes, I'm still scared...but in a different way.'

She gulped, not sure of what she wanted him to say next.

'Your eyes are unnerving, Arisa. *You* are unnerving. In a way I never anticipated. A way that makes me believe anything is possible. Arisa, I—'

Takai's words came to a shuddering halt as a group nearby erupted into shouts and laughter. They were pointing at a man performing a wobbly jig on the back of a cart. Arisa grinned instinctively, but her smile quickly faded as she realised Takai hadn't finished whatever he'd been planning on saying. By the time she turned back around, he already had his mask back on and was tying his bracelet to his wrist.

'What does it mean?'

He's talking about the bracelet, nothing else, Arisa had to tell herself.

She traced each of the knotted arms with her finger. 'Each of these represents the elements of air, water, fire and earth.'

'But there are five of them.'

'Yes, the fifth one is for balance. Balance and harmony in all.' She touched the empty centre of the knot and could feel Takai's pulse drumming beneath her fingertip. Her own heart-beat quickened to match his. 'This…' she started, a little shakily. 'This represents the aether – the space or soul that binds and connects us all.'

'I like it…' Takai's voice thickened. 'A lot.'

Arisa could only manage a whisper. 'I'm glad.'

His eyes went to his wrist, where her fingers were uncon-sciously tracing the knots. She snatched back her hand as if his skin had burned her.

Takai picked up the mug he'd left on the ground. 'Trouble. Nothing but trouble,' he said, laughing to himself.

Arisa's head was a whir of confusion. Did the Prince care for her? Were they more than friends? Could he accept that she was a silver-eyes?

'Come on.' Takai offered his arm to her. 'I thought we were here to be merry.'

She hesitated. Wasn't this exactly what she wanted? A Prince who was open-minded and kind? It didn't matter who the better person was. As long as they were together, they could balance each other out. Together, they were the fifth natural element. And tonight they could exist in the aether.

She threaded her arm through Takai's and let him lead her into the festival.

29

*T*akai took another swig from the mug in his hand. He wasn't sure if it was the home-brew, his anonymity, or Arisa's company, but he was actually enjoying himself. He was surrounded by strangers; there was no public scrutiny. To the revellers, he was another friend or neighbour. They were generous with their food, drink and laughter, and while they were curious about the Fisherman's friends, they welcomed him and Arisa among them.

He had never seen Arisa as alive as she was tonight. Her smile was infectious. Her Kengian eyes danced in the flickering light of the fire. Not even the mask she wore could hide her beauty. He was drawn to her more than ever, in spite of, or because of, everything that had happened. Who was she, really? What had happened to her when she was in the water? Takai still had so many questions. He'd put them aside when she'd given him the bracelet. He'd nearly declared himself to her then and there – but how could he? How could he truly love someone he didn't know?

Who is she? Takai needed to know. He couldn't wait a minute longer.

He stood up to approach Arisa on the other side of the

makeshift table, but the pressure of a firm hand on his shoulder stopped him in his tracks.

'Friends, there's someone I'd like you to meet.' The Fisherman had appeared by his side with a tall, dark-haired woman. She wore a half-mask that revealed the lower part of her face. Her skin shimmered as if it were covered in a layer of silver dust. She wore a crownlike headpiece of twisted twigs and budding flowers, and a robe trimmed with embroidered leaves and vines. She was strikingly beautiful.

'This is Laurel,' the Fisherman said proudly.

Takai gave Laurel a small bow, but instead of acknowledging him with an expected curtsey or nod, she reached out and clasped his hands in both of hers.

It was as if a bolt of lightning suddenly shot through him. His nerve endings were on fire. He wanted to pull his hands away, but one look from the woman immediately calmed him. She appraised him. Her eyes had the same all-knowing look of Arisa's, but they were blue, dark blue – not silver. They reminded Takai of the twilight sky.

'It is you.' Laurel's voice was sweet and smooth as nectar.

A shiver ran down Takai's spine. Had the Fisherman shared his identity with her? 'I'm sorry, I don't think we know each other.'

She smiled. 'But I do know you. Better than you know yourself. But that can change, given the right choice.'

Takai found her cryptic comment unnerving.

Laurel released his hands and redirected her gaze at a wide-eyed Arisa. 'Arisa. How have you been?'

Takai was a little taken aback that they appeared to know each other. What else wasn't Arisa telling him?

'I didn't think you'd recognise me,' Arisa said.

Laurel laughed. 'The Fisherman did tell me you were here, but no mask could have prevented me from recognising you. You're not easily forgotten.' Laurel reached out to take Arisa's hands, as she had done with Takai.

Takai watched closely to see if Arisa experienced the same reaction to Laurel's touch that he had. He didn't notice a change in Arisa, but he was surprised by Laurel. He thought he saw her stiffen for a moment before exchanging a swift glance with the Fisherman, who gave a small nod, as if he had expected Laurel's response. Arisa tilted her head to the side, a question forming on her lips, but Laurel immediately regained her composure and smiled back at her.

'May I sit?' she asked.

Arisa offered the seat beside her to Laurel, while the Fisherman sat down beside Takai.

Laurel stared across the table at Takai as if she could see through him. Then she turned to Arisa. 'You wish to ask me something?'

Takai got the distinct impression that Laurel was reading their minds.

'I want to ask lots of things.' Arisa looked as if she would burst. 'I have so many questions.'

Laurel nodded. Arisa glanced at Takai and shifted in her seat before continuing. 'I was wondering if it was true that Shamans can foretell the future?'

So Laurel was the Kengian Shaman. Half human. Half spirit. Yes, Takai had opened his mind to Kengians and silver-eyes – thanks to Arisa – but Shamans were an entirely different story: nothing more than charlatans.

'Some can see the future,' Laurel replied. 'Some can inhabit the bodies of animals.'

'Like wolves?' Takai said, almost without realising. He hadn't forgotten the day the Kengian snow wolf had beckoned him and Sar to follow it into a secret tunnel; the creature had appeared more human than animal.

Arisa tilted her head at his mention of the wolf, but Laurel appeared unfazed. 'Yes, some Shamans could inhabit a wolf. Every Shaman's gifts are different.'

'What about you? Can you see what will happen?' Arisa pressed.

Laurel shrugged. 'I have feelings – visions, sometimes – which I can't control. Whether they're from the past or a possible future, it's hard to tell.'

'That's helpful,' Takai muttered to himself.

'It cannot be any other way. The future is rarely fixed, and if I see something that may come to being, it's impossible to know exactly when it will come to pass. Time means nothing in the spirit world.'

'The spirit world.' Takai spoke a little louder this time, his voice laced with sarcasm.

Laurel was unperturbed. 'And you?' she asked him. 'What do you wish to know?'

He bristled. 'Nothing. I don't wish to know anything from you.'

'You wish to know much. You have many questions. That is clear.'

Takai didn't deny it.

'What can I answer for you?'

He shrugged. Arisa smiled encouragingly at him. The simplest gesture from her was capable of bolstering and incapacitating him at the same time.

'I don't know...' he said. 'What will become of Lamore? Will we go to war?'

'It is certain there will be war.'

Takai leant forward with sudden interest. 'Where will it happen? Will the Northemers invade us? Who will be the victor?'

Laurel shook her head. 'The details, the outcome – they are still unclear.'

Takai made a scoffing noise.

'What of Kengia?' Arisa asked.

Laurel turned toward her. 'It all depends.'

'On what?'

'It depends on the Water Catcher.'

Arisa's eyes widened. 'You believe there is a Water Catcher?'

Laurel placed her hands over Arisa's. 'Whether *I* believe or know something is not important. I cannot bring the Water Catcher into being.'

Arisa seemed transfixed by this woman, but her nonsensical talk put Takai on edge. 'Enough of your riddles.'

Laurel's eyes turned on him, and she dropped her voice to a whisper. 'You're wrong, Your Highness. It's not enough.'

Takai chortled. He wasn't impressed that she knew who he was. The Fisherman must have betrayed his identity.

As if hearing his thoughts, Laurel continued, 'The Fisherman didn't need to tell me who you were, Prince Takai. You told me when we first met. Your aura spoke to me.'

'Ridiculous!' he spat. 'Why are you saying all this? Are you trying to manipulate us?'

'I'm not trying to manipulate you. I'm trying to help you see that what you're doing isn't enough. It won't be enough to save your country or the people you love.'

Takai felt his face flush with anger. 'Is that the future-seeing you speaking, or your personal opinion?'

'I have seen it. I believe it to be true. You will find yourself on two paths. You will have to choose your path wisely. You must make the right choice. And then...only then...is there a chance of it being enough to save Lamore and yourself.'

'A path? *What* path?'

'You will know when the time comes. It will mean questioning everything you believe in. You'll be asked to take the biggest leap of faith you've ever made.'

Takai shuddered. There was something in her words and conviction that struck truth. He wanted to ask her more, but Laurel's attention was now on the Fisherman. He had moved away from them and appeared to be fielding questions from Sergei. The rebel leader was gesturing in their direction. Laurel stood up to join the men.

'About the Water Catcher—' Arisa cried out. 'If they do come to being, can they succeed in uniting the kingdoms?'

Laurel turned and gave one of her oddly serene smiles. 'Yes, that I'm sure of. If the prophecy comes to pass, the Water Catcher will possess the power to save Kengia and Lamore. But they can't do it alone. The Water Catcher is bound to another, and only together will they succeed.'

'You must have seen who the Water Catcher is,' Arisa pressed. 'You must know what will happen.'

'As I said, I can only see what's possible, not what *will* be. And it is not *I* who needs to know.'

Laurel looked one last time at Arisa before turning her back on them and joining the Fisherman. Takai couldn't hear what was being said, but Sergei soon stomped off, leaving Laurel and the Fisherman in deep conversation.

'I don't understand. What could I possibly know?' Arisa was mumbling to herself. 'I know nothing. Laurel must know more than she's saying.'

'Arisa.' Takai tried to get her attention, but she didn't seem to hear him.

'She has to know more. I have to talk with her again.' Arisa made to walk toward Laurel, but Takai took her by the arm.

'Arisa, we have to talk.'

'I need to speak with Laurel.'

'We have to talk about what happened today.'

Arisa stood stiff and silent.

'Don't pretend you don't know what I'm talking about.' Takai dropped his voice to a whisper, his hand still firmly grasping hers. 'What happened in the water today?'

'There's nothing to talk about.' She spoke in clipped tones.

'Nothing to talk about? Light came out of your hands. Your mouth. Your body. There was a huge spout of water that came from nowhere and shot us into the air. If I didn't know better, I would say it was magic.'

'Takai, there's nothing to talk about because I don't know

what happened.' Arisa's voice was strained. 'Truly, I don't know. I wish I did, but I don't.'

'Can you at least tell me about who you really are?' Takai could feel the secrets between them boiling over, all at once. 'Explain how you're Kengian. Tell me who your guardian is.'

'I wish I could answer all of your questions…' She took a sharp breath, as if she were trying to stop herself from crying. 'But I can't.'

Takai loosened his grip on Arisa's arm and turned her to face him. He had the sudden urge to pull her into his arms and hold her. He wanted to tell her everything would be alright, but he couldn't bring himself to say it – because it was a lie. Nothing was alright.

Instead, he tilted her face up to his, so she was looking right in his eyes. The moonlight caught beneath her cheekbones. He was struck again by her ethereal beauty.

She had completely disarmed him.

'I believe you,' he murmured. But he suddenly felt awkward, and released her. 'Right,' he began, in a take-charge tone of voice. 'We don't know what happened. But there must be a logical explanation. It was some natural force that caused the water to act strangely. Maybe the light was a trick of nature. Maybe I was seeing things…after all, I had been knocked out.' Takai stopped with a sigh. 'But you saw it too, didn't you?'

'Of course I saw it, but I can't explain it. Nothing makes sense.'

He reached out and squeezed her hand. 'We don't have to figure it out now. Tonight, let's enjoy this festival of yours. We can talk about it later.'

They sat back down at the table. Their hands intertwined, and Arisa leaned against him. Takai let himself get lost in the firelight and the warmth of her body next to his.

Secrets or not, they were bound to each other.

30

'Well! What do you have to say for yourselves?' Horace bellowed at his children.

A dishevelled Theodora and Guthrie had arrived back at the castle and delivered the news of Arisa and Takai's disappearance to their furious father.

'It's not my fault.' Guthrie pointed accusingly at his sister. 'She's the one who took off with the others.'

'Yes, and you're the stupid oaf who let them get away from you.' While getting rid of Arisa had always been her plan, the last thing Theodora had wanted was for Takai to go with her. 'Sar aided them. He was supposed to be protecting the Prince, and it is he who should be blamed.'

'And I will deal with him the first moment I get…as I will deal with you two,' Horace hissed. 'Tell me *everything* that happened. Don't spare a single detail.'

Theodora gave her father a comprehensive account of the day's events. She explained how Takai and Arisa had been swept down the Shizen River, and miraculously survived going over Riverend Falls before becoming stranded on a remote shore – all the while glossing over any mention of her own involvement in what had happened; of how it had been her foolish plan to get rid of Arisa once she'd realised the girl wasn't going to try to escape.

'You said they were unable to get back up the cliffside?' Horace asked.

'Their only option was to accept an offer from a fisherman to go to his home on the other side of the marshlands. We would have had to backtrack around the King's Forest to get to them, but it was impossible to make it before dark.'

'Yes…you said that. What I'm more interested in is this fisherman. What was his name?'

'He said he was only known as the Fisherman.'

Horace sat, steepling his fingers. 'I see. What did the Fisherman look like?'

'Like a fisherman.'

'Don't be obtuse.'

Theodora sighed. 'I personally paid little attention to him, but Selina rabbited on and on about him all the way home. Describing him as a bronzed giant of a man…which I suppose he was. I did find him quite arrogant. He spoke far above his station and was quite uncouth in his manner.'

'You're quite sure he was a fisherman?'

'He had fish, a fishing net and a spear.'

Horace appeared to turn the information over in his mind. 'I've heard rumours of a fisherman in the counties. Someone with an unknown past, but with all the appearance of being a warrior. I wonder…'

'Yes, Father?' Theodora said eagerly, wondering if now he would finally confide in her. 'You wonder…?'

Horace frowned. 'There's nothing for you to concern yourself with. Just know that if this man is who I think he is, he poses a threat to all of our plans – plans I had so painstakingly gotten back on track, before you two imbeciles ruined everything.'

Theodora dropped her head. 'Father, I'm sorry.'

'You should be sorry. I told you to stay close to the ward. It was the last thing I said to you before you left. It's bad enough you left her with the Prince, but worse than that, it puts our future at risk. She was the only leverage I had. The only way of getting the healer to cooperate with my plans.'

Theodora withheld a smirk. *I know your plan for firesky, Father, and you shall never have it if it means sacrificing my* own *plans.*

'Yes, Theodora,' Horace went on. 'You should be *very* sorry.'

Guthrie shot a smug look at his sister.

'I wouldn't be so pleased with myself if I were you, Guthrie,' their father added. 'You have also failed miserably. I don't think you realise how important it is that we get the ward back to the castle.'

Guthrie scowled. 'Who cares about that little wench?'

'I care.'

'Let me go get her tomorrow morning. I will make damn sure she doesn't leave my sight for a second.'

'I will send my personal guards at first light. I have other matters for you to deal with. I'm expecting there to be trouble from the workers I have dismissed from the hospital site.'

'You've cancelled the hospital project?' Theodora asked. 'How did you get the King to agree?'

'If you must know, I have the King's ear again. It seems he was none too happy that the Queen was only pretending to be his *true* wife again.'

'I'm just surprised it took him this long to work it out,' Theodora quipped.

'Well, now that he has, I have got him to agree to abandon the ridiculous alliance with Ivane and to negotiate with the Northemers instead. He also agreed to put an immediate stop to the hospital and his other charitable follies that have drained the treasury. We will implement tighter grain rationing and divert the supplies to the army that will invade Kengia with the Northemers.'

'A grand plan,' Guthrie said. 'Teach the people who's really in charge.'

Theodora resisted the urge to roll her eyes at her brother's lack of foresight. 'What about Sergei and his rebels? Surely they will rise against the King again?'

Horace tilted his head and gave his daughter a look that could be mistaken for admiration. 'Yes. We need to pre-empt any possible uprisings or attacks on the castle, and deal with the rebel leader once and for all. I am having the King recall the army from training. I will send the regiment at Talbot into the counties to find and punish Sergei and his supporters. The forces at Iveness will be mobilised and sent to protect the castle.'

'Will the Duke agree to it?' Theodora asked.

'He won't have a choice. I will see that a state of martial law is declared so no one can question my authority. I will have the King declare me the Lord Commander of his forces, and Guthrie will be my second-in-command.'

Guthrie puffed out his chest. Her buffoon of a brother. Second-in-command. Had her father lost his mind?

'First thing in the morning, Guthrie shall go to Iveness, then on to Talbot to deliver my orders under the King's seal.'

Guthrie's eyes went to the silver-and-brass seal featuring the King's peregrine falcon insignia. It was sitting back in its rightful place on Horace's desk.

'Our power is on the rise again, son,' Horace continued. 'And you never know what may happen. Remember, you're in line for the throne. In these uncertain times, anything could befall Lakeford and his sickly son.'

'And the Prince?' Guthrie's voice was tinged with hope.

'Now that your sister has failed in her task, perhaps the Prince is expendable.'

Guthrie smirked at Theodora. She dug her nails into her palms. How could her father reward Guthrie after all his signifi-cant failures, yet shame her for what had been virtually an impos-sible task? She was a thousand times more useful than her brother.

'What about Sar?' she asked. 'As Captain of the Guards, I expect he will try to stand in your way, Father.'

'Sar won't be doing anything or going anywhere. As soon as the King has calmed down, I will get him to agree to confine Sar, the Queen and the rest of our detractors to their rooms. I can't have anything else interfere with my plans.'

'Thank you for entrusting me with this honour,' Guthrie said. 'I won't let you down.'

'You'd better not. There is one final thing you can do for me.'

'Anything, Father.'

'You can inform the King personally of his son's whereabouts and your part to play in today's disaster. Assuring him, of course, that I have the matter in hand.'

Guthrie's face paled. 'Father?'

'It is about time there was at least some consequence for your actions. And to be frank, I don't have time to deal with the King right now. One minute he's screaming at everyone, the next he's a blubbering mess, calling out his wife's name while downing another jug of wine.'

'Perhaps it would be better if you—' Guthrie began, but Horace motioned for his son to leave.

'Should I leave as well, Father?' Theodora asked.

Horace's eyes narrowed. 'Not before you too obtain a lesson in consequences.'

A chill ran through Theodora as her father indicated for a guard to admit a 'guest'. She didn't need the guard to announce the pirate, as the smell of rum preceded his entry.

'Secretary.' Goldman bowed to her father. 'My lady.' Her skin crawled under the pirate's hungry gaze. She did not offer her hand, so he tipped his hat instead.

'You have a message for me?' Horace prompted.

'I do.' The pirate's eyes gleamed. He plonked himself into a plush chair, his fat belly spilling out of his velvet doublet and embellished lace shirt. The man's arrogance was incorrigible.

'And why did you see the need to deliver it in person?'

'So I could collect my reward. For bringing you the news you have been waiting for.'

'Stop playing with me,' Horace demanded. 'Say what you came here to say.'

Goldman reached into his doublet and retrieved a note, which he threw across the table. Theodora recognised Malu's serpent-head seal before her father ripped it open.

A smirk tugged at the corner of Horace's mouth as he read the message. Did he finally have his alliance with the Northemers?

'To my reward. Governorship of Ette…' The pirate nodded at Theodora. 'And your daughter's hand.'

Theodora's heart thumped in her chest. Surely her father wouldn't agree, no matter what the note said. He would not go through with his threat.

'You will be rewarded when everything we discussed comes to being,' he said.

She breathed a sigh of relief.

'And it shall.' Goldman glanced over at a partially drunk glass of wine on Horace's desk. 'Don't mind if I do.' Without invitation, the pirate snatched the glass with a grubby paw and gulped down its contents. A trickle of red wine ran down his pointed beard. To Theodora, it looked like blood.

'There is one final task, and you shall have what you ask,' her father said.

Theodora's heart stilled.

Horace went on to tell Goldman about the Fisherman, instructing him to go with his guards in the morning to fetch Arisa and Takai, but also to 'take care' of the man who was apparently a threat to Horace's unnamed plans.

Her father and the pirate shook hands, sealing Theodora's fate.

31

*A*risa didn't want to speak. Breaking the silence might ruin whatever was happening between her and Takai. As they sat hand in hand, she could finally admit it to herself: she had fallen completely under his spell.

While there were many things that remained unresolved, the magic of the night had made Arisa believe there was no obstacle that could keep them apart. Tonight, they could forget their differences and the uncertain future that lay ahead. So she wouldn't speak. She wouldn't taint this moment. Instead, she let her thoughts get lost in the firelight.

She would have remained like that indefinitely, had it not been for an unwelcome interruption. A man in farmer's dress, a rooster mask hanging from his neck, staggered past their table, making an unsteady beeline for Sergei, who was standing nearby. The man lurched up to the rebel leader, thumping his back and offering a crude greeting.

'What you got planned for that bastard…Horace,' he slurred, 'and his puppet…the King?'

Arisa felt Takai's hand tighten in hers.

'We're gonna flatten them,' the man continued. 'I'm ready to go now.'

He punched the air a few times, before falling over, to the amusement of the crowd. The farmer righted himself again.

'There's no time to waste…Serg-eiii.' He wobbled. 'We should attack straight away.'

The Fisherman was on his feet and had edged closer to the group, as Sergei attempted to placate the man.

'I admire your enthusiasm,' the rebel leader said, 'but while the King continues to be generous to the people, and provides work for our displaced countrymen, we have no quarrel with him.'

The farmer stabbed Sergei's chest with a pudgy finger. 'You're as yellow-bellied as the King.'

The part of Sergei's face that could be seen turned crimson. He shoved the farmer away. The man stumbled backward, falling toward Arisa and Takai. A murky smell of ale smacked her in the face.

Takai intercepted his fall, pushing the man back upright. 'Watch your step!'

The farmer reared up and raised his fists in challenge to Takai, before his unfocused eyes found Arisa.

'Evening, misss.' He made to tip a long-lost hat. 'You fancy a dance?'

'Leave her be,' the Fisherman growled from behind the farmer.

'Oi…Fisherman…How did…you get there? I'm takin' this – *hic* – lass – *hic* – for a dance.' He waved a flailing arm at Arisa.

'You'll do nothing but leave us,' Takai said, 'and go sober up. Somewhere else.'

The farmer turned his ruddy face toward Takai and squinted suspiciously. 'And who are you?'

'I'm someone you shouldn't mess with.'

Takai had stood to his full height, and Arisa feared he was about to reveal his identity. Thankfully, the Fisherman stepped in and grabbed the farmer by the shoulder.

'Enough!'

The music stopped mid-song. Every eye was on them.

'And who are your friends, Fisherman?'

The man, even in his drunkenness, appeared suddenly alert. Arisa noticed the Fisherman's grip tighten on his shoulder, until the man winced under the vice-like pressure.

'As you say, they are my friends. It would be wise not to bother them any further.'

After a moment's consideration, the farmer grunted and threw his arms back to indicate he was done. The Fisherman released him, letting the man stagger back into the shadows.

'Aren't we all here to enjoy ourselves? Let's have some music,' the Fisherman cried out to the band.

The musicians broke into a lively song with heavy drum beats. A woman sang with a raw savageness that quickly drew the crowds back in, diverting the attention away from Arisa and Takai.

'I suggest you two try to fit in a little.' The Fisherman pointed to the groups of dancers gathered in front of the musicians. 'Get out there. Have a dance.'

A fiddle had joined in, and pipes, both matching the fast beat of the tambours. The stomping of feet on the hard ground was deafening as the revellers immersed themselves in the music.

Arisa had become so accustomed to the refined and formal dances at court, she'd forgotten the carefree nature of this simpler kind of dancing. There was no choreographed line to display fancy footwork, twists and twirls. Instead there was much clapping of hands and spinning arm-in-arm in circles. Everyone danced until they were completely out of breath. It wasn't beautiful to watch. But it was an expression of pure joy.

The Fisherman prodded her gently on the shoulder. 'Go on, get out there.'

'Come on.' She grabbed Takai's hand and dragged him to join the other dancers. He started to protest, but she would hear nothing of it.

They negotiated their way to the centre and tried to imitate those around them. Arisa had experienced similar dancing in Obira City and was able to lead Takai. It didn't take him long to abandon himself to the music, throwing his head back in laughter, linking arms with the other dancers.

At one point, Arisa was sure she recognised the wild red hair of Lina, spinning arm-in-arm with someone nearby. It was hard to tell with the masks they were wearing, but she thought the woman smiled back at her. Arisa resolved to seek her out later, and if it was Lina, she would tell her the good news about Cynfor.

All too soon, the song came to an end, and she and Takai spun uncontrollably into each other's arms. Trying to catch her breath, Arisa was relieved when a ballad followed.

Takai pulled her closer to him and they fell into the slower rhythm. She closed her eyes and laid her head against his chest, getting lost in the music and the lyrics.

'We are not of one world,
Our thoughts are not the same;
You think you know it all,
So sure of who to blame.

But how much do we know?
How much can we learn?
I want to reach out to you,
Knowing I'll be burned.

Our differences can't divide us;
I'm drawn to you every day.
None of it makes sense –
You're close, but far away.

I am awake, yet it's a dream;
My enemy and my friend.

I find it hard to understand,
But I'll follow you till the end.

My heart is open to hope.
A hope that flows through you,
A river I want to swim in –
It's too good to be true.

Doubts crowd my thoughts,
Crashing down on me like waves.
I must give myself to you
So I can be saved.

In your arms I can't fight you.
I cannot back away.
I'll be swept up in the torrent,
If only you would stay.'

The music stopped. Arisa opened her eyes to find Takai staring wordlessly at her. She wondered – no, she *hoped* that he would kiss her. She was sure he wanted to. She moved her face closer to his—

Pain shot up the back of her heel. Arisa yelped, turning around to find the drunk farmer's glassy eyes on her.

'There you are, lass – *hic*.' He clasped her arm and pulled her toward him. 'Come with me for a spin.'

Takai reached out and prised the farmer's hands away. 'Leave her be.'

'Off with you, boy. The girl is with me.'

'Over my dead body.'

The farmer raised his fists unsteadily. 'Let's see 'bout that.'

'I'm not fighting you.' Takai turned his back on the man and made to lead Arisa away.

The farmer shoved him in the back.

Takai stumbled forward. He regained his footing and held up his fists—

'No!'

Arisa's protest was futile. She was ushered off the dance floor, and a space was cleared for the pair.

Panic coursed through her veins. The farmer might have been drunk, but that was the only advantage Takai had. His opponent was a heavyset man, with a tree trunk of a neck and meaty paws for hands. Years of working in the fields had made him more muscle than anything else.

He flicked Takai's fists out of the way as if they were nothing but a pesky fly, and wrapped him in a tight bear hug, lifting the Prince off his feet.

Takai brought his fists down hard on the man's head. The blow sent the farmer off balance enough for him to drop Takai to the ground. The Prince stood up and returned to his fighting stance. The farmer righted himself and charged toward Takai, who side-stepped, as Arisa had seen him do many times in swordplay with Sar. The crowd laughed as the farmer went flying into the crowd. Takai egged them on, acknowledging the cheers.

He didn't notice the farmer getting back onto his feet.

'Watch out!' she cried out in warning, but it was too late. The farmer had charged again, this time picking Takai up and throwing him into the crowd. Takai's mask went flying through the air.

Arisa rushed to retrieve the mask, knowing they were only seconds away from being discovered. The Fisherman appeared as if from nowhere and shoved his way through the crowd to confront the farmer.

'I told you not to make trouble for my guests. You fight my friends, you fight me.'

'Fisherman,' the farmer growled, 'my quarrel isn't with you.'

'But it is now.'

All eyes were on the Fisherman, giving Arisa a chance to

help a dazed Takai to his feet and lead him into the safety of the shadows.

The farmer ran hard at the Fisherman, but in one smooth action the Fisherman flipped him onto his back. He lifted the farmer into the air and spun him over his head, as if the man were nothing more than a twig. The crowd broke into hysterical laughter.

There was no question in Arisa's mind now. The Fisherman was a warrior.

He dropped the groaning farmer into a bale of hay and moved swiftly toward them. 'Time to leave.'

Takai and Arisa didn't argue. Together, they rushed to keep up with the Fisherman's pace as they left the festival behind.

akai was on edge after seeing the Fisherman fight. Who exactly had he and Arisa entrusted their safety to? He watched the man as he walked ahead of them, high up on the mountain path. The Fisherman was leading the way with a torch, and in the light thrown by the flames, Takai recognised the unmistakable gait of a warrior. He had seen warriors in his time, but none as impressive as this man. The Fisherman had a certain alertness about him, as if every sense were trained on its surroundings, anticipating any potential danger.

Takai's eyes kept flicking to the man's calf, where his fishing knife was sheathed. Its metallic rivets glinted back at him in the moonlight. Takai knew if the Fisherman intended them harm, they didn't stand a chance. He must gain control of the situation and get to the bottom of who the man was. He had to act when the Fisherman least expected it.

He had to act now.

Takai sprung forward and grabbed the knife from its sheath, holding it out in front of him.

The Fisherman spun back toward him. His stance was deceptively relaxed, but Takai knew he was ready to pounce.

'Takai!' Arisa cried. 'What are you doing?'

Takai stayed focused on the Fisherman. 'Who are you?'

'I told you. I'm the Fisherman.' The man's voice was terrifyingly calm.

'No fisherman I know can overcome a man as easily as you just did.'

'You're right.' The Fisherman held up his hands in surrender and smiled, and in one swift movement he had dropped the torch, reached out, twisted Takai's arm and retrieved the knife. He pulled Takai back into his chest and held the blade to his neck.

'No!' Arisa cried. 'Please stop—'

The Fisherman didn't acknowledge her appeal. 'Are you really sure you want to know who I am?'

Takai felt a trickle of warm blood run down his neck as the point of the knife broke his skin. 'Oh, yes. I'm sure,' he said through gritted teeth.

The Fisherman released him with a laugh. 'I suppose you will learn the truth, sooner or later. Yes. I used to be a warrior. A knight, in fact.'

Takai moved quickly out of the Fisherman's reach and rubbed the blood from his neck where the knife cut him. 'Impossible. Every one of my father's knights is known to me.'

'You don't know me, but I know you. I was at the castle when you were born. I was there when your mother and father got married. I was there when...' His eyes shifted to Arisa.

'You lie,' Takai said.

'How do you think I knew you on the shore? I haven't been to the city for years, but you are the spitting image of your mother. Actually, you're the spitting image of your grandfather, Arlo, the great Ivanian King.'

Takai's face flushed with anger. How dare the Fisherman pretend he was acquainted with Takai's family?

'I don't know what you're playing at, or what you want from us, but I demand to know who you really are.'

The Fisherman laughed again. There was something eerily familiar about his manner. 'I'm Elos.'

Takai heard Arisa gasp. There was only one Elos Takai knew of…Sar's father. But that man was long dead.

'You shall not use a great warrior's name for your own wicked gain. Elos died on a mission for the King.'

'Yes, that is exactly what you're meant to believe. My so-called mission was to kill the Kengian Prince, Alik.'

'*You* killed Alik?' Arisa's voice and whole body appeared to shake. 'It was you?'

'I said it was my *mission* to kill him.'

'But why would you do such a thing? What harm could he have done to the King…to Lamore?' Arisa cried. 'He had come to broker peace between Lamore, Ivane and Kengia. He didn't deserve to die.'

'Arisa,' the Fisherman said. 'I suspect you know as well as I do that Horace wanted Alik out of the way. He hated the Prince from the moment Alik arrived in the kingdom. He begrudged Alik's friendship with the King. When relations began to fail with Ivane, and the blood moon appeared, Horace saw his opportunity to use the prophecy as a means for Lamore to turn on all Kengians.'

Takai balled his fists. He didn't understand why this man was making up such elaborate tales. 'What are you talking about? Alik was a treacherous magician. He didn't want peace. He tried to bewitch my father and take power for himself and Kengia. He was the one in the Water Catcher prophecy that would bring death and destruction to Lamore.'

'That is what you have been led to believe,' the Fisherman said. 'Since the blood moon was the first sign of the prophecy, Horace wanted to convince everyone that Alik, and all Kengians, posed a threat to the kingdom. That is how Horace induced the King to order the Prince's death and encourage the people to hunt down Kengians. It wasn't difficult to persuade your father – he was as superstitious as he was ambitious. Once

Alik was gone, they knew there would be no protection over the mountain passage. It would leave Kengia open to invasion. It was an irresistible proposition for the King.'

Arisa was nodding, as if she had already heard this account. But Takai shook his head.

'Prince Alik left to go home when peace negotiations with Ivane failed, and he was caught up in the blood moon massacre. The massacre that was precipitated by the people, who, understandably, mistrusted Kengians. It was not my father's doing.'

'Do you really believe that?' the Fisherman asked.

Takai didn't know what he believed anymore. Arisa, though, appeared to be hanging off the Fisherman's every word.

'What happened to Alik?'

'There was an order to take him into custody, but he escaped.'

Her brow furrowed. 'The Prince never escaped. He died.'

'He did escape. I know this, because I helped him.'

'What?' Takai was struggling to absorb the absurdity of the man's claims. 'Why would you help him? You say you were a knight. You were duty-bound to the King.'

'I had a difficult choice to make. To uphold my promise to be loyal to the King, I would have to break my knight's oath to be fair and just. Alik was an innocent man. Ivane and Kengia were never ours to take. Helping Alik escape was the only honourable choice.'

'So now you're saying he escaped?' Takai demanded.

'He did. And I was ordered to find him, and kill him.'

'So you tracked him down and...?' Arisa's voice was shaking.

'I found him, but I didn't kill him. I tried to help him.'

She shook her head. 'It doesn't make sense.'

'I helped him as much as I could,' the Fisherman's face contorted, 'but he made a careless decision.'

'What decision?'

'It doesn't matter,' the Fisherman looked away, 'because the

Prince died anyway. Despite my best efforts to save him, he became a victim of the blood moon massacre. So the passage into Kengia was closed.'

Takai couldn't contain his indignation a moment longer. 'And we're supposed to believe this ridiculous story?'

'I believe him,' Arisa said in a quiet voice.

'But what of you?' Takai demanded of the Fisherman. 'If you're Elos, like you say you are, why didn't you return to the castle? Why didn't you return to your son? You abandoned Sar. He thinks you're dead.'

The Fisherman turned back to face them. 'I couldn't return.' A flicker of pain crossed his face. 'They would have made me lead the invasion into Ivane. I knew your mother. I respected her and her people. It didn't sit right with me. Besides, if they discovered I had helped Alik in his escape, and had failed my mission, there would have been consequences. While I didn't fear what they would do to me, I feared what would happen to Sar.'

Arisa laid her hand on the man's arm. 'Which is why you gave him to Gwyn for protection?'

'I knew before I started that my actions would put Sar at risk, which is why I went into hiding. If they thought I was dead, Sar would be safe.'

'You're lying,' Takai spat. 'I don't know why you've told this elaborate tale. I know not your motivations, but you're a liar.'

'I may be many things…' The Fisherman's face was threateningly close to Takai's now. 'But I'm not a liar.'

Takai stood his ground, not so much as flinching at the Fisherman's proximity. 'If what you say is true, you shirked your orders and duty to the King. You're a liar, or a traitor and a deserter – you pick.'

'I chose my duty to protect my son over my duty to the King.' The Fisherman's hands clenched by his sides. 'But I'm not a traitor to Lamore. What I did was in the best interests of my country and its people. *Your* people. Leaving my son was the price that had to be paid.'

'All that sacrifice for nothing.' Arisa's silver eyes were a lake of tears. 'The Prince died anyway.'

'Not for nothing, Arisa. I made a choice – the only choice I could have made. The right one.'

There was a familiarity in the Fisherman's voice now, an immovable sense of conviction that struck Takai. And there was something in the Fisherman's expression – a raw honesty that reminded him of Sar. How had he been so ignorant? He did know this man…or at least, part of him.

'You *are* Sar's father,' he murmured.

The Fisherman – Elos – grunted. 'So you believe me now?'

'I have only heard one other person speak about honour in the way you do. Your son.'

Elos's expression softened. 'He's a good man, then?'

'The best of men.'

'He is,' Arisa said. 'The best.'

Takai pushed aside the small twinge in his chest as Arisa spoke so highly of his friend. 'But I don't understand why you're telling us all of this,' he said. 'Why, after all this time?'

'There is war coming, and I won't be able to stand by much longer. I'll have to pick a side once again, and it won't be possible to hide my identity when that happens,' Elos replied. 'Hopefully, after all this is done, I might be able to get to know the son I left behind.'

'Pick a side? Do you mean in a war with the Northemers?'

Elos shook his head.

'The rebels?' Arisa asked. 'Is that what you and Sergei were discussing tonight?'

'Sergei wanted to know who you two were. He suspected you were spies sent by the King. I tried to reassure him that he has nothing to fear while the Queen is by the King's side. But he made some reference to having to act before it's too late. He says Horace has some sort of plan that will change the whole state of play, and that he would know when he had to act. That there would be a signal.'

Takai noticed Arisa clutching her neck, reaching for where her medallion usually hung. A nervous twitch he instantly recognised.

'Arisa, do you know what Sergei is talking about?'

She shook her head unconvincingly. The only other time she had been this evasive with him had been when he'd asked her about Erun's work—

That was it.

'Arisa, has Erun figured out how to deliver on his promise to the Secretary?' He didn't want to mention firesky in front of Elos. Sar's father or not, Takai didn't entirely trust him.

Arisa didn't answer.

Elos's brows knitted. 'Laurel told me what Erun has been forced to work on. Is it related to the signal?'

Arisa remained silent.

'Your guardian hasn't succeeded, has he?' Takai was desperate to know if there was a chance Horace would get what he needed to regain power over the King.

She shook her head. 'Erun will never hand over his secrets.'

'You can't underestimate Horace,' Elos said. 'He will get what he wants at any cost.'

Takai nodded in agreement.

'I need to go back to speak to Laurel. Potentially using firesky as a signal isn't worth the risk.' So Elos knew of Horace's plans after all. 'There must be another way to help the rebels and enact the prophecy.'

'The prophecy can never come to being,' Arisa said. 'You should be more worried about what will happen if Horace gets his hands on firesky.'

Elos frowned. 'Stick to the path. I'll catch up with you both soon.' He turned and headed back to the festival.

Arisa looked out across Lamore and the night sky hanging over Obira in the distance, as if she were searching for answers among the stars. As much as Takai cared for her, he knew she was hiding the truth from him, and he needed to know what it was. The time for secrets was over.

'Erun hasn't succeeded, has he?' he pressed.

Arisa bit her lip and turned to him. Her silver eyes swam with tears.

Takai should have been worried about the implications of Erun uncovering the secrets to firesky. His mind should have been on what that meant for his kingdom – but suddenly, all he could think of was her.

His hand instinctively went to her cheek, wet with tears. Arisa leant into his touch, her eyes never leaving his. He raised his other hand to cup her face, and before he realised what was happening, he was drawing her lips to his—

The moment their lips touched, there was an explosion of light and sound.

Takai drew back from her wordlessly. His gaze went to the distant sky, suddenly awash with colourful light. There were flashes of reds, yellows and oranges, and muffled booming noises that came from far away – from the direction of Obira City and the castle.

Firesky.

33

A drastic plan had formed in Theodora's mind to deal with the pirate once and for all. A plan that grated against her very core, but was the only way she could be sure she wouldn't have to marry her father's vile spy.

She arrived at the Queen's rooms to find the presence and privy chambers unguarded. At first she thought the Queen must be elsewhere, but the sound of excited voices within said otherwise. Theodora cautiously opened the privy chamber door and let herself in. Her eyes went immediately to the Queen, Gwyn and Willem, peering out a window that overlooked the Queen's gardens and the southern castle grounds. None of them had noticed her arrival. There was no sign of Erun or Sar.

What could they be looking at?

Theodora's question was answered by a great explosion of lights and colours in the sky. The visual spectacle was only equalled by the deafening sound that accompanied each burst of light.

'Firesky.' Willem pointed frantically out the window. 'It's *firesky*.'

Firesky? Why would the healer launch it? Why now, when

248

Arisa was safely away from the castle? What did this mean for Theodora's leverage over him?

'I can't believe Erun did it,' Gwyn said. 'There has been a blood moon, and now firesky. The prophecy will be as foretold.'

Simpleton, Theodora thought. Her father had made sure that there never could be a Water Catcher.

'I just hope it was worth the risk,' the Queen said darkly.

'As Erun said, he will never help Horace weaponise it,' Willem said.

'Do you think it worked?' Gwyn asked.

Theodora looked out the window, hoping to see an explanation for Erun's actions materialise in the night sky, but there was nothing other than a few wisps of smoke remaining from the fizzled-out light.

Such an obvious display, she thought. The sky was remarkably clear. Firesky must have been visible from miles away, maybe as far as the lowlands…or further.

The wheels in Theodora's mind turned over.

It's a signal.

To whom? Arisa? Someone else? She should speak to her father about it – but surely he had seen the same display, and Theodora had more important business to deal with.

She cleared her throat, revelling in the three wide-eyed gazes that fell on her.

'What are you doing here?' Gwyn snapped with an admirable sense of authority, given her situation.

'I'm here to help you.'

The Queen scoffed. 'I'm not sure spying for your father is much help to us at all.'

'But I'm not here on my father's account.'

'What, then?' asked Gwyn.

Theodora made a tutting sound. 'Really, you should be grateful I have even bothered to bring this information to you.'

'Out with it, Theodora,' Willem said.

She told them about the unscrupulous pirate who was being

sent with Horace's guards to ensure Arisa was brought back to the castle, and delivered into her father's custody. To serve her purposes, Theodora added her own embellishment – that Goldman had been told to use 'whatever force was necessary'. She told them how the pirate had also been instructed to kill the fisherman who'd helped Arisa and Takai. She was taking a gamble that this fisherman would dispatch of her pirate problem, based on what she had seen of the man and her father's suspicion that he was a warrior.

'Why are you telling us this? I thought you hated Arisa,' Gwyn said.

Theodora gave a simpering smile. 'Let's just say my dislike of the pirate is even greater.'

'I believe her,' Willem said. 'I know of this pirate. He is the one who held Guthrie and Sir Marcus for ransom and then took the Northem leader's brother as a hostage. He isn't a man to be trifled with.'

'Then we must send someone we can trust with this pirate,' the Queen said, 'to warn the Fisherman and make sure Takai and Arisa are not harmed.'

Gwyn cast a scrutinising look at Theodora, as if trying to see whether she had lied. Eventually, she nodded. 'We'll send Klaus. He can make sure Arisa is taken to safety and bring Takai back.'

A self-satisfied smile formed on Theodora's face. She had succeeded on two fronts: ridding herself of the pirate, and of Arisa. Perhaps her ambition to be Queen could still come to pass.

'One more thing,' she chirped. 'My father is issuing orders to have the Queen, Gwyn, Erun and Sar under house arrest. So you might want to leave while you still can.'

'I won't be going anywhere until my son is back here and safe,' the Queen replied.

'My duty is to remain at the Queen's side,' Gwyn said.

Theodora shrugged. 'Suit yourself.' Then she left the Queen's rooms, humming a merry tune to herself.

34

*A*risa woke and blinked a few times as her eyes adjusted to the early morning light. It took a moment for her to realise where she was. Scanning the room, she remembered she was on the stretcher in Elos's hut. On the ground was a makeshift bed made of rugs, where she assumed Takai had slept.

Elos and Takai sat at the roughly hewn wooden table, eating a breakfast of bread and pickled fish in silence. Elos, with his dark-rimmed eyes, didn't look like he had slept a wink. At her movement they both glanced at her, before going back to their breakfast.

'Did you find Sergei?' she asked.

Elos shook his head without looking at her.

They were both angry with her. And she didn't blame them. After the firesky display last night, Elos had come running back, and he and Takai had interrogated her. Much of what she said, they'd already guessed. That Erun would have launched firesky as a signal, warning that Horace would be moving against the people. She had confirmed that Sergei would have recognised the signal. They all knew the next logical step was for him to amass and mobilise his rebels.

Elos had returned to the festival to look for the rebel leader and try to prevent him from acting impulsively. Many of the rebels would have been at Ujej, and the majority would not have been in any state to mount an attack. Elos had to convince Sergei they were hopelessly unprepared, no match for any battle against the King's forces.

Takai and Arisa had been left alone. Their previous closeness, the memory of their kiss, had vanished with firesky's final puff of smoke.

'Why didn't you tell me?' Takai had asked, his face screwed up in hurt. 'Why didn't you trust me enough to share Erun's plans?'

'Hardly anyone knew. It was better that way,' she'd insisted. 'Firesky is not the kind of secret you want the whole world to know about.'

'I'm not talking about the whole world. I'm talking about me. Trusting *me* with your secrets. Do I mean that little to you?'

'No, Takai. You mean a lot to me, and given time I would have—'

'I could have helped,' he cut across. 'I could have made sure Erun never needed to use it as a signal. I could have helped keep it from Horace.'

'Once your mother was back in the King's good graces, we were sure firesky was safe. We were sure your father would never allow Horace to act against Erun or the rebels. Erun was prepared to risk his life before giving the secrets over. He still is.'

'But seemingly there is a good reason for him to launch the signal.'

'Something significant must have occurred. There must be real danger.'

'And now danger is heading toward the castle and my family.'

Arisa had nodded miserably.

'Don't you realise the consequences of this?' Takai had

demanded. 'You said it yourself – now that Horace has seen firesky, he will stop at nothing to weaponise it.'

'Of course I realise that. It's how I know something terrible must have happened.'

'And something even more terrible will happen.'

'No. I don't believe that. Just because Erun has revealed firesky, it doesn't mean he will give the secrets to Horace.'

Takai's eyes had widened in horror. 'The book! Horace already has the secrets, doesn't he?'

'Horace does have the Firemaster's book, but it is protected by a spell. He would need Erun's help to reveal the secrets, and to weaponise firesky. And my guardian will *never* do that,' she had cried. 'He would die first.'

'And die he may have to, because Horace will do whatever it takes to get his hands on firesky.'

Arisa hadn't argued.

'I can't believe this,' Takai had muttered. 'I can't believe you hid this from me, and put my home and my family at risk.'

'I'm sorry, Takai, but I wasn't sure what we were.'

His response had been filled with venom. 'There is no *we*. We are nothing, Arisa, and there is nothing between us. My only concern is protecting my people – that is, the ones who are not currently taking up arms against my family.'

Takai had stormed off outside the hut, and Arisa had sat up waiting for him. But he hadn't returned, at least not before she fell asleep in the wee hours of the morning.

Now, she picked up a piece of bread and nibbled on it distractedly. She was worried about what Takai might be planning to do.

'Takai, I don't think it's safe for you to return to the castle.'

He didn't look at her. 'Of course I'm going back to the castle. That is where my duty lies.'

'But it's not safe. Please don't.'

'Arisa, it is you who shouldn't return.'

The jagged edge in Takai's voice cut through her. 'I can take care of myself.'

'It's not that I'm worried about.'

The words were like a stab in her chest.

'If Horace gets hold of you, he will have what he needs to force Erun to comply and weaponise firesky.'

Elos grunted between bites of food. 'Erun would mean for you to go to safety.'

Arisa knew her guardian and that he wouldn't want her to return to the castle. She knew launching firesky was as much a signal to her as it was to the rebels, but she couldn't turn her back on everyone.

'I will not abandon Erun, and the people I care about at the castle.'

Takai finally looked at her, his eyes unblinking, his shoulders set determinedly. 'Erun may be prepared to give his own life, but he wouldn't be willing to put you in harm's way. You can't go back.'

'That is exactly why I need to go back. I can't let him make that sacrifice.'

Arisa meant it; she would do everything in her power to save Erun. She felt the flicker of familiar darkness reignite inside her, remembering how far she had been willing to go to protect what she believed in. She'd been willing to kill the King. She would kill anyone to save Erun if she had to.

Takai stood up and clasped her wrists. His eyes were filled with unexpected concern. 'Arisa, you have to stay safe.'

She jutted out her chin. 'I'm going to the castle with you.'

'No. We need to get you out of here, to safety. We should assume Horace's men are already on their way to make sure you go back.'

'Takai is right,' Elos put in. 'I will take you to Laurel's home.'

'No!' Arisa put her hands on her hips. 'You cannot make me.'

The distinct sound of hooves reverberated outside the hut, interrupting their argument. Elos leapt up and concealed a knife in the arm of his tunic.

'Wait here.'

Arisa and Takai moved soundlessly to the window and peeked through the gaps in the shutters. Arisa could make out a cart, pulled by draught horses and laden with bales of wool. Two peasants sat at the front of the cart; a man was on horseback beside them. The driver stared wordlessly at Elos before saying something that couldn't be made out, then handed him a bundle of cloth. On closer inspection, Arisa could see a sword tucked under one of the men's cloaks. She recognised the driver as Klaus and his companion on the cart as one of the Queen's regular guards.

Elos backed away, his eyes never leaving the man on horseback, until he was safely inside the hut again. 'Your escort has arrived.'

Arisa took a deep breath. 'Alright. Time to go.'

Takai spun toward her and made to protest.

'I'm going,' she said, as forcefully as possible.

'If you insist on going back to the castle, I believe you will be safe with that man.' Elos pointed at Klaus.

'We will be,' she said. Takai didn't contradict her.

'After you're gone, I'll go after Sergei,' Elos went on. 'I may still be able to catch him and the rebels.'

'What about *that* man?' Takai pointed to the one on horseback.

Elos grunted. 'He may be dressed as a farmer, but he's not like any I've seen before. Apparently, he has some…business with me.'

Takai narrowed his eyes as he looked at the man through the shutters. 'I think I've come across him before…I'm not sure where.'

'Me too…I think I saw him in Obira City once.' Arisa shivered as the man stared at the hut, a sneer forming on his lips, his gold teeth gleaming in the silvery sunlight. She knew she'd seen him before, but couldn't place him.

Elos was unperturbed. 'Here – put these on.' He handed over the bundle of cloth Klaus had given him, which turned out to be two hooded cloaks in simple peasant style.

Arisa and Takai pulled on the cloaks and the trio walked outside. As she reached the cart, Arisa turned back and cast a grateful look at Elos.

'Thank you. For all of your help. We're indebted to you.'

'Take care.' Elos reached out and hugged her awkwardly. Then he bent down and whispered in her ear. 'Remember what you've been told. You must *know* it. It's more important than ever.'

She would have asked him to explain what he meant, but Elos had already stepped away to shake Takai's hand.

Klaus gave Arisa a reassuring smile as he helped them up onto the cart. She and Takai sat side-by-side among the bales of wool, legs dangling over the end.

'Arisa?' Klaus said tentatively. 'You look...' His eyes were fixed on her silver ones.

'Kengian.' She smiled broadly. 'I look Kengian.'

It felt good – amazing, in fact – to say it openly for the first time in her life. But a sad echo reached out from her childhood: her brave silver-eyed friend, Rea, who'd been taken because of her Kengian identity. A constant ghost that reminded Arisa of her duty to always do what she could to protect her fellow Kengians.

Klaus shook his head to himself. 'As I've said before, the less I know about you and Erun, the better.'

She smiled at him. 'You're a wise man.'

'And I, for one, am glad to see you here, Klaus,' Takai said. 'I was sure Horace would have tried to send his own men.'

Klaus dropped his voice. 'He did, but one of the Queen's guards and I took their places before we left the castle. I'm afraid there are two guards who will wake up this morning with quite a headache. No doubt punishment will await us when we return.'

'It's alright,' Takai said. 'I'll get my mother to speak on your behalf.'

Klaus shook his head. 'I'm sorry, Your Highness, but the Queen is no longer in the King's favour. Horace has the King's ear again. He has stopped all work on the hospital. Horace has been made Lord Commander and he and Guthrie are mobilising forces against the rebels. He's in the process of declaring Lamore a state of martial law.'

'What?' Takai's shoulders stiffened. 'He can't.'

'He already has.'

Arisa's stomach churned. *This* was why Erun had launched the signal. 'What of the Queen?' she asked.

'She has been placed under arrest in her rooms, along with Erun, Gwyn...and Sar, as soon as they find him.'

'For *what?*' Takai demanded.

'I don't know, Your Highness. But we have quite a journey ahead of us, and I'm afraid it won't go quickly. We didn't want to bring attention to ourselves, so we picked up this cart and horses from Dunhin. They keep a dreadfully slow pace.'

'I understand, but I was hoping to get word back to the castle about some potential trouble. Could I get the man on horseback to take an urgent message? I understand he has other business, but this is more important.'

'He's one of Horace's men, who fortunately doesn't realise that I am not. He has business with your *friend*.' Klaus glanced back at Elos.

'The Fisherman?' Takai prompted.

'Yes...the *Fisherman*.'

'What about?' Arisa asked. Klaus shrugged, but she felt as if he knew a lot more than he was letting on.

'It's alright. Let's get back as quick as we can,' Takai said.

'Of course. But first, we have to get Arisa to safety,' Klaus said.

Arisa crossed her arms. 'I'm going back to the castle.'

'But your guardian—'

'I'm coming with you.'

Klaus looked to Takai, who shrugged. 'No point arguing with her.'

'If you say so.' Klaus hurried back to his seat at the front of the cart and urged the horses into action.

Arisa waved goodbye to Elos, but his watchful eyes were on Horace's man. She wondered whether she would see him again, or Laurel, and whether they would ever explain what they meant about her *knowing*.

ARISA TRIED to lose herself in the jolting movement of the cart, and the sunlight as it spread across the Nymoi Alps and warmed her body. She forced herself to push aside the terrible thoughts of what awaited them at the castle, and the danger they were walking into. Nothing, though, could distract her from one thing – one person. Takai.

'What shall we talk about?' she asked him.

'Huh?' Takai sounded as if he were a million miles away.

'We can't sit the whole way in silence. We'll drive ourselves crazy thinking about what we're going back to.'

Takai frowned. 'I'm not sure what you want me to say.'

Her heart plummeted. Had everything they had experienced together meant nothing? Was everything going to go back to the way it had been before?

'What do you mean, you don't know what to say? I could think of a thousand things to say.'

'Yes, I'm sure you could.' His words were acidic.

She bristled. 'What about Sar's father being alive? What about firesky and what it means? What about the Shaman and the things she said?'

Takai's brow furrowed. 'No, Arisa. I don't know what to say

because I don't know where to start. Everything I believed in has turned out to be wrong or a lie. I don't know what is fact and what is fiction. The truth is clouded in secrets.'

'I have no secrets from you.'

He arched a brow.

'Not anymore,' she insisted. 'You know everything.'

'Do I? What about what happened yesterday, when we went over the falls? I nearly drowned. I should have died. There was *light* coming from you. Then you conjured up a waterspout. Was it magic? Is it going to happen to you again?'

Arisa heaved a sigh. 'I don't know. Truly, I don't. I'm hoping Erun can explain…maybe he knows something.'

Takai shook his head to himself. 'Erun and his secrets aside, when it comes to Elos…I believe he is who he says he is, but I don't fully trust him. He betrayed the King's orders. He helped a dangerous Kengian escape.'

Arisa squared her shoulders. 'A Kengian Prince accused of things he didn't do.'

Takai waved his hand, as if to say it was a moot point. 'Now we know about Elos, we have to tell Sar. But once people know Elos is alive, and what he did, imagine what danger that puts them both in.'

'We can tell Sar, but it doesn't mean anyone else needs to know.'

Takai sighed heavily. 'There you go again with your secrets. They seem to come so easily to you.' He continued, not giving her a chance to defend herself. 'On top of all that, my father will be forced to launch his forces against his own people. Many of whom are not our enemy.'

Arisa nodded, realising the heavy burden Takai faced.

'So many things have changed over the last few months,' he mused. 'Actually, ever since I met you.'

She wasn't sure if she should be flattered by this. 'What will you do?'

'I will talk to Father. As soon as we get past this immediate threat of attack. I will make him forgive my mother, for whatever he thinks she has done. I will convince him to pardon the rebels. I have thought a lot about it, and I will urge him to maintain the alliance with Ivane. I will remind him how the Northemers can't be trusted after invading the castle, and how they have that girl rumoured to have unusual powers; that Horace's plan to join forces with them would lead to disaster. With Ivane – and perhaps even Kengia – we can fight the Northemers together. And somehow, I will persuade my father not to weaponise firesky…ever. No one can safely possess that sort of power. We must have peace at all costs, and help our people. They deserve my respect and protection, even if they're planning to attack my family.'

Arisa had never heard him speak with such conviction. But his tone soon changed, and he sounded as uncertain as she felt.

'I hope we're not too late. I hope my father will listen to me.'

'We'll figure it out,' she assured him.

'*We?*'

'I thought you may want some help,' Arisa offered, her voice just above a whisper.

'I don't *want* your help, Arisa.'

She felt as if a knife had been plunged into her chest.

'There are still so many secrets between us,' Takai went on. 'They form a wall I don't think either of us fully understand.'

He paused. Arisa dropped her gaze, trying to hide her pain. Then—

'It is a wall we must conquer,' he said. 'I have tried to fight this for too long, and argue it away with logic, but it's hopeless. I don't *want* your help. I *need* it. I need you, Arisa.'

She looked up again, daring to meet Takai's gaze with her tear-filled eyes. 'What do you mean?'

'I don't have all the answers. I have hardly any. But what I do know is that you must be by my side. I know this with every inch of my being. And together we will work through it.'

Takai clutched her hands in his.

'My admiration for you is beyond words. I am shamed by and in awe of your courage, your determination, your compassion. You believe I can be a better person. The best person. The best King. No one has ever believed in me like you have. But I can only do it…if you're by my side.'

Arisa realised she had been holding her breath. She exhaled shakily. 'I will help you.'

Takai's eyes darted across her face, searching for something. 'I know you will *help* me. But Arisa, I must know – will you *love* me? Do you think you could possibly come to love me? I know I'm not the kind of man you would choose to admire, but I'll spend every waking moment trying to become that person.'

She was stunned into silence. Takai's hands were shaking in hers.

He must have taken her lack of words to mean she needed more convincing, because he continued. 'I know we still have much to learn about each other, and need to fully earn each other's trust. No doubt we will disagree on many matters, on a daily basis, and there are obstacles we will have to overcome – but besides all of that, can you give me the smallest glimmer of hope that you can learn to love me?'

'You *love* me?' Arisa didn't dare to believe it was true.

'Yes. A million times, yes. I love you, Arisa.'

She took a deep breath, trying to absorb what she had heard, and her own feelings. 'For once…' she began hesitantly. She could see Takai hanging on her every word. 'For once I not only agree wholeheartedly with your sentiments…but I can fully reciprocate them.'

Takai's face came alive with light. 'And you reciprocate what, exactly?'

'You must hear the actual words?' she teased.

He nodded earnestly.

Arisa smiled at him. 'I love you, Takai, above all and everything. Is that what you wanted to hear?'

'More than anything,' he replied softly. Takai lifted her chin and pulled her face gently toward his. He pressed his lips to hers – softly at first, like he'd done the night before, and then harder, hungrily.

Tingles ran down Arisa's neck and spine. So this was what it felt like to be in love, and to be loved in return. It was everything. More than she had ever imagined.

The kiss finished all too soon, and they sat with their fingers entwined, keeping their thoughts to themselves. Part of Arisa wished that the trip could go on forever. That they could stay like this and would never have to deal with the frightening realities that lay ahead.

Takai then kissed her again and she let the warm touch of his lips drive away every thought other than the joy she felt in that moment.

MANY KISSES LATER, they reached the city gates – and realised immediately that something was dreadfully wrong.

There were no guards at the entrance gate to the city. In fact, there was no one around at all.

Takai sat up straight, suddenly alert. Klaus slowed the cart, turning to give them an anxious look. The guard beside him had his hand ready on the hilt of his sword.

There was fear in the air. Arisa could almost smell it. It had been the same the night of the last blood moon, and throughout the days that had followed—

A sickening realisation washed over her.

'I remember, Takai. I remember.'

'Remember what?'

'The man on horseback at Elos's hut. I saw him come out of the Lion's Den, the day I first fought Guthrie. The man was in the crowd, but I couldn't forget his face. He was dressed in seagoing clothes. He looked like a—'

'A pirate!' Takai finished. 'Yes, Theodora mentioned she met a pirate one day in her father's rooms…She described him as one of Horace's vile spies. Arisa, he's extremely dangerous.'

'Elos!' Arisa cried out, but it was too late. Right now, they had to come to terms with the dangerously deserted city.

A woman was running toward them, a crying baby in her arms.

'You there. Stop!' the guard beside Klaus shouted, but the woman kept running, not seeming to notice. 'Stop – I order you in the name of the King!' He held his sword out to obstruct her path.

'They've come,' she cried. 'They're here.'

'Who has come?'

'The rebels. They're marching on the castle. No one is safe. They're pillaging and destroying everything in sight.'

'Get to safety,' Takai said, 'as quick as you can.'

The woman ran past them and out the city gates.

'Unhitch the cart,' Takai ordered the guard. 'How fast can these horses go?'

'Not fast at all.'

Takai looked around desperately.

'The other guards' horses,' Arisa called, pointing toward the gatehouse.

All of them were on their feet, looking for the horses. Takai and the guard set off on one side of the gate while Klaus and Arisa searched the other.

That was when she noticed the trail of blood.

Arisa followed it to the lifeless bodies of two guards, slumped against the wall. Klaus ordered her back, but not before the images were embedded in her brain. One guard had a spear sticking from his chest. The other's throat had been cut.

She stood in shock, swallowing back the rising bile in her throat. Takai appeared next to her. He grabbed her by the arm and pulled her to him so she could no longer see the bodies.

'There will be worse to come,' he murmured. 'We need to get to the castle. Here, take one of these.'

He held the reins of two horses in royal regalia, offering one set to Arisa. Sensing the danger, the horses jostled, their nostrils flaring.

Takai gave the other set of reins to Klaus. 'Get back to the castle, as quick as you can, and tell them what is happening.' Klaus mounted the horse and was gone in an instant. 'If it's not too late,' Takai finished.

He turned to the other guard.

'You – find a horse somewhere and go to Iveness. If the army and Guthrie are still there, tell them to come back immediately, and to send word to the forces at Talbot.'

The guard nodded and sprinted away.

Takai was already on the remaining horse. He helped Arisa up in one clean movement, so she was sitting behind him. 'Maybe we can beat the rebels to the castle. If Sergei knows what he's doing, the main contingent will be marching in formation. They will need to take the wider streets, and will be heading uphill.'

'I know the backstreets,' Arisa said. 'I can find us a way.'

She directed Takai, reaching parts of the city where chaos reigned. There were screams in the distance. The sounds of windows being smashed, and people crying out for help, their running footsteps echoing through the streets.

They had to stop and start several times as they wound their way through Obira, backtracking when they needed to avoid being discovered. They were passing through the top part of the city when they caught a glimpse up a side street of a group pulling over a statue of the King. Its head smashed on the stone ground.

Takai pulled up the horse. Arisa could feel his whole body tense.

He spun around and shot her an accusatory look. 'These are your peace-loving Lamorians who don't want war? The people who need my protection and respect?'

'They are driven by desperation,' she cried. 'Don't you see?'

'Yes, I do see. I am beginning to see quite clearly again.' Takai's torso stiffened under her arms. She could almost feel his heart as it hardened against her – or, at the very least, against his people.

'Onward!' Takai dug his heels into the horse's belly. Arisa felt as if it were she who'd been kicked in the stomach.

Had she already lost him?

———————

akai dismounted the horse, leaving Arisa to be helped down by a waiting groom. He wiped the sweat from his brow, allowing himself to take a deep breath. Somehow, they had reached the castle unscathed. With Arisa's knowledge of the city, they had managed to weave their way to safety ahead of the rebels, leaving Obira via something known as the 'smuggler's gate' on the eastern side of the city. From there they had been able to get into the castle grounds through the north-east gate. It was a significant distance from the main gate and could only be accessed by negotiating a rocky outcrop – an impossible route for any large group, but their single horse had made light enough work of it.

Takai had caught a glimpse of the invading force as it gathered at the foot of the hill leading up to the castle. The rebels had taken refuge behind the half-built hospital. There were hundreds of them. Perhaps a thousand. He couldn't be sure. He had wondered how so large a group had gained entry to Obira without being challenged. But he soon realised they were a mix of farmers and peasants, as well as tradesmen from the abandoned hospital site. Some looked like merchants who may have joined the group from the marketplace. Many were riding workhorses and mules unhitched from carts or wagons. They would have looked like the usual crowd making their way to market. In fact, many of them may have already been heading to Obira's marketplace when Sergei had enlisted them along the way. Takai conceded a flicker of admiration for the rebel leader, who must have marched through the night with many of his fellow revellers from the festival.

The rebels, though, were terribly ill-equipped, armed with a ragtag collection of spears, bows, knives, pitchforks, pieces of timber – anything they could get their hands on. They also lacked the organisation one would expect from military-trained forces. But they would still be problematic for the castle.

The main gate had been closed and all the towers and walls were swarming with guards. Takai could not recall a time when the castle had been under attack. He expected they should be able to hold off the rebels until the King's forces made it back to the castle, but at what cost?

Takai's recent change of heart to favour peace and making amends with Lamore seemed a distant memory. His home was under threat from the same people he'd wanted to protect. While he hadn't forgotten about Arisa and Elos, firesky, or what had happened at Riverend Falls, all of it would have to wait. He headed straight toward the main keep, where he expected the King would have established his war room.

'Takai, wait—'

Even now, Arisa's voice could stop him mid-stride.

He turned and met her pleading gaze. The beautiful crea-ture to whom he had declared his heart stood before him, begging him with nothing more than her piercing silver eyes to remember his promise to be just to the people. Takai's heart ached at the thought of displeasing her. He knew that by fulfilling his duty to protect the castle and its inhabitants, he was effectively walking away from Arisa. He wasn't sure if he had the strength to give her up, but it didn't matter. His strength was needed elsewhere.

'I have to go,' he said. 'We have to mount our defence.'

Takai turned away before Arisa could argue.

He raced toward the entrance to the west wing, stopping only when Sar stepped out in front of him, as if he had materialised out of the shadows.

'Takai,' he said. 'Good to see you safe, friend.' He looked over Takai's shoulder in Arisa's direction. 'I really wish Arisa hadn't returned.'

'No time for that. We have to get to work.'

But Sar looked around, as if to see whether he was being watched, and walked straight past Takai, directing his next words to Arisa. 'I have to speak to you.'

'Sar, why aren't you in the war room?' Takai called after him. 'We're under attack.'

Sar's attention was fixed on Arisa. 'Your eyes…' He reached up and touched her face.

Takai's cheeks burned.

'It all makes sense,' Sar said dreamily.

'The rebels!' Takai implored. 'They're nearly at the main gate.'

Sar turned back to him. 'Horace ordered me to be restricted to the Queen's quarters. As soon as they find me, I'll be placed under arrest.'

'Don't worry about that. I will speak to the King.'

'It's no use. Horace is in control.'

'Klaus told us, but surely none of that matters right now—'

'It more than matters. Horace has declared us enemies of the state – your mother, Gwyn, Willem and me.'

'And Erun?' Arisa's voice was small and pinched.

'He is also under arrest. They caught him shortly after we launched firesky.' Sar faced Arisa again. 'Arrest orders have been issued for you as well.'

Takai had to speak to his father. Now. He couldn't let anything happen to those he held dearest. He couldn't let anything happen to Arisa.

'How did Horace manage it?' he asked Sar. 'When we left, my mother had the King's ear.'

'It's a long story, but the King and Queen are no longer reconciled.'

Takai nodded slowly. 'You two need to hide somewhere until this is all sorted.'

'You can trust me to take care of Arisa,' Sar said.

Ignoring the urge he felt to stay with her, Takai sprinted toward the main keep. He had almost reached the stairs that led to the King's apartments and council chambers when he ran headlong into Theodora.

'Takai! Thank goodness you're alright,' she cried. 'My father wants to see you.'

'I'm going straight to *my* father,' he replied. 'I assume they are together, establishing a war council.'

'The King is in his privy chamber, but my father, the *Lord Commander*, has taken charge. I will take you to him.'

Takai's temper flared at the mention of Horace's new title. 'Not now. I will see my father first.'

Theodora narrowed her eyes and scanned the area around them. 'Where's Arisa? I thought I saw her ride in with you.'

'I don't know where she is,' Takai lied.

Theodora pursed her lips. She seemed even more annoyed than usual about Arisa's presence. 'Father will find her soon enough,' she muttered, grabbing Takai by the wrist and trying to steer him up the stairs.

He flung her arm away.

'Please tell me you don't want to go after the ward,' she said. 'There is a near war going on outside the castle walls, no one is prepared, all our lives are under threat, and you're more worried about protecting some commoner.'

'She is no more a commoner than you're a lady,' Takai thundered.

'You're a bigger fool than her,' Theodora snapped. 'You deserve each other.'

Takai's jaw tensed. 'Fool or not, Arisa is a thousand times the woman – no, a thousand times the human being you will ever be. But rest assured, Theodora, I won't shrug off my duties. I will ensure the castle, and you, *my lady*, are protected.'

Takai spun on his heel and marched back in Arisa's direction. He knew he was being irrational, that his duty to the kingdom came first. But he needed to resolve matters with Arisa. What was the point of saving the castle, and his family's reign, if she wasn't by his side?

He had to know whether he had something, or *someone*, to fight for beyond this day.

36

'This way.' Sar led Arisa into the shadows under a set of stairs in the castle's west wing.

'I need to get to Erun,' she insisted, pulling away from him. She didn't have time to waste with whatever Sar had planned.

'We can't go to the Queen's rooms. It's not safe. We have to hide.'

She shook her head vehemently. 'I have to see my guardian.'

'Erun wants you to get to safety.'

'Sar!' She tried to extricate herself from Sar's grip.

'Shh. They'll find us. Arisa – there is something I need to tell you, and no one else can hear it.'

Only then did she notice that Sar was trembling. Whatever the news was, it had shaken this giant of a man, this seasoned warrior, to the core. With a jolt, Arisa remembered where she had just come from – or rather, who she had been with.

'Actually, I have something to tell *you*,' she said.

'It can wait. You must hear me at once.'

Sar reached into his coat and retrieved something. It made a metallic clinking sound as he handed it over.

Arisa squinted in the darkness at the objects in her hand. Kengian coins – three of them, strung together with cord. The cord was fraying at the edges, as if it were extremely old, but otherwise it looked as if it had been well cared for.

She raised the coins closer to her face. Each bore a different symbol – a yew tree seed, a phoenix, a starling – representing the natural elements of earth, fire and air. The only one missing was water.

Water…

The hairs on her arms stood on end. No – it couldn't be.

She flipped the coins over and found a letter on the reverse of each coin: an 'L', an 'I', and a 'K'.

Her fingers froze.

'They're the remaining coins, aren't they?' Sar asked. His face was terrifyingly serious.

Arisa reached into her gown and pulled out her medallion. She opened it to reveal the coin engraved with a koi – the fish symbolising water – and the letter 'A' engraved on the back.

Arisa assembled the letters in her mind.

Alik.

'Where did you get this?' she demanded, holding the string of coins up to Sar.

'It fell from Gwyn's book. The one she carries all the time.'

'The book of Kyprian tales?'

'Yes. It must have been hidden in the spine or something, because I've never seen it before.'

The bud of an idea started to form in Arisa's mind. An idea that petrified her.

'When I saw the coins and remembered your medallion,' Sar said, 'I knew immediately.'

'No, no, no—' She shook her head vigorously, not daring to believe it.

Sar grinned wildly. 'Arisa, if the coin you have is from your father…I think it's reasonable to assume your father was Prince Alik of Kengia.'

Arisa tasted bile rising in her throat as Sar went on.

'And if Gwyn has had the remaining coins all this time…the coins belonging to the Prince…she might be—'

'It can't be true,' she interrupted. 'My mother couldn't have been alive all this time. There must be another explanation.'

Arisa couldn't deny, though, the ring of truth in what Sar said.

'I have to get to Erun,' she murmured. 'I have to get answers.'

Sar put his hands on her shoulders. 'It's not safe.'

'You don't understand,' she cried, wrenching herself free from his grip. 'After all this time, to find out I may actually have a parent who's alive—' Sar's face crumpled, and with a start, Arisa remembered. She put her hands to his face. 'Actually, you may understand.'

Sar cocked his head to the side.

'That is what I had to tell you. It's a long story, but…I met your father, Sar. Well, you met him, too. It was the Fisherman who saved us at Riverend Falls.'

Sar's eyes widened for a moment. Then he clenched his jaw. 'My father is dead. He died on a mission for the King.'

'A mission to kill Alik' – her throat caught on the name – 'but one he couldn't carry out. He went into hiding.'

Sar shook his head. 'That doesn't make sense. Prince Alik died.'

'Yes, but not at your father's hands. Trust me, Sar. I know it sounds incredible, but it's true. Elos is alive.'

Sar slumped to the floor. 'My father is alive?' His voice was barely a whisper.

Arisa knelt before him. 'Yes, he's alive, and he misses you. He had good reason for leaving you, but it kills him that he had to do it.'

Sar's eyes welled up. She wrapped her arms around him like he was a small child. Sar started weeping into his hands, and Arisa held him against her chest, wondering if this was the first time in his adult life he had allowed himself to openly cry—

'So this is what happens when my back is turned!' came a roaring voice.

Takai stood before them, quivering with rage.

Arisa and Sar broke apart and stumbled to their feet. 'Takai, it's not what it looks like,' Sar said, waving his hands to placate the Prince.

'It's exactly as it looks.' Takai clenched his fist and swung out at his friend, hitting him square on the nose.

Sar doubled back, wiping blood from his nostrils. 'Takai, it's nothing.'

Takai ignored him and turned toward Arisa.

'I should have known everything between us was lies. I knew you still had secrets from me, but I had no idea one of them involved a tryst with my best friend.'

'That's not true,' she cried. 'I—'

Takai held his hand up to silence her.

'Thank you for making my choice easy.'

He turned his back on them and walked away.

Choice. Where had she heard that before? Laurel had told Takai he would have to make a choice…Arisa pushed it from her mind. Right now, she had to get through to him. She had to explain.

'Takai!' She made to run after him, but Sar grabbed her arm.

'He can wait. There's something else we have to deal with.'

'What else could there possibly be?'

'Don't you see? If you're Alik's child, you're the last remaining of Kengia's firstborn line. You could be the—'

'Don't say it, Sar. Don't.'

It was too much. The last pieces of the puzzle that was her life were dropping into place – but if what Sar was getting at was the final one, Arisa didn't want to know. She couldn't deal with it.

But…she *had* to know. And only two people could confirm if any of it was true.

She clasped Sar's hand. 'Come on. We have to speak to Erun and Gwyn.'

'We can't go to the Queen's rooms.'

'Sar, I must know. *We* must know the truth.'

After a long pause, he nodded.

THEY ARRIVED breathless outside the Queen's rooms, to be confronted by six open-mouthed guards.

'Sar?' It was one of his own men. The guard's face was a mixture of surprise and embarrassment. 'I'm sorry to say this, but Sar, you're under arrest. And you, too.' He pointed to Arisa. 'Both of you must remain in the Queen's rooms.'

'It's alright. I understand,' Sar assured the guards as they were ushered inside the Queen's privy chamber.

They found the Queen, Gwyn, Erun and Willem holding a silent vigil.

'You're here!' Erun cried as he and Gwyn strode across the room. Erun wrapped Arisa in his arms.

Sofia's brows bunched together. 'Takai – is he alright?'

Arisa disentangled herself from her guardian. 'He's fine.'

'But *why* are you here?' Erun cried. 'Didn't you get the signal? You must have known the dangers. Klaus was supposed to make sure you got to safety.'

'Don't blame Klaus. I made him bring me back,' she responded in clipped tones. 'Is it true?' She looked from Erun to Gwyn.

'Is what true?' Gwyn asked.

'*This!*' Arisa held up the string of coins so Gwyn and Erun could both see. Gwyn's face froze. 'Is this my father's?'

Gwyn glanced at Erun, and he bowed his head. When she answered, her voice was flat.

'It's true.'

It was as if the whole room was spinning. Arisa's head swam. She took a deep breath to try to regain her composure.

'My whole life has been a bigger lie than I thought.'

Erun reached out to her. 'Arisa—'

She stepped unsteadily away from him, still reeling. Every person she cared for, including the only parental figure she had ever known, had betrayed her. She glared at Erun. 'We need to talk, *Uncle Amund*.'

'Amund?' Willem enquired. 'Not like *Prince* Amund?'

Erun winced. 'It's better everyone calls me Erun within these walls.'

'Well?' Arisa was waiting for an explanation from her guardian, but she doubted there was anything any of them could say that would dispel her anger and hurt.

Gwyn reached out for the coins, but Arisa closed her fist around them.

'You're right,' Gwyn said. 'It's time you knew the truth.'

'Tell me everything,' Arisa ordered. 'And I mean everything.'

Erun and Gwyn nodded in unison.

'Arisa, I wasn't exactly truthful when you first came to the castle and asked me if I knew Prince Alik,' Gwyn said. 'I did know him. In fact, I knew him well. We were in love. Only a few people knew. The Queen, Lore. I also told Elos later, but we had to keep it a secret to protect Alik. We couldn't risk Horace finding out. He already begrudged Alik's friendship with the King, and he had feelings for me. And you have to remember – at that time, the prophecy was something that haunted the King. As much as he liked Alik, the fact that he was of Kengia's first-born line – and a potential threat – was never far from his mind.'

Arisa held up her hands, as if to protect herself from what was to come next. Once the words were said, there would be no denying her lineage, and the responsibility that came with it.

Gwyn continued undeterred, the long-unspoken words tumbling from her mouth.

'When the Queen went into confinement with Takai, he wasn't the only baby to be born. I had fallen pregnant with

Alik's child, but we had to keep that a secret as well – even from Alik, at least until we figured out what to do. It was the only way we could protect him and the child.'

'How did you manage to have a child without all the ears and eyes at court finding out?' Arisa demanded.

'It was easy to conceal while the Queen was lying-in. Lore attended us both. The child came a fortnight or so after Takai. On the night of the blood moon. And that child was—'

Blood pounded so loud in her ears that she hoped it would drown out Gwyn's next words. 'Don't say it.'

'It was you, Arisa.' Gwyn's eyes glittered with tears. 'The most beautiful baby girl I had ever seen. Eyes the colour of Shizen Lake. In my joy, I imagined we could live as a family with Alik. That somehow we could make it work.'

'You said yourself the child from the firstborn line would be a threat. How could you be so…' Arisa searched for the right words.

'Naive,' Gwyn supplied. 'I misjudged the situation horribly. Not long before we were due to come out of confinement, we discovered that Horace had used the blood moon to plant seeds of fear in the King's mind. He talked endlessly about the prophecy and claimed Alik was trying to bewitch Delrik. Before we knew it, orders had been issued against Alik, and I knew I could never let anyone know about his child. The Queen and I discussed trying to pass you off as a maid's, but that wasn't possible – not with your silver eyes.'

'What did you do with the baby?' Arisa didn't recognise her own voice as the strangled words squeezed out. 'What did you do with me?'

'After we learnt Alik had disappeared,' Erun said, 'and that his powers over the mountain passageway were gone, I set out from Kengia to look for him.'

'You've told me that before.'

'But what I didn't tell you was that I came to the castle and found the Queen. I was sure that being from Ivane – Kengia's ally – Sofia would help me find out what had happened to Alik. I discovered it was too late for my brother...but not for you, Arisa. I met Gwyn, and she asked me to take you to safety.'

Arisa understood why Erun had agreed to care for her, but she couldn't fully reconcile Gwyn's actions. 'Your child,' she forced out, turning to Gwyn. 'You gave away your own flesh and blood. You gave *me* away.' Her eyes burned from the tears starting to well.

Gwyn's face contorted with pain. 'It's the hardest thing I've ever done, but also the most important. It kept you safe.'

'But I was right here in Lamore. Why didn't you come looking for me?'

'You were supposed to be in Kengia. I had no idea that Amund was in Obira, living under another name. Not until you both came here the night of the Prince's accident. I knew the instant I met you that you were my child.'

Arisa took a deep breath, recovering enough to feel angry again. She had questions for Erun.

'Why didn't you take me to Kengia?'

'I intended to take you, but by then it was too late. Horace had already mobilised his army to march on Kengia. I only had enough time to send an urgent message to my father, so he could use his powers to close the mountain pass once and for all. But that action trapped both of us in Lamore, and I was determined that no one else would know of your location.'

'You couldn't tell my mother? You couldn't tell *me* the truth?'

'Erun made the right decision. As hard as it was for all of us, it was better that way.' The pain in Gwyn's eyes said otherwise.

'I know there is a lot I need to explain to you.' Erun held out his hands pleadingly. 'And apologise for. But my first duty has always been to protect you, and I will not fail.'

Sar, who had remained silent all this time, asked the question Arisa had been dreading to ask herself.

'Does that mean Arisa is the Water Catcher?'

Erun's face brightened. 'I believe it may be her destiny, but it is unknown what powers she has, and when those powers will arrive.'

'I think they may have already,' Arisa said in a low voice.

'*What?*' every person in the room cried out at once.

Arisa explained what had happened in the sea below Riverend Falls. She mentioned the references Laurel had made to *knowing* who she was, and *knowing* there would be a Water Catcher.

When she finished speaking, Erun laughed out loud, clasping his hands together.

'I fail to see how this is funny,' she cried.

He grabbed her gently by the shoulders. 'You're right. It's not funny, because this puts you in more danger. But don't you see? It's coming to being. First the blood moon, then firesky, now this. The known world is on the brink of war, and from what I hear, Lamore Castle will soon be under attack from the King's own people, just as foretold. But everything will be alright, because the Water Catcher can unite all the kingdoms. You are the bringer of peace.'

'No.' She shook her head. 'I don't know what these powers do, or how to control them.'

'That will all come in time. It is enough to know that you're the Water Catcher.'

Arisa stumbled back. 'No. It can't be true. I'm not the Water Catcher.'

Erun caught her hands. 'Arisa, it's your destiny.'

Everyone else looked at her, as if expecting to see a sign of her abilities. Her legs wobbled violently beneath her, and she sank into a nearby chair.

Erun's tone grew soft. 'Arisa, who else knows about what happened at Riverend Falls?'

'No one. Other than Takai, and maybe a fisherman, but we can...' She had been about to say they could rely on Takai to keep the secret, but that might not be true anymore.

'If Takai knows, we must assume Horace will know soon enough.' Sar hung his head. 'We have lost his trust.'

No one questioned why. Instead, Gwyn vocalised their collective fear.

'Horace will know the significance of Arisa's powers. He may have suspected my relationship with Alik, and I'm sure he will realise her parentage.'

Erun rubbed the nape of his neck. 'And he will conclude that he doesn't merely need Arisa to get me to hand over firesky and weaponise it. He needs to keep her close, and under his control, to stop her from fulfilling the Water Catcher prophecy.'

Gwyn strode over to Arisa and framed her face in both hands. '*Alia*, my beautiful girl.' Her voice broke. 'That's the Ettean name I gave you when you were born. I think Arisa suits you better.' She gave a wry smile that soon disappeared. 'We must part again. We have to get you out of the castle.'

'But where will she go?' Queen Sofia asked.

'To Elos.'

Everyone other than Arisa turned to Sar, their mouths agape.

It was her turn to reveal a secret.

'It's true,' she said. 'Elos is alive.'

37

$\mathcal{T}$akai shook his throbbing hand as he strode away. The pain extended all the way to his heart. The image of Arisa in Sar's arms was scorched on his brain.

How long had it been going on between them? He knew they had spent a lot of time together when Arisa had been helping Sar prepare for his knighting. She had given him lessons in Kengian. Had it started back then? Had they been laughing behind his back all this time? Did the betrayal run that deep?

Why, then, had Arisa gone as far as confessing her feelings for him? She had told him she loved him. Had she lied? But to what end? He racked his brain, trying to make sense of the madness of the last day. The last few months.

He thought back to when he had returned to the castle from Talbot. To how Sar had advised him against everything he'd been taught to pursue. He'd urged Takai to shirk his duty to Theodora. Had tried to convince him that Ette and Ivane were not Lamore's rightful territories. So Takai had stood up in support of the rebels and their leader. How had he been so foolish?

And then there was Arisa. The whole time he'd known her, she had tried to guilt him, manipulate him into supporting the same people who had turned against the King. She had dragged him to a forbidden Kengian festival and put him in the path of a Shaman. He'd believed Laurel and her cryptic references to *choices*. He'd thought the Shaman had meant choosing Arisa.

He had thought he loved her.

Sar and Arisa must have colluded. They'd worked together to persuade him to support Lamore's enemies. Everything they'd said to him had been against the kingdom's best interests.

And now he thought about it, it hadn't only been Sar and Arisa. His mother and Gwyn – and Willem, to some extent – had been by their sides, echoing the same sentiments and spouting the same virtues. His mother had even swayed the King from his lifelong ambitions of taking back Ette and Ivane.

It was as if the entire court had fallen under a spell. A spell that had started around the time of his accident. The same time Arisa and Erun, a Kengian, had appeared at the castle to save his life…using suspected magic.

Takai had been right all along. Everything he had learnt as a child. Everything that had happened to his family. Everything that had happened to him at Talbot, how he'd been treated – he'd known Kengians couldn't be trusted, especially silver-eyes. Their powers were unpredictable, and what they would do with them was just as uncertain. What Arisa had done at Riverend Falls was proof of that.

How had she done it? How had she gotten him to turn his back on his responsibilities? How had she made him fall in love with *her* – his polar opposite in every way?

The answer was obvious. Arisa had bewitched him, and probably others as well – Sar included. She must have put him under some form of enchantment – the same thing the Kengian Prince had tried to do to his father years before.

It all made sense. She was Kengian. Her alliances and motivations were clear. Kengians would do anything to destroy Lamore.

How could he have been so stupid?

Takai's self-admonishment would have to wait. Right now, everyone who had acted against him – whether under a spell or not – was under house arrest, or soon would be. At least it sounded as if his father was following Horace's advice again. With Horace's help, they would see to the Lamorian rebels.

Takai gritted his teeth as the sound of war cries came through the windows. There was a stampede of footsteps as the rebels advanced on the castle – on his home. He vowed to make the Lamorian traitors suffer. Exactly as Arisa and Sar had made him suffer.

He quickened his pace, taking the stairs to the second floor of the main keep, two at a time. He marched straight to the council rooms, where he found Horace with a handful of nobles and a Royal Guard from one of his personal security units. Lakeford and the Baron of Iveness were absent; they must still be en route from their properties.

Horace only gave Takai a cursory glance. He was pointing at a map of the castle, outlining the defence strategy. As Theodora had said, the King was nowhere to be seen.

'My father,' Takai demanded. 'Why isn't he here?'

The Secretary – Lord Commander, now – didn't deign to so much as glance at him. 'He's in his rooms.'

'I know that, but why?'

Horace shrugged. 'He's unwell.'

'Unwell?'

Horace fixed a steely gaze on Takai. 'He's unwell.' His tone didn't invite further comment, but Takai wasn't deterred.

'Where would you like me stationed?'

Horace cocked a brow.

'I will assemble Sar's units,' Takai said. 'Where do you want me to post them?'

'Under no circumstance can you put yourself in danger. As the heir and King's son, you must be protected at all costs.'

The nobles nodded in agreement.

Takai took a deep breath to calm himself. He was beyond tired of being told what to do.

'As the *heir*, it's my duty to protect the castle.'

'It's better you remain here and oversee the strategy,' Horace said.

'Surely that pack of poorly trained rebels doesn't present a real danger to us?'

'The castle has never been under attack in any of our lifetimes,' Horace replied. 'Our forces are still returning from Lakeford and Iveness. I'm not sure how long we can hold the rebels off in the meantime.'

'All the more reason I'm needed,' Takai said. 'You need every trained soldier you can get.'

Horace waved a hand smoothly. 'The defence is well in hand. The castle is in lockdown. I have deployed every available soldier and guard to the battlements and towers along the boundary and outer walls. Royal Guards have been stationed at the inner gatehouse and are working to barricade the entrances to the main keep in case the walls are breached.'

One of the nobles stepped forward. 'We need Sar, Lord Commander. He's experienced in battle. You should release him.'

'We will manage without him,' Horace said.

'But—'

'I, as Lord Commander, say we don't need Sar.'

'I agree,' Takai said. The next words he was about to utter cut him to the core, but were necessary. 'Sar can't be trusted.'

A flicker of intense interest flashed across Horace's face. 'You heard the Prince. We go ahead without Sar. Everyone knows what they need to do. Get to it.'

Horace turned to Takai as soon as the door closed behind the nobles and the guard.

'Explain yourself.'

Takai bristled at Horace's impudence. 'Explain myself?'

'I have neither the patience nor inclination to pander to a

stupid boy. My only concern is the protection of the kingdom, and what you know may affect it.'

'I don't know anything.' Takai tried to adopt a blank look. He may not trust his friends, his mother or Arisa, but it didn't mean he was ready to disclose anything to Horace.

Horace stepped closer to him. Takai could feel the man's hot breath on his face, and hear the clicking of his jaw.

'I warn you not to test me. You'll tell me everything you know about firesky, Arisa and Erun, and what their involvement is in this rebellion.'

'I wish to speak to my father.'

'You shall speak to me.' Horace's tone made it clear he was once again running the kingdom.

And maybe, said a voice in Takai's head, *that isn't a bad thing.*

He had never particularly liked the man, but it was a fortunate coincidence that right now Horace wanted what was best for the kingdom, and it just happened to be the best for him as well.

Takai sighed in resignation – or was it hurt over Arisa and Sar's betrayal? He supposed it would be a relief to unload some of what he knew.

'The first I knew of firesky – the reality of it – was when I saw it last night,' he began. 'Arisa had told me nothing. And the rebellion is as much as a surprise to me as it is to you.'

'What has she said about her guardian, Erun? What has she told you of him?'

'Nothing that you wouldn't already know.'

'There must be something,' Horace demanded. 'Has she ever mentioned something odd in passing? Maybe let something slip that was out of place?'

Takai shrugged. Should he tell Horace about Arisa being Kengian? Should he share his suspicions that she may have bewitched him? His gut told him to proceed carefully.

'This is important,' Horace pressed. 'The future of Lamore may depend on what you have to tell me.'

Takai had to decide who he trusted less: Horace, or Arisa. Before today, even just fifteen minutes earlier, it would have been an easy decision, but now…

Horace seemed to see the conflict in him.

'Think about it. Think about the consequences of a Kengian wielding the power of firesky and what they may be trying to do with it. Think about what they have done to this kingdom in the past. But most of all, think about your duty to protect your country…your family. What you decide to do, who you decide to side with, will have long-lasting impacts on Lamore, potentially threatening everything we have worked so hard for. If there is ever a time when you must make a critical choice…it is now.'

Choice. There was that word again.

'Tell me what you know,' Horace said.

Takai tried to remember what Arisa had told him. It hadn't really amounted to much. She still had so many secrets. The Fisherman – Elos – had asked her about things as well; she hadn't told him much either.

But she had mentioned a name by accident…

'Amund.'

'What?'

'I heard Arisa once refer to Erun as Amund.'

Horace licked his lips like a hungry cat. 'Amund, you say?'

'Yes, Amund. The name stuck in my head. It's so unusual. I knew I'd heard it somewhere before, but I couldn't quite recall.'

'Amund was the second son of King Leo. Prince Alik's brother.'

Takai's eyes widened. 'You don't believe Erun is the same man? A Prince?'

'Of course not.' Horace responded a little too quickly for Takai's liking. He rubbed his chin, apparently deep in thought. 'And you were saved by a fisherman?'

Takai paused. Should he try to protect Elos? The man was probably among the rebels as they spoke. He might have saved

Takai and Arisa's lives, but was that enough to warrant Takai's loyalty? His relationship to Sar certainly didn't inspire any confidence in Takai at this point.

'You must make a choice,' Horace said again. 'About what is more important to you: people who are enemies of the state, or the future of your kingdom.'

That word again. Takai was being asked to make a selfless choice. A necessary choice for the good of the kingdom.

He would choose, then.

Takai stood up a little taller and stared into Horace's cold eyes. He would not leave any doubt. He was not a traitor to his country.

'He wasn't a fisherman. He was the warrior known as Elos.'

Horace's eyes widened, then his mouth morphed into his characteristic smirk. 'Are you sure?'

'Positive.'

'Why would he have been in hiding this whole time?'

'Because he never killed Prince Alik,' Takai said. 'He failed in his mission.'

'*What?*' Horace took a step backward. 'He never killed Alik?'

'Not from what he says.'

'What does he say happened to the Prince?'

'He isn't sure.'

'But he must be dead. He must be,' Horace muttered himself. 'There's no other explanation.'

'Elos assumes that is the case,' Takai said. 'But he couldn't risk the King, or you, finding out he had ignored his orders.'

Horace clutched at Takai's arm, his fingernails digging in. 'Is there anything else? Anything else you can tell me?'

Takai's mind went back to Arisa. To her betrayal. If he was being honest with himself, he wanted to hurt her for it.

Before he knew it, the words were spilling from his mouth.

'There is something else.'

Horace's claw-like grip on his arm tightened.

'When Arisa and I were washed over Riverend Falls, something strange happened.'

'Strange, you say?'

'It's hard to explain, but...she saved me from drowning. I thought I was seeing things. I still think it can't have been real. Light burst from her hands and her mouth, her whole body, and she conjured up a giant spout of water. It was like she was *controlling* the water.'

Horace released Takai's arm and sat down at the table, nodding for him to continue.

'And soon after, I found out she is Kengian.'

'Kengian?'

'If you saw her now, you would see it yourself. She is a silver-eyes. She has been disguising her eye colour somehow, all this time. She is unmistakably Kengian.'

Horace's eyes danced as he began muttering to himself again. 'Of course. How hadn't I seen it sooner? She is the image of them both.' He paused and steepled his hands. 'Where is she now?'

'I don't know. She was with Sar when I last saw her.'

'She is here at the castle?'

Takai nodded.

'Good. Your instincts to tell me this were right. You may have saved us from imminent disaster.'

'I don't understand...'

'Considering what you have told me, we could be in graver danger than you know. As soon as this uprising is quashed, Arisa and Erun will be sent to the dungeons for inquisition, followed by execution.'

Inquisition. Execution.

A hard ball formed in Takai's throat. What had he done?

'That's unnecessary,' he said. 'We need to get to the bottom of who they are and what they've done, but they should be treated like civilised people.'

Horace stared at him. 'You don't know, do you?'

'Know what?'

A laugh burst from Horace's mouth. 'You foolish, lovestruck boy. You don't understand the value of what you've told me.'

Takai ignored the barb. 'You cannot send them to the dungeons. I order it.'

Horace leapt out of his chair and stood directly before Takai. His eyes narrowed.

'Why are you so keen to protect your enemies? I wonder if it is out of guilt that you come to confess all of this? Maybe you wish to protect yourself and hide your own involvement.'

'How dare you!' Takai growled.

'You know, it's interesting,' Horace went on. 'You visit the county known to harbour Sergei, and within a day of your visit, the rebels mount an attack on the castle.'

'I never—'

'Really? How else am I to understand your behaviour of late? How do you explain your blatant disregard for royal protocols? Your support of the Queen and her plans for dangerous alliances? Your total disrespect for the promises made to my daughter…your secret archery lessons with Arisa?'

'You've been spying on me?'

'You pathetic little boy. I have eyes and ears everywhere.'

Takai felt Horace zero in on him, as if he were an animal caught in a trap. He met the man's gaze with as much authority as he could muster.

'I'll go to my father, and demand an immediate stop be put to these accusations.'

Horace's eyes gleamed back at him. 'You really are stupid. You must know there is only one person the King will listen to. *Me.* The one who brought him firesky. The one who will bring him an alliance with the Northemers.'

'The Northemers? They will never agree to an alliance.'

'They practically have. Now that I'll have firesky, I will have the means of controlling our new friends. And after the Northemers have fulfilled my purpose for them, I'll take Ette back from them.'

Takai felt dizzy. 'I will counsel the King otherwise.'

'Be my guest. But I think you'll find the King is beyond reasoning. After finding out the Queen was lying to him, and his own people are mounting an attack on him, there isn't an untouched barrel of wine to be found in the castle. I think you'll find he is – shall we say – not of sound mind.'

'I will go to my mother, then,' Takai said. 'No matter what passed between them, I know she can get him to listen.'

Horace smiled. 'No, Takai. I don't think you will.'

He crossed to the door and opened it.

'Guards – please escort the Prince to his rooms. Ensure he doesn't come under attack from any traitors or rebels. No one is to come or go from his chambers. We must protect the heir at all costs.'

A pair of guards moved toward Takai.

'Wait!' He held up his hands. He had to play the situation as cleverly as Horace would. He needed to buy some time.

Takai dropped his voice so only Horace could hear.

'I'm sure this isn't necessary, considering how helpful I can be to your cause.'

Horace motioned the guards away. 'You have my attention.'

'You claim you have the King's ear again. That he has agreed to your plans. But what about Lakeford? He will be back soon, and it is he who has the support of the council. Not you. And the nobles would never agree to align themselves with the Northemers.'

Horace gave a dismissive wave. 'As I said, I have the King's support.'

'You also said my father is not of sound mind,' Takai countered. 'You will need Lakeford and the council's support, too.'

'And you would get that support for me?'

'I could.'

Horace sat and steepled his fingers again. 'The King will be well enough again soon, and he will order the council to agree to my plans.'

Takai wondered what else he could offer Horace. There must be something he desperately wanted…

After a moment, it came to him.

'I will cement your power once and for all…by marrying your daughter.'

Takai felt nauseous as the words passed his lips, but he saw from the way Horace sat up straighter that he had struck the right chord.

'Yes,' Horace said. 'Those may be acceptable terms to me. You agree to marry Theodora?'

'As I said.'

'Immediately after this rebellion is quashed?'

Takai nodded.

'Good. In the meantime, you will be confined to your rooms. I will not have you reneging on your promises to my daughter again.'

Bile flooded Takai's throat. He had failed, and Horace had everything he wanted. Erun, Arisa, control of the kingdom, a crown secured for his family…and Takai had handed it to him on a silver platter.

He didn't know what was worse: being bewitched by a beautiful Kengian girl, or manipulated by the most ruthless man in the kingdom. He made to protest but his objections were drowned out by Horace's orders to the guards to take him away.

38

*A*risa needed to breathe.

She felt as if someone were sitting on her chest, pushing the air from her lungs. The medallion and Gwyn's coins in her gown pocket were like a heavy weight, pulling her down, holding her to the spot. She took rapid breaths, willing herself to be calm enough to take stock of what she'd learnt.

Everything she knew, or thought she knew, had turned out to be lies.

Erun had kept Arisa from her own mother and led Gwyn to believe she was dead. Gwyn had been part of the same secret, and had deceived Arisa from the moment she'd met her at the castle. How long would they have gone on lying to Arisa, if she and Sar hadn't discovered the truth?

But even their betrayal wasn't nearly as distressing as finding out she may be the Water Catcher – that it was up to her to somehow save the kingdom and most of the known world.

The pain in her chest travelled to her head. Her trembling fingers went to her temple. She needed a moment to think, to process it all.

Erun was standing before her. Talking. She couldn't quite make out his words. It was as if he were speaking to her from far away. She caught enough from his gesticulating hands that he wanted to get her out of here.

Arisa shook her head. She couldn't go anywhere until she'd made sense of this.

Erun grabbed her by the shoulders and leant in to be sure she'd hear his words. 'If Horace learns your true identity, you and all of Kypria are in mortal danger.'

She shoved him away.

'I don't believe you. I'm not the Water Catcher.'

Gwyn approached her gingerly. 'You must believe you're the Water Catcher, Arisa. You must know it.'

She held up her hands to keep Gwyn away. She was sick of people saying she must *know it*. The idea that she was the Water Catcher was ludicrous.

'Yes, some weird things have happened to me,' she tried to reason. 'And I may be the daughter of Prince Alik. But the Water Catcher? That takes a whole new level of belief.'

Sar stepped toward her. Arisa let him near enough to put his arm around her. 'Arisa, I've been lied to as well, but I believe this. We all do. *We* know it – you must know in your heart that it is true.'

There it was again. *Know it.* The words of the Shaman, Laurel. Arisa had met her twice now, and both times, when she had questioned Laurel about the existence of a Water Catcher, the Shaman had said the same thing.

Did Arisa know it? Did she simply not want to admit it to herself?

'But if it is true...' she began hesitantly. 'If, and I said *if*, I'm the Water Catcher, what am I supposed to do now? How am I going to save everybody – save anyone, for that matter?'

Erun waved his hands dismissively. 'There will be time for all of that after we've got you out of here.'

The Queen nodded. 'We don't have much time. It has to be while everyone is occupied by the attack on the castle.'

Willem turned to Sar. 'Can you appeal to the guards outside for help?'

Sar frowned. 'There were six of them at last count. Two are loyal to me, but it still leaves four who are Horace's men. To overcome them…we'll need a diversion.'

Gwyn shot a swift look at the Queen, who immediately crumpled to the floor.

'Come quickly!' Gwyn shouted, banging her fists on the doors. 'The Queen is ill!'

Arisa could hear the guards arguing among themselves outside.

Sar joined in, thumping on the door. 'Get in here! You don't want the Queen to die on your watch.'

The Queen groaned loudly, and the doors flung open to reveal four guards. Arisa recognised them as Horace's.

'Step back,' one of the guards ordered, trying to examine the Queen. Then the room descended into chaos.

Willem struck the first guard over the head with a vase. The guard's eyes rolled back in his head before he hit the ground with a thud. Erun slammed a heavy book to the side of another guard's face, knocking him to the ground. Sar took advantage of the remaining two guards' confusion and tackled one to the ground. He rendered the man unconscious with a punch and grabbed his sword.

The last guard was already advancing, his sword at the ready. He ran at Sar with a flurry of strikes. Sar sidestepped, avoiding the blade. The guard pulled up awkwardly, but Sar was already upon him, pointing his newly acquired sword at the man's throat.

'Drop your weapon.'

The guard complied, and Sar struck him over the head with the hilt of his sword. Erun, Gwyn, the Queen and Willem banded together, kicking the guards' weapons away, then tying them up and gagging them.

Arisa stood immobilised. She didn't want to escape. As

angry as she was, she didn't want to leave them all behind at the mercy of Horace.

The two remaining guards, Sar's men, had entered the room but were standing back, hesitant to attack their Captain.

'Erun,' she appealed to her guardian. *Your suggestive powers,* she mouthed. But Sar, catching her meaning, shook his head. He sheathed his sword and walked slowly toward them with his hands up in surrender.

'I know it's your sworn duty to protect the realm before any one person. I know you must follow orders, even when you're asked to do something you don't agree with.'

It could have been Elos speaking, not his son. The guards' fingers hovered shakily above the hilts of their swords. Sar went on.

'Following orders is the duty of a Royal Guard and warrior. You are both great warriors, but also exceptional men. Men who I have trusted my life with, and whose lives I have defended. I'm going to ask you to do something difficult. I need you to trust me as your commander, as your friend, when I tell you the right thing to do is to let us pass. Let us go unharmed.' Sar indicated the other guards lying unconscious on the floor. 'They will never know.'

The two guards exchanged glances. After a collective sigh, they dropped their swords.

'Sar, you've put our lives before your own, more than once,' one of them said. 'We trust what you say.'

'Thank you. I will remember your faith in me.' He held up a length of torn linen taken from the Queen's bedchambers. 'Please forgive me for this.'

Both men lowered themselves to the ground and allowed their arms and legs to be bound. Sar avoided eye contact with the men as he gagged them.

Everyone was making sacrifices and risking themselves to protect Arisa. The thought shook her from her frozen reverie.

It had to be enough that everyone else believed in her – didn't it?

'Hurry,' Erun called, already at the open door.

Sar handed Erun, Gwyn and Arisa a sword each. Arisa shuddered, knowing she had no idea how to use it.

Queen Sofia picked up an abandoned blade, handling it as if she'd been born to it. 'How will we get Arisa out of the castle? Aren't we surrounded?'

Arisa thought quickly. 'The rebels hadn't reached the north-east gate when we came in.'

'The rebels and Lakeford's forces will be focused on the main gate. The north-east gate is our best bet,' Sar agreed.

'But the gate will still be guarded,' Erun said.

Sar looked pointedly at Gwyn. 'We will need another distraction.'

'Give me your cloak,' Gwyn said to Arisa. 'From a distance they will assume I'm you. I can make out I'm escaping with Erun. We can draw the guards away while you run.'

Erun nodded slowly. 'That could work. Sar, you have to go with Arisa.'

Sar's brow furrowed. 'I can't. You will need me to hold back the guards at the gate and buy her as much time as possible.'

'I can go,' Willem said.

'Sorry, my friend.' Sar touched his friend's shoulder. 'But we need you here. Once this is all over, we will need your father's representations to the King. You should stay here in the rooms and maintain the pretence of complying with Horace's orders.'

Arisa stiffened. She had never thought she'd have to attempt the escape alone.

Gwyn reached out and squeezed both of her hands. 'You'll be fine. You will go to Elos, and he will help keep you safe.'

Arisa wasn't so sure. 'Assuming I can make it all the way to Elos, then what?'

'You must go to Kengia,' Erun said.

'Kengia! How can I do that?' she cried. 'There won't be

time to find passage on a boat before I'm found. And the mountains are impassable.'

Erun gave one of his irritatingly serene smiles. 'You will find a way. You're the Water Catcher, Arisa. When you get to Kengia, make your way to Queen Mira. She will know what to do.'

'But what if I'm not the Water—'

Gwyn cut her off. 'Arisa, trust yourself. You will know what to do.'

Arisa looked desperately around at them all. 'I can't leave you. Any of you.'

'Don't worry about us.' Willem gave a crooked smile. 'I will plead your case with Father and do whatever it takes. It's more important you get away safely.'

'If you think it's our only chance,' she said slowly, 'I'll do it. But first I have to see Takai.'

Sar shook his head emphatically. 'There's no time. And he thinks we betrayed him.'

'I have to tell Takai everything before I go,' Arisa insisted. 'I have to see him.'

'No.' Erun used his firmest tone.

She folded her arms like a petulant child. 'I shall not go anywhere, then.'

'There will be too many guards in your path, and I don't think Takai is too inclined to listen to either of us right now,' Sar said. 'He may have already gone to Horace with what he knows, or suspects.'

She knew Sar was right, but it didn't matter. 'I have to try. He took a chance on me before, and I will take one on him.'

Erun scrutinised her face, reading the determination there. His lips thinned. 'Be quick.'

Sar went into action. 'Right. Gwyn and Erun, prepare the horses. Arisa, I will come with you to Takai. Queen Sofia, will you come with us too?'

Arisa gave Gwyn and Erun a quick hug. It wasn't a proper

goodbye, for she refused to believe this would be the last time she'd see her uncle and mother. She exchanged cloaks with Gwyn, squeezed hands with Willem, and they parted.

Sar led Arisa and the Queen through the castle, the sounds of battle carrying through the stone corridors. He peered out a window. 'Good. They haven't made it through the main gate.'

They passed no one on their way. Presumably, every available person was either locked in their rooms for safety or fighting the rebels. They were careful to take an indirect route to Takai's chambers, avoiding the King's council rooms.

Sar went ahead of Arisa and the Queen as they approached the Prince's rooms. He returned moments later.

'He must be within, because there are two guards outside. More of Horace's men. Stay out of sight. I'll try to get them to leave.'

Sar approached the guards as Arisa and Queen Sofia edged a little closer.

'You two,' he barked. 'Get to the main gate. On the Lord Commander's orders. I'll take over your post.'

'Sar?' one of the guards asked. 'Aren't you supposed to be under arrest?'

Sar let out a big belly laugh, designed to confuse the guards long enough for him to overpower the closest one. At the same time, the Queen leapt out from the shadows and hit the other guard over the head with the hilt of her sword.

Sar bound and gagged the unconscious guards before dragging them into an anteroom. Arisa grabbed a set of keys from one of their belts and locked them in the room.

'Go ahead.' Sar indicated the door to Takai's chambers. 'We'll keep watch out here.'

Arisa hesitated.

'Go on,' the Queen said. 'He needs to hear what you have to say.'

She pushed open the door.

Takai was in the far corner of his room. His eyes were on

the battle outside the window. He turned around as Arisa entered, and it appeared for a moment as if he were going to smile, before his gaze fell on the sword she was carrying. His eyes widened in alarm.

She dropped the weapon to the ground. 'No, no – I'm not here to hurt you.'

Takai gave an acerbic laugh. 'More than you already have? What are you doing here?'

'I had to see you.'

'To laugh at my expense?'

'Your expense?'

'As you can see, I'm a prisoner in my own rooms,' Takai snapped. 'And why? Because of you. Because of Sar. Because of my mother. Because of all of your treacherous lies. You have no idea the damage that has been done.'

Arisa's mind whirled at Takai's account of her betrayal – that he thought she was *with* Sar. 'Takai, I'm—'

'You're what, Arisa? Sorry? Sorry Horace has the King's permission to go after you and Erun to weaponise firesky? Sorry that Horace has entered an alliance with Malu, so they can invade Ivane and Kengia together?'

Malu? Kengia? Arisa pushed aside Takai's revelations for a moment. She had to get him to hear her out.

'Takai, you have to listen to me.'

'No, *Arisa*.' The way he hissed her name tore right through her. 'I don't have to listen to you. I'm done with you.'

The tears that she had somehow kept at bay before were streaming freely down her cheeks now.

'Tears!' Takai spat. 'Are you crying for me? I don't think so. You only cry for yourself. For your own fate. For the fact you will have to live out the rest of your days in a dungeon before Horace executes you as planned. I suppose with Sar as your cell-mate you'll be happy enough.'

Arisa wiped away the tears with the back of her hand. 'You're right. I have betrayed you,' a hint of anger then overtook her sadness, 'but not in the way you think. And not with Sar. Yes, there are some things I didn't tell you – some I didn't even know myself until now. But what was between us was real.'

'There's nothing real about living a lie.'

'The love I have for you isn't a lie.'

Takai scoffed. 'Don't you mean your love for Sar?'

'What you saw, what you *think* you saw between Sar and me, was nothing more than two friends comforting each after.'

He frowned. 'Comforting each other?'

'It's a long story, but I told him about Elos – and he showed me proof of who my father really was.'

'Your father?'

'Yes,' Arisa whispered. 'My father and mother. I'm the daughter of Gwyn…and Prince Alik of Kengia.'

Takai shook his head in disbelief. 'Impossible.'

'It is possible. Erun kept my identity secret all this time. It's why Elos appeared to know me. He knew my father.'

Takai paced the room. Arisa could see he was working through what she'd said, trying to determine what he believed. 'The messages from Kengia mentioning Gwyn,' he muttered to himself. 'All the secrets…'

Finally, he stopped right in front of her.

'Arisa, if that's true, you're of the firstborn line of Kengia.'

She nodded.

'It can't be.' Takai shook his head again, over and over, clearly trying to make sense of it all. 'No, it can't be true…' Abruptly, he reached out and grasped her shoulder. 'But it *could* be true. Everything that happened at the waterfall. The power you used to save me…Of course it's true! You *are* the Water Catcher.' His eyes were filled with a mixture of wonder and fear.

'I don't know if there is a Water Catcher—'

Takai stumbled away from her suddenly, his fists clenched. 'Horace knows.'

Arisa's heart missed a beat. 'He knows what?'

'He knows what happened at the waterfall. He knows you're Kengian.'

'You told him?' she whispered. *Horace*, of all people. It was unthinkable. 'Does he think I'm the Water Catcher?'

'Yes, I think he does. I don't know how he guessed all of it, but from his reaction, I believe that is what he thinks. You have to leave. Arisa, I'm sorry.' Takai's voice broke at the last words.

Arisa steeled herself. 'I can't leave. Not yet. Not until things are as they should be…not until you give me some hope that you may love me again.'

Takai's expression darkened. 'But I can't. Haven't you heard the news? I'm to be married.' A grim shadow washed over his face with his next words. 'I have agreed to marry Theodora.'

'You can't!' Arisa cried.

'It's practically done. I was trying to bargain with Horace, trying to help you.'

'You don't have to do it. Come with me. I'm going to Elos, and he will get us to Kengia.'

A look of pain engulfed Takai's face. 'I can't. I have to stay here. It's my home, my kingdom. I can't leave it in Horace's control.'

Arisa understood Takai's sense of duty, but it didn't make his refusal easier to bear. 'Then I won't leave,' she said.

'You must. It's the only way to stop Horace from weaponising firesky. The only way to keep you safe.' Takai gave a wry smile. 'And you never know – the Water Catcher may be able to save us.'

Arisa ignored his comment about the Water Catcher, focusing instead on what might become of her and Takai.

'I'm not sure if we will meet again. But if we do, I hope we can…' Her words trailed off, but Takai seemed to understand.

'That will depend,' Takai replied.

'On what?'

He looked back out the window. 'On what side you're on when we meet.'

Arisa took a great intake of breath, as if Takai's words had inflicted a physical blow. *It was over.*

Takai picked up the quiver of arrows and bow she had always practised with. 'You'll do better with this than a sword.'

Arisa slung the weapon over her back. Both of them were silent. As if each wanted to say something else, but neither knew what.

After a moment, Sar and the Queen entered. Sar nodded to Takai, who gave a small shrug in response. 'We have to go,' Sar said. 'Guards are heading our way.'

'You should take the secret passage,' Takai said.

'Of course. We can take the tunnel to the woodland.'

'Secret passage?' the Queen asked.

'Tunnel?' Arisa added. She had suspected Takai had some secret way in and out of his rooms ever since she had found him injured in the north-west tower, and he'd asked her to help him to a disused corridor. But a tunnel? If only she'd known about it earlier, maybe Erun could have escaped too.

'A while ago, Sar and I came across a secret tunnel that leads to the woodland. The Kengian snow wolf led us to it.' Takai smiled to himself. 'I thought nothing of it at the time, but with everything that's happened since then, I wonder if it was showing us the tunnel for a reason.'

'Reason or not,' Sar said, 'it's our best option.'

Takai pressed a panel in the wall. It swung open to reveal a tunnel of blackness. Sar grabbed a torch and motioned Arisa toward the passage.

The Queen reached out and hugged her, and Arisa hugged her back. She allowed herself one final glance back at Takai. She immediately recognised the expression on his face, for she felt the same. It was a look of aching loss.

If only she didn't need to leave. If only Horace wasn't the cruel man he was. If only...they might have stood a chance.

39

_T_he guards rammed the doors to Takai's bedchamber until the lock gave way. Finding no one other than the Prince and his mother, they mounted a search. One of the guards snatched the Queen's sword and the one abandoned by Arisa. He blocked the doorway as the others looked under the bed and behind the curtains, to no avail.

The guard sent his comrades in search of Arisa and Sar, with a quick warning. 'Don't tell anyone they're missing. We can't risk the Lord Commander discovering we've failed. We have to recapture them before he learns of this.'

Once the others were gone, the guard turned his icy stare on Takai and the Queen.

'You two, stay where you are.'

Takai let out a caustic laugh under his breath. 'Where do you expect us to go?'

In any case, he had no intention of trying to escape. What was the point? There was hardly anything worth fighting for now. Arisa had gone, and Takai had not said what he yearned to say. That even though he was hurt, he understood. He knew why she had hidden things from him. She had never bewitched him, at least not in the way he had feared. It was he who had betrayed her. He had practically handed her over to Horace. If by some miracle she managed to escape, Horace would stop at nothing to get to her – and it was all Takai's fault.

He turned his back on the guard and met his mother's eyes. She stood a few feet from him, but the distance between them might as well have been miles. He had betrayed the Queen as well. He had assumed she was working against Lamore and blamed her for their years of separation while he was at Talbot, when it had really been his father and Horace who'd kept them apart. Takai dropped his gaze as the shame ate into him. But before he knew it, his mother had him in her arms and was pulling him close to her.

The tears that had been threatening to come escaped freely now.

'I'm sorry.' Takai's voice wasn't his own; it was strangled, contrite. 'I'm so sorry.' It was the voice of an eight-year-old Takai seeking forgiveness and comfort from his mother.

'I know.' The Queen's wet cheek pressed against his. 'I am, too.'

They held their embrace a few moments longer before his mother wiped the last tears from her eyes and straightened herself up. 'There will be time for grieving later.' The Queen pulled Takai away from the guard's hearing. 'You can fix this,' she whispered.

'It's hopeless.'

'We will never be without hope,' she insisted.

'What do you suggest?'

'You already know the answer to that.'

Takai shook his head, not wanting to admit to himself that he wanted to leave all his duties behind to chase Arisa.

'Go to her,' the Queen whispered. 'You must.'

He winced. He couldn't leave – especially since he wasn't sure if he'd be able to forgive Arisa for keeping so much from him.

'It's my duty to stay here and protect the kingdom to the best of my ability.'

'You can't do anything while you're a prisoner in your rooms.'

His mother was right. He had to get out of his chambers. He had to see his father.

Takai turned toward the guard, mustering up his most authoritative tone of voice. 'The Queen and I will see the King now.'

The guard guffawed to himself.

'My mother is still your anointed Queen and demands to see her husband.'

'The Queen is under arrest,' the guard sneered.

'And I,' Takai drew himself up to full height, 'your Prince and future King, am releasing her from that arrest.'

The guard shook his head emphatically. 'Lord Commander's orders.'

'When this is over and the Queen is cleared of whatever ridiculous accusations Horace has dreamed up – and I say *when*, because it will happen – whose side do you want to be on?'

The guard's face paled. 'But it's my job to keep you safe in your rooms, Your Highness. The rebels are still out there.'

'Yes, and you should not neglect your duties. You will accompany us to the King's rooms, to ensure we are safe.'

The guard glanced around the room, as if he were trying to find someone to advise him on the best course of action. Eventually, he grunted, 'Come on.'

40

*A*risa felt as if they had been running in darkness for miles. The tunnel reeked of damp and decay, and she struggled to keep up with Sar's pace. They had used the secret passage from Takai's room to get to the abandoned corridor that led to the north-west tower. They'd taken the tower stairs all the way to the bottom and pushed open the stone entrance to the tunnel, all without passing another soul.

Arisa's eyes were on Sar's torch bobbing ahead when she tripped over the root of a tree. She fell heavily to the ground with a yelp, bringing Sar back to her at a sprint.

'Are you alright?'

She brushed the dirt from her grazed knees. The root had torn a hole in her dress, but she was unscathed. She caught her breath and managed to assure Sar between gasps that she was fine.

Sar helped her back to her feet. 'We must be close,' he said.

They went on. The ground started to incline upward, the roof looming toward them. Sar was hunched completely over, and Arisa was forced to duck her head as they trudged further along the tunnel. Her heart raced as an awful possibility occurred to her: the tunnel may have caved in ahead, trapping them. But when she couldn't bear the confinement a moment longer, hope arrived in the form of beams of light breaking through a patchwork of leaves and branches.

Sar shoved the undergrowth aside and the sunlight streamed in, temporarily blinding them. They emerged out of an over-grown alder bush. Arisa immediately recognised their location. They were on the southern edge of the woodland.

Forging ahead, they soon reached the northern tip of the woods. They clung to the shadows cast by the great oaks, elms and birch trees at the outskirts. Looking out, Arisa could see the north-east gate set into the boundary wall, a couple of hundred yards away. She leant against a tree and loudly sucked in gulps of air, trying to regain her breath. Sar signalled for her to shush—

An arm reached out from the shadows and grabbed his shoulder.

Arisa's first instinct was to scream, but she immediately quieted herself when she realised it was only Erun, with Gwyn beside him. They held the reins to Meteor and a grey stallion, both saddled up. Meteor let out a soft whinny of recognition and nuzzled Arisa's hand.

'You made it,' she sighed in relief.

'Thankfully,' Gwyn said, 'I still have some friends willing to help us…I found Klaus—'

'Klaus? He's safe?'

'For now…'

No doubt Horace would punish Klaus soon enough for disabling his guards and fetching Arisa from Elos.

'Klaus got us the horses and helped us get through the south gate,' Gwyn went on. 'We had to go all the way around past the Queen's garden, and back around the moat and the tiltyard… but we made it.' She smiled triumphantly.

'Everyone's attention seems to be on the main gate,' Erun said. 'Except for the guards over there.' He pointed to the dozen or so guards at the north-east gate.

Sar frowned. 'There's too many for us to take. I'll get their attention so Erun and Gwyn can make a break for it in the opposite direction. That will draw some of them away. I'll try to hold off the others while Arisa escapes.'

'Hold them off? There's only one of you, Sar,' Arisa cried.

He flashed a cheeky grin. 'But aren't I the most accomplished warrior in the King's service?'

'Sar—' She couldn't ask him to put his life at such great risk.

His smile dropped, and he patted the hilt of his sword. 'I'll be alright.'

'We'll all be alright.' Erun didn't sound quite as convincing. 'But no matter what happens, Arisa, you have to keep going and head for Elos. Go to Kengia. Don't turn back.'

She surveyed the trio ready to put their lives on the line for her. 'What will they do when they catch you all?'

'Horace will know my real identity soon, if he doesn't already,' Erun said. 'Which means I'm worth more to him alive than dead. And the Queen will plead for all of us. The only thing you need to worry about is getting to Kengia safely.'

'I told you. I don't know how to get to Kengia.'

Gwyn squeezed her arm. 'But you will know. You will figure out how to get there. You have to, for all our sakes.'

She had to do it. They were relying on her. 'I'll find a way,' she murmured. 'I'll go to Kengia and I'll send help.'

A shadow passed over Erun's face. 'Yes…send help.'

No one voiced out loud that help may never come, or at least not in time to save any of them.

Arisa embraced her mother, her uncle and her friend, not letting herself cry. She was determined she would see them all again.

'Right. We have a plan…' Sar sounded uncharacteristically nervous now. 'Of sorts.'

Erun mounted the grey stallion and helped Gwyn up behind him. She was still wearing Arisa's cloak. Gwyn pulled the hood up over her head and around her face, so only a general impression of her features could be made out.

Arisa gasped. Why hadn't she seen it before? From Gwyn's build to her olive skin, and even the shape of her mouth, Arisa bore more than a passing resemblance to her mother.

Sar helped her up onto Meteor and gave her a quick wink before running out into the clearing. He let out a loud whistle. 'Over here!' he shouted.

'Halt! Stop in the name of the King!'

Sar didn't look back. The guards started in pursuit. Arisa, Gwyn and Erun waited in the woods until Sar and the guards chasing him had vanished from sight.

'Come on.' Erun spoke softly to his horse, spurring him forward. He and Gwyn emerged from the woods at a full gallop and raced toward the gate.

The remaining guards struggled to collect themselves as Erun's horse nearly barrelled into them. They jumped out of the way. 'It's the healer and his ward!' one shouted. 'They've escaped!'

The remaining guards mounted their horses and followed Erun and Gwyn through the gate.

Arisa wasn't sure whether to be relieved or terrified that the ruse had worked. Now she had to play her part…and there was no turning back.

'Alright, friend,' she whispered into Meteor's ear. 'This is it.' She gave the mare a light nudge and they galloped out of the woods, Meteor's nose pointing straight at the gate.

They had just passed through it when the sound of a great commotion behind them made Arisa pull the horse to a stop. She looked back over her shoulder. Squinting, she could make out the group of guards, subduing Sar in the clearing. Every hand was on him as they tried to drag him back to the gatehouse. She watched in horror as the guards laid into Sar without restraint. Blood oozed from a gash on his head.

Meteor moved restlessly beneath her. The horse intrinsically understood her job: to get Arisa to safety. Arisa was wracked with indecision, knowing everyone expected her – no, *needed* her to escape. But she also knew the price they would pay for her actions. They may be willing to pay it, but she wasn't.

She could never live with herself if she abandoned everyone she cared about.

'I won't leave Sar,' she murmured to herself, and to Meteor. 'I won't leave any of them.'

She turned the mare back toward the castle – but they made it no further. A hand reached out from the shadows of the boundary wall and grabbed the horse's reins.

Arisa would have screamed, but the assailant leapt up and clamped his hand over her mouth. She struggled, but knew her efforts were futile. The assailant's hands were so large they nearly covered her whole face. The man leaned in closer to her – close enough that she was able to recognise him.

It was Elos.

'What are you doing?' he hissed, releasing her. 'You have to get out of here.'

'What am *I* doing? What are *you* doing skulking outside the castle walls? Why aren't you in there helping your son?'

'My concern right now is getting you out of here while we still can.'

'I won't go.' Arisa reached for the bow and arrow Takai had given her. 'Sar needs help.'

Elos stilled her hand. 'You forget, young Water Catcher…' She blinked in surprise. 'Yes, I know who you are. You forget that the whole reason my son is putting his life in danger is to help you get away. He's doing it to save you – to save the Water Catcher.'

'Someone needs to help him,' she pleaded.

'I will help him, as soon as I see you make your escape from here.'

'But I need you to come with me. I can't make it there alone.'

'There?'

'Kengia.'

Elos let out a low whistle. 'You're right. That will be tricky.' He looked back at Sar and the group, as if weighing up his options.

Sar had managed to take back a sword and break free from the group, but it was six against one. Not even he could beat those odds. One guard was writhing on the ground in pain, but five still circled Sar.

Elos shook his head before leading Meteor into the shadows of the wall. 'Give me five minutes. If I'm not back here by then, you promise me you'll make your own way out of here?'

Arisa nodded vigorously.

Elos unsheathed his sword and sprinted toward the group. His long legs covered the distance easily and he was upon the guards before they knew it. He charged at the closest guard, bringing the end of his sword down hard on the back of the man's head. The guard collapsed in a heap. Elos ran to his son's side, and, with a brief nod of acknowledgement, they stood back-to-back as the others surrounded them.

Despite the distance, Arisa could detect the nervousness in the guards' movements and voices. 'I'll be damned!' one of them cried. 'Elos, is that you? You're supposed to be dead.'

'Your eyes don't deceive you. It is me. And if you dare make a move against me, or my son, it is you who will be the dead man.'

The guard rushed forward, but Elos beat him back easily. One by one, the men charged at the pair, only to be pushed back by the superior swordsmanship of father and son. In what looked like a beautifully choreographed dance, they managed to knock the swords from two other guards and render them unconscious. Two of the remaining men paired off against Sar and Elos.

Sar's opponent managed to slice into his arm. Sar instinctively reached out to check the damage – but his momentary lapse meant he hadn't noticed the final guard coming up behind him, his sword raised.

Arisa yelled out in warning, but it was useless. Sar couldn't avoid the attack in time.

With the same unworldly speed she had felt at the riot in the marketplace, her hands flew into action, grabbing her bow and pulling an arrow from the quiver. She fired what she knew was her only shot as the guard readied to bring his sword down on Sar's shoulder.

But her speed wasn't matched with accuracy. The arrow whistled as it flew well overhead. Arisa reloaded her bow, knowing she had run out of time, knowing her efforts were in vain—

Then she heard it. A low growl.

The snow wolf had appeared between Sar and his opponent. The wolf glanced back at Arisa with its flashing green eyes, as if to say, *Allow me,* and advanced on the guard. Elos approached from the other side, disabling his son's attacker with a swift blow to the back of the head.

The last two guards eyed each other, and then the wolf, before racing back toward the gate. Arisa aimed her reloaded bow and arrow at them, and they dropped their swords.

The wolf looked back at her and dipped its head before running straight through the boundary gate toward the city.

Sar and Elos moved quickly, tying up the guards with ropes they found in the gatehouse, before returning to Arisa. She dismounted, assuring herself Sar was alright after a quick examination of his wounds.

Sar gave his characteristic dimpled grin. 'Now what?'

'To Kengia...I suppose,' she offered.

'I was planning on staying and facing the music, but I think you may need me.' Sar cast a suspicious eye toward Elos, who gave him a blank look in return. 'We'll need another horse.'

Elos whistled and a horse appeared from behind a large boulder on the hill leading up to the gate. Arisa thought it looked like the horse she had seen the pirate riding outside of Elos's hut. She shuffled forward on Meteor to make room for Sar, and they set off at a fast pace, down the rocky outcrop toward Obira, and the secret smugglers' gate she and Takai had used only a few hours earlier.

That felt like another life, now. A life she was leaving behind.

41

*T*he guard followed closely behind Takai and the Queen as they made their way to the King's chambers. The battle was well underway, but maybe not for much longer. A glimpse out a window showed the rebels facing fire on multiple fronts. The King's guards were launching showers of fire arrows into clusters of the invaders. Blood-curdling screams rang out, chilling Takai to the bone.

The King's Army was assembled in formation on the hill leading up to the castle, closing in on the attackers. Takai recognised Lakeford and the Baron of Iveness's banners at the head of the arriving forces. For a moment, he felt sorry for Sergei and his rebels. They didn't stand a chance.

Takai and the Queen continued on, striding purposefully through a series of anterooms until they arrived outside the King's bedchambers. Here, they found the main door guarded by Guthrie and two other men from his unit. His lip curled in disgust at their approach.

'Guthrie, I thought you would be leading the King's Army out there,' Takai said, wanting to humiliate him for his hateful actions against Arisa.

'Those were the Lord Commander's orders, but the insubordinate Duke refused to step down,' Guthrie sneered. 'I got back to the castle before the rebels made it here and told Father what he'd done. I have no doubt Lakeford will be punished accordingly, as soon as all this is finished.'

'And that's the only reason you're not fighting the rebels?' Takai taunted, a thinly veiled reference to Guthrie's cowardice in Ette.

Guthrie's face reddened and he gritted his teeth. 'I'm here to protect your father. Ensuring the King's safety is of the utmost importance.'

'Of course.' The Queen pinched Takai's arm in warning. 'And we're grateful to you, Lord Guthrie. But right now I'd like to see my husband.'

Guthrie turned to Queen Sofia and cocked his head, as if it were the first time he had noticed her presence. 'What is the Queen doing out of her rooms?' he barked at the guard who had accompanied them. 'She has been placed under arrest, and the Prince is to keep to his chambers.'

Takai didn't wait for the guard to respond. 'We *are* under guard, aren't we? And who are you to keep the King from his wife and son?'

Guthrie scowled, but finally nodded to the guard to admit them.

Takai and his mother found the King alone and mumbling to himself, his eyes glazed. After a few drawn-out moments, he fixed his unfocused eyes on them.

'Takai, son. Thank goodness you're here. They told me you were back, but Horace insisted you be kept safe.'

'I had to see you, Father.'

The King stumbled toward Takai and clutched his arm. 'The rebellion – the people have risen,' he slurred, his breath reeking of wine. 'And the prophecy. It has all come to pass. The Water Catcher is on their way. But not to worry.' He raised a wobbly finger and tried to wink. 'I have the Northemers on my side, and I have a secret weapon. I have—'

His words cut off as his gaze fell on the Queen.

'Sofia, my love. You're here.' He staggered over and embraced her. 'You've come back to me?'

Takai frowned. Had he forgotten his wife's so-called betrayal, and the fact that she'd been under arrest?

'I'm here. Your one true wife.' Sofia wore a frozen smile as the King stepped back to admire her.

Takai was about to raise his concerns about Horace assuming rule, but raised voices sounded outside. A harried-looking guard entered the room with Guthrie, not stopping to bow. He was breathing heavily.

'Your Majesty,' he puffed. 'I have come from – the north-east gate. The girl…' He bent over, trying to catch his breath. 'She escaped.'

Takai's chest tightened. *Arisa.* It must be her.

'What girl?' the King asked.

'The healer's ward.'

It *was* her. She was alright. She'd gotten away.

That was what Takai had wanted, wasn't it?

'How could this happen?' the King demanded. 'Last I heard, the ward and the traitors were all under guard in the Queen's rooms.'

'She is just one girl!' Guthrie bellowed. 'How did she manage to outsmart a whole unit of guards?'

The guard winced. 'She wasn't alone. The Kengian healer and Lady Gwyn drew some of our unit away. The rest of us were fully occupied with Sar, and would have overpowered him if it weren't for the snow wolf, and another man who appeared from nowhere.'

'The wolf?' Guthrie said incredulously. 'Another man?'

'Who was this *man*?' Takai asked.

'It was Elos,' the guard said.

Of course. Takai had to restrain a smile.

'Elos?' the King cried. 'But how can that be?'

'Elos!' Guthrie grabbed the front of the guard's armour and shook him. 'Don't be ridiculous. He's dead.'

'He is no more dead than you or I, my lord.'

'You're sure?' the King asked.

'It was him, Your Majesty. We managed to recapture Gwyn and the healer, but Sar and the girl left with Elos.'

'This level of incompetence is both unbelievable and inexcusable,' Guthrie spat. 'You and your fellow guards will be punished when this is over. I will personally see to it. Where are the escapees now?'

The guard shook his head helplessly.

'Gather every guard you can. We will leave at once,' Guthrie barked. 'I will lead a party to hunt down the girl, and won't rest until we have her…dead…or *alive.*'

'Yes, my lord,' the guard replied, and bolted from the room.

The gleam in Guthrie's eyes at the prospect of a hunting party, and the way he'd said 'alive' like it was an unlikely outcome, unnerved Takai. Horace's son had been waiting for this moment to get his revenge on Arisa.

He couldn't let Guthrie get to her.

Guthrie rounded up a handful of his guards from the King's apartments, casting a furious look at the Queen as he ordered two remaining guards to stay. 'Ensure the Queen remains here in the King's rooms. She is under arrest and is not to go anywhere unless my father, the Lord Commander, allows it.'

The guards nodded.

'Bring me back the traitor,' the King said.

'Your Majesty.' Guthrie bowed and left.

Takai locked eyes with his mother. He needed her help. He had to go after Arisa.

'Husband,' the Queen began, 'perhaps Takai could assist Guthrie…it's a very important task.'

The King shook his head vigorously. 'It's far too dangerous for my heir.'

His father would never let him leave. Takai had to think of something.

'But Father – I am *less safe* here.'

The King cocked his head to the side – so far that he stumbled a little. 'But you *are* safe. Safe here with me and your mother.'

'But the rebels we have just seen…They have nearly made it through the main gate.'

'No! It can't be true,' the King wailed. 'Lakeford arrived with my army!'

The Queen easily joined in with Takai's lie. 'I'm afraid he arrived too late. The attackers have already breached the castle's defences. It would only take one assassin to make it to the main keep and find us all here…I fear for Takai's safety. Our only heir.'

'Yes.' The King nodded knowingly. 'Of course you're right. What can we do?'

'Takai must leave immediately with Guthrie and the other guards. He must hide in the countryside until it is safe to return.'

The King's head continued bobbing slowly. 'You're right. We need to protect Takai. For the sake of the crown. I will summon Horace and get extra guards assigned.'

'But there is no time,' the Queen countered quickly. 'Takai must leave at once.'

'Very well.' The King turned to Takai, adopting a melodramatic air. 'My son, take care. If I perish, you must wreak vengeance upon those who dared to attack me.'

Takai gave a stoic nod.

His mother embraced him. 'Yes, son, take care.'

'I will, Mother…Father.'

Takai left at pace, hoping his father would be merciful when he sobered up and realised the Queen's deception. Somehow, Takai had to succeed in his task and make his mother's sacrifice worth it.

T<small>AKAI'S HANDS</small> moved quickly as he saddled up his horse. He didn't have a moment to waste. He had to be well away from the castle before anyone realised the King had been tricked into letting him go. And he had to find Arisa. He wasn't sure what he was going to do or say when he did – he wasn't even sure how he felt about her anymore. But that didn't matter right now. He just had to keep her alive.

Takai cast a sideways glance at Guthrie, checking he was moving with as much haste. The stare Guthrie gave him in return was icier than ever.

'I still don't understand why the King wants you to come with me.'

'Perhaps it's the fact you have failed in every task you've been given before now.'

Guthrie's nostrils flared. One obstacle – convincing Guthrie he was there to help – was overcome, though even if they made it away from the castle and the rebels, Takai didn't like his chances of evading Guthrie. But somehow, he had to do it.

They mounted their horses and convinced the perplexed guards at the castle's inner gate to lift the portcullis and open the heavy iron gate. They set a cracking pace as they passed the tilt-yard and headed into the woodland and then to the north-east gate. The first thing Takai noticed was the metallic smell of blood hanging in the air, then a single arrow lying on the ground. The few guards left at the gatehouse paid little attention to them, too occupied with nursing their wounds.

Clear of the castle, Takai searched his mind for a way to get away from Guthrie. But if he couldn't do that soon, he would have to lead him away from Arisa's route instead. The only way to protect her would be to get as far away from her as possible.

42

'The rebels have been brought under control.'

Lakeford was giving a report to Theodora's father, his blood-stained uniform testament to the battle he had just come from. The Duke was otherwise unscathed, his steely grey eyes glaring at Horace, full of distaste. Neither had noticed Theodora's arrival.

'Where are the rebels now?' Horace asked.

'Scores of them were killed, and the same number were captured and are on their way to the cells. Some survivors managed to get away and fled into Obira. We have a unit in pursuit to catch any stragglers, but most will probably go into hiding.'

'And their leader?'

'Escaped, from what I can tell. But I will personally—'

Horace held up his hand to silence the Duke. 'No, Lakeford.' Theodora noted his omission of the honorary address of *Your Grace*. 'I, the Lord Commander, will determine what happens next, and will tell *you* what to do.'

The Duke's square jaw clenched, but he remained silent.

'You may go. I will inform the King of *my* victory.'

Lakeford spun on his heel and stormed out without acknowledging Theodora.

'Father, you summoned me?' she ventured.

Only then did Horace divert his attention to his daughter. Something between a smirk and a scowl twitched on his lips. 'It seems you may have finally succeeded.'

'I have?'

'The Prince has agreed to marry you.'

Theodora stood up a little taller. 'I see,' she said, with a calm she didn't feel. How had her father managed it?

'And since the pirate has not returned to say he completed his task, you win, my dear. You will be Lamore's Queen. You can come with me to discuss the arrangements with the King.'

Theodora bowed her head so her father couldn't see the delirious grin on her face.

THE PAIR ARRIVED outside the King's chambers, but were surprised to find Guthrie wasn't at the guard's post, as instructed by Horace. Another guard was in his place. Horace dismissed his son's absence as unimportant, for he had 'much more serious matters to attend to'. They were shown into the King's bedchambers.

Horace appeared to do a double take when he realised the King was in the company of the Queen. Sofia was not only in the King's presence, but sitting serenely beside her husband, clasping his hand.

Horace and Theodora bowed, and Horace directed his gaze at the Queen.

'I'm surprised to see *you* here.'

'Surprised? Isn't a wife's duty to be with her husband at his time of need?'

Theodora watched her father bite back his retort. 'Sire, the attack has been quelled.'

'Are you sure?' the King cried dramatically. 'We're safe?'

'Safe for now, my love,' the Queen cut in. 'But it's only a matter of time before the rebels regroup and stage another attack on us.'

The King's brow furrowed. 'But we will have firesky,' Horace said with conviction, 'so—'

'*Will* you have firesky?' A knowing smile had spread across the Queen's face.

'Yes. With the healer's ward back at the castle, I have everything I need to guarantee his compliance.'

Queen Sofia lifted her chin. 'I find your confidence quite baffling.'

Horace shot her an odd look, then turned toward the King. 'There's something else I need to tell you, sire.' He paused. 'I have discovered that the ward, Arisa, is in fact the daughter of Gwyn and Prince Alik. And the healer, Erun, is actually Prince Amund. He has kept the girl's identity hidden all these years.'

The daughter of the Kengian Prince? Arisa was a princess. She was born to the firstborn prince. But that would mean…Theodora's head reeled.

The King shook his head in disbelief. 'Gwyn's daughter? Gwyn and the Kengian Prince? It can't be true. So fanciful. Sofia, my dear wife, say it can't be true.'

The Queen compressed her lips, but remained silent.

'But that would mean the girl is…' Theodora could see the cogs turning over slowly in the King's mind. 'It means she's of Kengia's firstborn line?' A look of horror washed over his face. 'The prophecy! But you said, Horace, that it was impossible…' The King cast a quick glance at the Queen before edging closer to Horace. He dropped his voice. 'You said the Prince was dead.'

'Yes, I believe he *is* dead. But Gwyn and Alik's relationship occurred before he died.'

'Then, the ward may be the Water Catcher?'

'Yes, which is why I'm relieved to know she is back at the castle.'

The King rubbed his chin. 'I dare not believe it.'

'Takai can confirm much of it. I will have him come here. Actually, I have a matter concerning the Prince and my daughter to discuss with you as well.'

It will be fine, Theodora thought. The Prince would want nothing to do with Arisa now, especially if she was linked to the prophecy. He would still want to marry her.

The Queen shot Horace an oddly triumphant look. 'I'm afraid you will find the Prince is unavailable.'

A heaviness formed in Theodora's gut.

'The Prince is safe. He's with Guthrie.' The King nodded assuredly. 'My son had to get away from the castle, and the danger posed by the rebels…but the Water Catcher… Guthrie must live up to his word.' He began pacing the floor.

'The Prince is *gone?*' Theodora screeched. Every eye in the room fell on her, but she didn't care. Her whole future was hanging on whether her brother was able to bring Takai back to the castle.

'He will be back…*with* the Water Catcher, if your brother can be relied on,' the King snapped.

'With the Water Catcher?' Horace asked, before turning on the Queen. 'Where's the girl?'

The Queen shrugged. So Arisa was gone. Perhaps there was still a chance for Theodora to get her crown.

'How could this happen?' Horace thundered. 'She was supposed to be under guard!'

'She tried to escape,' the King explained. 'Apparently she had help – the Kengian healer and Gwyn; Sar and…Elos, if you would believe it.'

Elos? Sar's father? How could that be?

Horace's jaw began clicking furiously.

'But Erun and Gwyn have been recaptured,' the King went on. 'Guthrie, with my son, has gone after the others.'

'Guthrie will prevail,' Horace said, almost convincingly. 'He will get the girl.' Then he caught the Queen's gaze and smiled slyly. 'Sire, one last matter of business. I trust, from what you have learned, that you realise the Queen was complicit in all of this. Her own lady-in-waiting, fraternising with a Kengian all those years ago…Not any old Kengian, but the same one who tried to bewitch you. And today she has aided all of your enemies in their escape. She has used you poorly. Again. The same woman who has refused to be your *true wife*.' He stressed the last words.

The King's face crumpled as he turned to the Queen. 'Say it's not so, my love. Say you are my true wife.'

The Queen looked at Horace defiantly.

'See? She has nothing to say in her defence. You cannot let your misplaced feelings prevent you seeing the truth for a moment longer. You have no choice but to take action against the Queen.'

Queen Sofia remained frustratingly stoic. She must have known the consequences she would face when she chose to help the others. Part of Theodora couldn't help but admire her bold, albeit foolish actions.

Horace pressed further, as King Delrik showed himself reluctant to give the order. 'Remember, this is the woman who betrayed you as far back as the earliest days of your marriage. She lied to you. Let you think she loved you again, when it was all a cruel trick. She has bewitched you somehow, the same as Prince Alik tried to do.'

The King nodded slowly. 'The Queen…must join her fellow traitors in the dungeons,' he said, his voice small. 'But she shall not be harmed,' he added, more forcefully.

Horace gave a nod. 'As you wish.'

Theodora withheld the smirk that was itching to spread across her face. Takai would be back soon enough. Even if her useless brother managed to capture Arisa, the troublesome girl would be imprisoned. So her marriage to the Prince would go ahead. In the meantime, the King had agreed to imprison the Queen, Gwyn and Erun. Her father was the Lord Commander and in control of all the King's forces, and would see that Arisa was punished.

No one would stand in her way now. Finally, everything would be exactly as it should be.

43

*A*risa, Sar and Elos kept a frantic pace. They had ridden through Obira's backstreets, shuddering at the destruction left in the rebels' wake. Broken glass from shop and apartment windows had littered the ground. Abandoned carts were upturned, their contents scattered. Obira's residents, adults and children alike, were wandering the city in a daze, many cradling bloody limbs and bearing the marks of other injuries. Arisa's heart had wrenched, knowing she couldn't stop and help. She had to keep going – her life, and others, depended on it.

They were well past the city gates and the village of Dunhin before they stopped at a stream to let the horses take water. Elos filled his flask and they passed it between one another. The afternoon sun was warm, and Arisa's face was damp with sweat. She slurped the water greedily, realising she hadn't stopped to eat or drink since she had left Elos's hut not long after dawn.

She took in a deep breath of the fresh country air, telling herself everything was alright, that they would get to Kengia somehow. She turned to Elos. It was the first opportunity any of them had had to speak to each other since escaping from the castle.

'Thank you for coming, Elos.'

He nodded in the same abashed way Sar often did. But Arisa wouldn't let his actions go unnoticed.

'You came when you didn't have to.'

Elos shrugged. 'As soon as I realised who you really were – that you were the Water Catcher – I knew it was my duty to protect you.'

She raised a perplexed brow. 'How could you have known? I didn't even know. I'm still not completely sure.'

'First of all, no one but the Water Catcher could have done what you did at Riverend Falls.'

So Elos *had* seen everything.

'And any fool could see you were Alik's daughter. You may resemble Gwyn in many ways, but you have your father's eyes. And you had Alik's horse with you. So when you said Amund's name, when you meant to say Erun, I knew for sure.'

Elos opened his mouth again, as if to say something else, but closed it just as quickly. He was keeping something from her.

'How did you know we needed help when we did?' she asked.

'I knew I wouldn't be the only person able to piece it together, and the danger that would put you in. I would have followed you sooner, if it hadn't been for the visit from Horace's man.'

'The pirate!' Arisa exclaimed.

'Pirate?' Sar and Elos said at the same time.

'Horace sent one of his men with the guards when they came to get me and Takai. I didn't remember until later that I had seen him before. He came out of the Lion's Den the day I saw Horace and Guthrie, a few days after the blood moon. He had the look of a pirate, and Takai confirmed as much.'

Sar scratched his head. 'I wonder if he was the same man who brought Guthrie and Sir Marcus back from Ette after the Northemers invaded – charged a King's ransom for them, from what I heard.'

Elos shrugged. 'Evidently Horace had learned, or at least

suspected, my real identity. Klaus warned me that the pirate had been sent to kill me.'

'Did you—?' Sar glanced at Arisa and stopped his question short.

Elos looked away. There was no need to answer. He had done what he needed to do to protect himself and get to her.

After an extended pause, Sar spoke. 'But you came to the castle anyway, knowing Horace was after you.'

'With the rebels on the way and Horace's eye on Arisa, I figured she could use my help.'

Sar squared his shoulders. 'I had it under control.'

Elos gave a wry grin. 'Clearly, you had it under control when I found you grossly outnumbered by those guards.'

Sar scowled. 'I could have had them.'

Elos must have read the hurt in Sar's face. He reached out clumsily and put his hand on his son's shoulder. 'No one could have held off that many men by themselves. No one.'

Sar shrugged his hand away. He clearly wasn't ready for a father returned from the dead.

'In truth,' Elos went on, 'you were pretty impressive back there.'

Sar's face brightened a little, his dimpled grin returning. 'And you weren't too bad either.'

'Don't get too carried away with yourself. I could still teach you a thing or two.'

'Maybe.'

Elos moved as if to ruffle Sar's hair, but stopped himself and stepped away awkwardly. 'Right. Enough talk. Off to Kengia, then?'

'Well…' Arisa said. 'That's what Erun— Amund says I need to do.'

Elos stroked his chin thoughtfully. 'The protection may be gone over the mountains, but it is still snowed in at the top of the Alps. It's impassable. There's no time to make it to the coast and find a boat, either. I don't know how we'll do it...' He laughed. 'But heck, why shouldn't we try?'

'Why not exactly,' Sar agreed, full of his usual confidence again.

'I'm glad you two think we can find a way into Kengia somehow,' Arisa said. 'But truly, I have no idea what to do.'

'Yes, you do,' Sar and Elos said in unison.

'You're the daughter of Prince Alik, aren't you?' Elos prompted.

'Well...yes.'

'And you're the Water Catcher,' Sar said, more than asked.

Arisa shifted her feet uncomfortably, still not wanting or willing to believe it. 'It's only a prophecy.'

Elos laughed again. He sounded eerily like Sar. 'Listen here. I'm not the type to believe in prophecies and such, but I believe in this one.'

Sar folded his arms. 'And so do I.'

'And so does Horace,' she added bitterly. 'Takai told him about everything that happened at Riverend Falls, and I guess, as you say, he put the pieces together.'

Elos snorted. 'Of course the Prince told him. I knew he was like the rest of them.'

'No—' Sar began, at the same time Arisa said, 'He's not like that.' Sar cast a sidelong glance at her. 'He would never have said anything if there hadn't been a misunderstanding.'

Elos raised a quizzical brow.

She wasn't prepared to elaborate. 'It doesn't really matter now. Takai is there, and we are here.'

Elos looked between them. 'The Prince can't be trusted. Agreed?'

Arisa was about to protest, but Elos signalled for her to be quiet. 'What is it?' she whispered.

He made a shushing sound. Sar cocked his head to the side.

'I can hear it too. Horses. And they're traveling fast.'

'Quick – behind here.' Elos led Arisa behind a thicket of bushes. Sar followed.

Arisa watched in horror as the riders edged right up to where they were hiding. The horses' flanks brushed against the branches directly in front of them. The two riders wore the uniforms of Royal Guards and looked as if they too were stopping to take water. Meteor and Elos's horse were unseen beyond a bend in the stream. But as if she had sensed danger, Meteor chose that moment to let out a loud whinny.

Arisa recognised the sound of swords being unsheathed, and the men dismounting.

'Come out from where you be hiding,' one shouted in their direction.

Sar turned toward her and shook his head to say, *Don't move.* His own hand was ready on the hilt of his sword. Arisa's heart quickened. She looked over to Elos for reassurance. He was peering through the bushes, a great smile spreading over his face.

'Alright.' Elos threw his sword out onto the bank. 'We're coming out.'

Sar grabbed his father's arm to stop him, but Elos pushed him away and stepped out to greet the riders.

'Sheesh. What are you, of all people, doing hiding in there?' one of the men cried.

'It's alright, you two. Come out,' Elos called back to Arisa and Sar. Sar stepped out cautiously, still holding his sword and standing protectively in front of her.

Arisa realised the two men weren't guards. She recognised them from the Ujej Festival. One was the surly man who had fought Takai and been bested by Elos. Both men bore bloody marks of battle and were peering suspiciously at her and Sar.

'It's alright. They're with me,' Elos told them, and they lowered their weapons slowly. 'What brings you two here?'

'We've come from battle. Sergei ordered a full retreat and we hightailed it out of there. Pinched these uniforms here to get us past the Duke's soldiers. The army will be on the main road as we speak.'

The other rider, the drunken farmer from the festival, had fixed his attention on Sar, who was still in his guard's uniform. He shifted his gaze to Elos. 'But you should already know this, Fisherman, for you should have been in battle with the rest of us.'

'I had other matters to attend to.' Elos's tone didn't invite further discussion.

'We haven't time to be questioning the Fisherman about his business,' the friendlier rider said. 'The Royal Guards are close on our heels.'

'Guards, you say?' Elos asked. 'Not soldiers?'

The rider nodded. 'As I said, the soldiers are on the main road. We veered off to avoid them, but these guards came from nowhere. Gave us a real fright – especially when we realised the Prince himself was among them.'

Sar and Arisa exchanged a look. Why had Takai left the castle? Was he looking for Arisa? If he was with the guards, he must be trying to capture her.

He had chosen his side after all.

'Where are they?' Elos asked. The frown on his face reminded Arisa where he believed the Prince's allegiance lay.

'On the hilltop yonder. They'll be wanting blood from anyone, I expect. But we won't be sticking around to find out.'

The men mounted their horses. 'I wouldn't hang around here too long if I were you, Fisherman,' the farmer called, as they rode away.

'Take care,' Elos shouted after them.

Sar's eyes narrowed as he looked back toward the road. 'This isn't a good sign. Takai knows where we're heading. I'll go back and try to buy you some time.'

'We'll keep going this way, toward Shizen Lake,' Elos said, as Sar retrieved his horse.

Sar nodded briefly at Arisa before galloping away, leaving a cloud of dust in his wake.

Elos had already mounted Meteor. 'This horse of yours – or should I say, your father's – how fast can she go?'

It sounded strange, Elos referring to Prince Alik as her father. It suddenly occurred to Arisa that the silver-haired man she'd seen with Meteor in her visions must have been him.

'Meteor and I are old friends,' Elos went on, patting the horse's neck. 'It's about time you got to go home, my girl.'

Pawing the ground, Meteor turned her nose toward the Nymoi Alps.

Elos pulled Arisa up behind him. Moments later, they were heading straight for the mountains on the horizon at a lightning-fast pace.

$\mathcal{G}$uthrie dismounted his horse and bent down to examine the tracks on the ground.

'It's them, I'm sure of it.' His lips curled into a grim smile. 'The Kengian mare's giant hooves are unmistakable. They passed through here within the last half hour, I'd say.'

They had stopped not far past Dunhin, and Takai was running out of time to veer Guthrie away from Arisa. He hadn't expected Guthrie to be good at tracking, especially when he was so unreliable when it came to almost everything else.

He had to buy Arisa more time. She needed to get far away from them.

'Guthrie, let's stop here a moment,' Takai said. 'We've been riding hard since we left the castle. The horses could do with a break – and frankly, so could I.' Indeed, the horses were covered in sweat and lathering at the mouth.

'What – stop now? When we're this close?' Guthrie tilted his head and cast a dubious look at Takai. 'If I didn't know better, I would say you're trying to help that little wench.'

Takai resisted the urge to tell him to shut his mouth. 'I have no loyalties to the ward,' he lied. 'But I'm not blinkered by revenge, either.'

'That cow broke my nose!'

Takai had to turn away from Guthrie and choke back a laugh. He looked at the guards who accompanied them. They looked as fatigued as Takai felt. One had dismounted with Guthrie and was shifting his weight from one foot to the other.

'Guthrie, we all need to take a break. Take a look yourself.' Takai gestured toward the guards.

'Speak up,' Guthrie roared at the men. 'Who here wants to stop?'

One guard dared enough to speak up quietly. 'Can we do as the Prince bids? Just a minute for a man to relieve himself?'

Guthrie screwed up his nose in disgust. 'A minute. Get to it.'

Two of the guards scuttled away behind a line of trees.

Guthrie's black eyes locked on Takai. They were filled with hate and distrust. Takai stared back at him, trying his best to maintain a blank expression.

With a grunt, Guthrie broke away from Takai's stare. He looked in the direction the guards had headed to see to nature's call. 'Where are those useless fools?' he muttered under his breath. 'Go fetch them,' he ordered one of the remaining two guards.

Takai was racking his brain for a way to slow Guthrie down when his horse let out a soft neigh. The hairs on Takai's neck stood on end. His hand went to the hilt of his sword. Guthrie had heard it, too, and unsheathed his blade.

A scan of their immediate surroundings didn't reveal anything, but a moment later there was a thud as the man that had been sent to collect his fellow guards collapsed. Takai caught a glimpse of a rock as it flew through the air toward the other guard next to Guthrie. The projectile found its target, hitting the man's head and sending him to the ground.

Guthrie spun around to face the direction the rock had come from. 'Show yourself, coward! See if you dare to attack the Royal Guards in the open!'

'With pleasure,' came the cry.

It was a voice Takai knew well.

Sar leapt from the cover of a bush, his sword at the ready.

'Traitor,' Guthrie sneered. 'You'll feel the wrath of my blade.'

Sar hadn't lost his cheeky grin, despite the injuries he bore – a bloody gash on one arm, and smaller cuts on all his limbs. 'I welcome the challenge, Guthrie. It's been too long coming.'

Guthrie stepped menacingly toward him. Takai wondered if a fresh and uninjured Guthrie could beat his friend – Guthrie was nearly the same height as Sar, but much wider.

Sar looked far from intimidated. Instead, he directed a forth-right look at Takai. 'And whose side are you on?'

'Do you need to ask?' Takai beamed as he moved to Sar's side.

'Yet another traitor.' Guthrie spat at the ground. 'I should have known.'

He charged headlong at them both, his sword raised.

Takai and Sar easily sidestepped and avoided his blade.

'Come on, Guthrie,' Sar said. 'Surrender yourself. You're outnumbered.'

'Outnumbered! I have four guards with me.' Guthrie charged again, and once more, they evaded his strikes.

Sar grinned. 'Four, you say? Two who are now off in sleepy-land...' He pointed at the two on the ground. 'And the other two, who are gagged and tied up back there.' He indicated the trees.

Guthrie screwed up his face and made another charge. This time, Sar reached out after him and landed the hilt of his sword on Guthrie's head. Guthrie's eyes rolled back and he slumped to the ground.

Sar and Takai made light work of tying up Guthrie and the unconscious guards and shifting them behind the trees. As they returned to their horses, Sar turned toward Takai with a hopeful look.

'You know there was never anything between me and Arisa.'

Takai grunted. 'But you both kept things from me.'

'Will that stop you from helping us? Come with us and see if we can make it to Kengia.'

Takai turned the idea over in this mind. He wanted to see Arisa, to speak to her again. He needed clarity. Seeing her might be enough to know exactly how he felt. He had to know…

But he couldn't do it. He couldn't turn his back on his kingdom.

'I can't leave Lamore,' he told Sar. 'My mother will have to face whatever punishment Horace has planned for her. Gwyn and Erun as well.'

'But you can't help them by staying,' Sar insisted. 'Horace is effectively Lord Commander of all of Lamore.'

'Trust me, I know the extent of Horace's current power. But I'm still the Prince. This is still my kingdom, and I can appeal to my father.'

'But what about Arisa? You can't leave her. You love her, don't you?'

Takai gritted his teeth. He couldn't answer.

Sar's brows knitted. 'What is it? Will you stay, or will you come with us?'

Takai looked up the road in the direction of the Nymoi Alps, then back the other way, toward the castle. It was an impossible choice.

'I don't know.'

45

at the base of Shizen Falls, Elos pulled up Meteor – or rather, the horse decided to stop of her own accord. Elos turned back to Arisa.

'We're here. What next?'

'I haven't a clue.'

They dismounted and looked up at the great force of water pummelling its way down the face of the mountain. Arisa's gaze was drawn upward, all the way to the top of the snow-capped Nymoi Alps.

Elos scratched his head. 'As I said, I can't see how we can get up and over. There must be another way…There must be.'

She shook her head miserably. 'But how?'

'The Water Catcher must be able to make it through.'

'And by *the Water Catcher*, I suppose you mean me?'

Elos raised his eyebrows, as if to say, *Who else can I mean?*

Arisa flung her arms up in exasperation. 'What do you expect me to do?'

'Use your powers, I suppose. How does it work? How do you control the water?'

'I don't know…Last time, it just sort of…happened.'

Elos grabbed her by the shoulders and looked right into her eyes. 'Arisa, this is serious. Think. Last time, when the light came out of you, what did you do?'

'I don't know.'

'Think harder.'

Arisa closed her eyes, trying to recall what had happened when she and Takai had gone over Riverend Falls. 'We went over the edge, and then I was in the sea. I couldn't see Takai. I ducked under the water and saw him sinking.' She winced at the memory.

'Good. Keep going.'

'I knew I had to do something. He was going to drown. We were both going to drown. And then there was all this light, and the water started churning upward, as if he was in an underwater whirlpool.'

'What was going through your mind when that happened? What were you thinking?'

She bit her lip, not sure if she wanted to share her intimate thoughts.

'What were you thinking?' Elos asked again, more forcefully.

'All I was thinking was that I couldn't bear to lose Takai.'

'Good. What else?'

She dropped her voice. 'I suppose I was thinking…that I loved him.'

Elos clapped his hands together. 'Ha!'

Arisa's eyes flung open.

'That's it,' he exclaimed. 'You have to think about what means the most to you. What makes you happy? What would make you happier? Think about all the things you have fought for, the things that are important to you. You have to conjure up all your feelings about those things, and those people, and what you would do if anything threatened them.'

'And then what?'

'I don't know. The rest is up to you.'

With a nod, Arisa closed her eyes again. She thought of Takai, hoping that once everything was over, whatever it was between them could be put right again. She thought about Lamore and Kengia, about peace, about all the things she and Erun – Amund – had fought so hard for. She thought about him, and about Gwyn. She thought about Queen Sofia and Sar.

Slowly, she raised her arms and reached out toward the falls. But nothing came to her.

'Focus,' Elos whispered in her ear.

Arisa opened her eyes and shot him an annoyed look. 'I'm trying.'

Again she closed her eyes, trying with all her might to concentrate on the things dearest to her, but nothing happened.

'It's no use,' she cried.

'You have to figure it out, and figure it out quickly, before Horace's flunkies find us.'

Elos was right. If they were caught, everything everyone had done for her would have been for nothing. The sacrifices made for her would be wasted. Everyone was counting on her. Counting on her to be the Water Catcher, to save Lamore and Kengia from the war and devastation on the horizon.

Arisa reached for the Kengian coins and medallion in her pocket, visualising each of the elements. The phoenix, representing fire and the last Firemaster's legacy to preserve Kengian magic. The yew tree seed for earth – the power of the last Kengian King. The starling for air – her father's magic. And finally, the koi, symbolising water – the power of the Water Catcher at her fingertips.

It was her inheritance. Her responsibility. Her power.

Arisa's gut churned violently, as if her insides were a spinning top. She could see, as much as feel, an energy and glowing warmth radiating from her torso, spreading into her chest. Her upper body was convulsing. She felt as if she had lost control over her limbs.

She closed her eyes tighter, focusing on the power inside her.

The warmth flowed down into her arms and her fingers. Arisa lifted her hands; they felt as if they were scorching. She reached out once more toward the falls. Her fingers began shaking uncontrollably. Her whole body was vibrating.

'Arisa—'

She could only just hear Elos's voice, as if it were coming from miles away. Then she caught the sound of Meteor's whinny.

Arisa opened her eyes slowly, trying not to lose the connection with the energy inside her. With a sharp intake of breath, she noticed the blinding white light radiating from her fingertips, consuming all of her body. It was so bright she had to look away. Her gaze landed on Shizen Falls – and at that moment, Arisa believed it for the first time. She believed what everyone else believed.

She was the Water Catcher, and she would not fail those who had faith in her.

The water parted, bending from the middle, as if someone had opened the falls like a set of drapes. The whole waterfall was alive with an effervescent light. Arisa moved her hands apart, and the gap in the centre of the falls grew wider. She was moving the water; she could manipulate it any way she wanted. She could push it, part it, pull it, throw it.

I am *the Water Catcher.*

The discovery brought new clarity to her mind, and she moved her hands further apart, knowing that whatever was happening, it was going to get them to Kengia. But the effort required to move the water was draining her. Her arms ached, as if someone had tried to yank them from their sockets.

'A bit longer,' Elos called.

Her body was overcome with an intense shaking sensation. It started in her ankles, running up her calves and her whole body, until she couldn't bear the exertion a moment longer. Her legs crumpled beneath her. Elos's arms flew out to catch her.

She had failed. She couldn't do what the prophecy required her to do.

Arisa looked up at Elos. 'I wasn't strong enough.'

'What are you talking about?' His eyes were wide, his voice full of wonder as he stared up at the falls. 'You *did* it.'

She got back to her feet and steadied herself before following Elos's gaze. The water was still parted, bathed in silver light.

Arisa squinted to get a better look. A dozen feet above their heads was a crevice in the mountainside. The opening looked wide and tall enough for a horse and rider to squeeze through, but whether it was a cave or a tunnel, she couldn't say.

The question was answered when a white shape appeared at the mouth of the crevice. The wolf – the Kengian snow wolf… It was here. Arisa's unlikely guardian was staring back at them, and with a swish of its tail, it turned and disappeared into the void.

'You're going to have to tell me more about that wolf sometime,' Elos said.

'We have to get up there.' Arisa pointed up at the mountainside, where there was a path wide enough to lead a horse.

'Are you sure you'll be alright?'

She was weak, but for the first time in her life, Arisa was able to say with complete confidence, 'Yes. I'm sure. Everything is going to be alright.'

Satisfied with her response, Elos started to lead Meteor toward the rocky hillside.

'Wait – what about Sar?' *And Takai,* she wanted to add.

'We can't wait for them. We have to go before the opening closes.'

Elos was right. Arisa didn't know much about her powers, but she did know her hold over the water couldn't last forever. Still… 'A few minutes?' she tried.

'No,' Elos replied. 'We don't know whether Sar found the Prince, or what might have happened if he did.'

She hesitated.

'Don't you realise, Arisa? The fate of all of Kypria rests squarely with you. Every choice you make from here on in will decide the future of thousands upon thousands of people. By staying here and waiting to be captured, you're not only putting yourself at risk. Every man, woman and child is counting on you.'

'What if I don't want everyone to count on me?' she demanded. 'What if I don't want this power? What if I don't want this responsibility?'

'Too bad. This is your destiny, and it seems it's my destiny to help you realise it.'

Arisa's eyes filled with tears. Elos rested his hand on her arm and softened his tone.

'We don't choose our destiny. We're born to it. You're the Water Catcher, and your path is through there.' He pointed through the opening in the mountain.

She nodded reluctantly. The water was starting to close in. After one final glance back the way they'd come, back toward the only land she had ever known, she hurried after Elos, and they headed up the rocky path.

With every step she took, Arisa was sure she could go no further. She stumbled over rocks and on loose gravel, again and again, but somehow found the strength to go on.

Stopping to catch her breath as they reached the landing at the crevice, she found Elos looking back out across Lamore, his brow furrowed with concern.

Arisa followed his gaze. She could almost see the whole kingdom from this vantage point. She could see where the land met the Kyprian Sea – a sea littered with boats. Dozens of them.

The Northemers.

She gasped. Not just at the sight of the invading fleet, but at the vision that appeared before her at that moment. A figure standing at the prow of one of the ships. A girl. Glimpses of a tattooed neck and hands. A red-and-gold feather tattoo extending up her wrist. A face marked with red warpaint.

Arisa couldn't make out her exact features, but there was something familiar in the girl's stance. An alertness. A sense of determination.

Almost as if the girl could see her, she turned her head and spoke.

'Arisa?'

Arisa's heart shuddered to a stop.

She looked again for the girl, but the vision was gone.

'Are you alright?' Elos asked. 'You look like you've seen a ghost.'

I think I just did, Arisa thought. Aloud she said, 'I'm fine.'

'Come on.' Elos urged her to follow him into the opening in the mountain. It was barely the width of two men. A chill ran down her spine. There was nothing but darkness ahead of them. Elos reached for his sword, and they edged their way into the passageway.

Arisa tried to ignore the dampness and cold surrounding them. *Please let there be an opening at the end.* She looked back, wondering if it was too late to return, but the curtains of water were closing. Could she open them again if she needed to? *Please, please let there be an opening.*

They had been trudging along for what felt like forever, but was probably only a few dozen steps, when a light appeared ahead. It started as a small pinprick and slowly widened. Arisa and Elos continued onward until she was sure they were in a tunnel. A tunnel through to Kengia. It had to be.

They pushed on. With every step, Meteor tugged at her reins, her nose pointed toward home. The rock walls groaned. *It is you,* they seemed to say.

As the darkness faded with the growing light, so did Arisa's apprehension. With light came hope. With light there was safety. With light there was home.

It is her, the waterfall gurgled behind her, announcing her arrival. What exactly she would find on the other side of the Alps, Arisa didn't know, but she was sure she would be welcome. She was of the firstborn line. She was the Water Catcher. The wait was over.

After a few dozen more steps, they reached the end. Arisa's racing heart felt as if it would burst from her chest. They emerged from the darkness, and she put a hand up to shield her eyes, giving herself a moment to adjust to the light before lowering it.

Kengia slowly came into focus.

Laid out before Arisa was a spectacular landscape. On either side, the Nymoi Alps extended as far as the eye could see. Ahead was a blue-and-green patchwork of valleys and hills, stitched together with snaking rivers and streams. There were dense forests and fertile plains. Things that looked like crops carved into a mountain. A sea in the distance. Signs of life everywhere. Birds dotting the clear blue sky. Animal sounds echoing up the mountainside.

It was everything Amund had promised and more. Everything that had happened up to now had been worth it. They had made it. They were in Kengia.

'I can't believe I'm here.' Arisa shook her head in disbelief. 'My father's homeland.'

Elos was strangely silent. He didn't look happy. He didn't look surprised. He looked sad, and apologetic.

'What is it?' she asked.

Elos looked down at his feet. 'Arisa, I have something to tell you.'

'What is it?'

He hesitated a moment before responding. 'It's about your father—'

But Elos's words cut off, his eyes suddenly wide with confusion.

He reached for the side of his throat, where a thin wooden

needle had appeared. His eyes rolled back in his head, and he dropped to the ground.

'*Elos!*'

But Arisa's cries were in vain. There was a sharp sting at the side of her neck as a dart pierced her skin, too. The hills of her father's homeland were the last thing Arisa saw before darkness claimed her.

DID YOU ENJOY THE WATER CATCHER'S RISE?

Thank you for reading *The Water Catcher's Rise*. We hope you enjoyed it and would appreciate if you could take a moment to leave a review.

Share your review via your favourite online bookstore or Goodreads.

Read on for a sneak peek of Book 3 in the Kyprian Prophecy Series – *The Air King's Return*.

THE AIR KING'S RETURN: THE KYPRIAN PROPHECY BOOK 3 – COMING SOON!

War has arrived in Kypria. Unlikely allies unite and mighty warriors clash. To protect the people and land she loves, Arisa must fulfil her destiny as the Water Catcher and defeat a powerful ghost from her past.

Read the first chapters of the *The Air King's Return* now!

THE AIR KING'S RETURN – THE KYPRIAN PROPHECY BOOK 3

AN EXCERPT

he Water Catcher has risen.'
The thread of whispered words penetrated his slumber.

'The Water Catcher walks among us.'

Was it a dream? There was a sense of reality to the words, but he was neither asleep nor awake. He was unable to prise his eyes open. It was as if his eyelids were glued together. But the words kept coming, over and over, beckoning him to wake.

He gripped the linen sheets in his hands, trying to summon the strength to break out of the in-between world. Chasing the words, he focused all his other senses on everything around him. He was conscious of the soft down mattress on which he lay and the beard scratching at his neck. He recognised the smell of dried lavender, rosemary and sage permeating the air, and between the whispered words, he heard the sound of a crackling fire – it too was speaking to him. *'The prophecy is upon us,'* it hissed.

That was when he knew he had to wake up. He was needed.

The words grew louder. He intensified his focus inward, upon the act of waking up. His eyelashes trembled as he returned to the waking world, blinking to adjust to the light. He tried to sit up but crumpled down again. The thin limbs attached to his body, the limbs of a stranger, felt as if they were filled with stones. He was himself, but the body was not his. There was something missing inside him. The warmth of energy that ran deep in his veins, that feeling of connection to the world, of being at one with the air he breathed – it was gone.

With a groan, he propped himself up on his pillow and scanned the room. He was alone.

'*The Water Catcher has arrived.*'

He turned his head in the direction of the voice, and managed an expression that was part smile, part grimace. There was a Kengian starling in a cage hanging from a roughly hewn rafter. It ruffled its iridescent feathers of gold, purple and blue, and cooed as if to say, '*About time*'. Then the starling spoke again, though its beak was unmoving. The bird planted the words in his mind.

'*The prophecy is upon us.*'

'But how?' he asked, his voice raspy and strained. The starling blinked its silver eyes. 'The Water Catcher couldn't have come to being…' he said to himself. 'Or *could* it?'

The starling tilted its head before letting out a loud squawk.

The bird's call brought a rush of footsteps toward the room. The door swung open to reveal a tall, dark-haired woman. Her hair hung in long waves. Her skin was luminous, as if covered in a silver sheen. She sat down beside his bed. Her dark blue eyes were all-knowing, hinting at untold wisdom. Her intense gaze probed his face and body. After a few moments she smiled, seemingly happy with his condition.

'Where am I?' he croaked.

'It doesn't matter right now.' Her voice was flecked with air and light. 'All that matters is that you're awake and you're safe.'

'Safe from what?'

'There'll be time for that later.' There was something about the calming effect of her voice and manner that tugged at a strand of memory.

'We've met before…What's your name?'

'A more important question is whether you know yours.'

He made a croaky scoffing sound at the absurdity of her question. Of course he knew his name. 'I'm Alik.'

The woman exhaled before bestowing one of her soothing smiles on him again. 'Yes, you are. Welcome back, Your Majesty.'

'Your *Majesty*?'

But he was a Prince of Kengia. The firstborn Prince. A Prince only. He was not the King.

Something was terribly wrong.

*P*rince Takai's breath hitched in his throat as he caught a glimpse of Arisa standing at the base of Shizen Falls. Her tiny figure was dwarfed by the glacier-fed waterfall hurtling down the face of the Nymoi Alps.

Takai and Sar had followed Arisa and Elos's trail all the way to Shizen Lake, riding through the Lamorian countryside to the point of exhaustion. They had finally come to a stop on a small rocky outcrop overlooking the lake and falls. Takai squinted in the setting silver sun reflecting off the glasslike water and snow-capped mountains. His eyes darted across the scene below, trying to catch a better view of Arisa. What was she doing? She appeared to be just standing there, gazing up at the mountain range that separated the kingdoms of Lamore and Kengia. It didn't make sense; she had to keep moving. The Royal Guards would be close now. Arisa had to escape. She had to make it to Kengia – somehow, she would have to negotiate the treacherous Alps, but standing there simply staring at the mountains wouldn't help.

Sar's loud intake of breath signalled the reason for her stillness.

Takai rubbed his eyes in disbelief. Arisa's long bronze hair billowed around her as she reached out toward the falls. Her outstretched hands gleamed. At first it was a soft glow, but it soon extended beyond her hands, cocooning her arms in a dazzling silver light. It was the same light that had overtaken her the day she'd saved him from the sea.

The glowing beams merged into an impossibly large arc that Arisa launched at the falls, illuminating the water. The falls looked like they were on fire. Sparks of light spat from the middle of the waterfall, as if she were burning a hole through the blanket of water.

'Whoa!' Sar cried. 'It's as if she can bend water…'

'As if she is the Water Catcher,' Takai murmured.

Sar slapped him on the back. 'Ha! There can't be any doubt now. She is the Water Catcher.'

Takai barely heard his friend's words as his eyes were drawn to the tunnel-like hole that had appeared halfway up the Shizen Falls. The hole was spinning and expanding like a whirlpool, until it formed a long, elliptical opening – an opening to what?

Takai could see what looked like a narrow crevice in the mountain. Arisa and Elos were already making their way up the rockface toward it.

'That's it. That's how they're going to do it.'

'A passageway through to Kengia?' Sar sounded as if he were in a dream.

'There's only one way to find out. Come on.' Takai urged his horse down the hillside, hoping to catch Arisa before she disappeared into the opening.

Takai and Sar moved quickly, but by the time they reached the bottom of the falls they had lost sight of Arisa and Elos. The pair must have disappeared into the void. A bolt of panic shot through Takai as he noticed the glow in the water dimming. The opening was shrinking.

He couldn't lose Arisa. Not now. Not after everything.

'We have to hurry,' he yelled over the roar of the waterfall. The void was closing rapidly. The water had already reclaimed much of the mountainside where Arisa and Elos had climbed up. There was just one narrow, slippery path remaining. They'd have to continue without the horses.

With every laboured step Sar and Takai took up the mountain, the opening shrank. Finally, they made it to a rocky ledge at the centre of the opening – the pounding curtain of water was almost skimming their shoulders. There was no sign of Arisa and Elos. Takai could only assume they'd gone into the crevice. He took one final glance back the way they had come, and a fresh bolt of fear sliced through him.

'Look!' He pointed in the distance to the Kyprian Sea,

where a fleet of ships was snaking its way down the Lamorian coast.

'The Northemers,' Sar confirmed.

Takai looked again into the dark crevice, leading presumably to Kengia, and back again at the Northem fleet. His country was in imminent danger from Malu and his fearsome army. He needed to warn his father. But he also needed to get to Arisa. Once again, he had to make a choice between the country he loved and the person he couldn't live without.

He ground his teeth back and forth. There was only one choice.

Takai shot his friend a look that said: *Let's do this.*

Sar nodded and ventured first into the opening. Takai took a deep breath and followed him into the darkness. He crept forth slowly, pursuing the sound of Sar's feet crunching on the gravel floor. Takai was acutely aware of the rumbling coming from the falls as the opening continued to shrink. There was little more than a sliver of a gap left in the water. They were committed to going wherever this cavern led – or didn't lead.

With a final resounding crash, the opening in the falls closed, sending shockwaves through Takai's body.

They inched further into the darkness. Just when Takai was sure they were destined to be entombed in the mountain forever, Sar let out a whoop. The source of his excitement became clear as Takai discerned the faint light ahead in the distance. They pressed forward, moving toward the growing light, until they reached the end of the tunnel.

Takai shielded his eyes from the bright light as they emerged. Slowly, Kengia came into view. Their position high up on the mountainside afforded a breathtaking panorama of the nation that had been closed off from Lamore for nearly two decades. Over Takai's shoulder were the familiar Nymoi Alps, extending for miles, but below him was a deep valley, with sparkling streams and rivers meandering their way through lush plains and hilly mounds. It was a kaleidoscope of the bluest blues and greenest greens. Woodland, a hundred times bigger than the King's Forest, lay at the bottom of the range on one side. On Takai's left, the sparkling sea winked back at him in the distance.

Sar whistled, echoing Takai's first impression of Kengia. The Prince had had no idea what to expect from the land that had closed itself off from Lamore after his father, King Delrik, had tried to invade it. It was a country full of people with magical abilities that he'd been taught to fear. Yet he had ventured willingly into this enemy territory, driven by his love for Arisa – a Kengian girl. And not just any Kengian girl. He'd fallen for one of the silver-eyes – the one from the prophecy.

It was hard to make sense of it all. All Takai knew was that he had to get to her. He had to see if there was still something between them. He hoped more than anything it wasn't too late to make amends for betraying her to Horace. But as his eyes fell on the scuff marks on the ground, and the footprints leading down a narrow track, he realised with a shudder that time may have already run out.

It was terrifyingly clear that Arisa and Elos had met with company when they'd arrived in Kengia.

Sar must have had the same thought, for he bent down to examine the ground. His hand closed around something. He held up a thin wooden needle for Takai to take a closer look at. There appeared to be a blood spot on its end.

'What do you suppose—' he started.

'A poisoned dart,' Takai said. He raced down the path with Sar in tow.

The pair were coming around a bend when a voice stopped them in their tracks.

'*Hur mayer!*'

Takai could tell from the tone of voice that it was a warning or threat. Blocking his path was a mountain of a man, with another four men standing behind him. Takai's eyes went to the long, curved swords each man held aloft. The blades' edges glinted razor-sharp. He noticed that each man had a second shorter sword tucked into a belt around his waist. They wore chest plates of metal scales and helmets that extended over their faces like masks. Each helmet featured a fearsome-looking beast or demon.

Takai searched his mind for the Kengian words he needed. He knew only the basics of their language from the time he spent at Talbot hearing the Kengian farmers speak. '*Igre rel? Igre Arisa?*' *Where is she? Where's Arisa?*

'Surrender your weapons,' the man barked in Kengian – more words Takai recognised.

His hand tightened around the hilt of his sword. 'What have you done with Arisa?'

'Surrender your weapons!' the man repeated.

Sar did exactly the opposite and unsheathed his sword, lunging toward the leader. In one lightning-fast movement the man swung his curved blade through the air, blocking Sar's strike – and slicing his broadsword in half. Sar's eyes widened as he stared at the sword stump left in his hands.

Takai leapt toward the leader to make his own strike, but the man blocked it with ease, the force ricocheting Takai's sword out of his hand and throwing him to the ground. Takai looked up in horror as his opponent raised his sword above his head, readying to bring it down on him. He held up his hands in a futile attempt to protect himself from the deadly blade—

Sar threw himself in front of his friend, holding up what was left of his sword. The Kengian blade cut through the remaining part of Sar's sword and sliced into his arm – the same arm that had been injured during his escape from the castle.

Sar groaned as he fell to the ground, clutching his bloody arm. The Kengian raised his sword again, ready to finish him off.

'*Hur!*' a girl's voice rang out. '*Hur!*'

Takai remembered then. It was the Kengian word for *stop*.

The Kengian's blade paused in mid-air and everyone turned

in the direction of the voice. It was Arisa, Elos with her, wobbling toward them with bound arms. They were being propped up by the vicelike grip of a fearsome-looking Kengian, followed by another in amour and a horned helmet. Sar's attacker looked to the armoured newcomer for direction, as if he were the leader.

'They're mine,' the assumed leader said in Kengian.

Sar's attacker grunted his assent and lowered his sword before backing away. The remaining Kengians yanked Takai and Sar to their feet and pinned their arms behind their backs.

'Unhand us!' Takai ordered with feigned confidence. 'Don't you know who we—'

'I don't care who you are,' the leader said in heavily accented Lamorian, 'but you should care who I am. For mine will be the last face you'll see, Lamorian scum.'

The Air King's Return will be released in October 2021 with the eBook available now for pre-order.

You can find out more about release dates for other platforms and paperback editions, and purchase any of Kylie's books via **www.kyliefennell.com** or the below QR code.

ABOUT THE AUTHOR

Kylie Fennell has made a 25-year career out of wrangling words, working as a journalist, editor and content creator, and more recently an author of speculative fiction. If she wasn't a writer, she'd be a superhero librarian – conquering the Dewey Decimal System by day and saving the world one book at a time by night.

As an Australian writer of European and Aboriginal (Gumbaynggirr and Bundjalung) descent she likes to explore culture and identity through her writing, as well as magic...always magic!

Kylie lives in Brisbane (Yuggera Country) with her husband, son and too many pets.

To find out more or purchase Kylie's books go to _www.kyliefennell.com._

If you want to stay up-to-date with Kylie's writing **or be part of her book review team** you can sign up to her mailing list via her website. All subscribers receive a **free book** – _Seeds from the Story Tree_ – a collection of award-winning speculative fiction stories and other short works, exclusive to Kylie's subscribers.

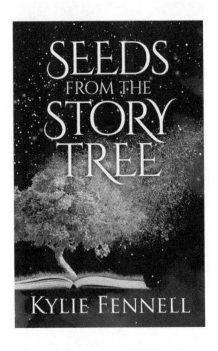

You can also connect with Kylie on social media.

facebook.com/kyliefennellauthor

twitter.com/kylie_fennell

instagram.com/kylie_fennell

BEGINNINGS: THE KYPRIAN PROPHECY – AN ORIGINS NOVELLA

Get it now for free!

No Email Address Required

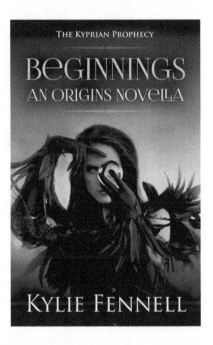

"Only a fool can't understand that there cannot be light without the darkness, and that power lies in harnessing the very thing people are scared of."

As a silver-eyes Laha has an extraordinary ability to harness the power within nature. She is also a royal companion to the Kengian Princess Mary, and with all of Kypria finally at peace Laha should be content…but she is far from it.

Laha has lost her powers and a darkness claws away inside her. She doesn't fit in at the Lamorian court, nor does she want to. She yearns for a life of excitement and adventure, but most of all she yearns to regain her powers and understand her dark urges.

The answer arrives in the form of a mysterious fortune teller whose prophecy and presence threaten to destroy everyone Laha cares about including the Lamorian Prince Emberto. Despite this she is drawn to the fortune teller and the woman's offer to help her realise the full potential of her powers...if she's willing to embrace her darkness.

Laha's choices lead to discoveries about her own identity and her friends being caught up in a deadly showdown between the most powerful of all Kengians – the Firemasters.

Beginnings is a stand alone novella that also sets the scene for the Kyprian Prophecy series and Book 1 – *The Firemaster's Legacy*.

Beginnings is **available for FREE** on all major online book retail sites including Amazon Kindle, Apple, Google Play, Kobo and Nook. No email address required!

CPSIA information can be obtained
at www.ICGtesting.com
Printed in the USA
BVHW071202051021
618194BV00002B/81